CHOCOLA

Hannah stopped several feet from the truck and called out, "Hi, Ron. Do you want me to phone for a tow truck?"

Ron didn't answer. Hannah walked closer, called out again, and moved around the door to glance inside the truck.

The sight that greeted Hannah made her jump back and swallow hard. Ron LaSalle, Lake Eden's local football hero, was lying face up on the seat of his delivery truck. His white hat was on the floorboard, the orders on his clipboard were rattling in the wind, and one of Hannah's cookie bags was open on the seat. Chocolate Chip Crunchies were scattered everywhere, and Hannah's eyes widened as she realized he was still holding one of her cookies in his hand.

At first Hannah's shocked mind refused to believe what she was seeing. Ron's body was stiff and lifeless, any fool could see that, and he had died eating one of her cookies . . .

Books by Joanne Fluke

Hannah Swensen Mysteries

CHOCOLATE CHIP COOKIE MURDER
STRAWBERRY SHORTCAKE MURDER
BLUEBERRY MUFFIN MURDER
LEMON MERINGUE PIE MURDER
FUDGE CUPCAKE MURDER
SUGAR COOKIE MURDER
PEACH COBBLER MURDER
CHERRY CHEESECAKE MURDER
KEY LIME PIE MURDER
CANDY CANE MURDER
CARROT CAKE MURDER
CREAM PUFF MURDER
PLUM PUDDING MURDER
APPLE TURNOVER MURDER
DEVIL'S FOOD CAKE MURDER
GINGERBREAD COOKIE MURDER
CINNAMON ROLL MURDER
RED VELVET CUPCAKE MURDER
BLACKBERRY PIE MURDER
DOUBLE FUDGE BROWNIE MURDER
WEDDING CAKE MURDER
CHRISTMAS CARAMEL MURDER
BANANA CREAM PIE MURDER
RASPBERRY DANISH MURDER
CHRISTMAS CAKE MURDER
CHOCOLATE CREAM PIE MURDER
CHRISTMAS SWEETS
COCONUT LAYER CAKE MURDER
CHRISTMAS CUPCAKE MURDER
TRIPLE CHOCOLATE CHEESECAKE MURDER
CARAMEL PECAN ROLL MURDER
JOANNE FLUKE'S LAKE EDEN COOKBOOK

Suspense Novels

VIDEO KILL
WINTER CHILL
DEAD GIVEAWAY
THE OTHER CHILD
COLD JUDGMENT
FATAL IDENTITY
FINAL APPEAL
VENGEANCE IS MINE
EYES
WICKED
DEADLY MEMORIES
THE STEPCHILD

Published by Kensington Publishing Corp.

CHOCOLATE CHIP COOKIE MURDER

A Hannah
Swensen
Mystery

JOANNE FLUKE

KENSINGTON BOOKS
http://www.kensingtonbooks.com

KENSINGTON BOOKS are published by

Kensington Publishing Corp.
850 Third Avenue
New York, NY 10022

All Kensington titles, imprints, and distributed lines are available at special quantity discounts for bulk purchases for sales promotion, premiums, fund-raising, educational, or institutional use.

Special book excerpts or customized printings can also be created to fit specific needs. For details, write or phone the office of the Kensington Special Sales Manager, Attn: Special Sales Dept. Kensington Publishing Corp., 850 Third Avenue, New York, NY 10022. Phone: 1-800-221-2647.

First Kensington Hardcover Printing: April 2000
First Kensington Mass Market Paperback Printing:
February 2001
First Kensington Trade Paperback Printing: October 2004
Revised Kensington Hardcover Printing: September 2006
Revised Kensington Mass Market Paperback Printing:
January 2008

50 49 48 47

Printed in the United States of America

This special edition is for our newest special addition, Kathryn Grace.

Chapter One

Hannah Swensen slipped into the old leather bomber jacket that she'd rescued from the Helping Hands thrift store and reached down to pick up the huge orange tomcat that was rubbing against her ankles. "Okay, Moishe. You can have one refill, but that's it until tonight."

As she carried Moishe into the kitchen and set him down by his food bowl, Hannah remembered the day he'd set up camp outside her condo door. He'd looked positively disreputable, covered with matted fur and grime, and she'd immediately taken him in. Who else would adopt a twenty-five-pound, half-blind cat with a torn ear? Hannah had named him Moishe, and though he certainly wouldn't have won any prizes at the Lake Eden Cat Fanciers' Club, there had been an instant bond between them. They were both battle-worn—Hannah from weekly confrontations with her mother, and Moishe from his hard life on the streets.

Moishe rumbled in contentment as Hannah filled his bowl. He seemed properly grateful that he no longer had to scrounge for food and shelter and he showed his appreciation in countless ways. Just this morning, Hannah had found the hindquarters of a mouse in the center of the kitchen table, right next to the drooping African violet that she kept forgetting to water. While most of her female contemporaries would have screamed for their husbands to remove the disgusting sight, Hannah had picked up the carcass by the tail and praised Moishe lavishly for keeping her condo rodent-free.

"See you tonight, Moishe." Hannah gave him an affectionate pat and snatched up her car keys. She was just pulling on her leather gloves, preparing to leave, when the phone rang.

Hannah glanced at the apple-shaped wall clock, which she'd found at a garage sale. It was only six A.M. Her mother wouldn't call this early, would she?

Moishe looked up from his bowl with an expression that Hannah interpreted as sympathy. He didn't like Delores Swensen and he had done nothing to hide his feelings when she'd dropped in for surprise visits at her daughter's condo. After suffering through several pairs of shredded pantyhose, Delores had decided that she would limit her socializing to their Tuesday-night mother-daughter dinners.

Hannah picked up the phone, cutting off the answering machine in midmessage, and sighed as she heard her mother's voice. "Hello, Mother. I'm ready to walk out the door, so we'll have to keep this short. I'm already late for work."

Moishe raised his tail and shook it, pointing his posterior at the phone. Hannah stifled a giggle at his antics and gave him a conspiratorial wink. "No, Mother, I didn't give Norman my phone number. If he wants to contact me, he'll have to look it up."

Hannah frowned as her mother went into her familiar litany on the proper way to attract a man. Their dinner last night had been a disaster. When she'd arrived at her mother's house, Hannah had encountered two additional guests: her mother's newly widowed neighbor, Mrs. Carrie Rhodes, and her son, Norman. Hannah had been obligated to make polite conversation with Norman over sickeningly sweet Hawaiian pot roast and a chocolate-covered nut cake from the Red Owl Grocery as their respective mothers beamed happily and remarked on what a charming couple they made.

"Look, Mother, I really have to . . ." Hannah stopped and rolled her eyes at the ceiling. Once Delores got started on a subject, it was impossible to get a word in edgewise. Her mother believed that a woman approaching thirty ought to be married, and even though Hannah had argued that she liked her life the way it was, it hadn't prevented Delores from introducing her to every single, widowed, or divorced man who'd set foot in Lake Eden.

"Yes, Mother. Norman seems very nice, but . . ." Hannah winced as her mother continued to wax eloquent over Norman's good qualities. What on earth had convinced Delores that her eldest daughter would be interested in a balding dentist, several years her senior, whose favorite topic of conversation was gum disease? "Excuse me, Mother, but I'm running late and . . ."

Moishe seemed to sense that his mistress was frustrated because he reached out with one orange paw and flipped over his food bowl. Hannah stared at him in surprise for a moment, and then she began to grin.

"Gotta run, Mother. Moishe just knocked over his food bowl and I've got Meow Mix all over the floor." Hannah cut off her mother's comments about Norman's earning capabilities in midbreath and hung up the phone. Then she swept up the cat food, dumped it in the trash, and poured in fresh food for Moishe. She added a couple of kitty treats, Moishe's reward for being so clever, and left him munching contentedly as she rushed out the door.

Hannah hurried down the steps to the underground garage, unlocked the door to her truck, and climbed in behind the wheel. When she'd opened her business, she'd bought a used Chevy Suburban from Cyril Murphy's car lot. She'd painted it candy-apple red, a color that was sure to attract notice wherever it was parked, and arranged for the name of her business—The Cookie Jar—to be painted in gold letters on the front doors. She'd even ordered a vanity license plate that read: "COOKIES."

As Hannah drove up the ramp that led to ground level, she met her next-door neighbor coming home. Phil Plotnik worked nights at DelRay Manufacturing, and Hannah rolled down the window to pass on the warning that their water would be shut off between ten and noon. Then she used her gate card to exit the complex and turned North onto Old Lake Road.

The interstate ran past Lake Eden, but most of the locals used Old Lake Road to get to town. It was the scenic route, winding around Eden Lake. When the tourists arrived in the summer, some of them were confused by the names. Hannah always explained it with a smile when they asked. The lake was named "Eden Lake," and the town that nestled next to its shore was called "Lake Eden."

There was a real nip in the air this morning, not unusual for the third week in October. Autumn was brief in Minnesota, a few weeks of turning leaves that caused everyone to snap photographs of the deep reds, gaudy oranges, and bright yellows. After the last leaf had fallen, leaving the branches stark and bare against the leaden skies, the cold north winds would start to blow. Then the first snowfall would arrive to the delight of the children and the stoic sighs of the adults. While sledding, ice-skating and snowball fights might be fun for the kids, winter also meant mounds of snow that had to be shoveled, virtual isolation when the roads were bad, and temperatures that frequently dropped down to thirty or even forty below zero.

The summer people had left Eden Lake right after the Labor Day weekend to return to their snug winter homes in the cities. Their cabins on the lakeshore stood vacant, their pipes wrapped with insulation to keep them from freezing in the subzero winter temperatures, and their windows boarded up against the icy winds that swept across the frozen surface of the lake. Now only the locals were in residence and the population of Lake Eden, which nearly quadrupled over the summer months, was down to less than three thousand.

As she idled at the stoplight on Old Lake Road and Dairy Avenue, Hannah saw a familiar sight. Ron LaSalle was standing by the dock of the Cozy Cow Dairy, loading his truck for his commercial route. By this time of the morning, Ron had finished delivering dairy products to his residential customers, placing their milk, cream, and eggs in the insulated boxes the dairy provided. The boxes were a necessity in Minnesota. They kept the contents cool in the summer and protected them from freezing in the winter.

Ron was cupping his jaw with one hand and his pose was pensive, as if he were contemplating things more serious than the orders he had yet to deliver. Hannah would be seeing him later, when he delivered her supplies, and she made a mental note to ask him what he'd been thinking about. Ron prided himself on his punctuality and the Cozy Cow truck would pull up at her back door at precisely seven thirty-five. After Ron had delivered her daily order, he'd come into the coffee shop for a quick cup of coffee and a warm cookie. Hannah would see him again at three in the afternoon, right after he'd finished his routes. That was when he picked up his standing order, a dozen cookies to go. Ron kept them in his truck overnight so that he could have cookies for breakfast the next morning.

Ron looked up, spotted her at the stoplight, and raised one hand in a wave. Hannah gave him a toot of her horn as the light turned green and she drove on by. With his dark wavy hair and well-muscled body, Ron was certainly easy on the eyes. Hannah's youngest sister, Michelle, swore that Ron was every bit as handsome as Tom Cruise and she'd been dying to date him when she was in high school. Even now, when Michelle came home from Macalester College, she never failed to ask about Ron.

Three years ago, everyone had expected the star quarterback of the Lake Eden Gulls to be drafted by the pros, but Ron had torn a ligament in the final game of his high school career, ending his hopes for a spot with the Minnesota Vikings. There were times when Hannah felt sorry for Ron. She was sure that driving a Cozy Cow delivery truck wasn't the glorious future he'd envisioned for himself. But Ron was still a local hero. Everyone in Lake Eden remembered his remarkable game-winning touchdown at the state championships. The trophy he'd won was on display in a glass case at the high school and he volunteered his time as an unpaid assistant coach for the Lake Eden Gulls. Perhaps it was better to be a big fish in a little pond than a third-string quarterback who warmed the Vikings' bench.

No one else was on the streets this early, but Hannah made sure that her speedometer read well below the twenty-five-mile limit. Herb Beeseman, their local law enforcement officer, was known to lie in wait for unwary residents who were tempted to tread too heavily on the accelerator. Though Hannah had never been the recipient of one of Herb's speeding tickets, her mother was still livid about the fine that Marge Beeseman's youngest son had levied against her.

Hannah turned at the corner of Main and Fourth and drove into the alley behind her shop. The square white building sported two parking spots, and Hannah pulled her truck into one of them. She didn't bother to unwind the cord that was wrapped around her front bumper and plug it into the strip of power outlets on the rear wall of the building. The sun was shining and the announcer on the radio had promised that the temperatures would reach the high forties today. There was no need to use her head bolt heater for another few weeks, but when winter arrived and the mercury dropped below freezing, she'd need it to ensure that her engine would start.

Once she'd opened the door and slid out of her Suburban, Hannah locked it carefully behind her. There wasn't much crime in Lake Eden, but Herb Beeseman also left tickets on any vehicle that he found parked and unlocked. Before she could cover the distance to the rear door of the bakery, Claire Rodgers pulled up in her little blue Toyota and parked in back of the tan building next to Hannah's shop.

Hannah stopped and waited for Claire to get out of her car. She liked Claire and she didn't believe the rumors that floated around town about her affair with the mayor. "Hi, Claire. You're here early today."

"I just got in a new shipment of party dresses and they have to be priced." Claire's classically beautiful face lit up in a smile. "The holidays are coming, you know."

Hannah nodded. She wasn't looking forward to Thanksgiving and Christmas with her mother and sisters, but it was an ordeal that had to be endured for the sake of family peace.

"You should stop by, Hannah." Claire gave her an appraising look, taking in the bomber jacket that had seen better days and the old wool watch cap that Hannah had pulled over her frizzy red curls. "I have a stunning little black cocktail dress that would do wonders for you."

Hannah smiled and nodded, but she had all she could do to keep from laughing as Claire unlocked the rear door to Beau Monde Fashions and stepped inside. Where could she wear a cocktail dress in Lake Eden? No one hosted any cocktail parties and the only upscale restaurant in town had closed down right after the tourists had left. Hannah couldn't remember the last time she'd gone out to a fancy dinner. For that matter, she couldn't remember the last time that anyone had asked her out on a date.

Hannah unlocked her back door and pushed it open. The sweet smell of cinnamon and molasses greeted her, and she began to smile. She'd mixed up several batches of cookie dough last night and the scent still lingered. She flipped on the lights, hung her jacket on the hook by the door, and fired up the two industrial gas ovens that sat against the back wall. Her assistant, Lisa Herman, would be here at seven-thirty to start the baking.

The next half hour passed quickly as Hannah chopped, melted, measured, and mixed ingredients. By trial and error, she'd found that her cookies tasted better if she limited herself to batches that she could mix by hand. Her recipes were originals, developed in her mother's kitchen when she was a teenager. Delores thought baking was a chore and she'd been happy to delegate that task to her eldest daughter so that she could devote all of her energies to collecting antiques.

At ten past seven, Hannah carried the last bowl of cookie dough to the cooler and stacked the utensils she'd used in her industrial-sized dishwasher. She hung up her work apron, removed the paper cap she'd used to cover her curls, and headed off to the coffee shop to start the coffee.

A swinging restaurant-style door separated the bakery from the coffee shop. Hannah pushed it open and stepped inside, flipping on the old-fashioned globe fixtures she'd salvaged from a defunct ice-cream parlor in a neighboring town. She walked to the front windows, pulled aside the chintz curtains, and surveyed the length of Main Street. Nothing was moving; it was still too early, but Hannah knew that within the hour, the chairs that surrounded the small round tables in her shop would be filled with customers. The Cookie Jar was a meeting place for the locals, a choice spot to exchange gossip and plan out the day over heavy white mugs of strong coffee and freshly baked cookies from her ovens.

The stainless-steel coffee urn gleamed brightly and Hannah smiled as she filled it with water and measured out the coffee. Lisa had scoured it yesterday, restoring it to its former splendor. Lisa was a pure godsend when it came to running the bakery and the coffee shop. She saw what needed to be done, did it without being asked, and had even come up with a few cookie recipes of her own to add to Hannah's files. It was a real pity that Lisa hadn't used her academic scholarship to go on to college, but her father, Jack Herman, was suffering from Alzheimer's and Lisa had decided to stay home to take care of him.

Hannah removed three eggs from the refrigerator behind the counter and dropped them, shells and all, into the bowl with the coffee grounds. Then she broke them open with a heavy spoon and added a dash of salt. Once she'd mixed up the eggs and shells with the coffee grounds, Hannah scraped the contents of the bowl into the basket and flipped on the switch to start the coffee.

A few minutes later, the coffee began to perk and Hannah sniffed the air appreciatively. Nothing smelled better than freshly brewed coffee, and everyone in Lake Eden said that her coffee was the best. Hannah tied on the pretty chintz apron she wore for serving her customers and ducked back through the swinging door to give Lisa her instructions.

"Bake the Chocolate Chip Crunches first, Lisa." Hannah gave Lisa a welcoming smile.

"They're already in the ovens, Hannah." Lisa looked up from the stainless-steel work surface, where she was scooping out dough with a melon-baller and placing the perfectly round spheres into a small bowl filled with sugar. She was only nineteen, ten years younger than Hannah was, and her petite form was completely swaddled in the huge white baker's apron she wore. "I'm working on the Molasses Crackles for the Boy Scout Awards Banquet now."

Hannah had originally hired Lisa as a waitress, but it hadn't taken her long to see that Lisa was capable of much more than pouring coffee and serving cookies. At the end of the first week, Hannah had increased Lisa's hours from part-time to full-time and taught her to bake. Now they handled the business together, as a team.

"How's your father today?" Hannah's voice held a sympathetic note.

"Today's a good day." Lisa placed the unbaked tray of Molasses Crackles on the baker's rack. "Mr. Drevlow is taking him to the Seniors' Group at Holy Redeemer Lutheran."

"But I thought your family was Catholic."

"We are, but Dad doesn't remember that. Besides, I don't see how having lunch with the Lutherans could possibly hurt."

"Neither do I. And it's good for him to get out and socialize with his friends."

"That's exactly what I told Father Coultas. If God gave Dad Alzheimer's, He's got to understand when Dad forgets what church he belongs to." Lisa walked to the oven, switched off the timer, and pulled out a tray of Chocolate Chip Crunches. "I'll bring these in as soon as they're cool."

"Thanks." Hannah went back through the swinging door again and unlocked the street door to the coffee shop. She flipped the "Closed" sign in the window to "Open," and checked the cash register to make sure there was plenty of change. She'd just finished setting out small baskets of sugar packets and artificial sweeteners when a late-model dark green Volvo pulled up in the spot by the front door.

Hannah frowned as the driver's door opened and her middle sister, Andrea, slid out of the driver's seat. Andrea looked perfectly gorgeous in a green tweed jacket with politically correct fake fur around the collar. Her blond hair was swept up in a shining knot on the top of her head and she could have stepped from the pages of a glamour magazine. Even though Hannah's friends insisted that she was pretty enough, just being in the same town with Andrea always made Hannah feel hopelessly frumpy and unsophisticated.

Andrea had married Bill Todd, a Winnetka County deputy sheriff, right after she'd graduated from high school. They had one daughter, Tracey, who had turned four last month. Bill was a good father on his hours away from the sheriff's station, but Andrea had never been cut out to be a stay-at-home mom. When Tracey was only six months old, Andrea had decided that they'd needed two incomes and she'd gone to work as an agent at Lake Eden Realty.

The bell on the door tinkled and Andrea blew in with a chill blast of autumn wind, hauling Tracey behind her by the hand. "Thank God you're here, Hannah! I've got a property to show and I'm late for my appointment at the Cut 'n Curl."

"It's only eight, Andrea." Hannah boosted Tracey up onto a stool at the counter and went to the refrigerator to get her a glass of milk. "Bertie doesn't open until nine."

"I know, but she said she'd come in early for me. I'm showing the old Peterson farm this morning. If I sell it, I can order new carpeting for the master bedroom."

"The Peterson farm?" Hannah turned to stare at her sister in shock. "Who'd want to buy that old wreck?"

"It's not a wreck, Hannah. It's a fixer-upper. And my buyer, Mr. Harris, has the funds to make it into a real showplace."

"But why?" Hannah was honestly puzzled. The Peterson place had been vacant for twenty years. She'd ridden her bicycle out there as a child and it was just an old two-story farmhouse on several acres of overgrown farmland that adjoined the Cozy Cow Dairy. "Your buyer must be crazy if he wants it. The land's practically worthless. Old man Peterson tried to farm it for years and the only things he could grow were rocks."

Andrea straightened the collar of her jacket. "The client knows that, Hannah, and he doesn't care. He's only interested in the farmhouse. It's still structurally sound and it has a nice view of the lake."

"It's sitting smack-dab in the middle of a hollow, Andrea. You can only see the lake from the top of the roof. What does your buyer plan to do, climb up on a ladder every time he wants to enjoy the view?"

"Not exactly, but it amounts to the same thing. He told me that he's going to put on a third story and convert the property to a hobby farm."

"A hobby farm?"

"That's a second home in the country for city people who want to be farmers without doing any of the work. He'll hire a local farmer to take care of his animals and keep up the land."

"I see," Hannah said, holding back a grin. By her own definition, Andrea was a hobby wife and a hobby mother. Her sister hired a local woman to come in to clean and cook the meals, and she paid baby-sitters and day-care workers to take care of Tracey.

"You'll watch Tracey for me, won't you, Hannah?" Andrea looked anxious. "I know she's a bother, but it's only for an hour. Kiddie Korner opens at nine."

Hannah thought about giving her sister a piece of her mind. She was running a business and her shop wasn't a day-care center. But one glance at Tracey's hopeful face changed her mind. "Go ahead, Andrea. Tracey can work for me until it's time for her to go to preschool."

"Thanks, Hannah." Andrea turned and started toward the door. "I knew I could count on you."

"Can I really work, Aunt Hannah?" Tracey asked in her soft little voice, and Hannah gave her a reassuring smile.

"Yes, you can. I need someone to be my official taster. Lisa just baked a batch of Chocolate Chip Crunches and I need to know if they're good enough to serve to my customers."

"Did you say *chocolate*?" Andrea turned back at the door to frown at Hannah. "Tracey can't have chocolate. It makes her hyperactive."

Hannah nodded, but she gave Tracey a conspiratorial wink. "I'll remember that, Andrea."

"I'll see you later, Tracey," Andrea said and blew her daughter a kiss. "Don't be any trouble for your aunt Hannah, okay?"

Tracey waited until the door had closed behind her mother and then she turned to Hannah. "What's hyperactive, Aunt Hannah?"

"It's another word for what kids do when they're having fun." Hannah came out from behind the counter and lifted

Tracey off the stool. "Come on, honey. Let's go in the back and see if those Chocolate Chip Crunches are cool enough for you to sample."

Lisa was just slipping another tray of cookies into the oven when Hannah and Tracey came in. She gave Tracey a hug, handed her a cookie from the tray that was cooling on the rack, and turned to Hannah with a frown. "Ron hasn't come in yet. Do you suppose he's out sick?"

"Not unless it came on suddenly." Hannah glanced at the clock on the wall. It was eight-fifteen and Ron was almost forty-five minutes late. "I saw him two hours ago when I drove past the dairy, and he looked just fine to me."

"I saw him, too, Aunt Hannah." Tracey tugged on Hannah's arm.

"You did? When was that, Tracey?"

"The cow truck went by when I was waiting outside the realty office. Mr. LaSalle waved at me and he gave me a funny smile. And then Andrea came out with her papers and we came to see you."

"Andrea?" Hannah looked down at her niece in surprise.

"She doesn't like me to call her Mommy anymore because it's a label and she hates labels," Tracey did her best to explain. "I'm supposed to call her Andrea, just like everybody else."

Hannah sighed. Perhaps it was time to have a talk with her sister about the responsibilities of motherhood. "Are you sure you saw the Cozy Cow truck, Tracey?"

"Yes, Aunt Hannah." Tracey's blond head bobbed up and down confidently. "It turned at your corner and went into the alley. And then I heard it make a loud bang, just like Daddy's car. I knew it came from the cow truck because there weren't any other cars."

Hannah knew exactly what Tracey meant. Bill's old Ford was on its last legs and it backfired every time he eased up on the gas. "Ron's probably out there tinkering with his truck. I'll go and see."

"Can I come with Aunt Hannah?"

"Stay with me, Tracey," Lisa spoke up before Hannah could answer. "You can help me listen for the bell and wait on any customers that come into the coffee shop."

Tracey looked pleased. "Can I bring them their cookies, Lisa? Just like a real waitress?"

"Absolutely, but it's got to be our secret. We wouldn't want your dad to bust us for violating the child-labor laws."

"What does 'bust' mean, Lisa? And why would my daddy do it?"

Hannah grinned as she slipped into her jacket and listened to Lisa's explanation. Tracey questioned everything, and it drove Andrea to distraction. Hannah had attempted to tell her sister that an inquiring mind was a sign of intelligence, but Andrea just didn't have the necessary patience to deal with her bright four-year-old.

As Hannah pulled open the door and stepped out, she was greeted by a strong gust of wind that nearly threw her off balance. She pushed the door shut behind her, shielded her eyes from the blowing wind, and walked forward to peer down the alley. Ron's delivery truck was parked sideways near the mouth of the alley, blocking the access in both directions. The driver's door was partially open and Ron's legs were dangling out.

Hannah moved forward, assuming that Ron was stretched out on the seat to work on the wiring that ran under the dash. She didn't want to startle him and cause him to bump his head, so she stopped several feet from the truck and called out. "Hi, Ron. Do you want me to phone for a tow truck?"

Ron didn't answer. The wind was whistling down the alley, rattling the lids on the metal Dumpsters, and perhaps he hadn't heard her. Hannah walked closer, called out again, and moved around the door to glance inside the truck.

The sight that greeted Hannah made her jump back and swallow hard. Ron LaSalle, Lake Eden's local football hero, was lying faceup on the seat of his delivery truck. His white hat was on the floorboards, the orders on his clipboard were rattling in the wind, and one of Hannah's cookie bags was open on the seat. Chocolate Chip Crunches were scattered everywhere, and Hannah's eyes widened as she realized that he was still holding one of her cookies in his hand.

Then Hannah's eyes moved up and she saw it: the ugly hole, ringed with powder burns in the very center of Ron's Cozy Cow delivery shirt. Ron LaSalle had been shot dead.

Chapter
Two

It wasn't the way that Hannah preferred to attract new clientele, but she had to admit that finding Ron's body had been good for business. The Cookie Jar was jam-packed with customers. Some of them were even standing while they munched their cookies, and every one of them wanted her opinion on what had happened to Ron LaSalle.

Hannah looked up as the bell tinkled and Andrea came in. She looked mad enough to kill and Hannah sighed.

"We have to talk!" Andrea slipped around the counter and grabbed her arm. "Now, Hannah!"

"I can't talk to you now, Andrea. I have customers."

" 'Ghouls' is more like it!" Andrea spoke in an undertone, surveying the crowd that was eyeing them curiously. She gave a tight little smile, a mere turning up of her lips that wouldn't have fooled anyone with its sincerity, and her grip tightened on Hannah's arm. "Call Lisa to handle the counter and take a break. It's important, Hannah!"

Hannah nodded. Andrea looked terribly upset. "Okay. Go tell Lisa to come up here and I'll join you back in the bakery."

The switch was accomplished quickly, and once she'd

slipped back to the bakery, Hannah found her sister perched on a stool at the work island in the center of the room. Andrea was staring at the ovens as if she'd just encountered a hibernating grizzly, and Hannah was alarmed. "Is there something wrong with the ovens?"

"Not exactly. Lisa said that the timer's about to go off and the cookies have to come out. You know I don't bake, Hannah."

"I'll do it." Hannah grinned as she handed her sister an individual carton of orange juice. Her sister would be more at home in a foreign country than she was in a kitchen. Andrea's culinary efforts were always disasters. Until she'd gone back to work and hired someone to come in to cook the meals, the Todd family had eaten nothing but microwave dinners.

Hannah grabbed a pair of oven mitts and removed the trays from the ovens. She replaced them with the unbaked Oatmeal Raisin Crisps that Lisa had prepared and then she pulled up a second stool and joined her sister at the work island. "What's wrong, Andrea?"

"It's Tracey. Janice Cox just paged me from Kiddie Korner. She said Tracey's telling all of her classmates that she saw Ron's body."

"That's true—she did."

"How could you, Hannah?" Andrea looked positively betrayed. "Tracey's impressionable, just like me. It's liable to scar her psyche for life!"

Hannah reached out and opened the carton of orange juice, slipping the little plastic straw inside. "Take a sip, Andrea. You look faint. And try to relax."

"How can I relax when you exposed my daughter to a murder victim?"

"I didn't expose her. Bill did. And all Tracey saw was the body bag. They were loading it into the coroner's van when he took her over to the preschool."

"Then she didn't actually *see* Ron."

"Not unless she has X-ray vision. You can ask Bill about it. He's still out in the alley securing the crime scene."

"I'll talk to him later." Andrea took a sip of her orange juice and a little color came back into her cheeks. "I'm sorry, Hannah. I should have known that you wouldn't do anything to hurt Tracey. Sometimes I think that you're a better mother to her than I am."

Hannah bit her tongue. This wasn't the time to give Andrea a lecture about how to raise her daughter. "Tracey loves you, Andrea."

"I know, but motherhood doesn't come naturally to me. That's why I hired the best baby-sitters I could find and went to work. I thought that if I had a real career, it would make Bill and Tracey proud of me, but it's just not working out the way I hoped it would."

Hannah nodded, recognizing the real reason behind her sister's unusual candor. "Your sale fell through?"

"Yes. He decided the property wasn't right for him. And when I offered to show him some of my other listings, he wouldn't even look. I really wanted that carpet, Hannah. It was gorgeous and it would have given my bedroom a whole new look."

"Next time, Andrea." Hannah gave her an encouraging smile. "You're a good salesman."

"Not good enough to convince Mr. Harris. I can usually spot a Looky-Lou a mile off, but I'm beginning to think that he was never serious about buying the old Peterson place."

Hannah got up to hand her a Chocolate Chip Crunch that was still slightly warm from the oven. Andrea had always loved Chocolate Chip Crunches and Hannah made a mental note to remind Bill not to mention that Ron had been eating them right before he died. "Eat this, Andrea. You'll feel better with a little chocolate in your system."

"Maybe." Andrea took a bite of the cookie and gave a small smile. "I just love these cookies, Hannah. Do you remember the first time you made them for me?"

"I remember," Hannah answered with a smile. It had been a rainy day in September and Andrea had stayed after school for cheerleading tryouts. Since there'd never been a freshman cheerleader on the varsity squad, Hannah hadn't held out much hope that Andrea would make it. So Hannah had rushed home from school to make chocolate chip oatmeal cookies for her sister, hoping to take the sting out of Andrea's disappointment, but she hadn't checked to make sure she had all the ingredients before she'd started to mix up the dough. The oatmeal canister had been empty and Hannah had crushed up some corn flakes as a substitute. The resulting cookies had been wonderful, Andrea had made the cheerleading squad, and she'd raved about Hannah's Chocolate Chip Crunches ever since.

"I guess there was no real way of knowing that he was just window-shopping." Andrea took another bite of her cookie and sighed. "He *seemed* like a real buyer. Even Al Percy thought so. I mean, we didn't even have to solicit him. He came to us!"

Hannah realized that it might be good for Andrea to talk about her disappointment. "How long ago was that?"

"Three weeks ago on Tuesday. He said he really liked the house, that it had a sense of history about it. I took him inside and he was even more impressed."

"But you couldn't get him to make an offer?"

"No, he said he needed to work out some details first. I figured that it was just an excuse and I wrote him off. Sometimes people don't like to say no and they give you some sort of lame excuse. I really didn't think I'd hear from him again, but he called me last week and said he was still interested."

Hannah decided that some sisterly comfort was in order. "Maybe he really wanted to buy, but he couldn't afford it."

"I don't think so. He told me that money wasn't the problem, that he'd just decided it wouldn't suit him. And then he got into his rental car and drove away."

"He was driving a rental?"

"Yes, he said he didn't want to damage his Jaguar by driving it over gravel roads. For all I know, he doesn't even have a Jaguar. If I ever see a man in a rug again, I'm not going to believe a single word he says! A man who lies about having hair will lie about anything."

Hannah laughed and went to take the Oatmeal Raisin Chews out of the ovens. When she turned, her sister was standing up to go.

"I've got to run," Andrea announced. "Mother told me that Mrs. Robbins is thinking about moving to the Lakeview Senior Apartments. I thought I'd drop in for a visit and see if I can convince her to list her house with me."

Hannah immediately felt better. Andrea seemed to have recovered her self-confidence.

"I'll just say hello to Bill and see if he can pick Tracey up after preschool. And I suppose I'd better find something to take to Mrs. Robbins. It's not very neighborly to arrive empty-handed."

"Take these. They're her favorites." Hannah filled one of her special cookie bags with a half-dozen Molasses Crackles. The bags looked like miniature shopping bags and they had red handles with "The Cookie Jar" stamped in gold lettering on the front.

"This is really sweet of you." Andrea sounded grateful. "I don't say it enough, but you're a wonderful sister. I don't know what I would have done if you hadn't come back when Dad died. Mother was a basket case and Michelle didn't know what to do with her. I tried to run back and forth, but Tracey was just a baby and I just couldn't keep it up. All I could think of was calling you and begging you to come home to bail us all out."

Hannah gave Andrea a quick hug. "You did the right thing. I'm the big sister and you were practically a newlywed. It was my responsibility to help."

"But sometimes I feel really guilty about calling you. You had your own life and you gave it all up for us."

Hannah turned away to hide the sudden moisture that sprang to her eyes. Perhaps losing a sale was good for Andrea. She'd never been this appreciative before. "You don't have to feel guilty, Andrea. Coming home wasn't a sacrifice on my part. I was having doubts about teaching and I really wanted to do something different."

"But you were so close to getting your doctorate. You could have been a professor by now at a really good university."

"Maybe." Hannah shrugged, conceding the point. "But baking cookies is a lot more fun than giving a lecture on iambic pentameter or being stuck in a deadly dull faculty meeting. And you know how much I love The Cookie Jar."

"Then you're happy here in Lake Eden?"

"My business is great, I've got my own place, and I don't have to live with Mother. What could be better?"

Andrea started to smile. "There's something to that, especially the part about not living with Mother. But what about romance?"

"Don't push it, Andrea." Hannah gave her a warning look. "If the right man comes along, that's great. And if he doesn't, that's fine too. I'm perfectly content to live by myself."

"Okay, if you're sure." Andrea looked very relieved as she headed for the door.

"I'm sure. Good luck with Mrs. Robbins."

"I'll need it." Andrea turned back with a grin. "If she starts bragging about her son, the doctor, I'll probably throw up."

Hannah knew exactly what her sister meant. Mrs. Robbins had come into her cookie shop last week, full of praise about her son, the doctor. According to his mother, Dr. Jerry Robbins was about to discover the cure for multiple sclerosis, cancer, and the common cold all in one fell swoop.

* * *

"I need to ask you some questions, Hannah." Bill stuck his head into the coffee shop and motioned to her.

"Sure, Bill." Hannah handed her apron to Lisa, grabbed two mugs of strong black coffee, and followed him into the back room. On the way, she admired the way his tan uniform shirt fit smoothly over his broad shoulders. Bill had been a football player in high school, never as famous as Ron LaSalle, but he'd helped to win his share of games. Now his waist was thicker, the result of too many chocolate-covered doughnuts from the Quick Stop on his commute to the sheriff's station, but he was still a handsome man.

"Thanks for the coffee, Hannah." Bill plunked down on a stool and cupped both hands around his mug of coffee. "It's getting cold out there."

"I can tell. You look positively blue around the gills. Did you find out anything?"

"Not much. The driver's window was open. Ron must have stopped his truck and rolled down the window to talk to his killer."

Hannah thought about that for a moment. "He wouldn't have rolled down his window if he thought that he was in any danger."

"Probably not," Bill agreed. "Whoever it was took him completely by surprise."

"Do you have any suspects?"

"Not yet. And unless we can find a witness, the only clue we'll have is the bullet. It'll go to ballistics right after the autopsy."

Hannah winced at the mention of the autopsy. To take her mind off the fact that Doc Knight would have to cut Ron open, she asked another question. "You don't have to tell anyone that he was eating one of my cookies when he died, do you? It might put people off, if you know what I mean."

"No problem." Bill looked amused for the first time that morning. "Your cookies had nothing to do with it. Ron was shot."

"I wish I'd found him sooner, Bill. I could have called for an ambulance."

"That wouldn't have done any good. It looked like the bullet hit his heart. I won't know for sure until the doc gets through with him, but I think he died instantly."

"That's good." Hannah nodded, and then she realized what she'd said. "I mean, that's *not* good, but I'm glad it was over quickly."

Bill opened his notebook. "I want you to tell me everything that happened this morning, Hannah, even if you don't think it's important."

"You got it." Hannah waited until Bill had picked up his pen and then she told him everything, from the time she'd first seen Ron at the dairy to the moment she'd discovered his body. She gave Bill the exact time that she had gone out through the rear door of the bakery, and the time that she'd come back in to call the sheriff's office.

"You make a good witness," Bill complimented her. "Is that all?"

"I think Tracey may have been the last person to see Ron alive. She said she was waiting for Andrea to pick up some papers at the realty office when Ron drove by in his truck. She waved at him, he waved back, and then she watched him turn at my corner. That must have been close to eight because Andrea and Tracey came into the coffee shop right after I opened and . . ." Hannah stopped speaking and began to frown.

"What is it, Hannah?" Bill picked up his pen again. "You just thought of something, didn't you?"

"Yes. If Tracey saw Ron at eight, he was already twenty-five minutes behind schedule."

"How do you know that?"

"Ron was supposed to be here at seven thirty-five. He delivers to the school and then he comes straight here. I've been on his route since I opened this place and he's never been more than a minute late."

"And that's why you went out in the alley to look for his truck?"

"Not exactly. We thought he'd broken down. Tracey said she heard his truck backfire right after he turned into the . . ." Hannah stopped in midsentence, her eyes widening in shock. "Tracey heard it, Bill. She thought it was a backfire, but she must have heard the shot that killed Ron!"

Bill's lips tightened and Hannah knew what he was thinking. It was terrifying to think that Tracey had come so close to the scene of a murder. "I'd better get out to the dairy and tell Max Turner what's happened," he said.

"Max isn't there. Ron told me that he was leaving for the Tri-State Buttermakers' Convention this morning. It's in Wisconsin and I think it lasts for a week. If I were you, I'd talk to Betty Jackson. She's Max's secretary and she'll know how to reach him."

"Good idea." Bill drained his coffee mug and set it down. "This case is really important to me, Hannah. I passed the detective's test last week and Sheriff Grant put me in charge."

"Then you've been promoted?" Hannah started to smile.

"Not yet. Sheriff Grant has to sign off on it, but I'm pretty sure he will, if I do a good job. This promotion would be good for us. I'd be making more money and Andrea wouldn't have to work."

"That's wonderful, Bill." Hannah was genuinely pleased for him.

"You don't think it's wrong to use Ron's murder as a springboard to my promotion?"

"Absolutely not." Hannah shook her head. "Somebody's got to catch Ron's killer. If you do it and if you get a promotion, it's only what you deserve."

"You're not just saying that to make me feel better?"

"Me? I never say what I don't mean, not when it's important. You should know that by now!"

Bill grinned, relaxing a bit. "You're right. It's like Andrea says: Tact isn't really one of your long suits."

"True." Hannah conceded the point with a smile, but it still stung a little. She thought she'd been very tactful with Andrea over the years. There had been countless occasions when she could have cheerfully strangled her sister, and she hadn't.

"There's one other thing, Hannah." Bill cleared his throat. "I hate to ask, but people tend to talk to you and you know almost everyone in town. Will you call me if you hear anything you think I should know?"

"Of course I will."

"Thanks. Just keep your eyes and your ears open. If Ron's killer is local, he's bound to say or do something to give himself away. We just have to be smart enough to pick up on it."

Hannah nodded. Then she noticed that Bill was eyeing the trays of Oatmeal Raisin Crisps with longing and she got up to fill a bag for him. "Don't eat all these cookies in one sitting, Bill. You're getting a roll around your waist."

After Bill left, Hannah thought about what she'd said. Andrea was right. She had no tact. A tactful person wouldn't have mentioned the roll around Bill's waist. It wasn't her place to criticize Andrea's husband.

As she walked back through the swinging door and took her place behind the counter, Hannah realized that she'd committed an even more serious sisterly infraction. She'd just promised to help Bill solve a murder case that might end up putting Andrea right out of a job.

CHOCOLATE CHIP CRUNCH COOKIES

Preheat oven to 375° F.,
rack in the middle position.

1 cup butter *(2 sticks, melted)*
1 cup white sugar
1 cup brown sugar
2 teaspoons baking soda
1 teaspoon salt
2 teaspoons vanilla
2 beaten eggs *(you can beat them up with a fork)*
2½ cups flour *(not sifted)*
2 cups crushed corn flakes *(just crush them with
    your hands)*
1 to 2 cups chocolate chips

Melt butter, add the sugars and stir. Add soda, salt,
vanilla, and beaten eggs. Mix well. Then add flour and
stir it in. Add crushed corn flakes and chocolate chips
and mix it all thoroughly.

Form dough into walnut-sized balls with your fingers and place on a greased cookie sheet, 12 to a standard sheet. Press them down slightly with a floured or
greased spatula.

Bake at 375 degrees for 8 to 10 minutes. Cool on cookie sheet for 2 minutes, then remove to a wire rack until they're completely cool. *(The rack is important—it makes them crisp.)*

Yield: 6 to 8 dozen, depending on cookie size.

(These cookies have been Andrea's favorites since high school.)

Hannah's Note: If these cookies spread out too much in the oven, reduce temp. to 350° F. and do not flatten before baking.

Chapter Three

"**T**hat's it, Lisa. I'm ready to roll." Hannah shut the back of her Suburban and walked around to climb into the driver's seat. "I should be back by four at the latest."

Lisa nodded, handing Hannah a container of lemons that had been washed until any germs courageous enough to light on their surface had fled in terror. "Do you want to take some extra sugar in case there's a run on the lemonade?"

"I'll just borrow some from the school kitchen if I need it. Edna doesn't leave until three-thirty."

When Lisa had gone back inside, Hannah backed into the alley and drove off toward Jordan High. It had been named after the first mayor of Lake Eden, Ezekiel Jordan, but she suspected that most of the students believed that their school's namesake had played pro basketball.

Jordan High and Washington Elementary were two separate buildings that were connected by a carpeted corridor with double-paned windows that overlooked the school grounds. The two schools shared a common auditorium and cafeteria to cut down on costs, and there was only one principal. The maintenance crew consisted of four people; two took care of the janitorial work and the other two were responsible for the playground, as well as the high school athletic fields.

The Lake Eden school complex worked well. Since the grade school and the high school were connected, older brothers and sisters were always available to drive a younger sibling home in the event of illness, or to calm a frightened kindergartner who missed Mom and Dad. This arrangement also provided a bonus for Jordan High students. The seniors who planned to become teachers were encouraged to volunteer as classroom aides during their free period. The early on-the-job training had produced several college graduates who'd returned to Lake Eden to accept teaching positions at the school.

As she turned on Third Street and drove past the city block that had been set aside for family recreation, Hannah realized that there were no preschoolers playing in Lake Eden Park. The chains on the swings were perfectly motionless, the merry-go-round was still laden with the colorful leaves that had fallen during the morning, and though the temperature had topped the predicted high of forty-eight degrees, there were no children on tricycles pedaling along the circular sidewalk around the playground.

For a moment this struck Hannah as odd. It was the type of weather that a mother of a preschooler prayed for. But then she remembered what had happened this morning and she understood why the park was empty. There was a killer loose in Lake Eden. Concerned parents were keeping their children inside, out of harm's way.

There was a long line of cars idling at curbside on Gull Avenue. It stretched for three blocks leading to and from the school complex, blocking access to driveways and fire hydrants in blatant disregard for the city parking statutes. Hannah inched her way past worried-looking parents waiting for the dismissal bell to ring, and as she neared the school, she saw that Herb Beeseman, his patrol car freshly washed and waxed, was parked diagonally in front of the entrance. He wasn't handing out any tickets for the infractions that were occurring right under his nose, and Hannah assumed that he'd placed the safety of Lake Eden's children at a higher priority than filling the city's coffers.

Hannah reached back between the seats and snagged a bag of Molasses Crackles. She always carried several bags of cookies with her for times like these. Then she pulled up beside Herb's patrol car and rolled down her window. "Hi, Herb. I'm going in to cater the Boy Scout Awards Banquet. Is it okay if I pull into the lot?"

"Sure, Hannah," Herb responded, his eyes on the bag of cookies in her hand. "Just make sure you park legally. Are those for me?"

Hannah handed him the bag. "You're doing a great job protecting the kids. I'm sure the parents appreciate it."

"Thanks." Herb looked pleased at her compliment. "Does your mother still hate me for that ticket I gave her?"

"She doesn't exactly *hate* you, Herb." Hannah decided that this wasn't the time to tell Herb precisely what her mother had called him. "But she's still a little put out."

"I'm sorry I had to do it, Hannah. I like your mother, but I can't have people speeding through town."

"I understand and I think Mother does, too. She's just not quite willing to admit it yet." Hannah began to grin. "At least one good thing came out of that ticket."

"What's that?"

"She stopped trying to fix me up with you."

Hannah was chuckling as she drove off. Judging from the surprised expression on Herb's face, he hadn't guessed that her mother had previously considered him for the position of son-in-law.

The wide gate that separated the teachers' parking lot from the school grounds was open and Hannah drove through. As she traveled down the lane between the rows of parked cars, she noticed a conspicuous absence of new or expensive vehicles. Teaching didn't pay well enough for any luxuries, and

Hannah thought that was a shame. There was something really wrong with the system when a teacher could make more money flipping burgers at a fast-food chain.

The strip of blacktop by the back door of the cafeteria was peppered with warning signs. Hannah pulled up by one that read: "NO PARKING AT ANY TIME BY ORDER OF THE LAKE EDEN PARKING AUTHORITY." In smaller letters, it warned that violators would be prosecuted to the full extent of the law, but Herb was the sole employee of the Lake Eden Parking Authority and he was out watching the front entrance. Hannah didn't feel guilty about violating a city parking statute. She was running late and she had to unload her supplies. In less than ten minutes a horde of hungry Boy Scouts would be clamoring for her cookies and lemonade.

The minute that Hannah pulled up, Edna Ferguson opened the kitchen door. She was a bird-thin woman in her fifties and she wore a welcoming smile. "Hi, Hannah. I was wondering when you'd get here. Do you want some help unloading?"

"Thanks, Edna." Hannah handed her a box of supplies to carry. "The Scouts aren't here yet, are they?"

Edna shook her hair-netted head. "Mr. Purvis called an all-school assembly and they're still in the auditorium. If their parents aren't here to pick them up, he wants them to walk home in groups."

Hannah nodded, hefting the large box of cookies that Lisa had packed, and followed Edna into the school kitchen. As she entered the large room with its wall-long counters and massive appliances, Hannah wondered what it would be like to be the last child in the group. You'd start off together, feeling safe by virtue of sheer numbers, but one by one your friends would peel off to go into their own homes. When the last one had left, you'd have to go the rest of the way by yourself, hoping and praying that the killer wasn't lurking in the bushes.

"There was no suffering, was there, Hannah?"

Hannah set the box down and turned to Edna. "What?"

"With Ron. I've been thinking about it all day. He was such a nice boy. If it was his time to die, I hope it was quick and painless."

Hannah didn't believe that everyone had a prearranged time to die. Thinking like that was too much like buying a lottery ticket and figuring that it was your turn to win the jackpot. "Bill told me he thought it was instantaneous."

"I guess we should be grateful for that. And to think that he was right here, only minutes before he was murdered! It's enough to give a body chills!"

Hannah placed her lemons on one of Edna's chopping blocks and began to cut them into paper-thin slices. "Then Ron made his delivery this morning?"

"Of course. That boy never missed a day. He was real conscientious and he took pride in his work."

Hannah added this tidbit to the small stockpile of facts she'd gathered. Ron had stocked Jordan High's cooler this morning, for whatever that was worth. "Did you see him this morning?"

"No. I never do. I don't come in until eight and he was long gone by then. But the cooler had been stocked."

Hannah unpacked her heavy-duty plastic punch bowl and handed it to Edna. She only used the glass one for formal functions like weddings and the senior prom. Then she picked up the huge thermos of lemonade and the bowl of lemon slices she'd cut, and led the way into the main part of the cafeteria. A table had already been set up for refreshments, covered with a blue paper tablecloth, and there was a cardboard file box at the head of another similarly covered table.

"Gil came down on his free period to set up," Edna told her. "He said to tell you that he's bringing a balloon centerpiece."

"Okay, I'll leave room for it." Hannah motioned for Edna

to put the punch bowl down. Then she opened the thermos and started to pour the lemonade into the bowl. "You didn't notice anything unusual about the way Ron left the kitchen?"

"Can't say as I did. What's in those ice cubes, Hannah? They look cloudy."

"They're made out of lemonade so they won't dilute it when they melt. I do the same thing with any punch I make." Hannah finished transferring the lemonade and floated the slices of lemon on the top. As she stepped back to admire the effect, she noticed that Edna was frowning. "Do you think it needs more lemon slices?"

"No. It looks real professional. I was just thinking about Ron."

"You and everybody else. Come on, Edna. I've got to unpack the cookies."

Edna followed her back to the kitchen and she gasped when Hannah lifted the lid on the box. "Just look at that! Those are real pretty, Hannah."

"I think so, too." Hannah smiled as she arranged the cookies on a tray. Lisa had piped on yellow and blue frosting in the shape of the Boy Scout logo. "Lisa Herman did the decorations. She's getting to be an expert with the pastry bag."

"Lisa's real talented. I swear that girl could do anything she put her mind to. It's just a pity she had to give up college to take care of her father."

"I know. Her older brothers and sisters wanted to put him in a nursing home, but Lisa didn't think that was right." Hannah handed Edna a box with small blue paper plates, gold napkins, and blue plastic cups. "You take this. I'll bring the cookies."

It didn't take long to arrange the plates, cups, and napkins on the table. Once everything was done, they went back into the kitchen for a cup of coffee. They were sitting at the square wooden table in the corner of the kitchen, waiting for the Scouts to arrive, when Edna gave another long sigh. "It's just such a pity, that's all."

"You mean about Ron?"

"Yes. That poor boy was running himself ragged with those routes of his. He was putting in a sixty-hour week and Max doesn't pay overtime. It was getting to him."

"Did Ron tell you that?"

Edna shook her head. "Betty Jackson did. She was there when Ron asked Max for an assistant. That was over six months ago, but Max was too cheap to put anyone else on the payroll."

Hannah knew. Max Turner had the reputation for pinching a penny until it screamed in pain. For someone who was rumored to have money to burn, he certainly didn't live the part. Max drove a new car, but that was his only luxury. He still lived in his parents' old house in back of the Cozy Cow Dairy. He'd fixed it up some, but that had been necessary. It would have fallen down around his ears if he hadn't.

"I just think it's a shame that Ron had to die on the day that he finally got his assistant."

"Ron had an assistant?" Hannah turned to look at Edna in surprise. "How do you know that?"

"I keep out a jar of instant coffee for Ron. He always liked something to warm him up after he came out of the cooler. There were *two* coffee cups on the counter when I came in this morning so I figured he finally got his assistant. But I never thought that Max would hire a woman!"

Hannah felt her adrenaline start to pump. Ron's new assistant might have witnessed his murder. "You're sure that Ron's assistant was a woman?"

"There was lipstick on the cup. She must have been young because it was bright pink and that color looks terrible on someone our age."

Hannah bristled at being lumped in a category with a woman who was at least twenty years older than she was. She had half a notion to remind Edna of that, but it might be counterproductive. "Did you wash the cups, Edna?"

"Nope. I threw them in the trash."

"You threw them in the *trash*?"

Edna laughed at Hannah's astonished expression. "They were the disposable kind."

"They could be evidence," Hannah informed her, and Edna's laugh died a quick death. "Bill's in charge of the investigation and he'll need to see them."

Hannah turned and headed for the wastebasket by the sink, but before she could start to rummage inside, Edna stopped her. "Mr. Hodges emptied my trash right after lunch. I'm really sorry, Hannah. I never would have thrown them away if I'd known that they were important."

Hannah realized she'd been abrupt. "That's okay. Just tell me what Mr. Hodges does with the trash."

"He throws it all in that big orange Dumpster in the parking lot. Somebody's going to have to dig through it before it gets hauled away."

"What time does that happen?"

"Around five."

Hannah muttered a curse under her breath. She couldn't stand by and let the trash truck haul away important evidence. She'd try to reach Bill, but if he wasn't here by the time the awards banquet was over, she'd have to go through the trash bags herself.

"Great job, Hannah!" Gil Surma, the Lake Eden scoutmaster and Jordan High counselor, gave her a friendly pat on the shoulder. "It's a good thing you brought extra cookies. I never thought that eighteen boys could eat seven dozen."

"That's less than five apiece and they're growing boys. I just figured that since I was catering a Boy Scout banquet, I'd better live up to the Boy Scout motto."

It took Gil a minute. As Hannah watched, the corners of Gil's eyes began to crinkle and he chuckled. "You mean, 'Be Prepared'? That's very clever."

Hannah smiled and carried the punch bowl out to the kitchen. When she came back, Gil was still there. "You don't have to stay, Gil. I can clean up."

"No, I'll help you." Gil began to gather up the plastic cups and plates and toss them into the trash. "Hannah?"

"Yes, Gil." Hannah paused to stare at him. Gil looked very earnest.

"You found Ron, didn't you?"

Hannah sighed. Everyone she met wanted to know something about Ron. She was becoming a local celebrity, but being catapulted to instant fame by virtue of Ron's murder made her feel rotten. "Yes, Gil. I found him."

"That must have been very upsetting for you."

"It wasn't exactly my idea of fun."

"I was just thinking . . . that's a terrible thing you had to go through and you might want to talk to someone about it. My office door is always open, Hannah. And I'll do my best to help you through this."

Hannah wanted to tell him that she didn't need a shrink. Even if she did, a Jordan High counselor who dealt with the heartbreak of acne and dateless Saturday nights wouldn't be the shrink she'd choose. But then she reminded herself that she'd vowed to be tactful, and she took a deep breath, preparing to lie through her teeth. "Thanks for the offer, Gil. If I need to talk to somebody about it, you'll be my first choice."

Edna had left by the time Hannah had packed up her supplies and carted them out to her Suburban. She'd tried to call Bill several times, but she'd been told that Bill was out in the field and couldn't be reached. Hannah glanced at her watch. She'd promised Lisa that she'd be back by four, and she had

only five minutes to make it. But finding the cup with lipstick was more important than getting back to The Cookie
Jar on time.

Hannah glanced down at her best dress slacks and sweater
set. She was catering the mayor's party tonight and she'd
planned to wear it.

The knit outfit was light beige, but it was washable. Giving a little groan for the load of laundry she'd have to do the
moment she got home, Hannah pushed up her sweater
sleeves and marched to the Dumpster, girding her loins to do
battle with the cafeteria leftovers that awaited her.

The Dumpster was huge. Hannah wrinkled her nose at
the stench that rolled out of the metal bin and muttered a
curse. The lip of the container came up above her armpits
and there was no way that she could lift all the bags out to
examine them. Muttering another curse, a more colorful one
this time, Hannah walked back to her Suburban and drove it
up nose-to-nose with the front of the trash bin. Then she
clambered up on the candy-apple red hood and reached into
the Dumpster to pull up the first trash bag.

Her first attempt yielded wadded napkins, globs of butterscotch pudding, and clumps of something brown that
looked like beef stew. At least she knew what the students
had eaten for lunch. Hannah was about to haul up the second
bag when she remembered that the kitchen wastebasket had
been lined with a smaller green plastic bag. She stretched
out over the hood and lifted the black bags one by one, drag-
ging them over to one side. Near the bottom—she should
have known that it would be on the bottom—she saw one lone
green bag.

Even though she scrunched forward until her entire upper
body was hanging over the edge of the Dumpster, the tips of
her fingers were still a good three inches from the top of the
green bag. Hannah sighed and then she did what any good
sister-in-law and dedicated amateur detective would do. She

turned around to dangle her legs over the lip of the metal bin, took a deep steadying breath, and slid down into the bowels of the Dumpster.

Now that she was on the inside, grabbing the green trash bag was simple. Climbing back out of the Dumpster wasn't. Hannah had to stack the big black bags in a pile so that she could scramble up on top of them, using them like a slippery and squishy staircase. One bag broke under her weight and she groaned as her shoes sank down into a morass of stew. By the time she emerged from the malodorous depths and pulled herself back up on the hood of her Suburban again, Hannah knew that she smelled every bit as bad as she looked.

"Bill's going to owe me big time for this," Hannah grumbled as she loosened the tie on the green plastic bag and began to search through the contents. Several crumpled bread wrappers and a slew of illicit cigarette butts later, she encountered two Styrofoam cups.

"Gotcha!" Hannah crowed. She was about to grab the cups when she remembered that movie and television detectives always used protective gloves and evidence bags. If there were fingerprints on the cup with the lipstick, she certainly didn't want to smudge them. Since Hannah didn't happen to carry gloves or evidence bags on her catering jobs, she settled for slipping a bread wrapper over her hand, plucking out the two cups, one by one, and depositing them inside a second empty bread wrapper.

With the evidence secured, Hannah slid down from the hood of her Suburban and climbed into the driver's seat. As she started her engine and drove out of the school parking lot, she felt a little foolish about the elaborate precautions she'd taken. Modeling herself after a television detective was crazy unless she was dumb enough to believe that the prefix of every telephone number in the entire country was five-five-five.

Chapter Four

Lisa was filling a bag with Peanut Butter Melts and her eyes grew as round as saucers as Hannah blew in the back door. "Hannah! What . . . ?"

"Don't ask. I'm going in to take a quick shower."

"But Bill's here and he needs to talk to you."

Hannah ducked into the bathroom and poked her head out the door. "Where is he?"

"Out in front. He's minding the counter while I pack up this order for Mrs. Jessup."

"Give him a mug of coffee and send him back here. I'll be out just as soon as I'm decent."

The moment she'd closed the bathroom door behind her, Hannah peeled off her filthy clothes and stuffed them into a laundry bag. Then she climbed into the minuscule metal enclosure that Al Percy had called an "added bonus" when he'd shown her the building, and cranked on the water. She'd used the shower once before, when a fifty-pound bag of flour had burst as she'd muscled it up to the surface of the work island. Her shower might be tiny and cramped, but it worked. Once she was as clean as she could get within the tight confines, she shut off the water and stepped out, toweling off in record time.

She put on the extra set of clothes she kept for emergencies: a pair of worn jeans with a threadbare rear and an old Minnesota Vikings sweatshirt that had faded from royal purple to a dull shade of pewter. The gold block letters had deteriorated into a peeling smudge, but at least she didn't smell like decaying food. After running a wide-toothed comb through her frizzy red hair, she slipped her feet into the pair of cross-country trainers she hadn't worn since the last time she'd fallen for the old "jogging is good for you" routine, and opened the door.

Bill was sitting on a stool at the work island. There were cookie crumbs on the otherwise sparkling surface and Hannah assumed that Lisa must have plied him with cookies to keep him from becoming too impatient.

"About time," Bill commented. "Lisa said you smelled worse than the panhandler that hangs around the Red Owl. What happened?"

"I was just helping you. Edna Ferguson told me that Max hired a woman assistant for Ron. I was collecting the coffee cups they used this morning."

Bill looked confused. "But Ron didn't have an assistant. I asked Betty about that. If there was a woman with Ron this morning, she wasn't hired by the dairy. Didn't Edna recognize her?"

"Edna didn't see her. Ron and this woman left before she came in to work."

"Wait a minute." Bill held up his hands. "If Edna didn't see this woman, how did she know about her?"

"From the cups. Edna always leaves a jar of instant coffee out for Ron and there were two cups on the counter this morning. One of them had a smear of lipstick on the rim and that's how she knew that Ron was with a woman. I collected them and they're right over there by the dishwasher in that bread wrapper."

"Why did Edna save them?" Bill looked puzzled as he got up to retrieve the cups.

"She didn't. I dug them out of the cafeteria Dumpster. They were all the way in the bottom and I had to climb in to get them."

"That's why you smelled like a panhandler?"

"You got it." Hannah gasped as Bill started to reach inside the bread wrapper. "Don't touch them, Bill! I went to a lot of trouble to preserve any fingerprints."

Bill's eyebrows shot up and he froze for a second. He took one look at her earnest face and then he began to laugh. "The lab can't lift prints from this kind of cup. The surface is too rough."

"I knew I never should have climbed in that Dumpster!" Hannah groaned. "How about the lipstick? Can you do something with that?"

"It's possible, unless it's such a popular color that half the women in Lake Eden wear it."

"It's not." Hannah was very sure of herself. "Most women look awful in bright pink."

"How would you know? I've never seen you wear lipstick."

"That's true, but Andrea bought a color like that once and it looked horrible on her. She's got every other shade there is, so I figure that this one can't be very popular."

"You've got a point." Bill started to smile. "Good work, Hannah."

Hannah was pleased at the compliment, but then she started thinking about the logistics of finding the Lake Eden woman who owned that color of lipstick. "What are you going to do, Bill? Inspect every powder room in town?"

"I hope it won't come to that. I'll start with the cosmetic counters and see if they carry this color. Whoever she is, she had to buy it somewhere. That's called legwork, Hannah, and I'll need your help. You may not know much about lipstick, but you've got to know more than I do."

Hannah sighed. Watching paint dry held more interest for her than cosmetic counters, and legwork didn't sound like very much fun.

"You *are* going to help me, aren't you?"

"Of course I am. I'm sorry I'm not more enthusiastic, but rooting around in all that garbage got me down."

"Next time just call me and I'll do it. I've got coveralls in the cruiser and I'm used to stuff like that."

"I *did* call you. I even left a message, but you didn't get back to me in time. And since Edna told me that the trash company was coming to empty the Dumpster at five, I figured that I'd better do it."

Bill reached out to pat her on the back. "You'd make a good detective, Hannah. Your dip in the Dumpster gave us the only real clue we've got."

Rhonda Scharf, her plump middle-aged body encased in a baby-blue angora sweater that might have fit her thirty pounds ago, leaned forward over the glass-topped cosmetic counter at Lake Eden Neighborhood Pharmacy to stare at the smudge of pink lipstick on the white Styrofoam cup. Rhonda was wearing a scowl that turned down the corners of her heavily rouged lips, and her too-long, too-thick, too-black-to-be-real eyelashes fluttered in distaste. "That lipstick didn't come from my counter. I wouldn't be caught dead displaying a product like that!"

Bill pushed the bag closer. "Take another look, Rhonda. We need to make sure."

"I did look." Rhonda pushed the bag back to him. "I do all the ordering and I've never carried that brand or that color."

"There's no doubt in your mind, Rhonda?"

Rhonda shook her head, her coal-black hair swaying from side to side. The strands moved together, like they'd been dipped in glue, and Hannah suspected that Rhonda must get a massive employee's discount on hairspray.

"See how it's smeared?" Rhonda poked at the bag with the pointed tip of a long, manicured nail. "I don't sell any lipstick that isn't smudge-proof, and the lines I buy from don't make garish shades like that."

Hannah looked up from the color charts that Rhonda had handed her. Her grandmother had always said that you'd catch more flies with honey than with vinegar, and she was about to put that old maxim to the test. "We really need your help, Rhonda. You're Lake Eden's only cosmetic expert."

"Then why did you go to CostMart? I know you did, Hannah. Cheryl Coombs called to tell me."

"Of course we went there," Hannah acknowledged. "We checked out every cosmetic counter in town. But we saved you for last because I told Bill you'd know more about lipstick than anyone else in town. Your makeup is always so perfect."

Rhonda preened slightly, giving Bill a sidelong glance that was definitely flirtatious. Since Rhonda had to be pushing fifty and Bill hadn't yet celebrated his thirtieth birthday, Hannah figured the gossip her mother had told her about Rhonda and the UPS driver might not be as ridiculous as she'd thought.

"I'll help any way I can." Rhonda simpered a bit, her violet-colored contacts trained on Bill. "What do you want to know?"

Hannah sighed, reminding herself again about flies and honey. "If you wanted to buy a lipstick like the one on the cup . . . and I know you wouldn't, having such good taste and all . . . but *if* you did, where would you go to buy it?"

"Let me think about that." Rhonda pursed her perfectly drawn lips. "No store in town would carry that lipstick, so I'd have to look elsewhere. Not that I would, of course."

Hannah agreed quickly. "Of course not. We're just pretending here, trying to get a feel for where the owner of this lipstick might have gone to buy it. You're helping Bill with a very important investigation, Rhonda, and he really appreciates it."

"Just a minute." Rhonda's eyes narrowed. "Does this have anything to do with Ron LaSalle's murder?"

Hannah kicked Bill and he took his cue from her. He leaned close and lowered his voice. "It's confidential, Rhonda. The only reason we asked is because we knew that we could trust you."

"I see." Rhonda reached out to pat Bill's hand. "If I wanted to buy this particular shade of perfectly awful lipstick, I'd just have to get it from Luanne Hanks."

"Luanne Hanks?" Hannah was surprised. Luanne had been in Michelle's high school class, but she'd had to drop out when she got pregnant. "I thought Luanne worked at Hal and Rose's Cafe."

"She does."

"They sell lipsticks at the cafe?" Bill asked.

"No, silly boy." Rhonda batted her unnatural lashes. "Luanne works at the cafe during the week and she sells Pretty Girl cosmetics on the weekends. I've seen her lugging her sample case around town."

Bill stepped back, preparing to go. "Thanks, Rhonda. You've been a big help."

"There's one more thing, Rhonda." Hannah put on her most serious expression. "Bill hasn't warned you yet."

Bill turned to stare at her with a perfectly blank face, and Hannah knew she'd have to take charge. She turned back to Rhonda and plunged ahead on her own. "It's like this, Rhonda. Bill doesn't want you to say anything about any of the questions he's asked you. If Ron's killer finds out that you helped, you could be in real danger. Isn't that right, Bill?"

"Uh . . . right!" Bill was a little slow on the uptake, but Hannah figured he was still rattled by Rhonda's attempt to flirt with him. "Mum's the word, Rhonda. Just keep in mind that Ron's killer has already committed the ultimate crime. He's got nothing to lose by killing again."

Rhonda's face turned so pale that Hannah could see the place where she'd blended her foundation. Rhonda deserved a good scare for flirting with Bill, but Hannah didn't want to be responsible for the damage if Rhonda fainted and crashed into the glass cosmetic counter.

"You don't have to be nervous, Rhonda." Hannah reached out to pat her arm and steady her at the same time. "No one overheard our conversation and we went to every cosmetic counter in town. As far as anyone knows, you just told us that you didn't sell this type of lipstick."

"Hannah's right," Bill said. "There's no cause for alarm, Rhonda. I'll protect your identity by keeping your name out of my notes."

"Thank you, Bill." A little color began to come back to Rhonda's face. "I won't breathe a word of this to anyone. I swear it."

Hannah was satisfied that Rhonda wouldn't blab, but she still looked awfully pale. "When the killer's behind bars, Bill will put in for a special citizen's merit certificate for you. You've been really helpful, Rhonda."

Bill echoed Hannah's words and picked up the plastic bag. With a final goodbye and a thank-you to Rhonda, they walked out of the store and climbed into Bill's county cruiser. They were driving back to Hannah's shop when Bill started to chuckle.

"What is it?" Hannah turned to stare at him.

"I was just wondering how I'd put in for a special citizen's merit certificate for Rhonda when the sheriff's department doesn't do things like that."

"No problem," Hannah assured him. "Gil Surma's got a bunch of blank award certificates for his Boy Scouts. I'll just ask him for one and you can fill it in with Rhonda's name."

"That won't work. Sheriff Grant will never sign his name to a trumped-up award."

"He doesn't have to." Hannah gave him a grin. "We're going to solve this case, Bill. By the time you get around to giving Rhonda her certificate, you'll be a detective and you can sign it yourself."

Chapter Five

Hannah hung her slacks and sweater on a hanger and reached out to catch Moishe before he disappeared into the still-warm interior of the dryer. "No, you don't. Dryers eat cats and I think you're already on your ninth life."

With Moishe tucked under one arm, she folded a towel one-handed and carried it out to the couch. The moment she set it down, Moishe jumped on top and started to purr.

"What's a little cat hair between friends?" Hannah asked, reaching down to scratch him under the chin before she went back to retrieve the rest of her clothes. Five minutes later, she was dressed and ready for the mayor's fundraiser at the community center.

"I've got to go, Moishe." Hannah stopped at the couch to say goodbye to him. "I'll turn on the TV for you. Do you want A&E, or Animal Planet?"

Moishe flicked his tail and Hannah understood. "Okay, I'll put it on A&E. *Emergency Vet* is on Animal Planet tonight and you don't like to watch that."

She had just flicked on the television when the phone rang. Hannah exchanged a glance with Moishe. "I'd better not answer that. It's probably Mother again."

Hannah listened as her outgoing message played: "Hello. This is Hannah. I can't answer the phone right now, but if you leave a message, I'll be glad to call you back. Wait for the beep." The beep sounded and then her mother's voice came through the speaker. "Where are you, Hannah? I've called six times already and you're never home. Call me the minute you step in the door. It's important!"

"Would you say that Mother sounds a little miffed?" Hannah grinned down at Moishe. His ears were laid back flat against his skull and he'd puffed up in anger at the sound of her mother's voice. She smoothed down his ruffled fur and gave him another scratch. "Don't worry, Moishe. She won't come over here. She just replaced the last pair of pantyhose that you shredded."

A rumble came from Moishe's throat, a deep self-satisfied purr. He was definitely proud of himself for chasing away the woman he'd labeled as the "bad guy." Hannah laughed and fetched him a couple of salmon-flavored kitty treats from the kitchen and then she rushed out the door. She had a stop to make before she could go to the mayor's fundraiser and she was running late.

Hannah gave thanks for Lisa once again as she started her Suburban, put it into reverse, and backed out of her parking spot. A neighbor was staying with her father tonight and Lisa had offered to cart the cookies and coffee urns to the community center for her. By the time Hannah arrived, the refreshment table would be set up and all she'd have to do was smile and serve.

Night had fallen and Hannah switched on her headlights. Once she exited the complex, she turned south on Old Lake Road and took the country road that led to the Hanks place. She'd promised Bill that she'd talk to Luanne tonight to see if the lipstick was one that she carried. Luanne had finished her shift at the cafe at six and she should be home by now.

Birch trees lined the sides of County Road 12, their white bark catching in the beams of Hannah's headlights as she drove. The Sioux had used birch bark to make canoes. When Hannah was still in grade school, her class had taken a trip to the museum to see one. Young Hannah had decided that if the Indians had built canoes so many years ago, it should be even easier to do using modern tools. Unfortunately, her mother had spotted the barkless patches on the stand of birch in their backyard. Her canoe hadn't gotten past the planning stage before Hannah had received the scolding of her life from Delores for attempting to kill her birch trees, accompanied by a spanking from her father for pilfering his best pocketknife.

Hannah's lights caught the metal reflective triangle that was nailed to a tree trunk at the mouth of Bailey Road and she slowed to take the turn. Bailey Road was gravel because it provided access to only three homes. Freddy Sawyer still lived in his mother's cottage at the edge of the puddle they called Lake Bailey. He was mildly retarded, but Freddy did just fine living by himself and doing odd jobs for the people in town. The second house on Bailey Road had been finished only last year. Otis Cox and his wife had built their retirement home on the site of his parents' old cottage. They'd told everyone in town that they liked the quiet and the solitude, but Hannah figured it had more to do with the Lake Eden statute that limited dog owners to three canines per residence. Otis and Eleanor were crazy about dogs and now that they lived outside the town limits, they could take in as many strays as they wanted.

Hannah grinned as she drove past the cozy three-bedroom house. Otis and Eleanor's matching Explorers were in the driveway, each sporting a new bumper sticker. They were rip-offs of the old "I ♥ New York" stickers. They read: "I ♠ My Dog."

The only other residence on Bailey Road, way down at the end where the snowplows had no room to turn around, was the old Hanks place. Ned Hanks, Luanne's father, had recently died of liver disease, the result of his years of alcohol abuse. Now that Ned was gone, the only occupants of the Hanks place were Luanne, her mother, and Luanne's baby daughter Suzie.

As she pulled up in front of the four-room cabin, Hannah thought about Luanne's strange reaction to Bill. He'd told Hannah that he'd stopped Luanne once, for a broken taillight on the old car she drove, and she'd seemed positively terrified of him. Hannah didn't understand that at all. Bill was a giant teddy bear, with his easy smile and his nonthreatening manner. He didn't have a mean bone in his body, and everyone in Lake Eden knew it.

Hannah really didn't know Luanne that well. She'd met her a couple of times when Michelle had brought her home from school and she'd seen her at the cafe, but they hadn't exchanged more than a few polite words. All the same, Hannah admired her. Even though Luanne had dropped out of high school in her senior year, she'd continued to study throughout her pregnancy and she'd passed the equivalency test for her diploma. Luanne was a hard worker at the cafe, always pleasant and neatly groomed, and now that her father was dead, she was the sole support of her mother and Suzie. Though there were rumors, no one really knew who had fathered Luanne's baby. Anyone who'd had gall to ask Luanne directly had received a perfectly polite, "I'd rather not say."

Naturally, Hannah had brought cookies. She'd packed up a bag with a dozen of her Old-Fashioned Sugar Cookies and she grabbed it as she got out of her Suburban. There was a mouthwatering aroma in the crisp night air and Hannah sniffed appreciatively. Someone was cooking supper and it smelled like fried ham and biscuits.

Luanne was clearly surprised to see Hannah when she answered the knock at the door. "Hannah! What are you doing way out here?"

"I need to talk to you, Luanne." Hannah handed her the cookie bag. "I brought some Old-Fashioned Sugar Cookies for Suzie."

Luanne's eyes narrowed perceptively, and Hannah didn't blame her. She was practically a stranger and after all Luanne had been through, it was natural not to trust people. "How nice. Suzie loves sugar cookies. But why do you need to talk to me?"

"It's about lipstick. Do you have a couple of minutes?"

Luanne hesitated for a moment, and then said, "Come on in. Just let me serve supper and then I'm all yours. I already ate at the cafe."

Hannah stepped through the doorway into a wide rectangular room. The kitchen was at one end, there was a table in the center for eating, and a couch, two chairs, and a television set were down at the other end. Though it was shabby, it was squeaky-clean and two-thirds of the floor was carpeted with carpet samples that had been sewn together in an attractive crazy-quilt pattern.

Mrs. Hanks was sitting at the table, holding Luanne's baby, and Hannah walked over to her. "Hi, Mrs. Hanks. I'm Hannah Swensen. Luanne went to school with my youngest sister Michelle."

"Sit down, Hannah," Mrs. Hanks invited, patting the chair next to her. "Nice of you to drop by. You need some of Luanne's lipstick?"

For a moment Hannah was floored, but then she remembered what she'd said at the door. Mrs. Hanks had sharp ears. "That's right."

"Why don't you get Hannah a cup of coffee, honey?" Mrs. Hanks motioned to Luanne. "It's nippy outside tonight."

Luanne walked over to set a plate of ham, a bowl of green beans, and a basket of biscuits on the table. "How about it, Hannah? Would you like some coffee?"

"Yes, if it's made."

"It's made." Luanne went back to the old wood stove and filled a cup from the blue enamel pot that sat at the back. She set it down in front of Hannah and asked, "You still drink it black, don't you?"

"That's right. How did you know?"

"From the cafe. The tips are bigger if I remember things like that. Just hold on a minute and I'll put Suzie in her highchair. Then we can talk about that lipstick."

Luanne slid her daughter into the highchair and pushed up the tray. She handed Suzie a biscuit and laughed as the little girl tried to push the whole thing into her mouth. "She's still not clear on the concept of small bites."

"They never are at that age," Hannah responded with a smile.

Luanne retrieved the biscuit and broke it into bite-sized pieces. Then she turned to her mother. "Will you feed Suzie, Mom?"

"Sure will. Go on, honey. Take Hannah back and show her what's in your sample case."

Hannah followed Luanne into one of the bedrooms. It was painted sunny yellow and there were frilly white curtains at the window. Suzie's crib was against the far wall, and a twin bed that Hannah assumed was Luanne's was against the other wall. Two plastic laundry baskets sat in a corner with a few toys in each. There were three children's books sitting on top of a child-sized table, and Hannah noticed a handful of crayons in an old bleach bottle that had been partially cut away to make a crayon carrier.

"That's Suzie's corner," Luanne explained, motioning toward the table. "I'm stenciling blue and white bunnies on the wall this weekend and I'm going to paint her table blue."

Hannah noticed that the table was longer than most children's tables. It was just the right height for a toddler like Suzie and there was plenty of room to work. "That table's perfect. Tracey used to have a little square one. It looked nice, but it was barely big enough for a coloring book."

"Suzie's used to be an old coffee table. I just sawed off the legs. Now all I have to do is find something that she can use for a chair."

Hannah remembered the things in her sister's garage, all

the clothing, toys, and toddler-sized furniture that Tracey had outgrown. "Andrea may have a chair for Suzie. I'll ask her."

"No." Luanne shook her head. "I know you mean well, Hannah, but we don't need charity. We're getting along just fine."

Hannah should have guessed that Luanne would be too proud to accept an outright gift. But there were ways around pride and as she stared at the table, Hannah had an idea.

"Believe me, it's not charity." Hannah gave what she hoped was an exasperated sigh. "I promised to help Andrea clean out the garage this weekend and cart all of Tracey's toddler things to the dump."

Luanne looked shocked. "To the *dump*? You should take them to the thrift store, Hannah. I'm sure somebody would be glad to buy them secondhand."

"I know, but this stuff has been stored for a couple of years and Andrea's too busy to go through it. It's easier for her to just dump it."

Luanne looked thoughtful. "It's a shame to think of all those things just going to waste. I could go through it for Andrea. Helping Hands always needs contributions."

"Would you? We could just haul it out here and you could sort it out one box at a time. But you have to promise to pull out anything that you can use for Suzie. You deserve it for doing all that work."

"I'll be glad to do it." Luanne sounded pleased at the prospect. "Sit down at the dressing table, Hannah.

Luanne gestured toward an old-fashioned vanity that was painted a pretty shade of blue. Its mirror was darkly spotted with signs of age, and a sampling of Pretty Girl cosmetics was arranged on the top. A battered old folding chair with a matching coat of paint sat in front of the vanity, and Luanne whisked a stuffed rabbit off the seat. Once Hannah was seated, she smiled. "You said you needed some lipstick?"

"Yes, I do." Hannah told herself that she wasn't really

lying. She'd already decided to buy some cosmetics from Luanne. Anyone who worked this hard to make a life for her mother and daughter deserved her help.

"What color did you have in mind?" Luanne asked.

"This color." Hannah reached into her purse and drew out the bag that contained the cup. "Do you have anything that matches this?"

Luanne stared at the cup for a moment and then she sighed. "You can't wear that color, Hannah. It'll clash with your hair."

"Oh, it's not for me," Hannah launched into the story she'd prepared. Bill had warned her not to mention the investigation, but Hannah had thought of a way around that restriction. "My mother just loves this shade. She was helping me take out the trash the other day and she spotted this cup with the lipstick on it."

Luanne looked relieved. "Then it's for your mother?"

"That's right. She told me she used to wear lipstick like this and she can't find it anywhere in town. I thought I'd surprise her with it the next time I go over there for Carb Tuesday."

"Carb Tuesday?"

"That's what I call it. I have dinner with Mother every Tuesday night and she's crazy about sweets. Last night we had Hawaiian pot roast with pineapple slices and candied yams."

Luanne started to grin. "I can see why you call it Carb Tuesday!"

"You haven't heard the rest of it. We also had a side dish of fried bananas and nut cake with chocolate frosting for dessert. Mother had ice cream on top of hers."

"Your mother sounds like a sugar junkie. Does she ever eat it right out of the bag?"

"I wouldn't be surprised." Hannah laughed. "I know she has a stash of fudge brownies in her freezer and a whole drawer filled with one-pound chocolate bars. I guess I should be grateful that she invited Carrie Rhodes and her son to join us for dinner. Norman's a dentist."

Luanne gave her a shrewd look. "I heard that Norman moved here when his father died. Is your mother trying to fix you up with him?"

"Of course she is. You know Delores. She's desperate to marry me off and she's leaving no single, divorced, or widowed stone unturned."

"And you don't want to get married?"

"I'm just fine the way I am. It would take the combined efforts of Harrison Ford and Sean Connery to change my mind."

"Me too," Luanne said. "I'm really glad that lipstick isn't for you, Hannah. I'd hate to miss out on a sale, but I'd already decided that I couldn't let you walk out of here wearing a color that's wrong for you. With that pretty red hair of yours, you need to choose from an earthier palette."

"But you *do* have a lipstick in this shade?"

"Sure, I do. And your mother's right. I'm the only one in Lake Eden who carries it. It's called 'Pink Passion' and I stock it for a lady in town."

"That's great, Luanne. This is going to win me points with my mother." Hannah was proud of herself. She knew where the lipstick had come from. Now all she had to do was get Luanne to tell her the name of the woman who wore it. "Tell me about the other woman who wears it. Mother gets upset if someone she meets is wearing the same hat or the same dress. She probably feels the same way about lipstick."

"Oh, that's no problem. I don't think your mother and Danielle belong to any of the same groups."

Hannah zeroed in on the name. The only Danielle she knew was married to Boyd Watson, the winningest coach Jordan High had ever had. "Are you talking about Coach Watson's wife?"

"That's right. I just about died the first time she ordered it, but it actually looks good on her. You've got to be a natural light blond to wear it. And Danielle's hair is so blond, it's almost white."

"Are you sure that Danielle Watson is the only woman in town who wears Pink Passion?"

"I'm positive. No one else orders it from me and I'm the only Pretty Girl distributor around."

"Thanks, Luanne." Hannah was grateful, more grateful than Luanne knew. "If you've got a tube of Pink Passion, I'll take it."

"I've got it. Just sit tight and I'll pull it out of my stock. And while we're at it, I'll give you a makeover. Let's see how attractive you'll look with the right foundation, a nice shade of eye shadow, and the perfect color lipstick."

"Okay," Hannah agreed. It would be rude to refuse and she could ask more questions about Danielle while Luanne played beautician. "Does Danielle order a lot of makeup from you?"

Luanne pulled out a huge sample case and set it on a table next to the dresser. It was much larger than a briefcase and it opened on both sides to expose several tiers. The top tier contained miniature sample tubes of lipstick, the second had small jars of foundation and blusher, and the third was filled with various shades of eye shadow, eyeliner, and mascara. Jars of nail polish were arranged in the bottom and there was a lift-out tray with brushes, cotton swabs, and sponges.

"Danielle's one of my best customers," Luanne answered as she pulled out a jar of foundation. "She orders from our theatrical line."

"She belongs to the Lake Eden Players?" Hannah named the community theater group that had opened a dinner theater in the old shoe store on Main Street.

"I don't think so." Luanne took out several old-fashioned hair clips, the ones that Bertie had stopped using at the Cut 'n Curl years ago, and gathered Hannah's hair back from her face. "Let's just get your hair out of the way."

"Why does Danielle wear theatrical makeup?"

"She has skin problems." Luanne began to apply foundation to Hannah's face. "Close your eyes, Hannah. I need to do your eyelids, too."

Hannah obediently closed her eyes, but she continued to ask questions. "What kind of skin problems?"

"Blemishes and rashes. Don't say that I mentioned it. Danielle's very self-conscious about her condition. She told me that she still breaks out like a teenager and it's not just on her face. She gets horrible rashes on her upper arms and her neck, too."

"And theatrical makeup covers that up?"

"Perfectly. Pretty Girl theatrical makeup will cover almost anything. Remember when Tricia Barthel got that black eye?"

"Mmm-hmm." Hannah did her best to answer in the affirmative without opening her mouth. Luanne was in the process of applying foundation around her upper lip. She remembered Tricia's black eye. Tricia had told everyone that she'd run into a door, but Hannah had heard the real story from Loretta Richardson. Loretta had told Hannah that her daughter, Carly, had thrown an algebra book at Tricia when Tricia had put the moves on Carly's boyfriend.

"Tricia's mother was really upset because they were taking senior pictures the next day. She called me in for a consultation and I used Pretty Girl's theatrical foundation on Tricia. It covered her bruises perfectly and she's ordered makeup from me ever since."

"That's amazing," Hannah risked commenting. Luanne had moved on to her chin. "I saw Tricia's picture when they ran all the senior photos in the paper and I didn't see any bruises."

"Pretty Girl theatrical foundation will cover anything from a bad bruise to a zit." Luanne sounded proud of her products. "But you don't need it, Hannah. Your skin is perfect. You must use just the right combination of moisturizer and night cream. If I were you, I wouldn't change a thing."

Hannah stifled a grin. She wasn't planning to change anything, especially since she'd never used a moisturizer or a night cream in her life. She washed her face with whatever soap was on sale at the Red Owl and never thought twice about it.

"Just lean back and relax, Hannah," Luanne said in a professional voice. "By the time I get through with you, you'll look better than you've ever looked before in your life."

Chapter
Six

When Hannah walked into the community center, the first person she saw was her mother. Delores Swensen was holding court at the far end of the room, surrounded by a circle of her friends. As Hannah watched, her mother reached up to pat her sleek dark hair and her tasteful diamond earrings glittered in the overhead lights. She was wearing the soft blue dress that had been in the window of Beau Monde Fashions and her purse and shoes matched perfectly. Hannah's mother was still a beautiful woman and she knew it. At fifty-three, Delores was winning the battle against time and only Hannah, who'd helped her mother with her finances for several months following her father's death, knew exactly how expensive that battle was. Fortunately, Delores had the money to spend. Hannah's father had left Delores in very good financial shape and she'd also inherited from her parents. There was no way that Delores could run out of money, even if she resorted to costly tummy tucks and face-lifts.

Hannah sighed as she made her way through the crowd. With the exception of her hair color, Andrea resembled Delores. And Michelle was another petite beauty. Both of her younger sisters had inherited their mother's beauty genes. Hannah was the only one in the family to take after her father. She was cursed with his curly, unmanageable red hair and she was at least four inches taller than her sisters. When strangers saw Delores with her daughters, they assumed that Hannah was adopted.

Delores was laughing at something that one of her friends had said. Hannah waited until the group of ladies had disbanded and then she walked over to tap Delores on the shoulder. "Hi, Mother."

"Hannah?" Delores turned to face her. Her eyes widened, her mouth opened in a round O of shock, and she dropped her purse to grab Hannah's hand.

"What is it?" Hannah began to frown.

"I don't believe it, Hannah! You're actually wearing makeup!"

Hannah was puzzled by her mother's reaction. She'd decided to wear the results of Luanne's makeover to the fundraiser, but if she'd known that Delores would react with such gaping-mouthed astonishment, she would have stopped at The Cookie Jar and washed her face. "You don't like it?"

"It's such a change. I don't know *what* to say."

"I can see that." Hannah bent over to pick up her mother's purse. "I guess I should have washed it off before I got here."

"No! It actually looks good. You surprise me, Hannah. I had no idea you even knew what eyeliner was."

"I must have hidden depths." Hannah grinned at her mother. "Tell me the truth, Mother. Do you really think it's an improvement?"

"It certainly is! Now, if I could only convince you to dress better, you might actually . . ." Delores stopped speaking and her eyes narrowed. "I know you hate makeup and there's only one reason you'd go to all this trouble. Tell me, dear. Did you do this for Norman Rhodes?"

"Norman had nothing to do with it. I drove out to see Luanne Hanks and while I was there, she gave me a makeover."

"Oh." Delores looked disappointed. "Well, I think it looks

very nice on you. If you'd put on makeup and get all dressed up more often, it might make a real difference in your life."

Hannah shrugged and decided to change the subject before her mother went into one of her lectures. "Have you seen Andrea? I really need to talk to her."

"She's here somewhere. I saw her over by the refreshment table a few minutes ago."

"I'd better go and find her." Hannah prepared to make her escape. "See you later, Mother."

Hannah searched the crowd, but she didn't see Andrea. She decided she'd look for her sister later and headed off toward the refreshment table, which was set up on the side of the room. She was shirking her duties and Lisa would probably be eager to get home to her father.

"Hi, Hannah. " Lisa smiled as Hannah came up to the table. "Everyone loves your cookies. Mrs. Beeseman's been back four times."

"That figures. She loves anything with chocolate. You've done a wonderful job, Lisa. If you want to leave now, I can take over."

"I don't have to leave, Hannah. My neighbor said he'd sit with Dad until I got home. Besides, I'm really having fun."

Hannah had trouble believing what she'd heard. "You think serving coffee and cookies at a political fundraiser is *fun*?"

"It's great. Everybody's coming over to talk to me and they're really friendly. Go ahead and circulate, Hannah. You might be able to drum up some new business."

"Okay, but consider yourself on overtime." Hannah gave her a long, level look. If this was Lisa's idea of fun, she really needed to get out more. "I have to talk to Bill. Have you seen him?"

"Not yet. Your sister said he'd be late. I guess there was a whole lot of paperwork for him to do. Do you want me to tell him you're looking for him when he gets here?"

"Yes, thanks." Hannah needed to tell Bill about Danielle Watson, but in the meantime, she might be able to find out why Danielle was with Ron when he stocked the school's cooler. "How about Coach Watson's wife? Is she here?"

"They were both here a couple of minutes ago. Coach Watson said that he just got back from a basketball clinic. He was gone for three days."

Hannah's mind was spinning as she set off to find Andrea. Coach Watson had been gone and Danielle had been with Ron, early this morning. Hannah didn't want to believe that Ron was the type to have an affair with another man's wife, but that was the obvious conclusion.

Andrea was talking to Mrs. Rhodes, but she excused herself when she saw Hannah. "What happened to you? You look fantastic!"

"Thanks, Andrea. Do you have a minute?"

"Of course I do." Andrea led the way over to a less populated corner of the room. "Why are you wearing makeup?"

"Luanne Hanks gave me a makeover and I didn't have time to wash it off. That's why I needed to talk to you. When I was out at Luanne's, I noticed that her daughter doesn't have many things. I was just wondering if you had any of Tracey's old furniture and toys that you could give her."

"Of course I do. I saved every single thing she outgrew. I'd give it all to Luanne in a heartbeat, but I know how she is about taking charity."

"No problem. I told her that you were hauling some of Tracey's things to the dump and I asked her if she'd mind if you dropped them off her at house instead."

"And she agreed?"

"Only after I said that you didn't have time to go through the boxes and it was a real shame that all that nice stuff would be rotting out at the dump. She's going to pull out what she can use and take the rest to the thrift shop."

"Good job, Hannah!" Andrea reached out to pat her on

the back. "I didn't think you had a devious bone in your body, but I guess you must have learned *something* from Mother."

Hannah spotted Danielle Watson from across the room. She was a part of a group that contained her husband, Marge Beeseman, Father Coultas, Bonnie Surma, and Al Percy. Danielle was wearing an ice blue dress, and her light blond hair was arranged in a fashionable twist at the nape of her neck. Several feathery curls hung down near her cheeks to make her hairstyle less severe and her lips were colored with the lipstick that Hannah now recognized as Pretty Girl's Pink Passion.

Hannah moved forward and joined the fringes of the group. The topic of conversation was Ron LaSalle and that didn't surprise her. Ron's murder was the biggest news to hit Lake Eden since little Tommy Bensen had released the brake on his mother's Ford Escort and crashed through the plate glass window of the First Mercantile Bank.

"My Herbie says he was shot clean through the heart," Mrs. Beeseman offered her tidbit of gossip. "Now Max is going to have to reupholster the truck because there was blood all over the place."

Coach Watson looked sad. "It's a terrible loss for The Gulls. Ron came to every practice and he was a real inspiration."

"Do you suppose it was some kind of sports vendetta?" Al Percy asked, his dark bushy eyebrows almost meeting in a frown. "After all, Ron was The Gull's star player for three years in a row."

Father Coultas shook his head. "That doesn't make sense, Al. Everybody liked Ron, even the boys on the opposing teams."

"You're right, Father." Coach Watson was quick to agree. "Ron was popular because he played fair."

Al continued to frown and Hannah could see that he wasn't ready to give up his sports vendetta theory quite yet. "Maybe it didn't have anything to do with high school sports. From what I heard, it was an execution-style killing and that sure smacks of bent-nose types to me."

"Bent-nose?" Bonnie Surma bristled and Hannah remembered that her maiden name had been Pennelli. "Are you talking about the Mafia?"

Al nodded. "It's not impossible, Bonnie. Everybody knows that they run the sports books and they could have recruited Ron to pick up bets with his milk orders. If Ron's take came up short, they might have put out a hit on him."

"You're crazy, Al." Marge Beeseman obviously didn't believe in mincing words. "Ron was one of ours and he never would have done something like that. Besides, my Herbie says that Mafia hit men always shoot their victims in the back of the head. Or they use that wire thing to choke them like they did in *The Godfather.*"

As Hannah watched, Danielle's naturally pale face turned a shade of sickly gray. The polite smile on her face crumpled and she looked as if she were struggling not to burst into tears. She turned to her husband, whispered a few words, and then she left the group. Hannah watched her as she pushed her way through the crowded room and headed out into the hallway that led to the ladies' room.

This was her chance and Hannah wasn't about to waste it. She set off after Danielle as fast as she could. Once she'd gained the hallway, Hannah headed straight for the ladies' room with only one purpose in mind. She had to find out exactly what Danielle knew about Ron's murder.

Chapter
Seven

As Hannah approached the door to the ladies' room, she heard the sound of muffled sobbing. Maybe it wasn't fair of her to take advantage of Danielle in her grief, but playing fair wasn't as important as helping Bill solve Ron's murder.

Hannah pushed open the door and found Danielle standing in front of the long mirror above the sinks. She was dabbing at her eyes with a soggy tissue and she looked helpless and frightened. As Hannah stepped into the pink-tiled room, she felt like Simon Legree confronting Little Eliza.

"Danielle?" Hannah remembered the old flies-and-honey maxim and she put every ounce of sympathy she could muster into her voice. "What's wrong?"

Danielle whirled around, looking terribly guilty. "Nothing. I just . . . uh . . . I got something in my eye, that's all."

"Both eyes?" Hannah spoke without thinking and instantly regretted it. She wouldn't get anywhere by alienating Danielle before she'd asked her first question. "It's probably dust. It's been really windy today. Do you want me to take a look?"

"No! Uh . . . thanks anyway, Hannah. I think I got it."

"Good." Hannah gave her the best of her friendly smiles. She knew that the excuse Danielle had given her was a bald-faced lie, but she was willing to ignore it, providing Danielle told her what she wanted to know. "Isn't it awful the way everybody's talking about Ron?"

Danielle's face blanched again. "Yes, it is."

"Did you see Ron in the past couple of days?" Hannah held her breath. If Danielle admitted she'd ridden along to the school with Ron, she'd be one step closer to gathering the facts that Bill needed.

"No. We don't take home delivery and I really didn't run into him all that much. I've got to go now, Hannah."

"You just got here." Hannah moved to the side to block Danielle. "Stay for a minute, Danielle. If I were you, I'd fix my makeup. Your mascara's starting to run."

"No, it's not. I just checked it. I've really got to go. Boyd's waiting for me and he doesn't like me to be gone for long."

"Why not?" Hannah could feel Danielle's panic and it didn't make sense.

"He . . . uh . . . he worries about me when I'm not with him."

Danielle was standing right under the overhead light fixture and Hannah noticed that the makeup on one side of her face was much thicker than it was on the other. Was it covering the skin problem that Luanne had told her about?

"We can talk later, Hannah. Boyd won't be happy if I don't get right back out there."

"Not quite yet." Hannah reached out to take Danielle's arm as she tried to brush past her. The flies-and-honey tactic hadn't worked and it was time to play hardball. "I know you were with Ron this morning and I need to know why."

Danielle's eyes widened in an attempt to look innocent, but a telltale blush rose to her cheeks. "Ron? You're mistaken, Hannah. I told you I haven't seen him for weeks."

"That's a lie and you know it. Why were you at the school with Ron when he stocked the cooler?"

"Who says I was?" Danielle turned to face her directly and there was a definite challenge in her eyes. It was clear she wasn't willing to give up the information without a fight.

"Nobody says it, but I know you were. Your coffee cup was sitting on the counter and you left a smear of lipstick on it. You're the only one in Lake Eden who wears that color, Danielle. Were you having an affair with Ron?"

"An affair?" Danielle seemed genuinely shocked. "That's ridiculous, Hannah! It's true I was with Ron, but we were just friends. He . . . uh . . . he helped me through some rough times."

Danielle's face had the very same expression Hannah had once seen on a trapped rabbit. She'd freed the rabbit, but Hannah wasn't about to let Danielle escape before she'd given her some truthful answers. "Let me see if I've got this straight, Danielle. Your husband was out of town, you spent the night with an attractive man who's just a friend, and your friend just happened to get murdered this morning only minutes after you had coffee together?"

"I know it sounds bad." Danielle sighed and all the bravado seemed to go out of her. "You've got to believe me, Hannah. That's exactly what happened."

"Does Boyd know that you spent the night with Ron?"

"No!" Danielle looked sick. "Please don't tell him! Boyd would never understand!"

"I won't have to tell him if you start being honest with me. If you and Ron weren't having an affair, why were you with him?"

Danielle glanced at the door and then she looked down at her arm where Hannah's fingers gripped it. She shivered and then she nodded. "All right. I'll tell you, Hannah, but you've got to respect my privacy. I . . . I can't let Boyd know where I was last night."

"Deal," Hannah agreed. "But if you know anything about Ron's murder, I'll have to give the information to Bill."

"It doesn't have anything to do with Ron's murder! At

least, I don't *think* it does. I lied to you, Hannah . . . Ron and I were more than just friends. He was my GA sponsor."

"GA?"

"Gamblers Anonymous. We meet every Tuesday night at the community college."

That confession threw Hannah for a loop. "You're a recovering gambler?"

"Yes, but Boyd doesn't know." Danielle reached out and steadied herself against the wall. "Could we sit down, Hannah? I don't feel very good."

Hannah led her over to the couch and chairs that were arranged in a corner of the ladies' room. When Danielle had taken a seat on the couch, Hannah pulled up one of the chairs. "You said that Boyd doesn't know about your addiction?"

"No. He's not an easy man, Hannah. He wants perfection from a wife. I think he'd divorce me if he ever found out the truth."

Hannah suspected that Danielle was right. Coach Watson demanded perfection from everyone around him. He was hard on his team when they made errors on the playing field or the court, and he'd be even harder on Danielle. Danielle might be exaggerating when she said that her husband would divorce her, but Hannah was willing to bet that he'd be plenty upset. "You said you go to GA meetings every Tuesday night. Doesn't Boyd ask you where you're going?"

"I told him I was taking an art class at the college. I had to lie to him, Hannah."

It was time to cut Danielle a little slack and Hannah knew it. "I can understand that. I'd probably do the same thing in your place. Were you at the GA meeting last night?"

"Yes, I was there."

"How about Ron?"

"Ron was there, too. He never missed a meeting."

Hannah zeroed in on the crux of the matter. "Did you go home from the meeting with him?"

"Of course not. I thought that Boyd would be back by then and we were going to drive out to The Hub to have a late supper together. Boyd really likes their steaks. He says an athlete doesn't get enough protein from chicken and fish, and he always makes his boys eat plenty of red meat when they're in training."

Hannah had seen the boys from Coach Watson's teams wolfing down hamburgers at Hal and Rose's Cafe and she didn't think there was much danger they'd be protein-deficient. But Danielle was digressing and Hannah needed to get her back on track. "Your husband didn't come home last night, did he?"

"No. When I walked in, there was a message from Boyd on the answering machine. He said he'd decided to stay over at his mother's house and he'd be home by noon today. He doesn't see her that often and I should have just taken it in stride, but I expected him to come home and . . . and it just threw me off."

Hannah gave her an encouraging smile. "Of course it did. What happened next?"

"I opened the mail and I found a check from my mother. We bought some stocks together and we made a good profit when we sold them. If that check hadn't come, I think I would have been all right. But just looking at that money made me want to gamble."

"That's understandable. What did you do?"

"I called Ron. We're supposed to call our sponsor right away when we think we're in trouble. But Ron wasn't home and—" Danielle swallowed hard. "I'm not proud of what I did next, Hannah."

Hannah figured she knew what Danielle had done, but she asked anyway. "You went out to gamble?"

"Yes." A tear rolled down Danielle's cheek and she wiped it away with her soggy tissue. "I used the ATM to deposit the check and take out some cash. And then I drove out to the Indian casino. That's where I ran into Ron."

"Ron was gambling at Twin Pines?"

"No." Danielle shook her head quickly. "Ron was a tower of strength, Hannah. He'd completely beaten his addiction. He told me once that he didn't even have the *urge* to gamble anymore."

"Then what was he doing there?"

"He was passing out brochures in the parking lot. One look at me and he knew I was in trouble, and he got his car and followed me back to my house. I was really glad he did. Boyd's Grand Cherokee wasn't running very well and I was afraid it would break down on the way back."

"Do you know what time that was?"

"Eleven o'clock," Danielle answered promptly. "The grandfather clock in the hallway was striking when I walked in the door."

"And Ron stayed there with you?"

"No, he waited around the corner for me. I was in pretty bad shape, Hannah. I almost scraped the side of my Lincoln when I pulled into the garage."

Hannah nodded and waited for her to go on. She could sympathize with Danielle, but this wasn't the time. She still needed more information from her.

"I went inside to check the answering machine again, and then I walked down the alley to meet Ron. He drove me to his apartment and we stayed up all night, drinking coffee. That's exactly what happened, Hannah. I swear it!"

"Why did you go to work with him?"

"Ron was late and he didn't have time to take me home until later. I went along on his home delivery route and then we went back to the dairy and he loaded up for his commercial customers. I only went to one commercial place with him. Right after we stocked the school cooler, he dropped me off at home."

"What time did Ron bring you home?"

"It was seven-twenty. I looked at my watch before I got out of his truck. I figured that my neighbors might be up by then, so I ducked in the alley and went in through the garage."

"Do you think you would have noticed if anyone was following Ron's truck?"

"I don't know." Danielle looked frightened. "I've been thinking about it all day, but I don't remember seeing anyone behind us."

Hannah leaned forward. If Danielle knew where Ron had been planning to go when he'd dropped her off, it could be very helpful. "Think hard, Danielle. Did Ron say anything about where he was going when he left you?"

"He didn't say anything except goodbye," Danielle's voice quavered and she dabbed at her eyes again. "I tried to talk him into going to the dentist for his tooth, but I don't think he did. Ron had this thing about being totally reliable and making his deliveries on time."

Hannah's eyebrows shot up. "His tooth? What was wrong with his tooth?"

"I think it was cracked. He got into a fight with one of the casino bouncers when he tried to hand out some pamphlets inside. His jaw was all swollen up and it was hurting him a lot. I made him put ice on it. That's good for the swelling."

Hannah flashed back to the last time she'd seen Ron alive. He'd been standing by his truck, cupping the side of his face. She'd thought that he looked pensive, but he could have been holding his hand over a cracked tooth. "Was Ron's cracked tooth on the left side, Danielle?"

"Yes!" Danielle gasped and stared at Hannah as if she'd just pulled a rabbit out of a hat. "How did you know?"

"I saw him loading the truck when I drove to work this morning and he was cupping the left side of his jaw. But I didn't see *you*."

"That's because I was scrunched down in the seat. I didn't want anyone to spot me with Ron and get the wrong idea."

That made sense. Hannah knew the local gossips would

have had a heyday if they'd seen Danielle with Ron. "Can you describe the bouncer who hit Ron?"

"I wasn't there. It happened about an hour before I got to the casino. I think you could find him, though. Ron told me he landed a couple of good punches and he was pretty sure he gave the guy a black eye."

"And that's all you know?"

"That's everything, Hannah." Danielle gave a deep sigh. "You don't have to tell Bill about this, do you? Boyd thinks I was home all night and I really don't want him to find out."

Hannah made one of her lightning decisions and she hoped she wouldn't regret it. "I'll tell Bill what happened, but I'm not going to use your name, Danielle. There's no reason he has to know."

"Oh, thank you, Hannah! You don't know how much I appreciate this. I wanted to say something sooner, but—"

"I understand," Hannah interrupted her. "You couldn't say anything without letting Boyd know that you were with Ron."

Danielle dipped her head in a nod. She still looked beautiful, even though her makeup was smudged and her eyelashes were stuck together in clumps from the tears she'd shed. Hannah was amazed at the difference between them. Every time she cried, which wasn't often, her nose turned as red as the light on top of Bill's cruiser and the skin around her eyes puffed up. It was pretty clear that when they'd handed out the gorgeous genes, women like Danielle and Andrea had stolen her share.

"Take a couple of minutes and fix your makeup." Hannah gave her a bracing smile. "Your mascara really *is* running now."

Danielle looked scared again. "But Boyd'll come looking for me if I'm not out soon."

"I'll find him and tell him that you got a piece of dust in

your eye." Hannah helped her up and propelled her toward the mirror. "Don't worry, Danielle. Your secret is safe with me."

"I know, Moishe. I was gone a long time." Hannah scooped up the orange blur that hurled itself at her ankles when she opened her condo door. That action seemed to appease the needy feline because he started to rumble, deep in his throat. He licked her hand and Hannah laughed. "I'm home to stay now. Just let me make one phone call and then we'll have our bedtime snack and hit the pillows."

Moishe followed her out to the kitchen and watched as she poured herself a glass of white wine from the green gallon jug of Chablis that sat in the bottom of her refrigerator. It was far from fine wine and Hannah knew the difference, but it was cheaper than Sominex or Bayer P.M. She opened the cupboard to grab one of the antique dessert dishes that her mother had given her as a Christmas present and filled it with Moishe's favorite brand of vanilla yogurt. Her mother would be horrified to learn that the only one who'd ever used one of the cut-glass dessert dishes was the cat who'd shredded her stockings.

"Okay, we're all set." Hannah clicked off the kitchen light and let Moishe precede her into the living room. He hopped up on the coffee table and waited for Hannah to set down the dessert dish. "You can start, Moishe. I'll drink my wine while I talk to Bill."

Hannah watched as Moishe began to lap up the yogurt. She didn't know if it was usual feline behavior since she'd never shared her home with a cat before, but Moishe had perfected the act of eating and purring simultaneously.

Bill hadn't arrived at the fundraiser by the time she'd packed up, and Hannah assumed that he was still at his desk, doing battle with the quadruplicate forms that were required by the latest paper-reduction act. She punched out the number of the sheriff's station and was rewarded when Bill answered on the first ring.

"Bill?" Hannah frowned. Her favorite, and only, brother-in-law sounded tired and out of sorts. "It's Hannah. I managed to identify the woman with the pink lipstick, but I can't tell you who she is."

Bill's reaction was loud and predictable, and Hannah set the phone down on the table. She knew she should have been more careful about the way she'd phrased that particular bit of information, but she'd exceeded her tact quotient for one day.

When the volume of irate squawks had diminished somewhat, Hannah brought the phone back to her ear. "Listen up, Bill. This woman doesn't have anything to do with the murder. I'd stake my life on it. And she split up with Ron right after they stocked the school cooler. The only way I could get her to tell me anything at all was to promise that I wouldn't reveal her identity."

The squawks were fewer this time around and Hannah settled for merely holding the receiver away from her ear. When they stopped, she continued. "I can't break my promise to her, Bill. You know how the people in Lake Eden are. If the word gets out that I betrayed a confidence, nobody'll trust me enough to give me the time of day."

"I don't like it, but I guess we'll just have to play this your way." Bill sounded mollified. "You can talk to this woman again if we need her, can't you?"

"Of course I can. She was cooperative and she's very grateful that I'm keeping her identity a secret."

"You'll probably get further with her if she thinks of you like a friend. Remember, Hannah, I don't want you to tell anybody that you're in on the investigation. You can talk to Andrea, but that's it. I'm not writing your name on my reports. I'm just referring to you as my snitch."

"Your *snitch*?" Hannah took a sip of her far-from-premium wine.

"A snitch is a person whose identity is protected by the investigating officer. You must have learned that from those detective shows you're always watching."

Hannah rolled her eyes at Moishe. "I know what a snitch is. Why can't I be your undercover agent?"

"My undercover agent?" That made Bill laugh, but once he realized that Hannah wasn't laughing with him, he backtracked fast. "All right. Consider yourself my undercover agent. What else have you got?"

"The woman with the pink lipstick told me that Ron got into a fight at Twin Pines last night. She thinks he cracked a tooth because his jaw swelled up. Remember when I told you I saw him cupping his jaw this morning?"

"Right. You said you thought he was thinking about something important. I've got it right here in your interview notes."

"Well, I was wrong. His tooth hurt and that's why he had his hand on the side of his face."

There was a moment of silence and Hannah heard a pen scratch. Bill was taking notes. Finally he said, "That makes sense. Did this woman know who Ron fought with at the casino?"

"No, it happened before she got there. I'll try to find out for you, Bill."

"I know I asked you to nose around, but this isn't a game, Hannah." Bill sounded worried. "Ron was murdered in cold blood and the killer won't hesitate to take you out if he thinks you're on to something."

Hannah swallowed hard, the image of Ron's lifeless body flitting across the screen of her mind. "You're scaring me, Bill. Do you really think it could be that dangerous?"

"Of course it could. Promise me that you'll be careful, Hannah. And call me right away with anything you learn, even if it's four in the morning."

"I will. Good night, Bill." Hannah shivered as she hung up the phone. She'd been thinking of Ron's murder as a puzzle to be solved, but Bill had reminded her that it was dangerous to try to uncover a killer. As she finished her wine, Hannah decided that she'd be a lot more cautious in the future.

There was a plaintive yowl from the direction of the coffee table and Hannah saw that Moishe was doing one of his incredibly wide kitty yawns. It was definitely time for bed. She scooped him up, carried him into the bedroom, and set him down on the mattress.

When she was ready for bed, Hannah climbed under the covers and pulled her roommate over for a cuddle. But Moishe had been a loner too long. Sweet words, ear scratches, and tabby treats would never turn him into a tame and obliging house cat. He permitted a few pets, but then he moved over to claim Hannah's other pillow and ignored her completely by going to sleep.

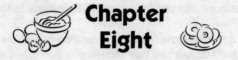

Chapter Eight

Hannah woke up with a start. She'd been having a nightmare and Norman Rhodes, an insane dentist with a drill that sounded like a dump truck backing up, had been grinding her teeth. Since she'd refused to unclench her jaw, he'd been doing his evil dentistry right through her cheek. When she opened her eyes, she was relieved to find that it was only Moishe, licking her face with his sandpaper tongue to wake her.

The alarm clock was serenading her with its irritating electronic beep, and Hannah moved Moishe over so that she could reach out and shut it off. It was still dark outside, but the security light on the side of the building had come on. Since it detected any type of motion, Hannah figured that it had been set off by a winter bird that had swooped down to peck at the birdseed bell she'd hung outside her window.

"Okay, I'm getting up. I know it's feed-the-kitty time." Hannah levered her head from the warm comfort of her pillow and sat up in bed. She dangled her feet over the side of the mattress and searched with her toes for the pair of slippers she kept there. She nabbed one, then the other, and wiggled her feet into the gray scuffs that had once been powder blue.

When she got to the kitchen, the coffee was ready, and Hannah gave thanks for the timer she'd rigged to the kitchen outlet. Some of the older women in Lake Eden called strong black coffee "Swedish plasma" and Hannah agreed with that definition. She couldn't even think, much less function, until she'd downed at least a cup. She poured herself a mug of the steaming, caffeine-laden brew, threw some kitty crunchies into Moishe's bowl, and sat down at the table.

There was something very important on the docket for today. Hannah took a big gulp of her coffee, hoping to dispel the morning cobwebs that had gathered in her head during the night. It wasn't a new catering job. She had her schedule set for this week.

The sound of loud chewing roused Hannah from her zombielike state and she turned to look at Moishe. His kitty crunchies were living up to their name. He was chomping so hard, he sounded as if he might break a tooth and . . . "Ron's tooth! That's it!"

Moishe gave her a startled look and then he buried his head in his food bowl again. Hannah grinned. He probably thought she was crazy for hollering out loud, but she'd just remembered what Tracey had told her, right before she'd discovered Ron's body. Tracey had said she'd waved at Ron and he'd given her a "funny" smile. People who'd just come from the dentist had "funny" smiles, especially if the dentist had given them a shot of novocaine. And Danielle had said that she'd urged Ron to go to the dentist.

Hannah reached out for the yellow pad she kept on the kitchen table and jotted down a note to herself. *Call every dentist in town. Did they see Ron yesterday morning?* Then she grinned at what she'd written. Every dentist? There were only two dentists in Lake Eden: Doc Bennett and Norman Rhodes. Doc Bennett was retired, but he still kept a few of his former patients in enamel, and Hannah hoped that Ron had been one of them. She certainly wasn't looking forward to the prospect of calling Norman. He might think that she was following up on her mother's attempt at matchmaking and nothing could be further from the truth.

It took a second mug of coffee, but at last Hannah felt she was ready to face the morning. She added a second note to her first—*Drive to Twin Pines to check out the bouncer*—and then she pushed back her chair. It was time to get ready for work.

Since she never ate breakfast, Hannah was usually ready to go in record time. She made quick work of her shower, dressed in faded jeans and a flowered sweatshirt, and hurried back to the kitchen to fast-forward through the messages on her answering machine. They were all from her mother. Delores sounded like a talking chipmunk at the increased-speed playback and Hannah was amused. She knew she'd have to return her mother's calls eventually, but that could wait until she got to The Cookie Jar.

"See you tonight, Moishe." Hannah grabbed her keys from the corkboard next to the phone and glanced at the African violet as she passed by the table. Its leaves were turning yellow and it looked in imminent danger of becoming mulch. She shrugged into her bomber jacket and snatched up the plant, carrying it with her out the door. Lisa was a wizard with plants. She might be able to resuscitate it.

It wasn't until Hannah was approaching the dairy that it hit her, and she winced as she drove past the white cinderblock building with the huge Cozy Cow sign on the roof. Ron was gone. She'd never see him loading his truck again.

That was a sobering thought and Hannah almost blew off the stop sign at the corner of Main and Third. She managed to brake just in time and she smiled guiltily at Herb Beeseman, who was lurking in the alley by the Cut 'n Curl. Herb just shook his finger in a good-natured "no-no" gesture, and Hannah breathed a sigh of relief. Herb was being very nice this morning. He could have given her a ticket for reckless driving, but he seemed more amused than angry. The Molasses Crackles she'd given him yesterday afternoon had been a very good investment.

As she turned the corner and drove into the alley behind her shop, Hannah wondered who'd hauled away Ron's truck. Max Turner would be livid if it had been impounded and he was one truck short for his delivery routes. She steered a wide berth around the place where Ron had been shot and gave a fleeting thought to the difference between the fronts of the shops and the backs. There were no decorative planters in the alley for shrubbery or flowers, no plate-glass windows for displays and signs. The backs of the shops were institutional-looking, just parking places, Dumpsters, and blank walls with small doors set in at regular intervals. It wasn't a nice place to die, but that raised another question. Was there a nice place to die? And did it really matter to the deceased?

Morbid thinking was getting her nowhere, and Hannah drove on down the alley. If Ron had been killed on the street, there might have been witnesses, but the alley was usually deserted and she hadn't seen any activity when she'd driven in yesterday morning. Even though she hadn't been paying much attention, Hannah was sure she would have noticed if there had been anyone prowling around the Dumpsters or standing near any of the doorways. The only other person she'd seen yesterday morning had been Claire Rodgers.

As Hannah unlocked her back door, she decided she'd have a chat with Claire. Bill or one of the other deputies must have already interviewed her, but it couldn't hurt to ask a few more questions. Hannah had the perfect excuse to talk to Claire. Just as soon as she mixed up her cookie dough, she'd dash next door and take a look at the cocktail dress that Claire had seemed so eager to sell to her.

She switched on the lights, fired up the ovens, and headed for the sink. After she'd slipped on her paper cap and given her hands a thorough scrub, Hannah reached for the book of laminated recipes that hung on a hook by the sink. She was catering the Lake Eden Regency Romance Club meeting at four this afternoon and she needed to make a batch of Regency Ginger Crisps.

Hannah read through the recipe before she began to work. She also used an erasable felt-tipped marker to check off the ingredients as she added them to the bowl. It was possible to leave out a critical ingredient when she was distracted, and Hannah was definitely distracted. She couldn't stop thinking about Ron's murder and the clues she'd gathered in the past twenty-four hours. The way she saw it, they had two suspects: Coach Watson and the unidentified bouncer at Twin Pines. Both of them had possible motives to kill Ron.

Coach Watson might have believed that Danielle was having an affair with Ron, and jealousy was a powerful motive for murder. And if Ron had landed the "few good punches" that Danielle had told her about, the bouncer could have decided to follow Ron and take his revenge.

As Hannah melted, measured, and mixed, she thought about the first of their suspects. She had to check out Coach Watson's alibi, and the Lake Eden Regency Romance Club was a good place to start. Coach Watson's sister, Maryann, would be at the meeting, and Hannah could pump her for information.

Identifying their second suspect would take a little work. Hannah planned to drive out to Twin Pines tonight and nose around. She'd find out which bouncer had fought with Ron and whether he had an alibi for the time of Ron's murder.

It was seven twenty-five by the time Hannah had finished her early-morning work. In addition to Regency Ginger Crisps, she'd also mixed up two batches of Chocolate Chip Crunches, three batches of Pecan Chews, and one batch of a recipe that Lisa had developed called White Chocolate Supremes.

"Hi, Hannah," Lisa called out cheerfully as she breezed

through the back door at precisely seven-thirty. She hung up her parka, tucked her hair inside a paper cap, and headed for the sink to wash her hands. "What do you want me to do first?"

Hannah stashed the last bowl of dough in the walk-in cooler and joined Lisa at the sink. "Would you mind putting on the coffee, Lisa? I've got a few phone calls to make. I mixed up a batch of your White Chocolate Supremes and you can bake them first. We'll try them out on the regulars today. And see what your green thumb can do with that African violet on the counter. I don't want to do jail time for houseplant abuse."

"No problem. I'll set up the tables and bring you a mug of coffee when it's ready."

When Lisa had left, Hannah picked up the phone and punched out Doc Bennett's number, listening to it ring.

"Doc Bennett."

Doc sounded curt and Hannah glanced at the clock. Perhaps seven forty-five was a bit early to call a semiretired dentist. "Hi, Doc. This is Hannah Swensen over at The Cookie Jar."

"Hello, Hannah. Still brushing the way I taught you?"

"You bet!" Hannah was relieved. Doc sounded a lot friendlier now.

"Do you have a dental emergency, Hannah?"

"No, everything's fine." Hannah hadn't been able to come up with a roundabout way to ask her question, so she just blurted it out. "I was wondering whether you saw Ron La-Salle yesterday morning as a patient."

"My office wasn't open, Hannah. I took the day off and drove up to Little Falls to see my sister. You'd better check with Norman Rhodes. I hear he's been coming in at the crack of dawn most mornings and taking walk-ins without appointments."

"Thanks, Doc. I'll do that. And drop in for a cookie one of these days."

Hannah hung up the phone and sighed. Things never worked out the way she wanted. Now she'd have to call Norman.

The smell of coffee from the shop was enticing, and Hannah walked in to fill a mug. It hadn't finished perking, but it was hot and she sipped it gratefully. She shouldn't have to call the man her mother had picked out for her without a full load of caffeine to sustain her.

"The coffee's not ready yet, Hannah." Lisa turned to give her a curious glance.

"That's okay." Hannah took another sip of the coffee-flavored water. Then she thought about Twin Pines and how seldom Lisa got out of the house. "Can you get someone to sit with your father tonight? I'm driving out to Twin Pines and I'll treat you to supper if you want to come along."

"I'd love to. The neighbors like to sit with Dad, now that we bought that big-screen TV. Why are you going out to the Indian casino?"

Hannah remembered Bill's caution about not telling anyone that she was doing legwork for him. "I've never been there and I've always wanted to see the place."

"Me, too. Herb Beeseman says they have great ribs."

"Then we'll have the ribs. And we'll take all the quarters in the cash register and feed the slots."

So Lisa had been talking to Herb. Hannah stored that away for future reference and walked back to the bakery feeling much better. Lisa was good company, and as far as anyone else was concerned, they were just going out to the casino to eat ribs and gamble.

It was time to call Norman. Hannah reached for the phone and punched out his office number. If Norman misinterpreted the reason for her call, Bill would owe her. She twisted the cord around her fingers as it rang several times and then Norman picked up.

"Rhodes Dental Clinic. Norman Rhodes speaking."

"Hi, Norman. It's Hannah Swensen."

"Hello, Hannah." Norman sounded pleased to hear from her. "Did you call your mother yet?"

"My mother?"

"She called me this morning to ask if I'd seen you. She said she'd left a bunch of messages on your answering machine, but you hadn't called her back."

"Guilty," Hannah admitted. "I didn't check my machine until this morning and then I was in a rush. I don't suppose you happen to know what she wanted?"

"Not really. But she did ask what my intentions were toward you."

"What?"

"Relax, Hannah. My mother's the same way. It must be in the genes. They never stop trying to control your life."

Hannah wasn't about to ask Norman what he'd said. She really didn't want to know. "I've got a question for you, Norman. Did Ron LaSalle come in to see you yesterday morning?"

There was a long pause and then Norman sighed. "I'm sorry, Hannah, but I can't tell you that. All information regarding a patient's visit is confidential."

"Then Ron *was* your patient?"

Hannah heard a distinct gulp on the other end of the line. "I didn't say that!"

"Of course you didn't."

"Then why did you assume that he was?"

Hannah smiled, very pleased with herself. Perhaps she'd actually learned something in that required logic course she'd taken. "If Ron wasn't your patient, you could tell me he wasn't. There's no breach of ethics in that. But you said that you couldn't tell me and that means he was."

There was another beat of silence and then Norman chuckled. "You're quick, Hannah. And you're right. I guess it can't do any harm to tell you now. Ron was my first appointment of the morning. He came in presenting considerable pain from a fissured molar."

"A cracked tooth?"

"Yes, in layman's terms. I'm sorry, Hannah. I've got a patient in the chair and I can't talk now. Just hang on and let me check my schedule."

Hannah waited, shifting from foot to foot. This was important. Norman might have been the last person to talk to Ron.

"Hannah?" Norman came back on the line. "I'm booked solid this morning, but I don't have anyone scheduled for one. If you come in then, I'll tell you all about it."

"You want me to come in?"

"I think it would be best, don't you? We really shouldn't talk about something this sensitive on the phone. I'll pick up salads and sandwiches at the cafe and we'll have lunch while we talk. I have something very important to ask you."

Hannah made a face. The last thing she wanted to do was have lunch with Norman, but if she wanted to help Bill solve Ron's murder, she had to gather all the facts. And the one person left alive who could tell her what had happened during Ron's dental appointment was the dentist himself.

"All right, Norman," Hannah caved in to the inevitable with all the good grace she could muster. "I'll see you at one."

REGENCY GINGER CRISPS

Do not preheat oven yet—
dough must chill before baking.

¾ cup melted butter *(1½ sticks)*
1 cup brown sugar
1 large beaten egg *(or two medium, just whip them
  up with a fork)*
4 tablespoons molasses *(that's ¼ cup)* ***
2 teaspoons baking soda
½ teaspoon salt
2 teaspoons ground ginger
2¼ cups flour *(not sifted)*
½ cup white sugar in a small bowl *(for later)*

Melt butter and mix in sugar. Let mixture cool and
then add egg(s). Add soda, molasses, salt, and ginger.
Stir it thoroughly. Add flour and mix in. Chill the
dough for at least 1 hour. *(Overnight is even better.)*

When the dough has chilled, preheat oven to 375
degrees F., rack in the middle position.

Roll dough into walnut-sized balls with your hands.
Roll the dough balls in white sugar. *(Just dump them
in the bowl with the sugar and shake the bowl gently to*

coat them.) Place them on greased cookie sheets, 12 to a standard sheet. Flatten them with a spatula.

Bake at 375 degrees F. for 10 to 12 minutes or until nicely browned. Cool on cookie sheets for no more than 1 minute, and then remove to wire rack to finish cooling. *(If you leave these on the cookie sheets for too long, they'll stick.)*

*** To measure molasses, first spray the inside of a measuring cup with Pam so that the molasses won't stick to the sides of the cup.

Served these at Mother's Regency Romance Club. They asked me for something from the Regency Period. Why not?

(Tracey loves these as a bedtime snack with a glass of milk.)

Yield: 6 to 7 dozen, depending on cookie size.

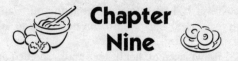

Her shop was every bit as crowded as yesterday, and Hannah was relieved when the predictable eleven o'clock lull arrived. It was the time of day when Lake Eden residents decided that it was too late for a breakfast cookie and too early for a lunch cookie. The break gave Hannah time to gather her wits and continue her unofficial, but deputy-sanctioned, investigation. She put on a fresh pot of coffee, wiped down the counter until it was sparkling, and went through the swinging door to the bakery to talk to Lisa.

Lisa had just taken the last pan of cookies from the oven and she greeted Hannah with a smile. "I'm finished with the baking, Hannah. And your plant's going to make it. Its roots just needed to be soaked."

"Thanks, Lisa." Belatedly Hannah remembered the instructions her mother had given her with the plant. African violets needed to be watered from the bottom and not from the top. She walked over to glance at the plant and saw that it looked much perkier. "I think it needs a new caregiver. Take it home with you, Lisa."

Lisa smiled, clearly delighted with the offer. "It's a hybrid called 'Verona's Delight,' and it'll be just gorgeous when it blooms. Are you really sure that you don't want it?"

"I'm positive. It'll be a lot happier with you. Can you hold down the fort for me while I run next door to talk to Claire?"

"Sure." Lisa whisked off her baker's apron and tied on the fancy one she wore when she handled the counter. "Go ahead, Hannah."

Hannah stepped out the back door and immediately shivered. The temperature had dropped at least ten degrees and the clouds were gray and ominous-looking. The radio weatherman had promised clear skies, but she'd been listening to a Minneapolis station and that was fifty miles away.

Claire's Toyota was in her parking spot and Hannah walked over to knock on the back door of Beau Monde Fashions. Claire didn't open until noon on Thursdays, but she was obviously here.

"Hello, Hannah," Claire greeted her with a smile. "Come in and I'll show you that darling dress. I had to pull it off the rack yesterday. Lydia Gradin asked to try it, but it wouldn't have been right for her. And Kate Maschler had her eye on it, too."

Hannah felt immediately guilty. Because of her, Claire had lost a potential sale. "You should have let one of them buy it, Claire. I haven't even tried it on."

"But you will. And it'll be absolutely perfect. Come in, Hannah. I'll show you."

Hannah sighed and stepped into Claire's tiny back room. There was an ironing board set up in a corner next to a stack of dress boxes ready to be assembled. The air smelled hot. Claire had obviously been pressing out the wrinkles in her new shipment, and Hannah followed her past racks of newly arrived clothing and stepped around the sewing machine that was set up for alterations. She was frowning as she stepped through the gap in the curtain that separated the back room from the dress shop. She knew she'd have to try on the dress that Claire had chosen for her. It would be rude to refuse.

"Here it is!" Claire opened the closet that held her most expensive dresses and removed a hanger that held a black silk cocktail dress. "Isn't it just darling?"

Hannah nodded. What else could she do? It looked like an ordinary dress to her, but she knew next to nothing about fashion, and Claire was the expert.

"Go right in and try it on." Claire led the way to one of her little dressing rooms. "Would you like me to help you?"

"No, thanks. I can manage." Hannah walked into Claire's posh little dressing room and shut the door. "Are you out there, Claire?"

"I'm here," Claire's voice floated in through the open transom. "Do you need me to zip you up?"

"No, I'm fine. I just wondered if you saw anyone in the alley yesterday morning."

"Just you, Hannah. Bill already asked and I told him the same thing."

"How about later?" Hannah unzipped her jeans and let them slip down into a denim pile around her ankles.

"I didn't go out again until I heard all the commotion."

Hannah kicked her jeans over to a spot near to the mirror and pulled off her sweatshirt. "Are you sure? You said you were unpacking a new shipment. Didn't you go out to throw any packing materials in the Dumpster?"

"I don't think . . . Yes, I did!" Claire sounded surprised. "You're right, Hannah. I broke down some cartons and carried them out. And there *was* someone in the alley. A homeless man was huddled up in the thrift shop doorway, waiting for it to open."

"Do you have any idea what time that was?" Hannah asked as she removed the black dress from the hanger.

"I think it was about a quarter to eight. When I got back inside, I pressed a dress and then Becky Summers called to ask if the alterations were finished on her new pantsuit. I glanced at my watch and I remember thinking that only Becky would have the nerve to call me a full two hours before I opened, so it must have been eight."

"What did this homeless man look like?"

"I'm sure you've seen him around town, Hannah. He's tall and his hair sticks up in spikes. It's this awful red. . . . " Claire paused and she sounded embarrassed when she spoke again. "It's not like your hair, Hannah. Yours is a lovely auburn color. This man's hair is so red, it's almost orange, like a clown."

Hannah added that tidbit to her memory banks as she lifted the dress over her head and stuck her arms through the sleeves. She wiggled, the silk slipped down with a slither, and she reached behind her to pull up the zipper by its little tab. The dress fit her perfectly. Claire had a good eye for size.

"Does it fit you, Hannah?" Claire's voice floated in again.

"Like a glove." Hannah took a deep breath and glanced in the mirror. The stranger that stared back at her looked shocked. Not only did the dress fit—it was stunning on her. And Hannah had never looked stunning before in her life.

"Do you like it?"

It took Hannah a moment to find her voice. "It's . . . uh . . . it's great."

"Come out and let me see if I need to do any alterations."

"You don't." Hannah kicked off her favorite old Nikes. They didn't exactly go with her new image. And then she opened the door and walked out.

Claire's mouth dropped open when she saw her. "I knew it would be perfect for you, but I had no idea it would turn you into a femme fatale. You have to take it, Hannah. I'll give you a huge discount. This dress was made for you."

"I think you're right." There was wonder in Hannah's voice as Claire led her over to the three-way mirror and she studied her reflection. She looked sophisticated, gorgeous, and utterly feminine.

"You want it, don't you, Hannah?"

Hannah turned to the mirror again. If she squinted, the woman who stared back at her looked a little like Katharine Hepburn. Her first instinct was to tell Claire to wrap up the dress, that price was no object, but reality intruded. Price *was* an object and she knew it. "Of course I want it, but I don't know if I can afford it. How much does it cost?"

"Forget what I said about the discount. I'll give it to you at my cost. Just promise that you won't tell anyone what you paid."

"Okay," Hannah promised. "How much is it?"

"It retails for one-eighty, but you can have it for ninety."

Hannah didn't hesitate. A dress like this came along only once in a lifetime. "Sold. I'll never have a chance to wear it and it'll probably hang in my closet for the rest of my life, but you're right. I've got to have it."

"Good girl!" Claire looked very pleased. "But what do you mean, you won't have a chance to wear it? The Wood-leys' annual party is tomorrow night."

Hannah blinked. She'd stuck her invitation in a drawer and forgotten all about it. "Do you think that I should wear this dress?"

"I'll tell everyone that your cookies are lousy if you don't," Claire threatened. "You're going to knock them dead tomorrow night, Hannah. And on Saturday morning, your phone's going to be ringing off the hook."

Hannah laughed. Perhaps Claire was psychic and her phone would ring off the hook. But ninety-nine percent of those calls would be from Delores, trying to find out which man she'd been trying to impress.

Hannah stashed the dress box in her Suburban and walked back into the bakery with a bemused expression on her face. She'd certainly spent a lot of money helping Bill investigate Ron's murder. She'd dropped fifty dollars with Luanne for the cosmetics and she'd spent ninety with Claire for the dress.

As she passed the work island, the phone on the wall started to ring. Hannah called out to tell Lisa that she'd get it and picked up the receiver. "The Cookie Jar. This is Hannah."

"Hi, Hannah." It was Bill and he sounded discouraged. "I'm just checking in with you. I'm out here at the dairy doing interviews."

"Did you learn anything new?"

"Not a thing. Everyone else came in at seven-thirty and Ron had already loaded up and left by then."

"How about Max Turner? Did you speak to him yet?"

"No. Hold on a second, Hannah." There was a lengthy pause and then Bill came back on the line. "Betty still expects him to call in today. I told her to get a number and I'd call him back to tell him about Ron. How about you? Do you have anything for me?"

"Yes, and it could be important. I talked to Claire Rodgers and she remembered that she saw a homeless man in the alley about seven forty-five. He was huddled in the thrift shop doorway and she gave me a description."

"Let me get out my notebook." There was another pause and then Bill spoke again. "Okay. Give it to me."

"He was wearing baggy clothes and he had bright red hair sticking up in spikes. Claire said she'd seen him around town before."

"Good work, Hannah." Bill sounded pleased. "I'll run over to the soup kitchen at the Bible Church and see if they know who he is. And I'll check with the thrift shop. They might have let him in. Anything else?"

"Maybe, but I'm not sure. Ron went to the dentist for that cracked tooth I told you about, and that was why he was running late. I'll get back to you the minute I know more."

Hannah hung up the phone and then she picked it up

again to punch out her mother's number. She couldn't put Delores off forever. As she listened to the empty ringing, she began to smile. Her mother was out and she left a brief message. "Hi, it's Hannah. I'm just returning your call. Guess you must be out. I'll see you later at the Regency Romance Club meeting."

Hannah had just hung up when Lisa stuck her head around the side of the swinging door. "Your sister's here, Hannah."

"Send her back here with two mugs of coffee," Hannah instructed, walking to the counter to pile a half-dozen White Chocolate Supremes on a plate. There weren't many left and she suspected that Lisa's new recipe had been a success. Then she sat down on a stool and wondered what new crisis had brought Andrea to The Cookie Jar for the second day in a row.

"Hi, Hannah," Andrea greeted her. "Here's your coffee." She plunked down the two mugs of coffee, saw the cookies, and grabbed one before she even sat down. "These new cookies are heavenly. Everybody's raving about them and they're all sold out up front. Lisa gave me the last one while I was waiting for you."

Hannah smiled. "I'm really glad they went over so well. Lisa worked a long time on the recipe."

"They're Lisa's?" Andrea looked surprised. "That's funny. She didn't say a word about it to me."

"She wouldn't. Lisa's still a little shy about her baking."

"Well, she doesn't have to be. These are winners." Andrea reached for another cookie.

"What brings you in, Andrea?" Hannah mentally prepared herself for another sibling crisis. "I just got off the phone with Bill and he sounded fine. Tracey's okay, isn't she?"

"Tracey's fine. Everything's fine. I don't have another showing until three and I just dropped in to say hello."

Hannah raised her eyebrows. Andrea never *just dropped in.* "I'm busy tonight, but I can be home by eight-thirty. Is that too late to drop Tracey off?"

"Why would I want to drop Tracey off?" Andrea looked confused. "What are you talking about, Hannah?"

"You don't need a sitter tonight?"

"No." A dull flush rose to Andrea's cheeks. "I've really been taking advantage of you, haven't I?"

"Of course not." Hannah shook her head. "I enjoy spending time with Tracey. She's a great kid."

"I know, but when I came in, you just assumed that I needed something. I'm not a very good sister, Hannah. I take and I take, but I never give back."

Hannah was uncomfortable. This was getting altogether too serious to suit her. "Oh yeah? You urged me to open The Cookie Jar. I'd call that giving back in spades."

"You're right. I *did* suggest it." Andrea looked pleased for a moment. "But I really should do more for you, Hannah. You help me out all the time and I never know how to return the favor. If you'd just ask me for something, I'd do it."

Suddenly Hannah had a brilliant thought. "That's about to change. If you really want to do something for me, you can come along with me to the dentist. My appointment's at one."

"Of course I'll come, but I didn't know you were afraid to go to the dentist."

"Believe me, I am," Hannah said with a grin, "especially when the dentist is Norman Rhodes."

Andrea's mouth dropped open. "But Mother said she tried to set you up with him! Why are you letting him work on your teeth?"

"I'm not. Right before Ron was killed, he had an appointment with Norman. I called him this morning and he confirmed that he'd seen Ron, but he refused to discuss it on the phone. He said he'd tell me all about it if I met him for lunch at his office."

Andrea lifted her eyebrows. "Very sneaky. And you're afraid that he's using this opportunity to put the moves on you?"

"No, that's not it. He seemed genuinely nice on the phone, but I don't really want to be alone with him."

"Why not? Unless . . ." Andrea stopped speaking and her eyes widened. "Do you think Norman's a *suspect*?"

Hannah shrugged. "No, but I can't entirely rule that out. Norman was one of the last people to see Ron alive, and I won't know if he's got an alibi until I ask him."

"I'll go with you," Andrea agreed quickly. "He can't try anything with both of us there. And while you're having lunch and grilling him about Ron, I'll snoop around to see if I can find any evidence."

"Uh . . . maybe that's not such a good idea, Andrea."

"Why? I'm a great snooper, Hannah. I used to snoop through Mother's things all the time and she never knew I did it. Besides, I'll be helping Bill, and a wife's supposed to help her husband."

"It could be risky, Andrea."

"Not if we work out a time schedule and stick to it. How long do you think you can keep him occupied?"

Hannah considered it seriously. "No more than twenty minutes."

"I've got to have longer than that. How about thirty?"

"Twenty-five and not a second more," Hannah said firmly. "I'll tell him I want to eat lunch in his office and your time starts the instant that I close the door."

"Okay. We'll synchronize our watches before we go in and I promise I won't get caught."

"I hope not. I think it's illegal." Hannah was already beginning to regret asking Andrea to go along.

"How can just looking through somebody's things be illegal? It's not like I'm going to steal anything, Hannah. If I find any evidence, I'll leave it right where it is and we can tell Bill."

"I'm still not sure this is such a good idea."

"Maybe it isn't, but we've got to do something to help

Bill solve Ron's murder. He won't mind, not when I explain it to him. Is it a go?"

Hannah agreed reluctantly. If Bill ever found out that she'd allowed Andrea to snoop through Norman's office, he'd do more than mind. He'd kill her first and ask questions later.

Chapter Ten

Hannah speared a piece of romaine lettuce with her fork and managed to glance at her watch. Only five minutes had passed since she'd closed the door of Norman's private office and he'd already told her all about his appointment with Ron.

Norman's account hadn't held any surprises. Ron had come in complaining of pain and Norman had given him a shot of Xylocaine. Ron hadn't wanted to take the time to repair the tooth right then, but he'd promised to come back to Norman's office right after he'd finished his deliveries. Of course he hadn't come back. Ron had been killed before the shot had even begun to wear off.

"Did Ron seem nervous about anything?" Hannah asked another question from the mental list she'd prepared.

Norman chewed and swallowed. "Not really. He was anxious about getting back to work, but that was all."

"Did he tell you how he cracked his tooth?"

"He said he'd been in a fight, but I didn't press him for the details. Now I wish I had."

"That's okay, Norman." Hannah gave him her friendliest

smile. "You didn't have any way of knowing that Ron was going to leave here and get himself shot."

"I guess not. I wish I'd paid more attention, though. I could have asked him more questions about it when I examined him. He was in the chair for at least twenty minutes."

"I don't think that would have done much good. With his mouth propped open and that little rubber sheet covering his tongue, he couldn't have told you very much."

"It's called a rubber dam," Norman corrected her, and there was a gleam of humor in his eyes. "You've got a point, Hannah. They taught us about conversing with patients in Dental Procedures 101. Never ask a question that can't be answered by *Gghhh,* or *Gghhh-Gghhh.*"

Hannah laughed. Norman's sense of humor was a pleasant surprise. Perhaps he wasn't so bad, after all. And he'd certainly spruced up his father's clinic. The institutional green walls in the waiting room had been freshly painted with a coat of sunshine yellow, the dusty and faded venetian blinds had been replaced with tieback curtains in a sunflower print, and the old gray couch and hard-backed chairs had given way to a new set of matched furniture that would have looked good in any Lake Eden living room. The only things that hadn't changed were the copies of outdated magazines that were stacked in the new wooden magazine holder on the wall.

"You've done a lot with this place, Norman." Hannah glanced around Norman's office appreciatively. He'd kept his father's old desk, but it had been refinished with a light oak stain and there was a fresh coat of pale blue paint on the walls. She looked down at the darker blue wall-to-wall carpeting and asked a question that had nothing to do with Ron's murder. "Did you install this same carpeting in the examining rooms?"

Norman shook his head. "I couldn't. The floors in there have to be washable. I replaced the linoleum and painted the walls, but that's about it."

"How about the windows?"

"I ordered some fabric vertical blinds, but they haven't come in yet. And I'm looking for new artwork for the walls."

"That's good. That old Rockwell print of the boy in the dentist's waiting room used to scare me half to death when I was a kid."

"It scared me, too," Norman admitted with a grin. "He looked so miserable with that big white napkin tied around his jaw. I told Dad I didn't think it was a very good advertisement for painless dentistry, but he seemed to think that it was funny. Dental humor, I guess."

"Like, I got my tongue wrapped around my eyetooth and I couldn't see what I was saying?"

"That was one of Dad's favorites," Norman laughed and took another Pecan Chew from the bag that Hannah had brought. "These cookies are really good, Hannah."

"Thanks. Next time I'll leave on the shells and you'll get lots of new patients."

"I've already got that covered, Hannah. I'm going to send out tins of taffy for the holidays with my office number printed on the lids."

Hannah laughed, but she reminded herself to get back on track with her questions. Norman seemed a lot different here in his office, and she was actually enjoying their visit. "Did you notice anything unusual about Ron when he came in? Anything at all?"

"No. I told you everything I could think of. I wish I could help you more, but Ron seemed like just an ordinary dental emergency to me."

"Will you call me right away if you remember anything else?"

"Sure," Norman agreed. "I know you're helping your brother-in-law solve the case, but I just don't have any more information to give you."

"Hold on, Norman. I haven't told anybody that I'm helping Bill. How did you guess?"

"Nobody's *that* nosy about a twenty-minute dental appointment," Norman pointed out. "And when your mother told me that your sister's husband was working on the case, I just put two and two together."

"Please don't tell anyone, Norman."

"Relax, Hannah. I won't give you away. Do you have any other questions for me? Or can I ask you my question?"

"There's one more." Hannah took a deep breath. She had to find out if Norman had an alibi for the time of Ron's death. "Did any other patients come in right after you treated Ron?"

"Just one. It was another fissured molar, but it was part of a bridge, so it was simple to repair. She was in and out in less than thirty minutes."

Hannah felt strangely relieved that Norman had an alibi. She was really beginning to like him. All she had to do was check with Norman's second patient of the morning and he'd be in the clear. "I need to know her name, Norman."

"You don't know?"

"How could I? Look, Norman, I know your patient list is confidential, but all I need is her name. I have to ask her if she saw Ron when she came in."

Norman began to grin. "I guess you haven't called your mother back yet."

"I called her. She wasn't home and I got her machine. What does my mother have to do with it?"

Norman's grin grew wider. "I thought she would have told you by now. Your mother was my second appointment."

"That's just great!" Hannah gave a deep sigh. "Mother left me a dozen messages saying that she had something important to tell me, but she's *always* got something important to tell me. Did she talk to you about seeing Ron?"

"Yes, but she didn't actually see him. And she didn't realize it was important until she got home from the mayor's fundraiser. She saw Ron's truck driving away when she parked in front of the office."

Hannah decided she would check with her mother at the Regency Romance Club meeting, but it seemed as if Norman had an ironclad alibi. If Delores had been with him, he couldn't have followed Ron and killed him. That made Hannah wish that there were some way to stop Andrea in mid-snoop.

"Now, Hannah?"

"Now what?" Hannah looked up at him, startled.

"Are you ready to listen to my question now?"

"Of course I am. What is it, Norman?"

"I was in dental school when my parents moved here and I only came to vist a couple of times. I really don't know much about Lake Eden."

"There's not much to know." Hannah grinned.

"But I'm invited to the Woodleys' party and my mother says it's the social event of the year. She's never had the chance to go. Mom and Dad always took their vacation the last week in October and they were out of town. She says that I should go and try to promote new business for the clinic."

"Your mother's right. All the important people in Lake Eden are invited and it's a great party. I think you should go, Norman. You need to meet all the local families if you want your practice to be a success."

"Then I'll go. Tell me about the Woodleys. I've never met them."

Hannah sneaked a peek at her watch again and she was surprised to see that twenty minutes had already passed. "Delano Raymond Woodley is one of the richest men in Lake Eden. He owns DelRay Manufacturing and the company employs over two hundred local workers."

"Delano?" Norman picked up on the name. "Is the Woodley family related to the Roosevelts?"

"No, but they'd like to be. From what I hear, Del's mother and father were strictly middle-class. His mother just wanted to give him a famous name. It must have worked because

Del married a Boston socialite. Her name is Judith and her family's in the social register."

"Judith, not Judy?"

Hannah laughed. "I called her Judy once and she nearly took my head off. She comes from 'old money,' but one of Mother's friends did some research and found out that Judith's father squandered it all away. All Judith has left is her social standing, and that's more important to her than anything."

"So he's a rich social climber and she's a destitute blue blood who married him for his money?"

"You got it. I couldn't have put it any better myself."

"You're going to their party, aren't you?"

Hannah thought of her new dress and smiled. "Of course I am. I do all right, but I'm still on a jug-wine and jelly-glass budget. This is my one chance to sip Dom Pérignon out of fine crystal."

"Do you have a date?"

"You must be kidding!" Hannah was amused. "Think about it, Norman. You saw Mother in action on Tuesday night. Would she try to set me up with every guy in town if I already had a date for the biggest party of the year?"

Norman shrugged, but he was grinning. "I guess not. Would you like to go to the party with me, Hannah? It'll get you off the hook with your mother."

Hannah wished she hadn't been so flippant. Her big mouth had gotten her into trouble again. Now Norman knew she didn't have a date and he was asking her for one. And she really didn't know what to say.

Norman reached out and patted her hand. "Come on. It'll be mutually beneficial. I'll drive so you can drink all the Dom you want, and you can introduce me to all the people you think I should know."

Hannah thought fast. There didn't seem to be any graceful way out, and going to the Woodleys' party with Norman might not be so terrible. He was funny, he seemed to like her, and it might make her mother back off a little.

"Okay, it's a deal."

Hannah drew a deep breath of relief when Norman escorted her back to the waiting room and Andrea was there. Her sister was seated on the new couch, idly flipping the pages of *National Geographic*.

"Hi." Andrea gave them a guileless smile. "Did you have a nice lunch?"

"Very nice." Norman smiled and then he turned to Hannah. "The Woodleys' party starts at eight. Shall I pick you up at seven-thirty?"

"Seven-thirty is fine." Hannah saw the startled look that Andrea gave her out of the corner of her eye, and she knew she'd have to do some explaining. "Do you need my address?"

"I've got it. It was nice to meet you, Andrea. Perhaps we'll see you at the party?"

Andrea put on a smile for Norman's benefit. "You will. Bill and I wouldn't miss it for the world. Goodbye, Norman. It was nice to meet you, too."

They walked out to Hannah's truck in total silence, and Andrea got into the passenger seat. But as soon as Hannah had slid in behind the wheel and closed the door, Andrea reached out to grab her arm. "You were just kidding around, weren't you? I mean, you're not actually going to the party with *him*!"

"Yes, I am," Hannah confirmed it.

"But you *can't*!"

Hannah started the engine, glanced behind her to make sure that no cars were coming, and pulled out into the street. "Why not?"

"Because he could be Ron's killer!"

"He's not." Hannah shifted into second gear. "Norman has an alibi. He was treating another patient when Ron was killed."

That seemed to take the wind out of Andrea's sails and she frowned. "Okay. Maybe he's *not* Ron's killer, but there's no way you should go out with him!"

"Relax, Andrea. It's not like it's a real date or anything. He's just picking me up and we're going to the party together. Norman's very nice."

"No, he isn't. It's not like you to be wrong about people, but this time you really blew it. While you were having lunch and accepting dates with this . . . this person you think is nice, I hit pay dirt in the storage room. I've got the goods on Norman Rhodes."

"What goods?" Hannah took her eyes off the road for a moment to glance at her sister. Andrea looked very proud of herself.

"I'll show you the minute we get back to The Cookie Jar."

Hannah's eyebrows shot up and she had all she could do to navigate the turn on Third and Main. "You'll *show* me? You didn't steal anything from Norman's office, did you, Andrea?"

"It wasn't exactly stealing. I know I promised not to take anything, but this was just too good to leave behind." Andrea sat back and gave a smug smile. "I'll tell you this much, Hannah. Mother didn't do you any favors when she introduced you to Norman. And he certainly isn't the man she thought he was!"

Hannah didn't ask any further questions. It was clear her sister wouldn't tell her any more until they'd arrived at The Cookie Jar. She turned into the alley, averted her eyes as she drove past the spot where Ron had breathed his final breath, and pulled into her parking spot.

When they came in the back door, Andrea was grinning like a Cheshire cat, and Hannah was beginning to feel very uneasy. She hoped that Andrea had found something trivial, like a patient's complaint that he'd been overcharged, or a stack of unpaid bills.

"Tell Lisa you're back and we need to be alone," Andrea advised as she hung up her coat. "Hurry up. This is important."

Hannah wasn't about to argue. She dashed into the shop, told Lisa to please handle the counter for a couple more minutes, and filled two mugs with coffee. Andrea didn't need the caffeine since she was jazzed enough as it was, but Hannah figured she might need a boost before all this was over. She raced through the swinging door to the back room, set the coffee mugs down on the work island, and slid onto a stool close to her sister's. "All right, Andrea. This has gone on long enough. Out with it."

Andrea was obviously enjoying this moment. She opened her purse with a flourish, pulled out a large manila envelope, and pushed it over to Hannah.

"What's this?"

"Open it," Andrea instructed. "And then tell me again how *nice* Norman is."

PECAN CHEWS

Preheat oven to 350° F.,
rack in the middle position.

1 cup butter *(2 sticks, ½ pound)*
3 cups brown sugar ***
4 eggs, beaten *(with a fork is fine)*
1 teaspoon salt
1 teaspoon baking soda
3 teaspoons vanilla
2 cups finely chopped pecans
4 cups flour

Melt butter and add brown sugar. Mix well and let cool. Add beaten eggs and mix. Add salt, baking soda, vanilla, and nuts. Mix well. Add flour and mix until flour is thoroughly distributed.

Form dough into balls with your fingers. *(Make them the size of a walnut with shell.)* Place them on a greased cookie sheet, 12 to a standard sheet. Press them down with a spatula. *(Spray it with Pam first, or grease it.)*

Bake at 350 degrees F. for 10 to 12 minutes. Let cookies set up on sheet for one minute, then remove them to a wire rack to finish cooling.

*** There's no need to keep brown sugar in stock. It can be easily made with white sugar and molasses, ⅛ cup molasses for every 3 cups of white sugar. *(That's how they manufacture it, really. And it'll save you from having to deal with all those lumps.)* Just add the molasses to the white sugar and stir until it is thoroughly and evenly mixed in.

(There's no problem if your recipe calls for dark brown sugar, or light brown sugar—just mix in molasses until it's the right color.)

(Norman Rhodes adores these, and so does Bill.)

Yield: 8 to 10 dozen, depending on cookie size.

Chapter Eleven

Hannah couldn't say a word. Her tongue seemed glued to the roof of her mouth. She stared down at the stack of Polaroids and blinked hard. No, she wasn't imagining things. The images were still there. There were no faces, just pictures of women's torsos, and every one was nude to the waist.

"Hannah?" Andrea reached out to grab her arm. "Are you all right?"

Hannah took a deep breath and nodded. "Who *are* they?"

"Dental patients. You can tell where they were taken from the background." Andrea jabbed her finger at the top print. "See that picture on the wall? It's in the room that Norman uses for cleaning teeth. I checked."

"This woman posed for Norman in his dental chair?"

"Make that *these women*." Andrea fanned out the pictures so that Hannah could see. "And I don't think they exactly posed. See the two canisters next to the chair? One is oxygen and the other is nitrous oxide."

"Laughing gas?"

"I studied it in chemistry class. If you mix it right, it's an anesthetic. A lot of dentists use it. But if you cut down on the oxygen, it can make you lose consciousness. A couple of whiffs of the increased mixture and these women would have passed out cold."

"He knocked them out and took nude photos of them?"

"That's what it looks like to me. When they came to, they wouldn't remember a thing."

Hannah shook her head. "I can't believe that Norman would do something like this. He seems so . . . normal."

"That's what they always say about perverts. You've heard those interviews on the news. All the neighbors say that they can't believe it, that he seemed like such a normal guy."

Hannah blinked and stared down at the photographs again. She still couldn't believe that Norman could have taken these pictures.

She picked up the stack of Polaroids and rifled through them again. "I wonder if . . ."

"What is it?" Andrea turned to stare at her sister when Hannah stopped speaking abruptly.

"It's this one." Hannah pointed to the picture. "There's a gold chain around her neck and that pendant . . . I know I've seen it before."

Andrea grabbed the photo for a second look. "You're right. I've seen it, too. It's a Celtic cross, isn't it?"

"That's right!" Hannah's eyes widened as she recognized the subject of the photograph. "Norman didn't take these pictures, Andrea."

"He didn't?"

"He couldn't have taken them. That's Miss McNally, our seventh-grade math teacher. And she left Lake Eden to get married three years ago."

Andrea stared down at the photo in shock. "Miss McNally is the only one who ever wore a cross like that. Norman's *father* must have taken these pictures. What are we going to do?"

Hannah's brain shifted gears. "First, we're not going to

tell anybody about them. Norman's father is dead. It's too late to do anything to him now. Making this public would just mortify his mother and embarrass the women. "

"That makes sense," Andrea agreed quickly. "Do you suppose Norman knows what his father did?"

"I don't know. Where did you find these pictures?"

"They were in the storeroom. I found them in a little box under a stack of old X-rays. It was filthy back there, Hannah. There must have been an inch of dust on those X-rays and . . ." Andrea stopped, realizing what she'd just said. "Norman doesn't know about them, Hannah. There was just too much dust. I'm almost positive that stack of X-rays hadn't been touched in at least a year."

Hannah breathed a sigh of relief. "Good. Do you think you got all of the photos?"

"I think so. I dumped the box in that envelope and I spent at least five minutes looking for more." Andrea reached out to gather up the photos and turned them facedown. "What are we going to do with them, Hannah?"

"We're going to destroy them. I'll throw them in my fireplace tonight."

"You can't do that," Andrea objected. "You've got a gas log. You're not supposed to burn anything in your fireplace. Maybe we should shred them. I'd do it at work, but Al would ask me what I was shredding."

"Let's try industrial-strength stain remover," Hannah suggested as she slid off her stool. "I used it to clean the rust stains off my bathroom sink and I've got some left in the bottle. It's supposed to take anything off anything."

Andrea followed Hannah to the sink and watched as she poured several inches of stain remover into the bottom of her stainless-steel sink. They dropped in one of the photos and Hannah moved it around with the handle of one of her long mixing spoons. It took a minute or so, but eventually the photo bleached out to white.

"It works!" Andrea sounded surprised. "How did you know to do that?"

"I saw something like it in a movie. Go ahead, Andrea. You put in the photos and I'll stir them around."

In less than five minutes the nude photos had disappeared, leaving perfectly white paper behind. Hannah pulled the plug, ran some clear water over the paper, and dumped the whole mess into the garbage.

"I guess I'd better get back to the office." Andrea glanced up at the clock. "I have to pick up the keys and some flyers before my showing."

Hannah gave her a little hug. "Thanks for all your help, Andrea. You're really a good snooper and I'm glad you found those pictures before Norman or his mother stumbled across them."

"So am I." Andrea gave her a sunny smile and headed for the swinging door. She stopped, her hand extended to push it open, and turned back. "Hannah?"

"Yes?"

"I think you should go to the Woodleys' party with Norman. I was wrong. He's boring, but he really *is* a nice guy."

Hannah managed to keep the polite smile on her face as the guest speaker extolled the virtues of Regency England, where men were "gentlemen" and ladies were "ladies in the true sense of the word." The plump, gray-haired lady in her frilly yellow dress, a retired English teacher from Grey Eagle who had written three Regency romances, stated that she was appalled and saddened by the "regrettable lapse of moral fiber" in the youth of today. She ended her speech by suggesting that parents be guided by the strict rules of polite society that had existed "on Albion's shores" at the beginning of the nineteenth century and make an effort to instill "Regency values" in their offspring.

There was a halfhearted smattering of applause when the guest speaker vacated the podium and then the meeting began. As she readied the refreshment table, Hannah wondered what Lake Eden's teenagers would do if their mothers tried to whisk them back to an era with no cars or video games, not to mention the absence of birth control. Matricide would soar, and Bill would certainly have his hands full.

Hannah started the coffee and arranged platters heaped high with Regency Ginger Crisps. She'd researched the period, but there were very few published recipes and none of them had sounded like cookies. She'd even paged through her mother's collection of Regency romances for any mention of desserts, but all she'd found were vague references to "duffs," "fruit compotes," and "seed cakes." Deciding that compromise was in order, Hannah had compiled a list of ingredients that had existed in Regency times and she'd discovered that an enterprising person could have baked ginger cookies. Whether they had actually done it was another question, but it would have been possible.

It didn't take long for the meeting to conclude and Hannah was relieved to see that the guest speaker had slipped out the door. That was good. The woman seemed to know a lot about the Regency period, and Hannah hadn't relished being exposed as a fraud. Most of the club members weren't that serious about authenticity. They liked to read Regency romances and talk about them, but club meetings were primarily an excuse to get out of the house and share gossip and refreshments with their friends.

The moment the gavel descended, there was a scraping back of chairs and a headlong rush toward the refreshment table. Hannah was ready. She had tea and coffee, both "leaded" and "unleaded," and her best silver platters heaped high with cookies. As she poured steaming beverages into bone-china cups—blue flowers for the decaf and pink flowers for regular—Hannah thought about the phone call she'd received from Bill before she'd left the shop. The homeless man, whose name was "Blaze," was no longer a suspect. Reverend Warren Strandberg had picked him up just after Claire had seen him and taken him to the Bible Church soup kitchen for breakfast. At the time of Ron's death, Blaze had been scarfing down pancakes with scrambled eggs in front of the reverend, several church volunteers, and some of his homeless peers.

"These are simply marvelous, Hannah." Mrs. Diana Greerson, wife of the local bank president and social climber par excellence, held a cup of herbal tea in one hand and nibbled on a cookie in the other, her pinkie extended.

"I'm so glad you like them, Diana." Hannah motioned toward the platter. "Do have another."

"Oh, I couldn't. I eat like a bird, you know."

The thought of a vulture tearing greedily at a carcass flashed before Hannah's eyes. The last time she'd catered an event that Diana had attended, she'd caught her dropping at least a half-dozen Date Delights in her purse.

While Hannah poured and offered coffee or tea to the women in Lake Eden, she kept a sharp eye out for her mother. Before she'd even reached kindergarten age, she'd discovered that Delores had a barometer face. If her eyes snapped, a storm of criticism was imminent. If her lips turned up, their encounter would be sunny with compliments. If there was a crease between her perfectly plucked eyebrows, a rain of judgmental questions was about to fall. Even a bland expression meant something. It warned of sudden change, and Hannah knew that she had to be prepared to either shiver under her mother's icy censure or bask in the warmth of her approval.

Hannah filled a cup with regular coffee for Sally Percy, the wife of Andrea's boss, and glanced at the end of the line again. What she saw made her relax for the first time that day. Her mother was standing in line with Carrie Rhodes, and both women smiled widely when they caught her eye. Hannah knew immediately that Norman had announced their plans to go to the Woodleys' party together. It was the old case of "I know, you know, and I know you know."

As the line snaked slowly past her, and Hannah concentrated on exchanging pleasantries with everyone she served, she noticed that Delores and Carrie seemed to be having a slight difference of opinion. They weren't arguing. It was much too friendly for that. But Hannah heard faint strains of "But I'd like to, really. This is so good for Norman" from Carrie, and "No, she'd never accept it from you" from Delores. Then Carrie's voice wafted down to Hannah, "I'll order the corsage. What type of flowers does she like?" And Delores answered, "She adores sunflowers, but those wouldn't do at all. How about orchids?"

By the time Delores and Carrie had arrived at Hannah's station by the coffee urns, they were both wearing identical "cat that got into the cream pot" smiles, a very useful phrase that Hannah had picked up while paging through her mother's Regency romances. Carrie took a cup of herbal tea, Delores selected black coffee, and then Delores leaned close. "We just came from Beau Monde and Claire told us you bought a new dress for the Woodleys' party."

"That's right, Mother." Hannah wasn't surprised that her mother knew about her recent purchase. It was almost impossible to keep secrets in a town the size of Lake Eden.

"I'd like to buy it for you, dear. Let's call it an early birthday present."

Hannah was surprised. Her mother usually wasn't this generous. "That's very nice of you, Mother, but my birthday's in July and that's over eight months away."

"All right then, Christmas. I'm just so pleased that you bought something in the 'first stare of fashion,' dear. Claire said it looked divine on you and everyone knows that Claire has exquisite taste. You must let me reimburse you. I insist."

Hannah stifled a grin, these club meetings always made her mother spout Regency phrases, but she wasn't about to look a gift horse in the mouth. Delores could afford to be generous. Hannah's grandfather had invested heavily in the fledgling Minnesota Mining and Manufacturing Company, and over the years 3M stock had split more times than Hannah could count. "Did Claire tell you what I paid for the dress?"

"I asked, but she said that it was just between the two of you. How much was it, dear? I'll write you a check."

Hannah sighed as she listened to the hoofbeats of the gift horse gallop off into the sunset. She couldn't tell her mother what the dress had cost. She'd promised Claire not to mention the price. "I can't say, Mother. Claire gave it to me at cost and I promised that I wouldn't tell anyone what I paid."

"Not even *moi*?"

"Not even you, Mother." Hannah had trouble keeping a straight face. Her mother sounded just like Miss Piggy when she referred to herself as *moi*.

Carrie leaned close to whisper something in Delores's ear, and her mother began to smile again. "That's a wonderful idea. You'll need a new purse and a pair of shoes, Hannah. Why don't you let me pick up the tab for those?"

"I have a black clutch, Mother. You gave it to me two years ago. And my black heels are perfectly—" Hannah stopped and began to frown as she remembered that her only pair of black dress shoes needed to be resoled. "You hit it on the nose, Mother. I could use a new pair of shoes."

"Then I'll buy them for you. Choose Italian, dear. They're the only ones that last. And make sure you walk around the store at least twice to make sure they don't pinch. I could go out to the mall with you and help you shop."

Hannah winced as she remembered the last shopping trip she'd taken with her mother. Delores had wanted her to buy a dress coat instead of her all-purpose parka. "That's all right, Mother. I know how busy you are. And that reminds me, how's your tooth?"

"My tooth?" Delores appeared startled, and Hannah bit back a grin. Did her mother think that the news on the gossip grapevine traveled in only one direction? "It's fine now, dear. Norman's a marvelous dentist. Did I tell you that I saw Ron LaSalle driving away?"

"No, but Norman did. You didn't talk to Ron, did you?"

"He was pulling out when I drove up and all I saw was the back of his truck. For all I know, it wasn't even Ron." Her mother looked very flustered. "Do you think that I should report it to Bill?"

"Definitely. Bill's trying to account for Ron's actions on the morning that he died, and what you saw might help."

Carrie shivered slightly. "It's frightening to think that someone we all knew could be shot down in broad daylight on our streets."

"I know." Delores sighed. "As far as I'm concerned, it's Herb Beeseman's fault. That boy spends all his time writing tickets and he's never where he's really needed. If he'd stuffed that citation book in his pocket where it belongs, he might have been there in time to save Ron's life!"

Hannah knew she should keep her mouth shut, but she couldn't do it. "Herb was hired to enforce Lake Eden's traffic regulations, not to patrol the streets hunting for would-be killers."

"She's right, Delores," Carrie said and then she turned to Hannah. "It must have been terrible for you, dear. Imagine something like that happening right in back of your shop!"

Delores didn't look very sympathetic. "Hannah can handle things like that. She's always been strong. She gets it from me. Isn't that right, Hannah?"

Hannah managed to keep her lips pressed firmly together. This from the woman who'd fainted when she'd found a dead squirrel on her back doorstep!

"We'd better move along, Delores." Carrie nudged her. "You know how upset these older women get when someone holds up the line."

Hannah came very close to losing it. With the exception of Mrs. Priscilla Knudson, the Lutheran minister's grandmother, Carrie was the oldest lady in the group.

After Hannah had served the remaining women in line, she picked up her cookie tray and stepped out to mingle. She had quite a few takers. Her Regency Ginger Crisps were going over big. She'd just finished serving Bertie Straub, the owner-operator of the Cut 'n Curl, when she overheard part of a conversation that Maryann Watson, Coach Watson's sister, was having with one of the secretaries at DelRay, Lucille Rahn.

"You have no idea how generous my brother is when it comes to Danielle," Maryann confided. "He paid an absolute fortune for her birthday present."

Lucille took a dainty bite of her cookie. "Really? How could he afford to buy something that expensive on a teacher's salary?"

"He's been saving all year. It's her thirtieth, you know, and he wanted to get her something special. He asked me to meet him at the Mall of America on Tuesday night to help him shop. I swear we went to every single jewelry store in the entire mall before he found something that he wanted."

Hannah slipped into her invisible caterer mode, setting her tray down at the far end of their table and busying herself by rearranging the stacked cookies on her tray. Neither woman seemed aware of her, but Hannah could hear every word they spoke.

"What did he buy?" Lucille looked very curious. "You can tell me, Maryann."

Maryann leaned forward, about to confide the delicious secret. She seemed perfectly oblivious to Hannah. Waiters, maids, and caterers were always treated to all the gossip, whether they wanted to hear it or not. "He got her a perfectly gorgeous ruby ring, but you can't tell a soul. It's supposed to be a surprise."

Lucille raised her eyebrows. "A ruby? That *does* sound expensive."

"It was," Maryann confirmed with a nod of her head. "It cost him over a thousand dollars. And Boyd even paid extra to have it engraved on the inside of the band."

"Is that why you missed the Dorcas Circle meeting on Tuesday night?"

"Yes, we had to stay over because the ring wasn't ready until the next morning. Boyd asked me to take it home with me for safekeeping, and you know what *that* means."

Lucille looked thoroughly puzzled. "What does it mean?"

"Danielle must snoop through his things."

"That doesn't really surprise me. Jill Haversham was Danielle's third-grade teacher, and she said that all the Perkins girls were nosy."

"I'll never understand why Boyd married her." Maryann sighed deeply. "He could have had anyone, and it wasn't like he *had* to, you know. But I guess there's no accounting for taste."

"That's what they say. Did you stay over with your mother?"

"Yes, and she was so glad to see us. Boyd went out to get doughnuts for breakfast the next morning and he came back with a huge box. That's so she'd have leftovers. We're not sure she's eating right, now that she's all alone."

Hannah stifled a grin. She didn't think that doughnuts for breakfast fell into the realm of "eating right," but she wasn't one to talk. A lot of her customers ate cookies for breakfast.

"She's lonely, now that Dad's gone," Maryann continued, "and she just rattles around in that house of hers. The neighborhood's turning industrial, and that's not good, either."

"Where is it?" Lucille asked.

"Right off the Anoka exit on the ninety-four. It used to be a nice quiet suburb before they put in the freeway, but it's going downhill in a handbasket. Boyd and I think she should sell and move into one of those nice apartment buildings for seniors."

Lucille raised her eyebrows. "Wouldn't she rather move in with you or Boyd?"

"My place isn't big enough. You've seen my apartment. I barely have room to turn around. Boyd's got plenty of room, but I don't think that Danielle wants her. Not that he's said anything about it. He wouldn't, you know. Boyd's as loyal to that woman as the day is long. He treats her like a princess, dressing her up in expensive clothes and buying her everything she could possibly want. He even bought her that house, you know, and let me tell you, that's got to be a real drain."

"Financially?"

"Their mortgage payments must be sky-high, and there's always something that needs to be fixed. Boyd tries to do it all himself, but heaven knows he's not a plumber or an electrician. I swear Danielle doesn't appreciate how hard he works, but what else can you expect, coming from a family like hers?"

"She doesn't work, does she?" Lucille asked.

"Of course not. She wouldn't lift a finger to help them out. Boyd says he doesn't *want* her to work, but I think he's just covering up for the fact that she's too lazy to hold down a job."

Hannah had heard quite enough criticism about Danielle. She picked up her tray, stuck on her "May I serve you" smile and walked over to tap Maryann on the shoulder. "More cookies, ladies?"

"Hello, Hannah." Maryann seemed surprised to see her. "These are wonderful cookies, dear. And to think that they're authentic! I was just commenting on how delicious they were, wasn't I, Lucille?"

Lucille smiled. "We're so lucky to have you back in town, Hannah. I don't know how the Lake Eden Regency Romance Club ever managed to serve refreshments without you."

"Thank you. I'm so glad you like the cookies." Hannah waited until both Maryann and Lucille had taken another cookie and then she moved on to another table. The Mall of America didn't open until eleven and Coach Watson had been with his sister until then. One more suspect had been eliminated and if her luck ran true to form, the bouncer at Twin Pines would have an alibi, too. Then she'd be back to square one.

Hannah sighed as she finished serving the cookies and went back to fetch the carafes of coffee and tea. Solving crimes certainly wasn't as easy as they made it seem in the movies.

Chapter Twelve

Hannah pulled into the parking lot at the Tri-County Mall and turned to Lisa with a frown. "I *hate* to shop!"

"It won't be so bad, Hannah. All you need is a pair of shoes. And it's really nice of your mother to pay for them."

"Oh, yeah?" Hannah turned to her with lifted eyebrows. "Mother's gifts always have strings attached. The shoes have to be Italian and they can't have more than a three-inch heel."

Lisa shrugged. "Italian is good and you never wear high heels anyway."

"Wait, there's more. I'm not supposed to buy anything except fine leather, no man-made materials allowed, and I have to ask the salesman to guarantee that the color won't run if it gets wet. She made me promise to put them on and walk around the store twice to make sure they don't pinch my feet."

"That doesn't sound so hard. Come on, Hannah. The mall closes at seven and it's already six-thirty."

Hannah sighed and got out of her truck. A light snow was falling and the temperature had dropped ten degrees since the sun had gone down. She didn't like to go to the mall at the best of times and this was the worst. The parking lot was packed with cars, she was pressed for time, and she needed to buy the shoes tonight. As far as Hannah was concerned, this hasty shopping trip to buy a last-minute item was a perfect recipe for disaster.

Lisa led the way across the slushy lot and into the rear door of Sears. They cut through the hardware, paint, and household appliance sections and sped down the path of green indoor-outdoor carpeting to the indoor entrance of the mall itself.

As they walked into the huge dome-shaped area, Hannah's eyes were immediately drawn to a giant red plastic sleigh and eight plastic reindeer frozen in midprance. She blinked twice and then she turned to Lisa. "It's not even Halloween yet and they're all decorated for Christmas!"

"They put up the decorations right after Labor Day. I guess a lot of people like to do their Christmas shopping early and they buy more if the mall's decorated."

"Has your father seen it yet?"

"I bring Dad out every Sunday. There's an animated Santa's Workshop in the lobby of Dayton's and he's just fascinated by it. He must have seen it a half-dozen times, but he always points out what all the elves are doing for me."

"That must be the upside of Alzheimer's. Every time your father sees it, he thinks he's seeing it for the first time." Hannah's words popped out before she could think about them, and she winced when she realized that she'd sounded flippant. "I'm sorry, Lisa. I didn't mean to joke about such an awful disease."

"That's okay, Hannah. You *have* to joke about it. I do it, too. And it could be a lot worse. Dad's not in any pain and he's forgotten about all his problems. Most of the time he really enjoys himself."

"Where should we start first?" Hannah decided it was time to change the subject.

"Let's go to Bianco's. They're new. Rhonda Scharf was in the other day and I heard her telling Gail Hanson that they had a better selection than any of the other shoe stores."

Hannah followed Lisa through the crowd of shoppers without seeing a familiar face. That wasn't surprising. The Tri-County Mall was twenty miles from Eden Lake and it served all the small towns within a forty-mile radius. She saw several teenage boys wearing Little Falls Flyer team jackets and a group of giggling girls, standing near the video store, were sporting Long Prairie High School sweatshirts.

Lisa ducked into a brightly lit store displaying the Italian flag as a background in its window. Rows of shoes lined the shelves on the wall, and every few feet a round plastic display shelf jutted out with a pair of shoes arranged at eye level. Hannah followed and she immediately spotted a pair of black shoes near the back of the store. They had low heels, they were probably made of leather, and they looked comfortable.

"I think I'll take these, Lisa." Hannah walked over to point to the pair of shoes. "They look just right."

"They're too plain, Hannah. You need something fancier to go with your gorgeous dress."

"How much fancier?" Hannah wasn't willing to cave in quite so easily. The black shoes would go with almost anything, and plain was fine with her.

"Try this pair." Lisa snatched a pair from the display and handed them to Hannah. "They'll be perfect. Trust me."

"Trust me" was the same phrase her mother had used when she'd talked Hannah into buying a totally ridiculous velvet skirt one Christmas, and Hannah was leery as she examined the shoes. They met all the requirements, but the thin leather strap that buckled around the ankle would draw attention to her legs.

"Just try them, Hannah. If you don't like them, you can choose something else."

"Fine." Going shopping with Lisa was a lot like shopping with her mother. "I wear a nine and a half narrow."

"I'll get a clerk."

Lisa hurried off and within a few moments she came back with a man with black hair and a mustache. He was wearing white pants and a striped shirt and he looked exactly like Hannah's conception of a Venetian gondolier.

"This is Tony," Lisa introduced him. "He'll help you."

In record time Hannah's feet were measured, and Tony had slipped the shoes on her feet. Hannah stood up gingerly, took a few steps, and started to smile. Lisa was right. The shoes would be perfect with her black cocktail dress. "I'll take them."

"Not so fast," Lisa warned. "You have to walk around the store first. You promised."

Hannah sighed and walked up and down the aisles. She was glad she did, because she noticed a sign near the register that advertised a second pair of shoes for five dollars. She rushed back to Tony and gestured toward the sign. "A second pair is only five dollars?"

"That's right. It's still our grand opening. You want to look at a second pair?"

Hannah shook her head and pointed at Lisa. "No, *she* does and I'm paying. She'd like to try . . ." Hannah glanced around. She'd noticed that Lisa had been staring at a pair of shoes when they'd first walked in, and there had been a wistful expression on her face. She located the shoes, a pair of gold sandals with five-inch heels, and hurried over to retrieve them and carry them back to Tony. "She wants to try this pair."

"You'll be wasting your money," Lisa objected. "They're beautiful, but I wouldn't have anywhere to wear them."

"So what? I want you to have them. Every woman needs a totally fantastic pair of shoes once in a while, even if they just sit in her closet."

"But, Hannah . . ."

"Don't forget that I'm your boss," Hannah interrupted her. "And I'm ordering you to get those shoes."

Lisa began to laugh. "You win. Do you have them in a six, Tony?"

Twin Pines was only ten miles from the Tri-County Mall and the snow was still falling as Hannah pulled into a recently vacated spot near the entrance. It wasn't snowing hard, but she wondered what it would be like to get snowbound at a casino. Perhaps it was a good thing she hadn't brought any of her credit cards with her.

"It's huge, Hannah. And it looks nice." Lisa eyed the flashing neon signs as they walked up to the entrance, and there was a childlike wonder on her face. "I'm glad you asked me to come with you. I've never been inside a casino before."

A bouncer was stationed at a spot just inside the front door and Hannah held her breath. She hoped that Lisa was old enough to gamble. Then she noticed a sign that read: "YOU MUST BE 18 OR OLDER TO GAMBLE." She breathed a sigh of relief. She turned to look back at the bouncer again. His face was free of scratches and bruises and he certainly didn't have a black eye. There was no way that he'd been the recipient of Ron's punches, and Hannah decided to wait until they'd eaten before she asked any questions about the bouncer who'd been on duty Tuesday night.

"What a nice restaurant!" Lisa smiled happily as a waitress led them to a wooden booth in the rustic-looking dining room. "Just look at those Indian blankets on the wall. They're gorgeous."

"Yes, they are." Hannah glanced at the vividly colored blankets. Though they added coziness to the cavernous wood-paneled room, their woven designs didn't look anything like the Sioux blankets she'd seen on her trip to the museum. Perhaps authenticity didn't really matter to a gambler.

"Do you think we should take Herb's suggestion and try the ribs?" Lisa looked up from her menu. It was printed on a type of plastic that resembled birch bark and there was a stick drawing of a teepee on the front.

"That sounds good to me. If Herb recommended them, they must be good. He always had a knack for ferreting out the best item on a menu when we were classmates in high school."

When the ribs came, they were tender and juicy, slathered with a sauce that reminded Hannah of aromatic wood smoke and sweet vine-ripened tomatoes. As they ate, occasionally wiping their hands on the wet napkins the waitress had provided, Hannah thought about the best way to identify the bouncer who'd fought with Ron. If she asked the management, they'd be paranoid about possible lawsuits. She had to think of some nonthreatening excuse to convince them that she needed the bouncer's name.

By the time they'd wiped their hands the final time and shared an excellent cranberry cobbler, Hannah knew exactly how to proceed. She paid their tab, got Lisa settled in front of a quarter slot machine with the change from The Cookie Jar, and set out to find the manager.

After being referred to several employees, Hannah finally found a security guard who agreed to escort her to the manager's office. The guard was tall, broad-shouldered, and perfectly impassive as he blocked a lighted security panel with his body and punched numbers on a keypad that opened the door to an inside corridor.

Hannah gave him a friendly smile as he motioned her through the door, but he didn't smile back. It was obvious that a stern demeanor topped the list of requirements for casino security guards.

Once she'd arrived at the proper door, the guard knocked

twice and then opened it. "A Miss Swensen to see you. She says it's personal."

A voice from the interior told Hannah to enter and she stepped into the office. The room was large and beautifully decorated. Three walls were ivory and the fourth was painted an attractive shade of Chinese red. It contained an ivory silk-covered sofa and two matching chairs that flanked a black lacquer coffee table with gold inlay dragons. The decor was an odd choice for an Indian casino, and Hannah was surprised. There wasn't a single Native American blanket or artifact in sight.

An older man with carefully styled gray hair rose from his chair behind a black lacquer desk. "Miss Swensen? I'm Paul Littletree, the casino manager. Won't you sit down?"

"Thank you," Hannah replied and took the chair in front of his desk, a lovely black lacquer armchair upholstered in Chinese red silk.

"You can leave us, Dennis." Paul Littletree waved a dismissal to the security guard.

Hannah waited until the door had closed behind the security guard and then she launched into the speech she'd prepared. "This is really embarrassing, Mr. Littletree. I'm afraid my brother got a little out of hand the last time he was here. My parents sent me out to apologize and offer to pay for any damage that he did."

"When was this?"

"On Tuesday night. When he got home, he told my mother that he'd been in a fight with one of your bouncers." Hannah lowered her eyes and attempted to look embarrassed about her mythical brother's actions. "We think it's that new girlfriend of his. She's involved in some kind of antigambling movement and she talked him into driving out here to pass out brochures. My brother just has some scratches and bruises, but my parents asked me to check to make sure that your bouncer's all right."

"That would be Alfred Redbird. I noticed that he had some bruises and a black eye when he came in from the parking lot."

"I'm so sorry." Hannah sighed deeply. "Of course we'll be glad to pay his medical expenses and make up for any time he lost from work."

"That's very generous, but it's not necessary. Alfred didn't need more than a couple of Band-Aids."

"I'm so glad to hear that. My mother's been worried sick about it. Was Mr. Redbird able to finish his shift on Tuesday night?"

"No," Paul Littletree chuckled, "but that had nothing to do with your brother. His wife called at midnight and Alfred left to take her to the hospital. Their first baby was born at eight the next morning."

Hannah smiled, even though she felt more like frowning. The bouncer was sounding less and less like a viable suspect. "I'd still like to apologize to him personally. Is he working tonight?"

"No, I gave him the rest of the week off with pay. He'll be back on Monday and he should be used to being a new father by then. Relax, Miss Swensen. Your brother didn't do any real damage, but I'm afraid we'll have to ban him from the casino for a while."

"I certainly can't blame you for that. You have a very nice place here, Mr. Littletree. My friend and I just finished having the ribs at your restaurant and they were delicious."

"I'm glad you're enjoying your evening with us." Paul Littletree rose from his chair and Hannah knew that her interview was over. "Tell your parents that we appreciate their concern. And come out to see us again soon."

When Hannah emerged from the office, the security guard was waiting for her. He wore the same unsmiling visage as he escorted her back into the main part of the casino, and Hannah fought the urge to do something to rattle his composure. If he ever decided to move to England, he'd be a shoo-in to replace one of the guards at Buckingham Palace.

Lisa was right where Hannah had left her, sitting in front of the same slot machine. There was a pile of quarters in the tray and Hannah was surprised. "Are you winning, Lisa?"

"I think I'm a couple of dollars ahead." Lisa glanced down at her tray. "Why don't you try it? It's really a lot of fun."

"All right, but only for a few minutes. I want to get back before nine. Just let me get some change."

"Take some of these." Lisa scooped some quarters out of the tray and handed them to her. "Maybe they'll bring you luck."

The machine next to Lisa was empty and Hannah sat down. Her last suspect had been eliminated. If the bouncer had been at the hospital with his wife, there was no way he could have shot Ron. As Hannah pulled the handle and lost her first quarter, she wondered what people found so fascinating about slot machines. They weren't really interactive, but the man across the aisle from her was patting his machine with his left hand while he pulled the handle with his right.

It must be superstitious behavior, Hannah decided, and as she glanced at the people around her, she realized that every one of them was doing something to try to change their luck. The lady in the red dress talked to her machine, murmuring endearments as the reels spun around. The older man in the polo shirt held down the handle until the reels stopped moving and then he released it to fly back with a jerk. The young brunette in the pink sweater was cupping her left hand in the coin tray as if she could will the coins to fall. Hannah was amused as she turned back to her machine. Everything was mechanized. Didn't they realize that nothing they could do would change the outcome?

Prompted by the thought that the sooner they left, the

sooner she could get home to Moishe and her comfortable bed, Hannah noticed that it was possible to drop five quarters into the coin slot before she pulled the handle. That was nice. She'd get rid of her money five times faster that way. Hannah concentrated on dropping in multiple coins, pulling the handle, and waiting to drop in more.

"Isn't this fun, Hannah?"

Lisa turned to grin at her and Hannah put on an answering smile. Some fun. As far as she could see, the only benefit that might come from playing the slots was a possible strengthening of the muscles in her right arm.

Hannah dropped in her last five quarters. One more pull of the handle and she'd be finished. She yanked down the lever and turned to Lisa to ask her if she was ready to leave, when a siren wailed, red lights flashed, and quarters began to spew out of her machine.

"You hit a jackpot!" Lisa jumped up from her chair and rushed over to watch the hailstorm of coins bouncing down. "How many quarters did you put in?"

Hannah just stared at the avalanche of coins clanking noisily into the metal tray. "As many as it could take. I just wanted to finish so that we could go home."

"You did it, Hannah!" Lisa's mouth dropped open as she looked up at the flashing numbers above the machine. "You just won one thousand nine hundred and forty-two dollars!"

Hannah stared at the flashing numbers with absolute amazement. Then she looked down at the reels and saw that they were all lined up on the jackpot icons. No wonder people liked to play the slot machines. It was a lot more fun than she'd thought.

Chapter Thirteen

"**H**ey, Moishe. How about some grub?" Hannah tossed her purse onto the couch and carried Moishe out to the kitchen. She draped her parka over a chair, set Moishe down next to his food bowl, and poured in a generous serving of Meow Mix. Then she remembered that she'd just won a slot machine jackpot and she opened a can of fancy albacore tuna and dumped that in, too. Moishe meant more to her than any of the other males in her life. He should enjoy the fruits of her good fortune.

She'd already shared her winnings with Lisa. Hannah had given her a bonus of two hundred dollars, making her promise to buy a fancy dress to go with her new shoes. Lisa hadn't wanted to take it, but after Hannah had convinced her that she never would have played the slots if Lisa hadn't urged her, she'd accepted the money.

Hannah had done some mental arithmetic as she'd driven home, taking into account the money she'd spent investigating Ron's murder for Bill. Even after she'd subtracted the cost of the makeup from Luanne, the dress from Claire, and the money they'd spent at Twin Pines, she'd still come out over a thousand dollars to the good.

While Moishe munched and rumbled his contentment, Hannah marched to the kitchen phone to call Bill and tell him that she'd eliminated the bouncer as a suspect. Bill wasn't at his desk at the sheriff's station, but she left a message there and another with Andrea, who promised to prop up a note by the phone. Hannah hung up, her duty done, and went to her bedroom to change into the oversized sweatshirt and sweatpants she'd bought when the furnace had gone out last winter.

Ten minutes later, Hannah was sitting in her favorite spot on the couch, sipping her wine and holding Moishe. He was always starved for affection when she'd been gone for hours, and tonight was no exception. She scratched him under his chin until he purred in ecstasy and she sang the silly little song she'd made up for him. She'd never been able to carry a tune, but as long as she kept on scratching, Moishe seemed to enjoy it. Perhaps it was a very good thing that she lived alone. If anyone had heard her singing about how much she adored her "big strong puss," she'd be locked up as a nutcase.

The condo complex had free cable and Hannah surfed through the channels. There were fifty, but there was still nothing she wanted to watch. She settled for a documentary on forensics. It was possible she might learn something. But all the expert talked about were the new advances in fingerprint technology. Hannah listened to him expound on the use of superglue in subzero temperatures to lift prints from a victim's skin and then she switched to the classic movies channel. *Klute* was playing and she'd seen it before, but she didn't feel like channel-surfing any longer and she left it on.

Hannah thought about the crime for a while, but that was depressing. None of her sleuthing had done a particle of good. The cup with the lipstick had been promising at first, and she'd managed to find out that Danielle had been with Ron right before he'd been murdered. But what Danielle had told her really hadn't mattered in the long run. She'd checked out Coach Watson and the jealousy motive, but he'd been with Maryann at his mother's house when Ron had been shot. Norman was no longer a suspect, now that Delores had confirmed his alibi, and the homeless man that Claire had seen had been eating breakfast at the critical time. The bouncer that Ron had fought with at Twin Pines would be in the clear just as soon as Bill checked with the hospital, and Hannah was fresh out of suspects. She had to come up with some other suspects, but she didn't have any idea where to start.

She reached for the notepad she kept by the couch and scrawled a list of names: Coach Watson, Norman, Blaze, and Alfred Redbird. Then she sighed and drew a line through each of them. As an afterthought, Hannah added Danielle to the list, but she really didn't think that Danielle had shot Ron. All the same, she decided to check to see if she had an alibi.

Hannah picked up the phone book and paged through to find Danielle's number. If Coach Watson answered, she'd just hang up.

Danielle picked up on the second ring and Hannah breathed a sigh of relief. "Hi, Danielle. It's Hannah Swensen. Can you talk?"

"Just a minute, Hannah." Hannah heard Danielle say something to Boyd about ordering cookies and then she came back on the line. "We'll need five dozen for my art class Halloween party, Hannah. I was thinking of something with orange frosting."

"No problem," Hannah answered quickly. "If I ask you yes or no questions, will that be all right?"

"Yes."

"Great. Did you see anyone or make any calls after Ron dropped you off on Wednesday morning?"

"Yes. I'd love to see a sample, Hannah, but I can't come in

that early on Wednesday morning. The Sparklettes man delivers our water between eight and nine and I have to be here
to let him in."

"Can you figure out any way to tell me exactly what time
he was there?"

"I hate those morning deliveries, too. Last Wednesday he
was here at eight and I almost overslept."

"Thanks, Danielle." Hannah hung up and jotted down a
note by Danielle's name. She'd check with the Sparklettes
driver and if he'd delivered water to Danielle at eight, she
could cross Danielle's name off the list.

It was another dead end. Hannah sighed and tried to think
of something positive. Positive thoughts were supposed to
lead to pleasant dreams and she didn't want a repeat of last
night's nightmares. At least she was getting along with Andrea much better lately. Perhaps all the old resentments were
fading with the years and they could actually become friends.

Hannah had to admit that she'd been a pretty hard act to
follow in school. Andrea had taken a lot of criticism from
her teachers about the fact that Hannah had been a straight-
A student. Instead of competing with Hannah's academic
record, Andrea had thrown herself into extracurricular activities. She'd starred in school plays, sung solos at concerts,
and edited the school paper and yearbook. And Andrea had
certainly been more popular with the boys than Hannah had
been. Andrea's Friday and Saturday nights had been booked
from her freshman year through her senior year.

Hannah sighed. She could boast of only two dates during
her entire time in high school. One had been a study date at
her house with a classmate who was about to flunk chemistry and it had taken some very broad hints from Delores
before he'd agreed to take Hannah out for pizza to thank her
for his passing grade. The other had been her senior prom
date. Hannah had found out later that it had entailed a
promise of a part-time summer job in her father's shop for

Cliff Schuman to show up at her door with a corsage in his hand.

College had been different. There she hadn't been treated as a pariah because she read the classics and knew who Wittgenstein and Sartre were. In college, the ability to do an algebraic equation in her head wasn't considered a personality defect, and no one thought less of her if she knew the atomic number of einsteinium. Of course, there had been a group of incredibly gorgeous, bubbleheaded girls who'd turned male heads, but most of them had either flunked out or left to get their MRS degrees.

Hannah had finally started to date as a sophomore in college. She'd gone out with a too-tall, too-thin history major for several months. After that, there had been an intense art major who'd confided that he was celibate right after she'd begun to think they'd had something going, and a master's candidate who'd wanted her input on his thesis. True love, or perhaps it was true lust, hadn't found her until November in her second year of postgraduate work. That was when Hannah had met the man she'd thought would be her soul mate.

Bradford Ramsey had been the assistant professor in Hannah's poetry seminar, and the first time he'd given a lecture, she'd been spellbound. It hadn't been his manner of speaking or the way he'd read stanzas from Byron and Keats. It had been his marvelous, soul-searching dark blue eyes.

Social meetings after class with the professor had been frowned upon by the administration unless several students were in attendance, but Brad had found ways around the rules. Hannah had gone to his office for several student-professor conferences. After he'd told her that he thought he was in love with her, she'd wound up at his apartment, sneaking through the lobby at eleven at night with the hood of her parka obscuring her face. That night, and the nights that followed, had been memorable. Hannah had discovered that sex was a lot more fun than she'd thought it would be. But the last night she'd spent with her handsome professor had been memorable in a way she'd never anticipated. His fiancée had driven in for a surprise visit, Brad had panicked, and Hannah had been forced to vacate his bed by way of an icy fire escape.

Hannah had broken it off and told herself that she was wiser for the experience, but that hadn't made it any easier. Seeing her former lover stride across campus with a gaggle of young, impressionable girls in his wake had been almost too painful to bear. It had come as a relief when Andrea had asked her to leave college and come back to Lake Eden to help settle her father's affairs. That didn't mean that Hannah had given up on men. She was just taking a breather, waiting for one she could love and trust to come along. In the meantime, she had her family, her work, and her loyal cat. And if her bed was lonely and she sometimes wished that she had someone without furry paws to cuddle, she could deal with it.

The phone rang and Hannah reached out to answer it. "Hi, Bill. It's about time."

"How did you know it was me?"

"Who else could it be? Mother never calls me this late and Andrea told me she was going to bed an hour ago. Did you find out anything new about Ron?"

"Not a thing." Bill sounded depressed. "Ron had no known enemies, he didn't owe any large amounts of money, and there were no deposits to his bank account that couldn't be explained. I've got zilch."

Hannah was quick to commiserate, "Me, too. I talked to the manager at the casino and I think we have to eliminate the bouncer as a suspect. His name is Alfred Redbird and you should check with the hospital. His wife had a baby that morning. If he was with her the whole time, he couldn't have shot Ron."

"Okay." Bill sounded even more discouraged. "I'm fresh out of leads, Hannah. If we had a motive, we'd have something to go on, but we don't even have that."

Hannah's eyes were drawn to the television screen. *Klute* was still playing and that gave her an idea. "Maybe we *do* have a motive. What if Ron saw something that morning, something that could incriminate his killer in some way? That might be why he was shot."

"And Ron was murdered before he could implicate his killer in another crime?" Bill was silent for a long moment and Hannah knew he was thinking it over. "You could be right. But how do we find out what Ron saw?"

"I'll go back to my source, the one with the pink lipstick. She can tell me if anything unusual happened that morning."

"Okay." There was another long silence and then Bill sighed. "Maybe you'd better warn her to be careful. If you're right and she saw what Ron saw, the killer might come after her."

"He won't. I'm the only one who knows who she is and she's sure that no one spotted her with Ron. If the killer wanted to murder her, he would have done it by now."

"Maybe."

Bill didn't sound convinced and Hannah frowned. For Danielle's sake she certainly hoped that she was right.

"You've been a big help, Hannah. By the way, did you know that your mother saw Ron pulling away from Norman's dental office right before she went in for her appointment?"

"Norman told me about it. I questioned him, but he said that Ron was only in his chair for twenty minutes. He gave Ron a shot of Xylocaine for his cracked tooth and Ron was supposed to come back to get it fixed. I'll get back to you as soon as I talk to my source. I'm sure she'll be at the Woodleys' party. And if you want to talk to Norman, he'll be there, too."

"Andrea told me that you were going to the party with Norman. Is it serious?"

"Serious? With *Norman*?"

"I was just teasing you, Hannah. I'll see you at the party and we can compare notes."

Hannah hung up and flicked off the television. She scooped up Moishe, carried him into the bedroom, and deposited him on the pillow she'd designated as his on the first night he'd spent in her condo. Then she went back for her wineglass and flicked off the lights, taking a seat in the old wing chair she'd placed in front of her bedroom window. The snow was still falling and it created lovely halos around the old-fashioned streetlights that lined the brick walkways between the units. It was a perfect winter scene, worthy of Currier and Ives. According to her college art professor, people who lived in warm climates loved winter scenes with their glittering expanses of unbroken snow and yellow light spilling out from the windows of snug, cozy homes. Minnesotans who bought scenic art usually avoided winter scenes. Hannah didn't find that surprising. Minnesota winters were long. Why would they want to buy a painting that would constantly remind them of the bone-chilling cold, the heavy snow that had to be shoveled, and the necessity of dressing up in survival gear to do nothing more than take out the garbage?

Hannah had finished the last of her wine and was about to rouse herself to climb in under the covers when she noticed that one of the cars in the visitors' parking lot was idling, its exhaust pipe sending up plumes of white against the dark night sky. Its headlights were off and that was odd, unless someone was taking a very long time to say goodbye to his date. She could see only one occupant, a bulky figure behind the wheel that she assumed was a man. As she watched, she saw a reflection glinting off two round lenses in front of his face. Binoculars? Or eyeglasses? Hannah couldn't tell at this distance, but the fact that no one else was in the car made her nervous.

Hannah stared at the car, memorizing its shape. It was a small compact in a dark color, but it was parked too far away to identify the manufacturer. The roof looked lighter than the body, and Hannah assumed that it was covered with snow. This car had been parked for a while and the driver appeared to be watching her building.

There were only four units in her building. Phil and Sue Plotnik lived below her and there was no earthly reason why anyone would sit in a parked car to watch their place. Phil was home tonight. She'd seen his car in the garage when she'd driven in and she'd heard their new baby fussing softly as she'd climbed the stairs to her unit. Hannah's other neighbors were equally unremarkable. Mrs. Canfield, an elderly widow, had the bottom unit next to the Plotniks. She lived on her husband's retirement money and gave piano lessons during the week. Above her were Marguerite and Clara Hollenbeck, two middle-aged unmarried sisters who were very active at Redeemer Lutheran Church. As far as Hannah knew, there wasn't a breath of gossip about them, except for the time they'd washed the altar cloths with a red blouse of Clara's and they'd come out pink.

Hannah felt a chill as she stared at the car and its motionless driver. There was only one unit the man could be watching and it was hers.

Ron's killer! The thought struck Hannah like a lightning bolt of dread. Bill had told her to be careful about asking questions and she thought she had. But what if the killer had the misguided notion that she was hot on his trail? Bill's words came back to haunt her: *If he killed once, he won't hesitate to kill again.*

The security light had been on this morning. Hannah shivered as she remembered. She'd assumed that a bird had set it off, but perhaps she'd been wrong. Had Ron's killer attempted to get into her condo?

Hannah swallowed past the lump of fear in her throat, took a deep breath, and forced herself to think rationally. She really hated to call Bill and roust him out of his comfortable bed. Bill would race right over here to question the guy, but she'd feel like a fool if the driver had some perfectly good reason for being there. But what reason could there be for sitting in a car in the dead of night, alone in the snow?

She thought about it for several minutes and she came up with only one possible scenario. The driver was locked out of his condo. But why would he park in the visitors' lot if he lived here? It was a lot warmer in the garage.

Hannah didn't think she was in any actual danger. Bill had installed a police-recommended deadbolt on her door when she'd first moved in and he'd put extra locks on all the windows. She even had an alarm system, installed by the previous owner, that boasted a siren, clanking bells, and two keypads, one by the front door and another in her bedroom. Hannah had never bothered to turn it on before, but tonight she would. She hadn't been born with nine lives like her feline roommate.

She was about to go to the keypad to activate the system when she had a brilliant idea. The moment she thought of it, she jumped up and rummaged through the closet for her camera. She'd take a picture of the car. It was sitting right under the streetlight and the license plate would show. And she'd turn the film over to Bill in the morning.

Her camera was out of film and it took a frantic search to find a roll. Hannah turned off the flash, knowing it would just glare off her windowpane, and used the zoom lens to snap several shots of the car. Then she activated the security system and sat down in her chair. She'd done all she could, with the exception of alerting Bill, but she'd never be able to sleep peacefully. She might as well resign herself to an all-night stint of surveillance.

Several minutes later, armed with a freshly made cup of coffee and a box of white cheddar cheese crackers, Hannah sat down in her chair again. As she alternately crunched and sipped, Moishe opened his good eye to give her a curious stare and promptly went back to sleep again.

"Some attack cat you are!" Hannah complained. And

then she heard the sound of another car approaching the visitors' parking lot. As it drove past one of the old-fashioned streetlights, Hannah recognized Bernice Maciej's yellow Cadillac.

Bernice, who lived in the building directly across from Hannah, turned in to park next to the snow-covered car. She got out, the man got out, and they embraced in the parking lot. Hannah punched in the code to turn off the security system and opened the window to listen in on their conversation. She heard Bernice say: "Sorry, honey. I didn't think I'd be out this late." And the man replied, "That's okay, Mom. The traffic was light and I got here sooner than I thought I would."

Feeling more than a bit foolish, Hannah closed the window, set her alarm clock, and climbed under the covers. She rousted Moishe from the nest he'd made on her pillow and plunked him down on his.

"I must be getting paranoid," Hannah murmured as she reached out to pet Moishe's soft fur. "I should have taken my cue from you and just curled up and gone to sleep."

Chapter Fourteen

When Hannah woke up the next morning, she was in a foul mood. She was used to getting along without the recommended eight hours of sleep, but she'd spent a very restless night and some of her dreams had been disturbing. Ron's killer had chased her in a yellow Cadillac bearing a striking resemblance to the one Bernice drove. Her final nightmare hadn't been so bad. She'd dreamed that she was being held down and tickled by a furry monster. By now, Hannah knew what that dream meant. Moishe had crawled onto her pillow. She'd managed to rouse herself enough to shove him over, and the rest of the night had been relatively peaceful.

There was a list on the pad of notepaper she kept on her night table and Hannah switched on the light to read it. The words *Fluffy Dreams* were written at the top and they were in her handwriting. She must have been dreaming about cookies again.

Oh, yes. Hannah began to smile. She remembered the dream now. She'd been catering a reception at the White House and the president, a young Abe Lincoln, had raved about her cookies. His wife, Barbara Bush, had asked for the recipe and she'd written it out right there in the Oval Office.

Hannah laughed out loud. Abe Lincoln and Barbara Bush. She guessed she shouldn't be surprised. It had been a dream, after all. But she *had* written down the recipe. Perhaps her unconscious had come up with something delicious.

The words were written in an untidy scrawl. Obviously, she hadn't bothered to turn on the light. Hannah made out the word *butter* and a bit farther down *sugar.* Between the two words was a scrawl that looked like *pooches.* It must be *peaches,* and peach cookies were an intriguing concept. She also made out *marshes* for marshmallows, and *cuckoo,* which could be either cocoa or coconut. Perhaps she'd experiment a bit with the ingredients and see what she could make.

Hannah carried the notebook out to the kitchen and poured herself a fragrant cup of coffee. After several bracing sips, she noticed that there was another line scrawled at the bottom of the recipe. It said: *D—ask not with.*

There was a plaintive yowl from the direction of the food bowl, and Hannah got up to dump in the kitty crunchies. As she filled Moishe's water bowl with filtered water, she thought about that last cryptic note. The *"D"* was Danielle. Hannah was almost certain of that. But what was "ask not with?"

It came to her in a flash of brilliant insight. Her mind had been working overtime last night. She'd wanted to remind herself to ask Danielle if there had been any time, during their night and early morning together, that Ron had gone somewhere without Danielle.

Hannah set Moishe's water bowl down on his Garfield rubber mat and went back to the table to finish her coffee. If yesterday and the day before were any indication, today would be hectic. She reached for the notepad, turned to a fresh page, and wrote down a list of things to do.

The first item Hannah wrote was *Sparklettes.* She had to call to find out what time Danielle's water had been delivered on Wednesday morning. If what Danielle had told her was true, Danielle was in the clear.

Hannah made another note: *Herb—Lisa.* She wanted to corner Herb Beeseman on her way to work and convince him to call Lisa to invite her to the Woodleys' party. It was late notice, but Hannah was almost sure that Lisa would accept. When she'd asked last night, Lisa had told her that she'd received an invitation to the Woodleys' party, but that she wasn't planning to go. It wasn't because of her father—one of the neighbors had volunteered to sit with him—but Lisa really didn't want to attend the biggest party of the year by herself. She hadn't wanted to tag along with Hannah and Norman, either, and that was when Hannah had decided to talk Herb into asking Lisa.

The third item on her list was *Lisa—dress.* Hannah planned to take Lisa to Beau Monde during their slow time between eleven and twelve. She'd put a sign on the door and if anyone was that desperate for a cookie, they could come next door to get her.

The next line on Hannah's list said: *Clue Claire.* She'd dash over this morning, while Lisa was baking, to tell Claire that the dress Lisa chose should be "on sale" for sixty dollars. She'd make up the difference and they could settle up later, when Lisa wasn't around.

Moishe gave another yowl and Hannah noticed that his food bowl was empty again. Her cat was a regular feline garbage disposal, but he didn't seem to be gaining any weight. Perhaps he did kitty aerobics when she wasn't home.

"That looks lovely on you," Claire announced as Lisa walked out of the dressing room wearing a wine-red dress. "What do you think, Hannah?"

Hannah laughed. "You're asking *me*? You should know better, Claire. How many times have you wanted to tell me that all my taste is in my mouth?"

"Too many times to count." Claire laughed lightly and then she turned to Lisa. "What do you think, Lisa?"

"I'm not sure. I really like this one, but the emerald green is such a wonderful color."

"Too bad they're not twofers." Hannah winked at Claire, hoping that she'd take the hint. It was unlikely. Beau Monde was a boutique, and Claire thought of herself as a fashion consultant, several cuts above an owner or a saleslady. Hannah doubted that her high-fashion neighbor had ever considered having a two-for-one sale.

"It's strange that you should mention it, Hannah." Claire surprised Hannah by taking the hint immediately. "As it happens, I just marked these two particular dresses down. The wine satin sheath has a slight imperfection in the bodice and the button on the back of the green silk doesn't quite match the color of the dress."

Lisa's eyes opened wide. "I didn't even notice!"

"Perhaps not, but I did. And I refuse to let my customers pay full price for something that isn't absolutely perfect."

"How much are they now?" Lisa asked.

Hannah held her breath. If Claire mentioned a price that was too low, Lisa would suspect that they were in cahoots.

"They're both on sale for sixty. That's two-thirds off the regular price. Believe me, Lisa, you'll be doing me a favor if you take them off my hands. Returning things to my supplier is a nightmare."

"Then I'll take them both." Lisa was so excited her voice squeaked.

"There's only one condition." Claire looked very serious. "You have to promise that you won't tell anyone else how much they cost. If the other women find out that you paid only sixty dollars for a Beau Monde dress, they'll all ask for special prices."

"I won't tell anyone. Even if I did, they'd never believe me. Thank you, Claire. This is really my lucky day!"

While Lisa changed back into her working clothes, Hannah dashed back to The Cookie Jar. She'd been gone less than fifteen minutes, but there were several people waiting to get in. One of them was Bill, and Hannah pulled him aside, once she'd waited on her customers. "Why didn't you come next door to get me? I was just helping Lisa buy a dress."

"That's okay. You didn't find out anything new, did you?"

"Not since I talked to you last night." Hannah shook her head. She'd called the Sparklettes office and confirmed Danielle's alibi, but there was no reason to tell Bill about that. "Did you check on the bouncer?"

"The maternity ward nurse said that he was at the hospital until nine on Wednesday morning. I just dropped by to remind you that the sheriff's department's open house is tomorrow. You're going to bake cookies for us, aren't you?"

"Of course I am. It's on my calendar." Hannah led the way into the back room and pointed to the huge calendar that hung on her wall.

"What kind are you making?"

"Black and Whites. I might as well start mixing them up right now."

"Black and Whites?"

"They're fudge cookies with powdered sugar on top," Hannah explained. "I developed the recipe last week and I'm naming them after your new squad cars."

"The guys will like that. Are you going to bake them now?"

"No, not until tomorrow morning. The dough has to chill overnight. I'll have them out at the station before noon."

"That's another reason I came in. Sheriff Grant's driving the new guy around and he said they'd come in to pick them up."

"New guy?"

"He's coming in tomorrow morning. Sheriff Grant hired a really good detective away from the MPD."

"Why would a Minneapolis detective want to come

here?" Hannah was flabbergasted. "It's got to mean a big salary cut."

"I know. We only make half as much as the MPD guys do, but I heard that he wanted to move here for personal reasons."

"Personal reasons?"

"Yeah, he wanted to get out of Minneapolis. I know his wife died. I figure he probably wants to make a fresh start where things don't remind him of her."

That made sense, but Hannah was still worried. Winnetka County was big, but did the sheriff's department really need *two* new detectives?

"There's a lot I can learn from his guy, Hannah. I got a chance to peek at his personnel jacket and he's solved a ton of tough cases."

Hannah nodded and got out her mixing bowls, arranging them in a row. What Bill had just told her disturbed her deeply. If this new man had been hired as a detective, it didn't bode well for Bill's promotion. "Do you have time to watch the shop for me while I mix up this dough? Lisa should be back any minute and I'll pay you in cookies."

"Sure." Bill gave her a big grin. "I'm on my lunch break."

Once Bill had left, Hannah gathered the ingredients for the cookies she'd named Black and Whites. While she worked, she thought about the new detective. Bill had said that his wife had died, and Delores was bound to zero in on any new unattached man in town.

Hannah did her best to practice positive thinking as she mixed up the dough. She'd won a jackpot last night, and if her luck held, Bill's new colleague wouldn't be the type of man that her mother would consider as a prospective son-in-law. Unfortunately, as far as Delores was concerned, any ambulatory male without a felony conviction was a viable candidate.

BLACK AND WHITES

Do not preheat oven yet—
dough must chill before baking.

2 cups chocolate chips
¾ cup butter *(1½ sticks)*
2 cups brown sugar *(or white sugar with a scant 2 tablespoons molasses mixed in)*
4 eggs
2 teaspoons vanilla
2 teaspoons baking powder
1 teaspoon salt
2 cups flour *(not sifted)*
approx. ½ cup confectioners' sugar *(powdered sugar) in a small bowl*

Melt chocolate chips with butter. *(Microwave on high power for 2 minutes, then stir until smooth.)*

Mix in sugar and let cool. Add eggs, one at a time, mixing well after each addition. Mix in vanilla, baking powder, and salt. Add flour and mix well.

Chill dough for at least 4 hours. *(Overnight is even better.)*

When you're ready to bake, preheat oven to 350 degrees F., rack in the middle position.

Roll walnut-sized dough balls with your hands. (*Messy—wear plastic gloves if you wish.*) Drop the dough balls into a bowl with the powdered sugar and roll them around until they're coated. (*If the dough gets too warm, stick it back in the refrigerator until you can handle it again.*)

Place the balls on a greased cookie sheet, 12 to a standard sheet. (*They will flatten when they bake.*) Bake at 350 degrees F. for 12 to 14 minutes. Let them cool on the cookie sheet for 2 minutes, and then remove to wire rack to finish cooling.

Made these for the Winnetka County Sheriff's Department Open House, in honor of their four new cruisers.

Yield: 6 to 8 dozen, depending on cookie size.

Chapter Fifteen

Hannah stepped back to assess her reflection. Her new dress was exquisite. She'd pulled her frizzy red hair back in the ebony clasp her younger sister Michelle had sent from an art and jewelry fair they'd held on the Macalester campus, and it actually looked good. And Lisa had been right. Her new shoes couldn't have been more perfect. Hannah looked sophisticated for the first time in her life, and it was a bit of a shock. She also looked sexy, which was even more of a shock, and she hoped that Norman wouldn't think she'd worn this dress just for him.

Moishe yowled from his spot on the bed and Hannah turned to give him a thumbs-up. "You're right. I know I've never looked this good before. It's a real change, isn't it?"

Moishe yowled again and Hannah assumed that it was a change he didn't appreciate. He also knew that she was going out again and he didn't appreciate that, either. She dabbed on a bit of perfume from the bottle of Chanel No. Five that her old college roommate had given her years before, and headed off to the kitchen to appease the beast that lived under her roof.

Several kitty treats later and Moishe was happy again. Hannah paced across the floor, waiting for Norman. She didn't dare sit down. Her new dress was black and every chair in her apartment was inundated with orange cat hair. She was just crossing the living room for the sixteenth time when her doorbell chimed.

"Stay!" Hannah used the command voice the dog trainers on television used and Moishe looked startled. It probably didn't work on cats, but there was really no danger of Moishe escaping when she opened the door. He had a full food bowl and he knew when he had a good thing going.

"Hi, Hannah." Norman looked a little nervous as he thrust out a florist's box. "Uh . . . these are for you."

Hannah smiled and ushered him in. To her surprise, Norman looked much better in his formal clothing than she'd thought he would. "Thanks, Norman. Just let me get my coat and I'll be ready to go."

"You'd better put those in water first." Norman gestured toward the box. "My mother wanted me to get you a corsage, but I told her that this wasn't a prom date."

Hannah laughed and led the way to the kitchen to get out a vase. She filled it with water, opened the box, and smiled as she took out a large bunch of pink, white, and yellow daisies. "Thank you, Norman. They're beautiful and I like them much better than a corsage."

"You didn't tell me you had a cat." Norman stared at Moishe, who had lifted his head from the depths of his food dish to examine the stranger who had invaded his kitchen.

Hannah quickly thrust the flowers in the vase and turned to Norman in alarm. "Sorry. I didn't think to tell you. You're not allergic, are you?"

"Not at all. Cats are some of my favorite people. What's his name?"

"Moishe."

"After Moshe Dayan?"

"That's right. He's blind in one eye."

"Perfect name." Norman bent down and extended his hand. "Come here and meet me, big guy."

Hannah watched in amazement as Moishe padded over to Norman and rubbed up against his hand. Her cat had never been this sociable before. Norman scratched him under the chin and she could hear Moishe's purr all the way across the kitchen. "He *likes* you."

"I guess he does."

Hannah watched as Norman scooped Moishe up and tickled his belly, something Moishe usually hated. But her cat just lolled in Norman's arms and looked as blissful as a cat could look.

"Okay, Moishe. We have to go." Norman carried him out to the living room and set him down on the couch. "Do you leave the television on for him?"

Hannah nodded, hoping Norman wouldn't think she was crazy. "It's company for him when I'm gone."

"That makes sense. I'll do it while you get your coat. Which channel does he like?"

"Anything except Animal Planet. They run vet programs and he hates vets." Hannah went to the closet and grabbed the coat she'd chosen, a previously owned cashmere that she'd found at Helping Hands. When she came back into the room, Norman was frowning. "Is there something wrong, Norman?"

"I was just kicking myself for forgetting to tell you how gorgeous you look. I should have said that right away. Mother would have a fit if she knew."

Hannah laughed. "So would my mother. Delores made me promise to tell you how nice *you* looked and I forgot. If we run into them at the party, we won't mention it. How's that?"

"Good." Norman opened the door and waited for Hannah to step through. "Uh . . . Hannah?"

"Yes, Norman?" Hannah double-locked the door with her key and they walked down the stairs to the ground floor.

"We're going to run into them at the party. As a matter of fact, we'll see them before that."

Hannah winced. "Don't tell me we're picking them up!"

"Not exactly. I did that already, before I came to get you. They're both waiting for us in the backseat of my car."

Hannah felt as if she were stuck in a time warp as they drove to the Woodleys' mansion. It was a lot like being a kid again, dragged off to a party by her mother. To make matters worse, Norman's mother had brought a camera and she'd blithely announced that she planned to take pictures of them. Hannah had feared that this evening might turn out to be an ordeal, but it was going to be even worse than she'd anticipated.

The Woodley mansion was ablaze with lights and when they pulled up, a red-jacketed valet came forward to take Norman's car. Another parking attendant opened the doors, and Hannah and their mothers were assisted out of the car and up to the front entrance.

Hannah gazed around her as she entered the foyer on Norman's arm. It had been decorated for the occasion with banks upon banks of tropical blooms. Of course they were imported. Birds of Paradise, Royal Poinciana, and Chinese Hibiscus didn't grow in Minnesota, even in the summer. They had been transported from warmer climates, and Hannah knew they had to have been outrageously expensive.

There was a harpist, seated in an alcove, playing classical music. Hannah thought that was a nice touch. Leave it to Judith Woodley to provide a touch of class from the moment they entered the door.

"Your coat, ma'am?" A pretty maid, dressed in a dark green uniform and a frilly white apron, helped Hannah out of her coat. "Would you care to freshen up in the ladies' powder room?"

"Yes, thank you," Hannah replied, and then she turned to Norman. "I'm just going to run a currycomb through my hair."

Norman chuckled at her reference to the tool that was used to groom horses. "I *like* your hair, Hannah."

"Ma'am?" The maid touched Hannah's arm. "If you'll just follow me, please."

Hannah made arrangements to meet Norman at the bar and went off with the maid. She was an attractive brunette that Hannah didn't recognize, though she thought she'd seen her at last year's party. The Woodleys always hired outside help for their parties. Judith complained that the local girls simply weren't capable of being trained for such a special event. Hannah turned to the maid and asked, "You're not from Lake Eden, are you?"

"Minneapolis, ma'am. I work for Parties Plus, the service that Mrs. Woodley uses."

"That's a long way to drive for one party," Hannah commented, giving her a friendly smile.

"Oh, that's no problem. Mrs. Woodley arranges for our transportation, and this is one party I wouldn't want to miss. I've been here for three years in a row."

"I thought I recognized you from last year. What makes this party better than other parties?"

"It's a five-day assignment and we have the use of the indoor pool and spa. Mrs. Woodley even caters our meals while we're here. It's almost like a party for us."

Hannah was fishing, but she never knew when information like this might come in handy. "I guess your regular assignments aren't this nice?"

"No way. Usually we're in and out in less than six hours and we work like dogs while we're there. Mrs. Woodley always allows plenty of time for us to set up."

Hannah was curious. "How long have you been here?"

"Since Tuesday morning. We spent two days cleaning, and yesterday we set up the tables and made sure that all the glassware and dishes were ready. Today we just helped the caterer."

"When do you go back?"

"Right after we do the cleanup tomorrow morning. We're usually on the road by noon. I'll be back home by two at the latest, but Mrs. Woodley pays us for the whole day."

They had arrived at the ladies' powder room and Hannah went in to take stock of the damage. Her hair looked all right and she just patted down a few loose curls. Then she refreshed the lipstick that Luanne Hanks had decided was just perfect for her and went back out to find Norman.

Norman was standing by the bar, almost lost in a sea of taller faces. As Hannah moved toward him, she was glad her heels were only three inches high. "Hi, Norman. I'm back."

"And just in time." Norman took her arm and moved her away from the crowd. "Our mothers are headed this way. Let's go over and pay our respects to the Woodleys."

The reception line wasn't long, and Hannah and Norman took their places at the end. As they approached their host and hostess, Hannah admired Judith Woodley's dress. It was made of lilac silk and the bodice was beaded with tiny pearls. Her light brown hair was caught up in an elaborate twist on the top of her head and she looked lovely, as always. She was smiling and chattering with her guests and she appeared quite animated. Del, on the other hand, looked surprisingly glum, and Hannah noticed that there were dark circles under his eyes.

"Hannah." Judith extended her hand. "How lovely to see you."

Hannah had the insane urge to reply that it was lovely to be seen, but she thought better of it. She searched her mind for something appropriate to say and pulled out a standard compliment. "You look lovely tonight, Judith. I had no idea that Claire had such wonderful dresses in her shop."

"Claire?" Judith's green eyes widened, and Hannah knew she'd just stuck her foot in the mud. "This isn't from Beau Monde, Hannah. Billy designed it especially for me."

"Billy?"

"Billy Blass. He's a close personal friend of mine. And I see that you have a date this year. How nice."

Hannah cringed and introduced Norman to the Woodleys, making sure to mention that Norman had arrived to take over his father's dental practice. They chatted with the Woodleys for another brief moment and then they moved on.

"Billy Blass." Norman chuckled as he took Hannah's arm. "I wonder if he calls her Judy."

Hannah laughed appreciatively. This party might be fun if Norman kept making jokes. She accepted a glass of champagne from a passing waiter and they wandered through the crowd for a few minutes, hailing the people that they knew. Then they walked over to view the appetizer table.

"Caviar." Norman pointed to the black tapioca-looking substance in a large cut-glass bowl that was nestled in a larger bowl of shaved ice.

"It's beluga," Hannah informed him. "I asked last year and the waiter told me that the Woodleys wouldn't serve anything else."

Norman was obviously impressed because he accepted a caviar-laden toast point from the waiter and smiled in anticipation as he raised it to his mouth. Then he looked over at Hannah and froze. "I'm sorry, Hannah. I should have asked. Would you care for some caviar?"

"No, thanks. I know that beluga's the best that money can buy, but I grew up right next to a lake. It's still all just fish eggs to me."

While Norman busied himself with the caviar, Hannah walked over to survey the rest of the buffet. She'd heard that Judith had hired the best caterer in Minneapolis. Hannah could believe that as she walked past evenly fanned slices of beef fillet, platters of Smithfield ham, a whole poached salmon on a bed of dill, and several massive plates of carved chicken and turkey breast. There was a silver platter of tender baby asparagus, each tip pointing outward to form a giant wheel with a silver pitcher of hollandaise in the center, and a large crystal bowl that was filled to the brim with glazed carrots. Hannah spared only a passing glance for the tiny red potatoes that had been steamed in their colorful jackets and the deviled quail eggs. Her area of interest was the dessert table.

The desserts were gorgeous. There were small bites of cake that were frosted and decorated with tiny edible flowers, an array of truffles on a platter strewn with rose petals, chocolate-dipped strawberries with their stems intact, and a large silver basket filled with sugar cookies. Her professional interest aroused, Hannah selected a cookie and tasted it.

The cookie crunched in her mouth, just the way it should, but it was definitely on the dry side. The anticipated burst of butter that should have exploded on her taste buds was lacking. There was no vanilla taste, either, and Hannah began to frown. These cookies looked nice, but they really had no taste at all.

"Excuse me?" The female caterer, dressed in an expensive suit, walked over to give Hannah a nervous smile. "I couldn't help noticing your reaction to the cookies. Don't you like them?"

Hannah thought about tact. Then she thought about new business. New business won out and she decided that she wouldn't be doing the caterer any favors if she didn't tell her the truth. She stepped closer and lowered her voice so that none of the other guests would hear. "The cookies are disappointing. I hope you didn't make them."

"You don't pull any punches, do you?" The caterer looked amused.

"Not really. Did you make them?"

"No. I bought them from a supplier."

Hannah was relieved. At least she didn't have to tell the caterer that her own recipe was at fault. "Don't buy from them anymore. They use cheap shortening instead of butter and they're much too light on the vanilla. They overbake them, too. They probably set their ovens low to keep them from browning and leave them in for too long."

"How do you know they use shortening?"

"There's no butter taste," Hannah explained. "A sugar cookie without butter is like a car without gas. It looks good, but it doesn't work."

The caterer laughed. "You've got a point. How could you tell that they're overbaked?"

"That's easy. They're as dry as sawdust. Taste one—you'll see."

"I already have and you're right. Are you in food service?"

"Just cookies. I own a place called The Cookie Jar. If you give me your card, I'll send you a sample box of good sugar cookies."

The caterer reached into her pocket and handed Hannah a card. "I've been thinking about switching suppliers. Could you handle a standing order?"

"That depends on the order." As Hannah opened her dress purse and stuck the card inside, she wished that she'd had cards made. She really hadn't thought it was important until now. "Call me if you like the cookies and we'll discuss it. I'll include my card when I send them."

After the caterer had left, Hannah turned to look for Norman. She found him standing a few feet behind her and he was grinning from ear to ear. "What is it, Norman?"

"You. You're amazing, Hannah." Norman took her arm and walked her toward the grouping of small tables that were set up for dining. "If I went after new business the way you do, I'd have to enlarge the office and put in a revolving door."

Hannah laughed. "I guess you're right. When it comes to my cookies, I know they're the best and I'm not shy about telling people. But I almost goofed, Norman. I never thought about having cards made before."

"You don't have business cards?"

Hannah shook her head. "I just didn't think it was important. I told that caterer I'd include one with the cookies, so I guess I'll have to order some."

"I'll do some for you on my computer," Norman offered. "That's how I print mine."

"Thanks, Norman." As they neared the tables, Hannah thought again about how nice Norman was. Then someone stood up and waved, and Hannah recognized Lisa and Herb. "There's Lisa. She's my assistant at the shop. And you must know Herb Beeseman. He's our town marshal."

"Marshal? I thought he was in charge of parking enforcement."

"He is, but the job doesn't pay much. Herb was the only applicant and they let him choose his own title. He's always been fascinated by the Old West."

"I see. Well, let's go over and say hello."

Lisa and Herb had staked out a four-person table, and Hannah and Norman joined them for a moment. The two men immediately started talking about the traffic problem on Main Street, and Hannah turned to Lisa. "You look wonderful, Lisa. Are you having a good time?"

Lisa smiled, and Hannah noticed that her eyes were sparkling with excitement. "I saw your mother and Mrs. Rhodes. They asked if I'd seen you."

"If they ask again, lie."

Lisa laughed. "You can't avoid them forever. Mrs. Rhodes told me that she wants to take pictures of you and Norman for a memento."

"I know. That's one of the reasons I'm avoiding them."

"Grin and bear it." Lisa leaned closer and lowered her voice. "Doesn't Herb look handsome in his suit?"

Hannah glanced over at Herb. He was wearing a black suit with a Western cut and it reminded her of something

Marshal Dillon might have worn at a fancy wedding on *Gunsmoke*. It fit so perfectly, Herb could have been one of the mannequins in the display window of an old-fashioned men's clothing store. It was quite a change from the rumpled tan uniform that he usually wore. "He certainly does."

Just then a tall figure in another impeccably cut suit caught her eye and Hannah's eyebrows rose. "I don't believe it! There's Benton Woodley!"

"The Woodleys' son?"

"Yes. I thought the heir apparent was still back east, trying to buy his degree at some Ivy League school."

Lisa stared at Hannah curiously. "You sound like you don't like him very much."

"I don't. Or at least, I didn't." Hannah sighed deeply as she remembered the buckets of tears that Andrea had shed when Benton had dumped her. "Andrea used to date him when she was in high school. I wonder if she knows that he came back for the party."

"Maybe you should tell her. I know that she's married now, but it's always uncomfortable to run into an old boyfriend."

"Good idea. Have you seen her tonight?"

"She was over by the buffet tables a couple of minutes ago."

"Thanks, Lisa. I'll see you later." Hannah stood up and waited for a break in the conversation. When it arrived, she tapped Norman on the arm. "I have to find Andrea. Would you like to come with me?"

"Sure."

Norman said goodbye to Herb and Lisa and they started across the room. They were just crossing the space that would be used for dancing, when Hannah heard someone call her name.

Hannah stopped in her tracks and turned toward the warm and friendly voice. It was Benton Woodley and he was smiling at her.

"Who's that?" Norman glanced at Benton and then he turned to regard her curiously. "An old boyfriend?"

"Yes, but not mine. Come on, Norman. I'll introduce you."

It only took a moment to perform the introductions. As Benton chatted with Norman, Hannah wondered if he'd gone to the same charm school as his mother. He was polite, he seemed interested in hearing about Norman's practice, and he told her that she looked ravishing. The spoiled, know-it-all rich kid had grown up to be the perfect host.

"I'm glad to hear that you've reopened your father's practice, Norman. One never knows when one will need dental work." Benton sounded sincere and Hannah had the urge to laugh. She was willing to bet that if Benton ever needed dental work, he'd fly off to the fanciest, most expensive dentist in the country. "And how are you, Hannah?"

Hannah smiled her best party smile. "Just fine, Benton. I haven't seen you for years. Are you just here for the occasion?"

"No, Father's been a bit under the weather." Benton lowered his voice and moved a step closer. "I've come back to help him run the business."

Hannah remembered the dark circles under Del's eyes. Perhaps Benton was telling the truth. "I hope it's nothing serious."

"No, it's just that he's been working too hard. Now that I've moved back home to lend a hand, he should be fine."

"You're staying here?" Hannah was surprised. She seemed to remember that Benton had hated Lake Eden when he'd lived here.

"For a while. And it's wonderful to be back. I've always liked the ambience here, such a friendly, small-town feel. And that reminds me, I ran into Andrea and her husband a few moments ago and she mentioned that you'd opened a business. It sounds like such a quaint little shop. I'll have to make a point of dropping in soon."

Hannah bristled. Her business was a business, not a "quaint little shop." The tone in Benton's voice suggested that it was something a socialite might do as a hobby. Hannah opened her mouth to tell him that she'd worked very hard to make The Cookie Jar profitable, but she remembered about tact just in time. "It's been nice chatting with you, Benton, but we have to rush off to find Mother."

Norman waited until they were several feet away. "You want to find your mother?"

"Of course not. I just wanted to get away from Benton before I wrung his neck."

Norman grinned. " 'A quaint little shop'?"

"You got it." Hannah was impressed. For a dentist, Norman was quick. "Let's go find Andrea. I really need to talk to her."

They found Andrea and Bill by the buffet tables, and from the satisfied look on Bill's face, Hannah suspected that he was about to enjoy his second or third helping of food.

"Hi, Hannah. Good to see you, Norman," Bill greeted them. "Some spread, huh?"

Hannah turned to Norman. "Will you keep Bill company, Norman? I really need to talk to Andrea for a minute."

Bill gave her a conspiratorial smile, and for a moment Hannah was confused. Then she realized Bill thought she was giving him the opportunity to ask Norman about Ron's dental visit.

Hannah took her sister's arm and led her away to a relatively private place by the side of the room. "I'm sorry, Andrea. I came over to warn you the minute I saw Benton, but it was already too late."

"Warn me?"

"Yes." Judging from the puzzled expression on her sister's face, Hannah knew she'd better explain. "I just thought it might be uncomfortable for you to run into Benton again."

Andrea stared at her for a minute and then she began to

smile. "I get it. That was nice of you, Hannah, but seeing Benton didn't bother me at all. I got over him ages ago."

"Good! I never liked his attitude and I still don't. Do you know that he called The Cookie Jar 'a quaint little shop'?"

Andrea sighed and shook her head. "Don't mind Benton. He was always a snob. Did he tell you that he came back to help his father at DelRay?"

"That's what he said."

"He told us the same thing, but it was a lie. He was flicking his fingernail with his thumb when he said it."

"What?"

"It's something Benton does when he's lying," Andrea explained. "I picked up on that when we were dating and it came in handy. It's one of those unconscious gestures that people make when they're trying to pull something over on you."

"Did Benton tell you any other lies?"

"He told us he was glad to be back home in Lake Eden and that he was really looking forward to working at Del-Ray."

"And he was flicking when he said it?"

"Click, click, click. The only time he didn't flick was when he said that I looked ravishing."

"You always look ravishing." Hannah smiled at her sister, but she thought back to when Benton had told her the same thing. Perhaps it was a good thing she hadn't known about the fingernail-flicking lie detector test until now. "Did he tell you how long he'd been in town?"

"Bill asked him that. Benton said he'd flown in on Wednesday and taken the shuttle from the airport."

"Was he flicking then?" Hannah was curious.

"I couldn't see. He turned toward Bill to answer him. Can we talk about something else, Hannah? Benton Woodley bores me to tears."

"Sure." Since Andrea was so observant, Hannah decided

to ask her about Danielle Watson. "I talked to Coach Watson's wife at the mayor's fundraiser. What do you think of her?"

"Danielle?" Andrea looked thoughtful. "She seems nice enough, but I can't help feeling sorry for her."

"Why?"

"Because Boyd is such a control freak. I've seen them at parties and he doesn't like to let her out of his sight. It must be stifling. I bet Danielle has to ask his permission before she can even go to the ladies' room."

Hannah remembered how Danielle had whispered in her husband's ear right before she'd left him at the mayor's fundraiser. "I think you're right."

"I know I am. Thank God Bill's not like that!"

"Would it work if he were?"

"No way!" Andrea laughed and then she gestured toward a corner of the huge ballroom. "There's Danielle over there. I guess Boyd doesn't mind how much she spends on her clothes. She's wearing the peach dress that I saw at the mall, and I know it cost over five hundred dollars."

"Where?" Hannah's eyes searched the crowd.

"Right by that flowering hibiscus tree. She's standing there with a perfectly polite little smile on her face, waiting for Boyd to finish talking to Queen Judith."

Hannah grinned. Her sister had started to call Judith Woodley "Queen Judith" right after she'd begun to date Benton. "I see her."

"I really don't understand women like Danielle. She's got a great figure and she always covers it up. Either Boyd's the jealous type, or she's really shy about her body."

Hannah realized that her sister was right. She'd never seen Danielle wear anything even close to revealing. Tonight was no exception. The peach dress had long sleeves and a high mandarin collar. "Can you and Bill keep Norman amused for a couple of minutes? I really need to talk to Danielle."

"All right. Just don't take too long. If Norman starts telling me that I need to have my teeth cleaned, I'm going to run for the hills."

"He won't. Norman's not like that at all. He's got a great sense of humor. If you just get to know him, you'll like him."

"If you say so."

Andrea shrugged and headed back to the table while Hannah made her way through the crowd toward Danielle. As Hannah moved closer, she saw that Coach Watson was deep in conversation with Judith Woodley, and judging from the intense look on his face, Hannah figured that he was trying to drum up a donation for new team uniforms.

"I have to talk to you, Danielle." Hannah moved in to claim her before the coach could. "Let's go to the ladies' powder room."

"But I'm waiting for Boyd. He told me to stay right here and he'll be angry if I go off without—"

"It's important, Danielle," Hannah interrupted her. "Just tell him you need to fix your face or something."

"Is there something wrong with my face?"

"No, it's fine. I just need to talk to you about a mutual friend."

Danielle stared at her for a moment and then the light dawned. "All right, Hannah. Just let me tell Boyd and I'll be right with you."

Less than a minute later, Hannah led Danielle into the ladies' powder room. She was in luck. The large space was deserted and she flipped the lock on the door. "I need more information, Danielle."

"But I've told you everything I know. You shouldn't lock the door, Hannah. What if someone needs to get in?"

"They'll wait. You told me that you were with Ron from eleven until seven-twenty the next morning."

"That's right. I was. I told you the truth."

"I'm sure you did, but I need you to think back to the time

you spent with Ron. Did you see anyone else? Anyone at all?"

"No. All of his home delivery customers were still asleep and we didn't meet anyone at the school. That's why I said I'd go along. Ron promised that no one would see me."

"Was there any time that Ron was out of your sight?"

Danielle frowned as she thought about it. "Only when he was loading the truck, but there wasn't anybody else around."

"Then Ron didn't meet anyone at all?"

"No, I don't think . . ." Danielle stopped and her eyes widened. "Wait! After Ron loaded up for his commercial route, he had to run back inside the dairy for another box of pens with the Cozy Cow logo on them. He was leaving them with every order and it was some kind of promotional thing. When he came out, he said that Max had better get a move on or he'd be late for the Buttermakers' Convention."

"Then Ron saw Max?" Hannah felt a prickle of excitement. "What time was that?"

"Six-fifteen. Ron asked me to check to make sure he was on schedule. He was so organized, Hannah. He . . . he had everything worked out to the minute so he wouldn't b-be late."

Danielle's voice quavered and Hannah reached out to pat her on the shoulder. Danielle couldn't break down now— there wasn't time. "You're helping a lot, Danielle. Ron would be very proud of you."

"You're right. I think he would." Danielle took a deep breath and let it out in a quivering sigh.

"Do you know why Max was at the dairy so early?"

"He was meeting with someone in his office."

"Max was in a meeting at six-fifteen in the morning?"

"That's what Ron said. I don't know who was with him, Hannah. Ron didn't say."

Hannah drew a deep breath. She wished she had time to think about how this new information fit into the picture, but there would be time for that later. "Try to remember what everything looked like at the dairy when Ron drove in to re-load the truck. Did you see any cars in the parking lot?"

"I know Ron's car was there. That's where we parked when we got there at four in the morning. I don't know about later, Hannah. The parking lot's in the rear, behind the building. When Ron came back to load up for the second time, he used the truck road at the side. That's where the loading dock is."

"How about when you left? Did you drive around the building?"

Danielle shook her head. "There's a turnaround on the side, and Ron used that. We didn't drive past the parking lot at all."

"Thanks, Danielle." Hannah walked over to unlock the door. "You've been very helpful."

Danielle gave Hannah a timid little smile. "I feel really bad that I didn't ask Ron who was with Max in his office."

"That's okay."

"But it's important, isn't it?"

"It could be, but you had no way of knowing. Besides, we can always ask Max."

"That's right." Danielle looked very relieved. "I'd better get back to Boyd. And I suppose you need to get back to Norman."

After Danielle had left, Hannah sat down on the cush-ioned bench in front of the mirror and thought about what she'd learned. Ron had seen Max at six-fifteen, meeting with someone in his office. It could be something, or it could be nothing. Only time would tell.

Chapter
Sixteen

Hannah groaned as she approached Andrea and Bill's table. Somehow Delores and Carrie had found them, and both mothers were looking impatient. She felt like turning around and going back to the ladies' powder room, but her mother raised her hand and wiggled her fingers. It was too late. She'd been spotted.

"There you are, dear!" Delores gave her a wide smile. "We're ready to take the pictures now."

"That's just wonderful." Hannah's reply sounded sarcastic, even to her own ears, and she smiled to take the edge off her words. She glanced at Norman. He didn't look at all upset about the upcoming photo session, but perhaps he was one of those lucky people who were photogenic. Hannah knew she wasn't. No trick of the light or instruction from the photographer could make her look good on Kodak paper.

The mothers led the way across the room. Norman left Hannah to take his mother's arm, and Bill followed suit with Delores. Hannah pulled Andrea back just a bit so that she could apologize. "I'm sorry, Andrea. I didn't mean to be gone so long."

"That's okay. You were right, Hannah. Some of the things

that Norman said were really funny. We were having a good time until the mothers found us. They want us to pose, too."

"Great." Hannah was more than happy to have company in her misery. "Maybe you'll make me look good by osmosis or something."

Andrea laughed. "Come on, Hannah. You know you look wonderful tonight. That dress is so perfect on you, it even makes your hair look nice."

"Thanks . . . I think." Hannah grinned. Then she realized that the mother brigade was turning down the hallway that led to the ladies' powder room. "Where are they going?"

"I'm not sure. Mrs. Rhodes said she found the perfect setting for the pictures. I just hope we're not going to barge into someplace we shouldn't be."

The group stopped at the end of the hall and waited for Hannah and Andrea to catch up. Then Carrie opened a door and ushered them into a large room lined with bookshelves. It was done in a masculine style, with leather couches and armchairs, a massive wooden desk, and hunting prints on the walls. There was an incredible river-rock fireplace in the corner, and Hannah stared at it in awe.

"This is Del Woodley's den," Carrie announced.

"Should we be in here?" Bill looked very uneasy. "I mean, it's not off-limits to the guests, is it?"

Carrie shook her head. "I asked him and he said it was perfectly all right."

Hannah exchanged an amused glance with Andrea. Norman's mother was a lot like Delores. Not only had Carrie waltzed into Lake Eden's only formal affair with her camera, she'd even asked their host if they could use one of his private rooms to take pictures.

"Stand over by the fireplace with Bill." Delores motioned to Andrea. "We'll do yours first, just in case Bill gets called away."

Hannah watched as her sister posed with Bill. Then Carrie decided that the two couples should stand together, and Hannah and Norman joined them. They arranged themselves obediently—Hannah and Andrea in front, Norman and Bill in back, while Carrie clicked away. Then she took another series with the four of them lined up in a row like soldiers, the "girls" in the center flanked by the two "boys."

"Let's take a few on the couch," Delores suggested. "That always looks nice."

Hannah suffered through more photos, wondering how soon Norman's mother would run out of film. As soon as this ordeal was over, she had to pull Bill aside and bring him up to speed. Bill was tracing Ron's movements on the morning of the murder and he didn't know that Ron had gone into the dairy at six-fifteen and seen Max Turner in his office. It might not relate to Ron's murder at all, but it was a new piece of information and Bill could ask Max about his early-morning meeting.

"You look distracted, dear." Delores waggled a finger at her. "Concentrate on looking pretty and say cheese."

"Gorgonzola," Hannah muttered under her breath, and Andrea started to giggle.

"You're moving, Andrea," Delores warned. "Carrie can't focus if you're moving."

Hannah rolled her eyes just as Norman's mother snapped the picture. Didn't Delores know that most cameras were auto-focus these days? If she had to endure another minute of flashes and admonitions about smiling from her mother, she was going to explode in sheer frustration.

"We'd better take that one again." Delores turned to Carrie. "I think Hannah squinted."

Just as Hannah was about to rebel, Norman stood and held up his hands. "That's enough, Mother. Sit on the couch with Mrs. Swensen and I'll take a couple of you."

"Turnabout's fair play," Hannah murmured to Andrea as they stood off to the side and watched Norman take pictures of their mothers. "Let's tell Mother her lipstick's on crooked."

Andrea looked horrified at the thought. "Don't! Then she'll have to get out her mirror and fix it, and that'll take even longer."

Hannah was about to point out that they'd taken enough pictures to paper the entire back wall in her shop, when she heard a low beeping noise. She turned to Bill and asked, "Is that your pager?"

Bill retrieved his pager from his pocket. He glanced at the display and frowned. "I've got to call in."

"You don't have to go, do you?" Andrea grabbed at his sleeve. "We haven't even danced yet."

Bill gave her a little hug. "I know, but the dispatcher punched in the emergency code. Where's the nearest phone?"

"Right here." Hannah pointed to the one next to the couch. "Go ahead, Bill. We want to know what's happening."

Bill punched out the number and talked to someone at the sheriff's station. Hannah listened to his end of the conversation, but *Okay, right away,* and *I'll do that* didn't tell her much.

"There's a big accident out on the interstate," Bill informed them as he hung up the phone. "They're calling everyone in."

"Shall I take you?" Andrea offered.

"No, you can stay. I'll catch a ride out with one of the other guys." Bill patted her shoulder. "Have a good time for me, okay?"

Reading the glum expression on Andrea's face, Hannah doubted that she was going to have a good time without Bill, but her sister nodded. "Okay, honey. Be careful and I'll see you at home."

After Bill left, they all trooped back to the party. Hannah had seen Norman rewind the film and drop it into his pocket, and she was curious. "Are you going to put the film in the night drop at the drugstore, Norman?"

"No." Norman shook his head. "I'll develop it myself when I get home. I just finished setting up my darkroom."

"You're a photographer?"

"Just an amateur. I caught the bug when I was in Seattle. It's a great hobby. I'll bring the prints by The Cookie Jar on my lunch break tomorrow so you can see them."

The orchestra was playing by the time they reentered the ballroom, and Norman asked Hannah to dance. She couldn't refuse without seeming rude and Hannah found herself suffering through an agonizingly slow waltz. Norman was, at best, a tentative dancer and Hannah really wanted to lead. But she didn't want to hurt Norman's feelings and she endured their dance with a smile on her face.

When the dance had ended, Norman escorted her back to Andrea and their mothers. As they were standing there talking, Hannah spotted Betty Jackson. She wanted to ask Betty if she knew about Max Turner's early meeting, but Bill wouldn't like it if she dragged Norman along.

"Would you like to dance again, Hannah?" Norman offered, holding out his arm.

Hannah tried not to flinch at the thought. There was no way she wanted to dance with Norman again. She was just trying to think of a tactful excuse when she had a brilliant idea. "Why don't you ask Andrea? I heard her tell Bill that she wanted to dance."

"Good idea." Norman turned to Andrea with a smile. "How about it, Andrea? Would you like to dance?"

Andrea shot Hannah a wounded look as she danced off with Norman, and Hannah knew she'd have some explaining to do. She'd point out that dancing with Norman, no matter how painful, was better than getting stuck with the mothers.

Betty was standing near the orchestra, tapping her foot in time with the music. She looked as if she wanted to dance, but it was doubtful that any of the local men would ask her. Betty was what Hannah and her friends in high school had unkindly called "heavy-duty." She weighed close to three hundred pounds and she wasn't known for her grace on the dance floor. Hannah's father had once quipped that a man needed steel-toed boots to dance with Betty, and more than one man in Lake Eden had nursed an injured foot after an obligatory turn around the floor with her.

As always, Betty was dressed in vertical stripes. Someone

must have once told her that they were slenderizing and they might have been, for someone less bulky. Betty's stripes were wide tonight, and they were dark green and burgundy. The colors were pretty, but that didn't stop Betty from resembling the side of a circus tent. As she walked closer, Hannah made a mental vow to go on a diet and shed the ten extra pounds she'd been carrying around since last Christmas.

"Hi, Betty," Hannah called out a cheerful greeting. Since there was no one else around, it was obvious the local males feared for their insteps, and Hannah knew she'd never have a better chance to interview Betty about Max's meeting.

Betty reached out to pat Hannah's arm. "You look gorgeous tonight, Hannah."

"Thanks." Hannah knew it was only polite to return the compliment, but what could she say? Then she spotted Betty's shoes and she had her answer. "Your shoes are great. They match your dress perfectly."

Betty smiled, apparently satisfied. "Is there any news about poor Ron?"

"Nothing yet. I'm glad I found you, Betty. I need to talk to you about Max."

Betty swallowed and her face turned pale. "I knew it! There's something wrong, isn't there?"

"Wrong?" Hannah was puzzled. "Why do you think there's something wrong?"

"Max hasn't called in yet and that's not like him at all. He's a very hands-on manager. Last year he called me three times a day."

"There's nothing wrong as far as I know," Hannah reassured her. "I just wondered if he knew about Ron, that's all."

Betty fanned her face with her hand. "You practically gave me a heart attack. I'm probably just imagining things, but it's just so strange that Max hasn't called. Shirley, over at the Mielke Way Dairy, said Gary's called in every morning."

"Did Gary mention seeing Max at the convention?"

"No. And Shirley can't call him to ask, because Gary

won't tell her where he's staying." Betty's face crinkled in a huge smile and she moved closer. "Gary's a bachelor and this is his big chance to live it up a little, if you know what I mean. At least that's what Shirley thinks."

"Shirley's probably right. Do you think that Max is doing the same thing?"

"Max?" Betty looked utterly astounded. "If you knew him as well as I do, you wouldn't even think it. Max has only two pleasures in life: money and more money."

Hannah gave the appropriate laugh, even though she'd heard that particular comment about Max about a million times before. "Did you know that Max had an early-morning meeting in his office on Wednesday?"

"He did?" Betty seemed genuinely surprised. "But he was supposed to leave at five-thirty, and that's awfully early for a meeting. Are you sure?"

"That's what I heard."

Betty thought about it for a moment and then she shrugged. "Anything's possible, especially if it was about money. I know that Max was in the office early. They asked him to give the opening speech and I typed it up for him on Tuesday night. I left it on my desk and it was gone when I came in the next morning."

"You're sure that Max picked it up?"

"I'm positive. He left a yellow sticky, reminding me to order new file folders."

Hannah decided not to tell Betty that Max had still been at the dairy at six-fifteen. It would only worry her. "Have you tried to call Max at the convention?"

"Of course I have. They told me he wasn't registered at the Holiday Inn, but I didn't expect him to stay there. Max is very picky and he just hated his room last year. It was right next to the ice machine."

"How about the other hotels in town?"

"I tried them, but they all say he's not registered."

"Could Max be sharing someone else's room?"

"Max?" Betty laughed so hard, her ample bosom shook. "Max isn't the type to share. He always stays alone."

"Did you have him paged on the convention floor?"

"Of course I did. They're having a big banquet tonight and I called before I left home. Max didn't answer my page."

Hannah began to frown as an idea formed in her head. "Was Max driving to Wisconsin alone?"

"Yes. Gary Mielke asked him to carpool, but Max didn't want to ride with him. And if you're thinking that he was in an accident, I already checked with both highway patrols and he wasn't. I really expected him to call in before now and it's got me worried."

Hannah was worried right along with Betty, and she wondered if Max had made it to the convention at all. "You said that Max didn't want to ride with Gary Mielke. Do you know why?"

"Yes, but I really shouldn't tell you." Betty began to twist the handle of her burgundy clutch purse, a sure sign that she was uncomfortable. "It's . . . uh . . . confidential."

"If you want me to try to find Max for you, you'd better tell me. I promise I won't tell anyone else."

"All right, Hannah." Betty twisted her purse handle again, and Hannah wondered whether the thin strip of leather would snap. "The Mielke Way is our biggest competitor and Max is working on a way to take over Gary's operation. That's why he didn't want to ride with him."

"Then Gary doesn't know about Max's plans?"

Betty gave her a look that had *"idiot"* written all over it. "Max doesn't let anybody know what's going on until it's a done deal. That's the way he operates."

"But Max told you?"

"Not exactly. I just happened to pick up the extension in my office when Max was talking to some loan company about buying up the paper on one of Gary's loans."

Hannah didn't believe that Betty had just happened to

pick up the extension. Betty was nosy and that was why she was such a valuable contact. "Has Max ever done anything like this before?"

"Are you kidding? You don't get as rich as Max is by selling cream and butter."

"How do you know for sure?"

"You can't work for a man for twenty years without picking up a word here and there. Max is a regular shark when it comes to buying up businesses, foreclosing properties, and turning big fat profits on them."

Hannah was about to ask another question when she saw Andrea waving at her. She patted Betty on the arm and made her excuses. "Andrea's waiting for me and I've got to run. Thanks, Betty."

"But how about Max? Do you think he's all right?"

"I'll find out," Hannah promised, and then she quickly added up the new facts she'd learned. Ron had seen Max on Wednesday morning and now Ron was dead. And Max was supposed to be at the Buttermakers' Convention, but no one had seen him and he hadn't called in. Had Max shot Ron and fled the country? It was a distinct possibility. It was also possible that Max was lying low at the convention and he'd call Betty when all the excitement had died down. If Max thought he was safe, he might even waltz back into town as big as you please and act all shocked and saddened about the horrible crime that had cost Ron his life.

"What is it, Hannah?" Betty looked anxious.

"I'm just thinking. When is Max due back?"

"On Tuesday night."

If Max decided to call in, Betty might tell him about the questions she'd asked. That would alert him and he'd hop the first plane out of the country. Hannah couldn't let that happen. Somehow, she had to keep Betty silent.

"I just realized something, Betty. You'd better not mention that you talked to me. If Max finds out that we've been discussing him, he'll get really upset."

"That's true," Betty agreed.

"If he calls in, don't mention that I told you about his meeting. He'll just think that we were nosing into his personal life. I'm concerned for your job."

"You're right, Hannah!" Betty's eyes widened. "Max would fire me if he thought I was gossiping about him, even if I wasn't!"

"Exactly. If anybody asks you what we were talking about tonight, just say that we were making small talk about the buffet table. I'll say the same thing."

"Thanks, Hannah." Betty looked very grateful. "I sure don't want to risk my job. I just love it at the dairy. My lips are sealed—you can count on that."

"Mine too." Hannah walked away, confident that Betty wouldn't repeat their conversation. She'd also discovered a wonderful new tool for social intercourse. It was intimidation and it worked. And if the glower on Andrea's face was any indication, Hannah knew that she was in for a dose of it herself.

Andrea sighed as they walked down the hall together. She still didn't look happy about being left to dance with Norman for so long, but when Hannah had whispered that she'd been doing legwork for Bill, Andrea lightened up a little. "I still can't believe that you stuck Norman with the Hollenbeck sisters. You know they're going to chew his ear off for at least fifteen minutes."

"That's what I'm counting on. Norman said he wanted me to introduce him to prospective patients, and Marguerite seemed really interested in having her teeth whitened. If she does it, she'll tell all her friends at the church and they'll do it, too."

"Here's the ladies' room." Andrea stopped at the door.

"I know, but that was just an excuse. I need you to make a phone call for me, Andrea. You're a lot better at sweet-talking people than I am."

"You can say that again!" Andrea laughed and Hannah could tell that the last vestige of her anger had disappeared. "Who am I calling?"

"The Holiday Inn in Eau Claire, Wisconsin. That's where they're holding the Tri-State Buttermakers' Convention."

"You want me to talk to Max Turner?" Andrea sounded very reluctant. "I don't think I should do that, Hannah. Bill hasn't talked to him yet and he doesn't know about Ron."

"I don't want you to talk to Max. I want you to get Gary Mielke from the Mielke Way Dairy on the phone. I need some information from him."

Andrea looked dubious. "Does Bill know about this?"

"No. I just learned something from Betty and I have to confirm it with Gary."

"But are you supposed to . . . I mean, shouldn't Bill be the one to—"

"Bill's not here and I am," Hannah interrupted her. "This could be important, Andrea. It can't wait for Bill to get back from the accident scene. We'll use the phone in Del Woodley's den. That's private, and God knows the Woodleys can afford one long-distance call to Wisconsin."

Andrea thought about it for a minute. "Okay, I'll do it. Bill always says that I can sweet-talk anybody into anything."

Hannah led the way to the den and got Andrea settled behind Del Woodley's desk. Then she took a seat on the couch and listened in awe as her sister charmed the desk clerk into leaving his post to search for Gary Mielke. Bill was right. Andrea could talk anyone into anything, and knowing that caused a heavy load of guilt to drop from Hannah's shoulders. Bill might want Andrea to quit her job, but her sister would just sweet-talk him into letting her go right on selling real estate.

Chapter
Seventeen

Hannah was frowning as she approached the ballroom entrance with Andrea. What she'd learned had confirmed her suspicions. Max Turner wasn't at the Buttermakers' Convention. He'd been scheduled to give the opening speech, but he hadn't shown up and Gary Mielke had filled in for him. Gary had arrived at the Holiday Inn on Tuesday night to meet some friends of his. They'd gone out to a late dinner and spent the night with some "other friends." Hannah hadn't asked whether those "other friends" had been male or female. It didn't really matter. The point was that Gary Mielke had an alibi and he couldn't have had anything to do with Max's disappearance or Ron's murder.

"Come on, Hannah." Andrea took her arm. "We have to rescue Norman before the Hollenbeck sisters drive him crazy."

"I know. I just wish I could go home and think about this. There's something I'm missing."

"Later. I'll come over and you can run your theories past me. Bill won't be home until late, anyway."

"How do you know that?" Hannah turned to her in surprise.

"Reverend Knudson told me."

"How does *he* know?"

"Sheriff Grant paged him a couple of minutes ago. He said that some of the crash victims needed spiritual comfort."

"Uh-oh." Hannah winced. "They don't bring in the reverend unless it's really bad."

"I know. Sheriff Grant paged all *three* of them. Reverend Knudson is driving out there, and Father Coultas and Reverend Strandberg are riding with him."

Hannah figured it must be a truly massive pileup. It would take a disaster of that magnitude to get all three local clergy into a common car. Father Coultas hadn't spoken to Reverend Knudson since the Lutherans had beaten the Catholics at softball, and Reverend Strandberg had been privately denounced by the other two as a Bible-thumping zealot.

They found Norman still talking with the Hollenbeck sisters. He motioned for them to wait for just a moment and then he turned back to Marguerite. "I'll see you at ten tomorrow, Miss Hollenbeck. I know you'll be pleased with the new technique. It's completely painless and you'll walk out of the office looking so beautiful, your own sister won't recognize you."

Hannah waited until they had walked away and then turned to Norman. *"Your own sister won't recognize you?"*

"Okay. Maybe I was laying it on a little thick, but I know she'll be happy. Say, how about coming in for—"

"Forget it, Norman," Hannah interrupted him. "I know you're in recruiting gear, but don't even try. How about hitting the buffet tables before they pack up the food?"

Andrea, catching Hannah's attempt to change the subject from dentistry to food, agreed. "Good idea. I had a bite with Bill, but I'm hungry again."

Norman took Hannah's arm. "That's fine with me. My mother's on a health kick and she doesn't cook anything except chicken and fish. If I don't get some red meat soon, I'm going to lose every ounce of my fabulous muscles."

Andrea burst into delighted laughter and then she took Norman's other arm. "You know, I'm really beginning to like you, Norman."

"That's what they all say." Norman looked smug. "I tend to grow on people."

"Like mold?" both Hannah and Andrea asked in unison and then broke into laughter with Norman.

As Hannah filled her plate from the array of food, she mulled over the new facts she'd learned tonight. Gary Mielke had told her that delivering the opening speech was an honor and there was no way that Max would have willingly missed it. Gary had also told her that he'd looked for Max when he'd noticed that his convention pass was still behind the counter at the hospitality booth. Since it was impossible to get into any of the meetings without it, he'd assumed that Max was ill and hadn't been able to come.

Hannah followed Norman and Andrea to a table and began to eat her food. While she ate, she thought about the events that had occurred on the morning that Ron had been shot. Ron had seen Max in a meeting at six-fifteen. He'd even mentioned it to Danielle. But that was the last time anyone had spotted the owner of the Cozy Cow Dairy. She needed to find out who had been meeting with Max, but that seemed impossible.

Andrea and Norman were carrying on a conversation as they ate, but Hannah was silent. She was too busy thinking about where Max might have gone. She really didn't know much about his private life and she wasn't even sure if he had any friends. She'd have to remember to ask Betty about that.

Hannah finished eating and dabbed at her lips with a napkin. She glanced down at her plate and was surprised to find that she'd eaten every morsel.

"You must have liked the cod in aspic," Andrea commented, noticing Hannah's empty plate.

"That was cod?" Hannah made a face. She'd never liked cod and she despised tomato-based aspic. "I thought it was a Jell-O mold!"

Norman looked concerned. "You seem preoccupied, Hannah. Is there something wrong?"

"No, not really." Hannah knew she had to think of some explanation. She didn't want Norman to think that she wasn't enjoying his company. "I was just thinking about Max. I really need to talk to him."

"Max Turner?" Norman stared at her in alarm. "Whatever you do, don't get involved in any business dealings with that man!"

"Why?" Hannah was puzzled by the angry note in Norman's voice.

"He'll eat you alive! I could tell you stories about—" Norman stopped, and looked embarrassed. "Sorry. It's water over the dam now, but I still see red whenever I hear that man's name."

Hannah reached out to touch Norman's sleeve. "Tell us about it, Norman."

"My father borrowed some money from Max Turner and it was the biggest mistake of his life. He'd only been in business for a couple of months and he needed to set up his second examining room. Dental equipment is very expensive and he didn't have the money for it."

"Why didn't your father go to the bank for a business loan?" Andrea asked.

"He did, but they told him that he hadn't been in business long enough to establish an earnings basis. Max Turner offered to take my parents' house for collateral, even though they'd just bought it and they didn't have any equity. He told them that all they had to do was convert their mortgage to fifteen years and make every house payment. He even offered an interest-only loan on the money for the equipment, with payments on the principal whenever they had a good month."

Andrea winced. "Uh-oh. I know something about loans, and that's too good to be true."

"It was, but my parents didn't know that. My father believed Max when he said he wanted to encourage new business in Lake Eden and the town really needed another dentist."

"What happened?" Hannah asked, even though she guessed how this story was going to turn out. Betty had said that Max was a shark.

"Max waited until my parents were only a year away from paying off their house. Then he called in the full amount of the loan."

"Is that legal?" Hannah asked.

"Yes. There was a clause that entitled Max to call in his loan early. And since it was a personal loan, ordinary regulations didn't apply."

"That's terrible, Norman." Andrea looked very sympathetic. "But your mother still owns the house, doesn't she?"

"Yes. Dad called me in a panic and told me that they could lose their house and their business. I was working at a big dental clinic in Seattle at the time, and I managed to get a loan through my credit union. I wired them the money and they paid Max off just a day before the deadline."

Hannah felt sick. *Shark* was too tame a word for Max Turner. It made her wonder how many other Lake Eden residents Max had nearly ruined. She had a feeling that all this somehow related to Ron's murder, but she couldn't quite figure out how the pieces fit together.

"You won't mention this to anyone, will you?" Norman asked. "Mother's still embarrassed about it. She'd die if anyone found out that they were so naïve."

"We won't mention it," Hannah promised. "It's over now. Nobody needs to know."

Norman looked relieved as he stood up and pushed back his chair. "If you'll excuse me, I'd better dance with Mother. She made me promise. And just because I'm such a nice guy, I'll dance with your mother, too."

"Norman?" Hannah got up and took his arm. "Would you be terribly disappointed if I left now? There's something I have to do and it can't wait. You can stay. Andrea will drive me."

"Okay." Norman didn't look crushed with disappointment, and that made Hannah's ego twinge a bit. "Is it something about Ron's murder?" he asked.

"Yes. I'm sorry, but I can't tell you any more than that."

"Go ahead, Hannah, but we'd better think up a really good excuse for our mothers. Somehow I don't think that a headache will do it."

"How about a migraine?" Andrea suggested. "A migraine's always worked for me."

Hannah shook her head. "I don't get migraines, and Mother knows it."

"No, but I do." Andrea turned to Norman. "Just tell our mothers that I was in such bad shape, I begged Hannah to drive me home and stay with me until Bill got back."

"That should work," Norman said. "But what if she calls you and you're not there?"

"No problem." Andrea looked triumphant. "Mother knows I always turn off the phone when I have a migraine. I told her that I couldn't stand the ringing."

Norman patted Andrea on the back. "Very smart. I think you're covered. I'll go find the mothers and tell them."

"Norman?" Hannah remembered her manners just in time. "Thank you for a lovely evening. I had a wonderful time."

"Me too. You'd better move it, Hannah. And take Andrea's arm and pretend you're helping her walk. Here come the mothers and they look loaded for bear."

Andrea climbed in behind the wheel and they drove down the long, winding driveway. When they reached the bottom, she turned to Hannah. "Where are we going?"

"To my place. You can drop me off there."

"Drop you off?" Andrea slammed on the brakes and they skidded to a stop at the base of the driveway. "What do you mean, *drop you off?*"

Hannah sighed. She was the one who'd gotten Andrea interested in Bill's case in the first place and she should have known that there would be trouble. "I have to do something and it could be dangerous. I don't want to get you in trouble."

"But you don't care if *you* get into trouble?"

"Of course I care. I'll be very careful. But you've got a husband and a daughter. You have to think of them."

"I *am* thinking of them and I'm going along." Andrea glared at her. "We're talking about Bill's promotion here. If there's any way that I can help, I'm going to do it."

"But, Andrea . . . you know that Bill would—"

"Let me take care of Bill," Andrea interrupted her. "Where are we going, anyway?"

Hannah sighed and caved in. There was no dealing with Andrea when she got a bee in her bonnet, and this bee was as big as a buzzard. "First we're switching to my Suburban. I've got two of those big flashlights in the back. Then we're driving to Max Turner's house."

"Why are we going there?"

"Because Max didn't leave for the convention when he was supposed to leave. He was still in his office at six-fifteen, having a meeting with someone. Ron saw them."

"So?"

"So Max doesn't have an alibi for the time of Ron's death. We know he's not at the convention and no one's seen him since six-fifteen on Wednesday morning."

"I get it. You think that Max killed Ron and then he took off. But why would Max kill Ron?"

"Think about what Norman just told us and you'll have a possible motive."

Andrea was silent for a moment. "I got it. You think that Ron overheard Max making some kind of shady business deal? And Max followed Ron on his route and killed him so that he couldn't tell anyone about it. But how do you know that Ron saw Max?"

Hannah frowned. She should have known that Andrea was going to ask that. "My snitch told me."

"Your *snitch*?"

"Actually, she's more of a witness. The woman with the pink lipstick told me about it. She didn't see Max or the other person, but when Ron came back out to his truck, he told her that Max was in his office, meeting with someone."

Andrea stared out through the windshield for a long moment and then turned to Hannah with a frown. "There's something I don't understand. Norman said that what Max did was legal. Why would Max kill Ron if his business deals were legal?"

"I don't know," Hannah admitted. "All I *do* know is that I have to check out Max's house."

Andrea put the Volvo into gear. "You're absolutely right. Your place first?"

"That's right."

They started off for Hannah's condo complex. They'd only driven a mile or so when Andrea started to laugh.

"What's so funny?" Hannah asked.

"You. Checking out Max's house won't be dangerous at all. Max isn't stupid. If he killed Ron he wouldn't hole up there, just waiting for someone to put the pieces together and arrest him."

"That's true."

Andrea took her eyes off the road to shoot her a curious glance. "Then why did you tell me that it could be dangerous?"

"Because Max's house will be locked up tight, and Bill might just kill both of us if we get arrested for breaking and entering."

Chapter
Eighteen

Hannah turned off the highway and onto the access road that ran past the Cozy Cow Dairy. The huge cinder-block building was deserted this time of night and its white paint gleamed in the thousand-watt glow from the security lights that had been installed on poles around the perimeter. The security lights weren't really necessary. No thief in his right mind would break into a dairy to steal butter or cream vats, but Hannah supposed that Max had gotten a break on his insurance by lighting the place up.

"It's creepy out here at night." Andrea's voice was shaking slightly and Hannah suspected her sister was having second thoughts about demanding to come along. "Doesn't Max have a night shift?"

"No. There's nothing to do until the tanker trucks come in from the farms in the morning. Except for his deliverymen, nobody comes in until seven-thirty."

"I feel silly, dressed like this." Andrea glanced down at the black pullover sweatshirt and jeans that Hannah had insisted she wear. "Your jeans are too big for me. I had to roll the legs up three times and pin them at the waist. And this hooded sweatshirt smells like it came out of a trash bin. Why did we have to dress up like a couple of cat burglars, anyway? Max's house is at least a half-mile from the road. There's no way that anyone will spot us."

"Sorry, Andrea. My wardrobe isn't as extensive as yours. That's all I had that would almost fit you, and I didn't think you wanted to wear your party dress."

Andrea let her breath out in a long sigh. "You're right. I'm just a little nervous, that's all. I keep thinking about how mad Bill's going to be if we get caught."

"We won't. I told you before, if we have to break in, I'll do it. And if worse comes to worst, you can tell him that you tried to stop me, but I wouldn't listen."

"That'll go over like a lead balloon." Andrea sighed again, and then she winced as they bumped over a rut in the road. "With all Max's money, you'd think he'd have his driveway graded once in a while."

They rode in silence for another minute or so. As they neared Max's house, Hannah cut her lights and drove the rest of the way by moonlight.

"He must be gone. There aren't any lights," Andrea whispered as Hannah pulled up in front of Max's garage and shut off the engine. "I told you Max wouldn't be home."

"I didn't really expect him to be, but I'm going to ring the doorbell, just in case."

"What if someone answers?" Andrea sounded scared.

"Who?"

Andrea shivered. "I don't know. Just someone."

"Then I'll think of something to say." Hannah got out of her Suburban and marched up to the doorbell, wishing she were as confident as she'd sounded. If Max answered the door, she'd have some tall explaining to do. But Max didn't answer and Hannah walked back with a smile on her face. "Nobody's there. Come on, Andrea. Let's check out his garage. We can peek through the windows."

"How?" Andrea got out of the Suburban to stare up at the

high narrow windows that ran in a strip across the top of the garage door. "They're too high for us to see in."

"No problem." Hannah climbed up on the hood of her Suburban and motioned for Andrea to hand her a flashlight. She directed the powerful beam through the narrow strip of windows and what she saw made her gasp in surprise.

"What is it?" Andrea whispered. "What's in there, Hannah?"

Hannah climbed down, trying not to look as shocked as she felt. "Max's car is still there."

"If his car is there, he's got to be home!" Andrea was so astonished, she forgot to whisper. "Let's get out of here, Hannah!"

Hannah's instinct to flee was every bit as powerful as her sister's, but her sense of duty took over. "We can't just leave. If Max is inside, he could be sick, or injured, or . . . even worse."

Andrea gasped, and Hannah knew she'd understood the reference to "even worse."

"Don't be a fool, Hannah. Let's go get Bill."

"You go. The keys are in the ignition. I'm going in to check on Max."

"B-But . . ." Andrea started to stammer, and Hannah knew she was scared spitless. "I can't leave you here alone, Hannah. What if Max is dead and his killer is inside?"

"If Max is dead, his killer is long gone. Be reasonable, Andrea. If you killed someone, would you stay in the house with him for two whole days?"

"No," Andrea admitted. "But I just can't help feeling that something really bad is going to happen. Remember Charlie Manson?"

"That was California. Just stay here and be a lookout for me. If you see any headlights coming down the driveway, ring Max's doorbell."

"No way, Hannah. I don't want to say here alone."

"Then come with me." Hannah knew they were wasting precious time. "Make up your mind, Andrea. I'm going in."

"I'll come with you. It's better than staying out here by myself. How are we going to get in?"

"I don't know yet." Hannah stepped back to survey the house. There wasn't any easy way inside. "I guess I'm going to have to break a window."

"Don't do that. Bill says lots of people leave the door that connects their garage to their house open and that's how burglars get in. Maybe Max left his unlocked."

"That's great, but how are we going to get in Max's garage without a clicker? He's got an automatic garage-door opener. I saw the hardware when I looked inside."

"I know how." Andrea sounded very proud of herself. "I watched Bill do it once, when our clicker didn't work. He pulled up really hard on the door handle and it slid up a couple of inches, just enough for me to wiggle through. I think we could do it if we lift together."

"It's worth a try. Let's find something to prop it open after we lift it."

"How about those boxes?" Andrea pointed to the pile of old-fashioned wooden milk boxes that were stacked at the side of Max's driveway.

"They'll do." Hannah walked over to retrieve a milk box. She positioned it next to her foot and then she grasped the handle of the garage door. "Come over here and help me lift. If we can get it open, I'll kick the milk box under with my foot."

It took a couple of tries, but they managed to lift the door almost a foot. Hannah propped it open with the milk box and stepped back to eyeball the opening. "It's pretty small. I don't think I can get under there."

"I can." Andrea sounded frightened, but she managed to give Hannah a grin. "I'm only a size five. Just hand me a flashlight when I get inside."

Hannah watched as her sister stretched out on the driveway at the corner of the door, where the opening was larger, and began to wiggle through. Andrea hadn't wanted to break in, but here she was, inching her way inside the dark garage.

"Okay, I'm in." Andrea stuck her hand out of the opening. "Give me the flashlight."

Hannah handed her the flashlight and watched the light grow fainter as Andrea moved deeper into the garage. A few moments later, the garage door slid smoothly open and Hannah stepped inside.

"Hannah?" Andrea motioned her over to Max's car with the beam of her flashlight. "I think you'd better look at this."

For a minute Hannah didn't know what her sister was talking about. Max's new Cadillac looked perfectly all right to her. But then she noticed that there was a see-through garment bag hanging on the hook in the backseat. Two suitcases were standing near the truck, as if someone had planned to stow them inside later, and a briefcase sat open on the passenger seat.

"Max was packing his car, but he didn't finish." Andrea gestured toward the suitcases.

"Because something or somebody stopped him," Hannah stated the obvious conclusion. Max had intended to go to the Buttermakers' Convention. His suits were hanging in the garment bag, his suitcases were ready to stash in the trunk, and his briefcase was on the seat. "Turn on the garage light, Andrea."

Once the garage was flooded with light, Hannah walked around the Cadillac and opened the passenger door. She glanced down at Max's briefcase and took a deep breath. Max's wallet was inside and she picked it up.

"Do you really think you should snoop through his personal things?"

Hannah turned to give her sister a long, level look. "Why not? It didn't seem to bother you in Norman's office."

Andrea's cheeks turned a dull red and she snapped her mouth shut. She didn't say a word as Hannah opened the wallet and counted the bills inside.

"Twelve hundred in cash, his driver's license, and a folder of credit cards," Hannah reported.

"Then Max didn't kill Ron and run away." Andrea sounded very sure of herself. "He might have left the credit cards and his driver's license, especially if he was afraid of being traced. But the cash? He would have taken the cash."

"You're right." Hannah flipped through the papers in the briefcase and pulled out an agenda for the Tri-State Buttermakers' Convention. A line was highlighted in yellow and it read: *Opening Address by Maxwell Turner—10 A.M.*

"Look at this, Andrea."

Andrea stared at the highlighted line. "The speech Max didn't give."

"I wonder where it is." Hannah began to frown. "Betty said she worked late Tuesday night, typing it up. She left it on her desk for Max, and it was gone when she came in to work on Wednesday morning."

Andrea looked puzzled. "It's not in Max's briefcase?"

"No. Let's check out the house."

Andrea looked as if the last thing she wanted to do was go into Max's house. "Do we have to?"

"I think we do. Max may have left something behind that'll give us a clue to where he is."

"Okay," Andrea reluctantly agreed. "Do you think we should arm ourselves, just in case?"

"Good idea." Hannah grabbed a claw hammer from the workbench by the door and handed Andrea a rubber mallet. A hammer and a mallet were no match for a killer with a gun, but she was almost positive that no one was inside. If arming themselves with carpenter's tools made Andrea feel safer, that was fine with Hannah.

Hannah tried to turn the knob on the connecting door, but it wouldn't budge. "Oh, great! Max *did* lock his door. See if his keys are in his Cadillac, will you? I think I noticed them in the ignition."

Andrea hurried back to the Cadillac and came back with the keys. She handed them to Hannah and watched as her sister unlocked the door.

Hannah stepped into the kitchen, flicked on the light, and jumped slightly as the refrigerator kicked in. "Nice kitchen. I guess Max had a thing for cows."

Every round handle on the row of kitchen cabinets was painted with black and white patches like a Holstein cow. There was a collection of china cows in various poses on the shelves of the greenhouse window over the sink, and a large painted plate with frolicking cows around the border hung over the stove. There were cow magnets on the refrigerator door, a cow creamer and sugar bowl on the table, and a cow cookie jar sitting on the counter. A farm dog would have gone crazy in Max's kitchen, trying to round all the cows.

"It's a little much for my taste," Andrea admitted, "but I guess Max had to do something with all the cow things that people gave him. That's the trouble with collections. Once people know you're collecting something, they give it to you for every occasion."

There was a strange burning odor in the kitchen and Hannah noticed that the red light was glowing on the coffee-maker. She reached out to shut it off and realized that the pot was dry, just inky sludge that once had been coffee in the bottom. "Max left the coffee on."

"Don't run water in it," Andrea warned. "I did that once and the carafe cracked."

Hannah set the glass pot on one of Max's burners to cool. Then she noticed a thermos on the counter, right next to a dishtowel with happy-looking bovines grazing across its green terrycloth surface. The thermos was empty and its cap was off. "Max must have planned to come back here. He made a pot of coffee so that he could fill his thermos. He probably wanted to take it with him for the drive."

Andrea looked sick as she stared at the empty thermos, and Hannah knew she was thinking about what might have happened to Max. She grabbed her sister's arm and propelled her past the cabinets with their cow-painted knobs and into the deserted living room.

Hannah flicked on the lights, but there was no sign that anyone had been here since Max had left early Wednesday morning. She glanced at her sister—that sick look was still on her face—and decided that she'd better do something fast. Andrea's face was pale, her knees were shaking, and she looked as if she might faint.

"Andrea? I need you to help me out here," Hannah ordered in the same tone of voice that Delores had used when she'd told them to clean their rooms. "Have you ever been in Max's house before?"

Andrea blinked once, twice, and then she turned to Hannah. She looked disoriented and more than a little frightened. "What did you say?"

"Have you ever been in Max's house before?"

Andrea nodded. A little color was beginning to come back to her cheeks, now that Hannah had given her something else to focus on. "Al sent me out with some papers last fall. Max bought some property over in Browerville and Al handled the paperwork for him."

"Can you remember what the house looked like then?"

"Of course I can. I'm a real estate agent." Andrea's voice was less tentative. "Max even gave me a tour. It was right after he fixed it up and I wanted to see it. I thought he might want to put it up for sale later on and move to a bigger place in town."

Hannah smiled and patted her on the shoulder. "I knew I could count on you. Just keep your eyes open for anything that looks out of place. How about this room? Does it look the same as it did then?"

Andrea looked around. "Everything's the same, except for the couch. He used to have a black one with cow pillows on it. See that painting up there over the fireplace? He told me that his mother painted it from an old photograph. That's Max's grandfather standing in front of the original dairy."

"I didn't know that Max's mother was an artist." Hannah stared at the painting. It wasn't very good.

"Obviously, she wasn't." Andrea recovered enough to smile. "It's from one of those original paint-by-the-number sets. They were very big in the fifties. She mailed in the photograph and they sent back the canvas with little numbers in the spaces so she'd know what color to use. I had all I could do not to tell Max how bad it was."

Now that Hannah had moved closer, she could see some of the numbers showing through the paint and she doubted that Max's grandfather had sported a seventeen tattooed on his forehead. "Let's go through the other rooms. Tell me if you see anything that you don't remember."

With Andrea following, Hannah stepped briskly out into the hallway and they proceeded to go through every room in the house. Andrea pointed out new curtains in the den, a slightly different furniture arrangement in Max's home office, and new wallpaper in the dining room. Max's bedroom had been painted since Andrea had seen it. He'd changed the color scheme from blue to green, and the guest bedroom had a new braided rug on the floor. Every room had at least one cow in some shape or form.

"How can you remember what everything looked like?" Hannah asked. She was amazed at the amount of information Andrea had remembered from a single tour of Max's house.

Andrea shrugged modestly. "I've always had a good eye. That's why I could tell when Mother had been in my room. If one tiny thing had been moved, I noticed it."

"And there isn't one tiny thing out of place in Max's house?" Hannah kept talking as they made a full circle and approached the kitchen again. She didn't want Andrea to think about what might have happened to Max.

"Not that I can see, except . . ." Andrea stopped by the connecting door that led to the garage and reached up to touch an empty hook by the side of the doorframe. "Wait a minute, Hannah. There's supposed to be a key right here."

"What kind of a key?"

Andrea closed her eyes for a moment and then they snapped open again. "A shiny blue metal key on a cow key chain. It was hanging right here when Max showed me his kitchen. The cow was really cute, brown and white with a lit- tle—"

"Do you know what the key was for?" Hannah inter- rupted her sister's description.

"The dairy. Max said he used it when he walked to work and he didn't want to carry his whole key ring. He told me he just grabbed that key and his garage-door opener and—" Andrea stopped speaking and turned to Hannah. "That must be what he did on Wednesday morning! When I went back to his car to get the keys, I noticed that his garage-door opener wasn't clipped to the visor."

"I think you're right. Max started to pack his car Wednes- day morning, but he didn't have time to finish before his meeting. He left his briefcase open because he needed to pick up the speech that Betty typed up. When his meeting was over, he planned to come back here and leave for the convention. But Max didn't come back. The last time anyone saw him he was in his office at Cozy Cow. His trail ends at the dairy."

Andrea winced. "I hope you're not going to say what I think you're going to say."

"I am." Hannah closed up the garage and ushered her sis- ter out Max's front door. "We don't have a choice. We've got to check out the dairy."

Chapter
Nineteen

Hannah started her Suburban, reached for the bag of cookies she always carried in the back, and tossed them to Andrea. "Have a cookie. You need some chocolate. It'll make you feel better."

"I don't need chocolate. What I need is a shrink! It would take a psychiatrist to figure out why I ever agreed to this harebrained, idiotic idea of yours to . . . to—" Andrea stopped speaking, too rattled to go on. Then she reached into the bag, pulled out a cookie, and bit into it savagely. She chewed, swallowed, and then she sighed. "These are really good, Hannah."

"They're called Chocolate-Covered Cherry Delights. Mother gave me the idea for the recipe when she told me how Dad used to always bring her chocolate-covered cherries whenever she was mad at him."

Andrea reached into the bag for another and took a huge bite. "Are you absolutely sure we need to go inside the dairy?"

"I'm sure." Hannah turned at the end of Max's access road and into the Cozy Cow parking lot.

"We can't just *try* to call Bill first?"

"He's got his hands full," Hannah answered. She parked in the darkest corner of the lot and turned to her sister. Andrea looked a lot better and her hands weren't shaking anymore. "Relax, Andrea. Max isn't inside. He couldn't be. Betty or one of the other employees would have found him by now. All we're going to do is look for clues in his office."

"That's true." Andrea managed a shaky smile.

"Then you're coming in with me?"

"I'm certainly not going to sit in the parking lot alone, not with a killer on the loose! And it's not like we're actually breaking in or anything. You've got Max's keys."

"Right." Hannah knew that this wasn't the time to remind Andrea that they'd broken into Max's garage to get those keys. "Grab the flashlights. I don't want to turn on any lights inside. Someone might see them from the road."

Andrea reached into the back for the flashlights. "You're going to owe me a whole batch of cookies for this, Hannah. I'll take the Chocolate-Covered Cherry Delights."

"Deal." Hannah grabbed her flashlight from Andrea's hand and got out of the truck. The temperature had dropped in the past hour and she shivered as they walked across the parking lot to the rear door. She glanced down at the keys in the glare from the security lights and blessed Max for labeling them. She selected the one marked "Rear Door," and was about to insert it in the lock when Andrea gasped.

"What?" Hannah turned to look at her sister.

"I just thought of something. What if the dairy has a security system? We could set it off."

"Are you kidding? A security system for a place this big would cost a bundle. Do you really think that Max would spend that kind of money?"

"No, maybe not." Andrea breathed an audible sigh of relief. "Go ahead, Hannah. It was just a thought, that's all."

Hannah didn't mention that she'd thought of the same thing. She'd even glanced at Max's birth date on his driver's license. If there was a keypad by the inside of the rear door, she planned to enter the numbers two, three, and forty-nine. She'd read somewhere that most people used their birth dates as a code for their security systems. If bells started to clang and sirens began to wail, they'd hightail it back to her Suburban and leave as fast as they could.

The key turned, the door opened, and Hannah stepped in. No keypad, no flashing red lights, no buzzing or clanking or wailing. That was good. It would have been out of character for Max to fork out the extra money for an alarm system, but Hannah hadn't been one hundred percent sure.

"Come on, Andrea." Hannah motioned to her sister. "His office is down this hall and to the right."

Andrea stepped inside rather gingerly. "How do you know that?"

"I took the grand tour when I was in sixth grade. We came out here on a field trip and Max showed us around."

"We didn't get to go when I was in grade school." Andrea sounded a little miffed.

"I know. They stopped the tours right after my class went through. I think it had something to do with Dale Hoeschen. He tripped over a box and almost fell into a cream vat."

Andrea grinned. She was clearly in better spirits now. "I knew there was something I didn't like about Dale."

Hannah led the way down the hall and into the main part of the dairy. It was large and cavernous, not a comfortable place to explore at night. Their flashlights were powerful, but the twin beams did nothing to dispel the looming shadows. Hannah was sure that the place would seem very ordinary if they could turn on the overhead lights, but several rows of glass-block windows peppered the face of the building and she didn't want to take the chance that someone on the highway would notice the light.

"Are you sure you know where you're going?" Andrea's voice sounded unnaturally loud in the stillness.

"I think so," Hannah replied. "There should be another hallway—there it is." Hannah trained the beam of her flashlight on the entrance to the second hallway. "Max's office should be the second door on the left. Betty's office is the first door."

As they entered the second hallway, Hannah noticed that Betty had posted the delivery schedules on a corkboard right outside her door. The drivers' names were listed and their routes were marked with the times of each delivery. Ron's name was still on his route. Betty must be waiting for instructions from Max before she changed the name of the driver.

Max's office was right where Hannah remembered and it was marked with a brass nameplate on the door. Hannah opened the door, stepped inside, and played the beam of her flashlight over the walls. There were no outside windows. If they closed the door behind them, they could turn on the lights.

"Come in and shut the door," Hannah called out to her sister.

Andrea stepped in quickly and shut the door. "Good. It's creepy out there."

Hannah agreed. Her knees were still shaking slightly, but she decided to make light of it for her sister's benefit. "That's only because it's so big and dark. You can turn on the lights. There's probably a switch right by the door."

"Are you sure?" Andrea sounded very nervous.

"I'm positive. I checked and there aren't any windows. No one will notice the light if we keep the door closed."

Andrea located the wall switch and a moment later, bright light flooded down from an overhead fixture. Both sisters breathed a sigh of relief as they gazed around the room. Max's office was huge and it was tastefully decorated with dark gray wall-to-wall carpeting and pale yellow grass cloth on the walls. There were several framed prints of flowers hanging in strategic positions, and the upholstered furniture, done in a striped pattern of muted coral, dark green, and gold, picked up the colors from the flower prints.

"It's a nice color combination," Andrea commented. "The only thing that doesn't match is Max's desk chair."

Hannah glanced at the old brown leather swivel chair that sat behind the modern, executive-style desk. "I guess Max was going for comfort, not style."

Two smaller chairs faced the front of the desk for visitors and there was a small round table between them. A conversational grouping was arranged at the side of the room and there were three doors: the one they'd just entered, another that Hannah assumed connected to Betty's office, and a rough-hewn antique door in the center of the back wall.

"What's that door?" Andrea pointed to the only door that didn't match the decor.

"That leads to the old dairy," Hannah told her, "the one in the picture that Max's mother painted. It's the original door and Max told us about it when we took the tour. He said the old dairy was a landmark and he decided to preserve it, even though it cost more money to incorporate it into his expansion plans. He called it his contribution to the history of this area."

Andrea laughed. "And you bought it?"

"Bought what?"

"Max didn't keep the old dairy intact out of the goodness of his heart. He got a huge tax break for preserving a historical landmark. All you have to do is connect one of the original walls to the new construction."

"I guess I shouldn't be surprised." Hannah just shook her head. "Everyone's always said that Max is a shrewd businessman."

Andrea reached down to touch the velvety carpet. "Max must have spent some of the money he saved to buy this carpet. It's the deepest pile they make and it's just like walking on pillows. I wanted it for our bedroom, but I decided that it would be too hard to keep up. It marks every time you step on it. It's hideously expensive, too. For the price you'd think they could make something that's easier to care for."

Hannah spotted a leather-bound appointment book on the credenza near the door and she walked over to page through it. Wednesday's date was marked: *TSB Convention.* She recognized Betty's handwriting. There was another note at the top, scrawled in what she assumed was Max's untidy hand. It said: *Meet W.*

"Look, Hannah." Andrea sounded insistent. "See all the footprints on this carpet?"

Hannah looked down at the carpet and saw footprints in the deep pile. "You're a genius, Andrea. If you hadn't mentioned it, I might have trampled right over them. Follow me and keep to the sides of the room. Let's see if we can find any footprints in front of Max's desk."

Hugging the wall, Hannah moved forward until she was even with the front of Max's desk. Andrea was right behind her, and Hannah pointed to the tracks in front of one of the chairs. "There! That proves someone was in here with Max."

"And we know Max was here. See those marks from the wheels of his chair?"

"I see them," Hannah acknowledged, and then she pointed to another series of tracks. "But I'm more concerned about those."

Andrea studied the indentations in the pile of the carpet. "They're going right to that door."

"The original dairy. Max must have taken his visitor in there. We'd better check it out."

"Why would he take someone in there?"

"He told us that he used it for the storage of old records," Hannah explained. "Come on. Let's see if it's open."

With Andrea following at her heels, Hannah pushed open the door and found the light switch. She gestured toward the shelves of file boxes lining the small brick building. "I guess he's still using it for storage."

"Is that the original safe?" Andrea pointed to the old safe in the corner.

"It must be. It looks old." Hannah walked over to examine the safe door. It was standing open, but it didn't look damaged in any way. "Max must have opened it for some reason."

As Hannah searched through the contents, she kept up a running commentary so that Andrea would know what she was doing. "There's no sign of a robbery or anything like that. Here's a bundle of cash and a jewelry box." Hannah snapped open the box and looked inside. "It's a pair of gold cufflinks. They look like antiques. Maybe they belonged to Max's grandfather. And here's an antique pocket watch and a man's diamond ring. There's a Rolex, too. That must be fairly new. I don't think they made them when Max's father was alive. I didn't notice any kind of a safe in Max's house, so I guess this is where he keeps his personal valuables."

Her eyes were drawn to a few stapled papers on one of the shelves, and Hannah reached out for them. "Here's the speech that Betty typed for Max, just sitting on top of these files. Max must have picked it up from Betty's desk before he came in here."

Hannah set the speech aside and opened one of the files. There were legal papers inside and it looked like a loan agreement. Her eyes widened as she read the name. "I found the loan papers that Norman's parents signed. They're stamped 'Paid In Full' and Max initialed it. Hold on a second and let me look through some of these files. I want to see if there's anyone else we know."

"Here's one for Frank Birchum." Hannah glanced at the contents of another folder. "And his papers are stamped 'Foreclosed.' The Birchums moved away about six years ago, didn't they?"

Andrea didn't answer and Hannah frowned. "Andrea? You knew the Birchums, didn't you? They lived right next to the fire station, and Frank used to own the lumberyard before the Hedins took it over. Do you remember when they left town?"

There was no answer and Hannah turned to see what her

sister was doing. Andrea was standing near the door and she seemed rooted to the spot. There was a glazed look in her eyes and she was staring off into the far corner of the room.

"Andrea?" Hannah walked over to take her sister's arm. She gave it a gentle shake, but Andrea didn't seem to notice. "You're scaring me, Andrea. Talk to me!"

But Andrea didn't say a word. She just shuddered and stared off into the far corner with an expression of horror on her face. Hannah swiveled around and looked in the direction of her sister's fixated gaze. No wonder Andrea was speechless. There was a pair of feet sticking out from behind one of the shelves of file boxes!

"Stay right here." Hannah realized how unnecessary that warning was, but she couldn't think of anything else to say. "I'll go over and check it out."

Even though Hannah expected the worst, the sight that greeted her was still a shock. It was Max, and he was on his back. There was a hole, very similar to the one she'd seen in Ron's Cozy Cow Dairy shirt, in the center of Max's chest. And his eyes were wide-open and staring up at nothing, just as Ron's had been.

Max was dead. Hannah didn't need a doctor to tell her that. The blood on his shirt had dried thoroughly, and Hannah assumed that he'd been dead for quite a while, probably since shortly after his meeting on Wednesday morning.

Hannah walked back to her sister and took her arm. There wasn't any pleasant way to tell her. "It's Max and he's dead. Let's go and find Bill."

"Bill." Andrea managed to choke out his name.

"Right. Come on, Andrea. I'll drive out to the accident scene and we'll find him. How about Tracey? Do you need to get home to her?"

Andrea shook her head. It was a jerky, almost automatic kind of motion, but Hannah was relieved. At least she was responding. "With Lucy. Overnight. At the farm."

"Good." Hannah understood what Andrea was trying to

say. Lucy Dunwright was Andrea's friend, and her daughter, Karen, was Tracey's age. Tracey was spending the night with Karen at the family farm.

Hannah glanced over at the safe and made one of her snap decisions, the kind that frequently got her into trouble. This was a crime scene and all of Max's papers would be taken as evidence. Hannah knew that she shouldn't touch anything, but Norman had told them how embarrassed his mother would be if anyone found out about the loan papers they'd signed with Max. Their loan had been paid off more than five years ago. The date was right on the papers. It had nothing to do with the crime and there was no reason why anyone else had to know about it.

It only took a second to grab the file and stuff it inside the front of her jacket. Hannah collected her flashlight and then she went over to take Andrea's hand. "Come on, Andrea. We're leaving now."

Andrea was in shock and the sooner they got out of here, the better. Hannah pulled her into Max's office and guided her around the perimeter of the carpet and out the door. They walked back the way they'd come, across the large open space and out the back entrance. Hannah led the way to her Suburban and opened the passenger door. She tucked Andrea inside, walked around, and slid in.

"Eat another cookie, Andrea." Hannah plunked the bag on her sister's lap. "It'll help."

Andrea reached into the bag and took out a cookie. She stared at it for a second and then she took a bite. Hannah started the engine and drove out of the parking lot, turning onto the highway and heading for the interstate. Bill shouldn't be that hard to find. She could hear sirens in the distance and all she had to do was head toward the sound.

They'd driven about five miles when Andrea made a strange chortling sound. Hannah turned to stare at her and reached out to pat her arm. "Just take it easy, Andrea. I can see flashing lights up ahead. We'll be there in a minute."

Andrea nodded, and then she made the sound again. Hannah realized that it was a chuckle, and as she listened, it turned into a fairly normal-sounding giggle. "What is it, Andrea? You're not getting hysterical on me, are you?"

"No." Andrea giggled again. "I really do feel much better. I hate to say it, but maybe you're right. It could be the chocolate."

"Chocolate helps." Hannah stated her theory again, about how the caffeine and the endorphins in chocolate calmed nerves, heightened awareness, and provided a sense of well-being. And then her thoughts turned to Bill and how furious he'd be when she told him that they'd broken into Max's house, searched the dairy, and found Max's body.

"Andrea?" Hannah turned to her sister. "I think I need a dose of my own medicine. Hand me one of those cookies."

CHOCOLATE-COVERED CHERRY DELIGHTS

Preheat oven to 350° F.,
rack in the middle position.

1 cup melted butter (2 sticks)
2 cups white sugar
2 eggs
½ teaspoon baking powder
½ teaspoon baking soda
½ teaspoon salt
2 teaspoons vanilla
1 cup cocoa powder
3 cups flour (not sifted)
2 small, 10-oz. jars of maraschino cherries ***
1 pkg. chocolate chips (6 oz. pkg.—2 cups)
½ cup condensed sweetened milk

Melt butter and mix in sugar. Let mixture cool and add eggs. Mix it thoroughly and then add baking powder, baking soda, salt, vanilla, and cocoa, stirring after each addition. Add flour and mix well. *(Dough will be stiff and a bit crumbly.)*

Drain cherries and remove stems, reserving juice.

Pat dough into walnut-sized balls with your fingers. Place on greased cookie sheet, 12 to a standard sheet.

Press down in center with thumb to make a deep indentation. *(If the health board's around, use the bowl of a small spoon!)* Place one cherry in each indentation.

In a saucepan over simmering water *(double boiler)* combine the chocolate chips and the condensed milk. Heat on low until the chips are melted. *(You can also do this in the microwave, but you'll have to keep zapping it to keep it from hardening.)*

Add approx. ⅛ cup of the reserved cherry juice and stir to a thick sauce. If sauce is too thick, add more juice in small increments. *(Test it with a teaspoon. If it doesn't glob off, it's too thick.)*

Spoon the sauce over the center of each cookie just enough to cover each cherry. Make sure it doesn't drip down the sides.

Bake at 350 degrees F. for 10 to 12 minutes. Let cool on cookie sheet for 2 minutes, then remove to rack to finish cooling.

*** For those who don't like cherries, substitute well-drained pineapple tidbits, using the juice to thin the frosting. You can also use pecan halves or macadamia nuts and thin the frosting with cold coffee or water. If you don't have anything to go on top, just glob the chocolate mixture into the indentations. That's good, too.

Yield: 7 to 8 dozen, depending on cookie size.

A plate of these should be in every psychiatrist's office—two Chocolate-Covered Cherry Delights will lift anyone out of a depression.

Chapter Twenty

Hannah poured two glasses of chilled wine from the green jug in the bottom of her refrigerator and carried them into the living room. Her sister was seated on the couch, still looking rattled, but the color had come back to her cheeks. Moishe was nestled in her arms, and Hannah could hear him purring as Andrea absently stroked his head. Her resident feline was uncanny. He seemed to sense that Andrea was in need of comfort and he was doing his best imitation of a lap cat. Hannah handed one of the glasses to Andrea and said, "Here. Drink this."

"What is it?" Andrea eyed the stemmed glass suspiciously.

"White wine. Don't ask about the label. I'm sure you've never heard of it."

Andrea reached for the glass and expertly sloshed the liquid in a tight circle. "Nice liquor line." Then she took a small sip. "Light and somewhat fruity with an undertone of oak. It's not a true Chardonnay, but it's very interesting. I like it."

Hannah just smiled and kept her comments to herself. If Andrea knew that the wine had come from the Lake Eden

CostMart, and a gallon barely put a dent in a ten-dollar bill, she'd decide that it was pure vinegar.

"I think it's domestic." Andrea took another sip. "Am I right?"

Hannah decided it was time to switch to another subject. "You were incredible with Bill. I still can't believe that he isn't mad at me."

"Bill can't stand it when I cry." Andrea gave a smug smile. "He just falls apart when my lip starts to quiver."

"And you can quiver on command?"

"Of course." Andrea's smile grew wider. "I learned how to quiver right after Mother bought me my first bra. It always works with the guys."

"You're amazing," Hannah said with real admiration. Because of her practice at dealing with doting men, Andrea had managed to avoid the lecture that they'd both deserved.

Hannah had done her best to explain things to Bill. She'd told him that they were so worried about Max, they'd simply had to check on him. And then, when they'd found Max's Cadillac half-packed for his trip to the Tri-State Buttermakers' Convention, they'd had no choice but to use his key to search his office at the dairy, the last place that anyone had seen him.

That hadn't quite done it. Bill had still been upset about the fact that Hannah had led his wife into a potentially dangerous situation. But Hannah had posed a question: Wasn't it lucky that they'd found Max's body before the trail had gone cold?

Bill had reluctantly agreed, but he'd laid down some ground rules. The next time Hannah decided to follow up a lead, she should check with him first. Hannah had promised and she'd meant it. Finding two dead bodies was more than enough for one lifetime. But then Bill had started to ask questions about exactly why they hadn't come out to the ac-cident scene to get him earlier, and Andrea had gone into lip-quivering mode. One glance at Andrea's close-to-tears countenance and Bill had melted. He'd hugged Andrea and told her that he'd get a ride to Hannah's condo so that he could drive her home. And then he'd assured her that he wasn't angry with her or with Hannah.

"Moishe is a very comforting sort of pet." Andrea's fingers strayed toward the sensitive spot behind Moishe's ear and he purred even louder. "It's really amazing that he's so domesticated, considering the kind of life that he used to lead. He's just sitting here and purring. I never knew that he was so sweet."

Hannah wasn't about to tell Andrea how Moishe acted when he was hunting. She doubted that any small rodent or flightless bird would describe him as sweet. "I need to talk to you about Mr. Harris, Andrea. You said he was waiting at the Peterson property when you got there on Wednesday morning?"

"That's right. I met him at nine-thirty, but he said he was there a lot earlier than that." Andrea thought about it for a moment, and then her eyes widened. "Do you think he might have seen something?"

Hannah shrugged. "That depends on what time he got there. He didn't tell you if he knew Max or Ron, did he?"

"No. He said he didn't know anyone in—" Andrea stopped and stared at Hannah as the light dawned. "Do you think Mr. Harris killed Max and Ron?"

"The time frame works, but Mr. Harris doesn't have a motive as far as we know. I'd certainly like to talk to him about it. You don't happen to have his home phone number, do you?"

"Of course I do. I'm a real estate agent. I always carry my clients' numbers with me. Just hand me my purse. I don't want to disturb Moishe."

Hannah walked over to get the purse from the chair near the door and handed it to Andrea. When her sister had opened it, Hannah admired the way the interior was organized. Andrea's makeup was in a see-through pouch so that she could easily find the item she wanted, her keys were clipped to a leather strap, and her wallet was neatly stowed away in a leather holder on the side. There was even an inside pouch for the glasses that Andrea needed for reading, but refused to wear.

Andrea reached inside another pouch and drew out a small address book. She flipped to the proper page and handed it to Hannah. "Here it is. You're not going to call him now, are you?"

"There's no time like the present."

"But it's almost midnight. What are you going to say?"

"I don't know yet, but I'll think of something." Hannah grabbed the phone. "Relax, Andrea. I won't mention your name."

As she punched out the number, Hannah considered her options. Mr. Harris would be more likely to give her information if she had some sort of credential. She could say that she was a reporter with the *Lake Eden Journal,* but that might backfire. If Mr. Harris had anything to hide, he'd simply hang up on someone who said they worked for the town newspaper. As her call was connected, Hannah made a snap decision. Mr. Harris wouldn't dare to hang up on the police.

"Hello?"

The voice on the other end of the line sounded groggy, as if she'd awakened him, and Hannah did her best to sound official. "Mr. Harris? I'm sorry if I woke you, but this is Miss Swensen from the Winnetka County Sheriff's Station. We're investigating a crime that occurred at the Cozy Cow Dairy on Wednesday morning, sometime between six-fifteen and eight. We need to know if you happened to observe anything that could relate to the crime. I understand that you were in the area at that time?"

"Yes, I was. What happened?"

Hannah smiled. Mr. Harris sounded cooperative. "I can't give you the details, but I need to know the time that you arrived in Lake Eden and what you saw while you were there."

"Let me see. I got to Lake Eden about a quarter to seven and drove straight out to the Peterson farm. I did see one thing that was odd, but I'm not sure if it's helpful."

"Tell me anyway, Mr. Harris." Hannah maintained her professional voice.

"As I approached the dairy, a car pulled out of the driveway. The driver was in a real hurry. He skidded over the centerline, and I had to swerve to avoid him."

"You said *he,* Mr. Harris. The driver was a man?"

"I'm not sure. I didn't actually see him. The sun visor was down."

"Very good." Hannah grabbed the notebook and pen that were sitting on the coffee table and made a note. "Could you describe the car?"

"It was a small black compact with a rental sticker on the window. The sticker was white with red lettering, but I didn't see the name of the company. I always use Hertz, myself. My company gets a special rate from them."

"Then you don't own a car, Mr. Harris?" Hannah winked at Andrea. Her question had nothing to do with the investigation, but she wanted to find out if he'd told Andrea the truth.

"I have a vintage Jaguar, but I prefer not to drive it out of the city. I'm certainly glad I didn't drive it on Wednesday! That other driver came very close to hitting me. I just wish that Marshal Beeseman had been there to give him a ticket."

Hannah's eyebrows rose and she jotted another note. "You're acquainted with Marshal Beeseman?"

"Yes. He saw my car parked in front of the Peterson place and drove up to ask me what I was doing there."

Hannah wrote down Herb's name. "What time was this, Mr. Harris?"

"A minute or so past eight. I was listening to the radio and the eight o'clock news had just started."

"You've been very helpful, Mr. Harris." Hannah turned to wink at Andrea before she asked her final question. "Perhaps this has nothing to do with our case, but could you tell me why you decided not to buy the Peterson property?"

For a moment Hannah thought that Mr. Harris would refuse to answer, but then he cleared his throat. "My fiancée said she wanted to live in the country, but she broke off our engagement on Tuesday night. That's why I came to Lake Eden so early. I couldn't sleep and I decided that driving might make me feel better. I suppose I should have told Mrs. Todd the reason that I passed on the house, but I really didn't want to discuss it."

"That's certainly understandable." Hannah made a note on her pad and passed it to Andrea. "Thank you, Mr. Harris. We appreciate your cooperation."

Andrea waited until Hannah had hung up the phone and then she pointed to the note. "Mr. Harris was buying the Peterson place for his girlfriend?"

"That's what he said. She broke off their engagement on Tuesday night. You would have sold it if she'd hung on for just one more day."

"Oh, well. You win some and you lose some." Andrea shrugged and drained the last of her wine. "After all I've been through tonight, I think I deserve another glass of wine. It's really excellent, Hannah. I wasn't sure at first, but it definitely has legs. There's more, isn't there?"

Hannah went off to fetch her sister another glass of Chateau Screw Top. If Andrea wanted to get a little smashed, that was fine with Hannah. She just hoped that when Bill arrived, Andrea wouldn't need to be slung over his shoulder like a gunnysack and carried down the stairs.

The night wasn't peaceful, not by a long shot, and when Hannah's alarm went off at six the next morning, she felt as if she'd just closed her eyes. Her dreams had been peppered with bullet holes, blood, and stiff, cold legs sticking out like boards behind couches, chairs, and bookcases. There had even been a cow in her dreams—a huge, homicidal Guernsey that had chased her over fences and past bubbling vats of cream.

Hannah groaned and sat up in bed. Duty called. She had to bake the Black and Whites for the sheriff's department's open house.

As she padded into the kitchen, stepping carefully to avoid Moishe's morning rubs against her ankles, she wondered about the new hotshot detective from the Minneapolis Police Department. Would he approve of the way that Bill was handling the double-homicide case? Sheriff Grant had obviously been impressed with the new man. According to Bill, he'd set up an interview the day that his application had come in the mail.

"Here's your breakfast, Moishe." Hannah dumped dry crunchies into Moishe's bowl and gave him fresh water. Then she stumbled toward the coffeemaker and poured her first cup. She must be a caffeine addict. She really couldn't function without a wake-up cup, or three, in the morning. She just hoped the FDA and the president's drug czar didn't ever turn her into a criminal by classifying coffee as a drug.

Some days it was easier to operate on automatic pilot. Hannah didn't want to wake up to the point where she recognized how tired she really was. She slugged down only one cup of the steaming brew, enough so that she wouldn't fall asleep and drown in the shower, and then she went back to her bedroom to get ready for work. When she had showered and dressed, she came out to empty the rest of the coffee into the large-sized car caddy that Bill had given her for Christmas. She refilled Moishe's food bowl, grabbed her jacket and keys, and stepped out into the predawn freeze.

The blast of cold air that greeted Hannah caused her eyes to snap open all the way. Her breath came out in white puffs and she shivered her way down the outside stairway to the garage. It was time to break out her full winter gear.

The garage was deserted, the cars lined up in even rows

against the painted cinderblock walls. Hannah hurried to her Suburban and jumped inside, cranking the motor over twice before it started. Time to plug in her truck, too.

The heater kicked in about the time she turned onto Old Lake Road. Hannah reached over and turned the levers on both vents to direct the warm air to her side of the vehicle. As she zipped down the dark road, she flipped on the radio, and the impossibly cheery voices of Jake and Kelly, the crazy duo that hosted KCOW's "News At O'Dark-Thirty Show," assaulted her ears. She switched to WEZY's mellow strains and thought about the peculiar call letters of Minnesota radio stations. If the transmitter was east of the Mississippi River, the call letters started with a W. If it was west of the Mississippi, the call letters started with a K. The same was true for television stations. It was all controlled by the FCC. Hannah wondered what the bureaucrats would do if a station built a bridge over the Mississippi and mounted their transmitter in the middle.

Deliberately averting her eyes from the dairy as she passed it, Hannah made her way into town. There was no way she wanted to be reminded of Max's lifeless body this early in the morning. She spotted Herb Beeseman a block from her shop and flagged him down. Plying him with the rest of the Chocolate-Covered Cherry Delights in exchange for information, she verified that he'd talked to Mr. Harris at the Peterson farm at eight on Wednesday morning.

Hannah pulled into her parking place at six forty-five. After she'd locked up her truck, she plugged in the head-bolt heater and opened the back door to the bakery. The sweet dark scent of chocolate greeted her, and Hannah began to smile. Next to coffee, chocolate was her favorite aroma.

After she'd flicked on the lights, fired up the ovens, stuck on her cap, and scrubbed her hands at the sink, Hannah got out a mixing bowl. She had to make a sample batch of Old-Fashioned Sugar Cookies for the woman who'd catered the Woodleys' party.

Hannah poured herself a cup of coffee from the car caddy and read over the recipe while she ingested more caffeine. Mixing cookie dough was something she never did on automatic pilot. She'd tried it once and left out an ingredient that was essential to every cookie: sugar.

When the dough was ready, Hannah covered it with plastic wrap and stashed it in her walk-in cooler. The dough for the Black and Whites was thoroughly chilled and she grabbed a bowl and carried it over to the work island. She'd just finished rolling enough dough balls for two sheets of cookies when Lisa came in the back door.

Hannah glanced at the clock. It was only seven-thirty and Lisa wasn't scheduled to come in until eight on Saturdays. "Hi, Lisa. You're half an hour early."

"I know. I just thought you might need some help with the customers this morning. We'll be packed."

"We will?"

"You bet. They'll all come in to find out what you know about Max."

Hannah's eyebrows shot up in surprise. "How did *you* find out so fast?"

"I was listening to Jake and Kelly, and they said that Max was dead. Those two guys are crazy. They were making bad cow jokes and calling it a tribute to Max."

"Bad cow jokes?" Hannah looked up from her task of rolling the dough balls in powdered sugar.

"You know the type," Lisa explained as she hung her jacket on the hook by the door. " 'Why did Farmer Brown buy a black cow? Because he wanted to get chocolate milk.' That was the best of them. The rest were so bad, I don't even remember them. Do you want me to start the coffee and set the tables up in the shop?"

Hannah nodded and slid the first two cookie sheets into the ovens. She set the timer for twelve minutes and walked back to the work island to start rolling more balls. Lisa was right. If Jake and Kelly had discussed Max Turner on their show, The Cookie Jar would be flooded with customers this morning. And when the news got out that she'd been the one to find Max's body, it would be standing room only. Hannah sighed as she rolled more dough balls in powdered sugar. If she were ever unlucky enough to find a third body, she'd probably have to buy the building next door and expand.

OLD-FASHIONED SUGAR COOKIES

Do not preheat oven yet—
dough must chill before baking.

2 cups melted butter *(4 sticks)*
2 cups powdered *(confectioners')* sugar *(not sifted)*
1 cup white *(granulated)* sugar
2 eggs
2 teaspoons vanilla
1 teaspoon lemon zest *(optional)*
1 teaspoon baking soda
1 teaspoon cream of tartar *(critical!)*
1 teaspoon salt
4¼ cups flour *(not sifted)*

½ cup white *(granulated)* sugar in a small bowl *(for later)*

Melt butter. Add sugars and mix. Let cool to room temperature and mix in the eggs, one at a time. Then add the vanilla, lemon zest, baking soda, cream of tartar, and salt. Mix well. Add flour in increments, mixing after each addition.

Chill dough for at least one hour. *(Overnight is fine.)*

When you're ready to bake, preheat oven to 325 degrees F. and place rack in the middle of the oven.

Use hands to roll dough in walnut-sized balls. Roll dough balls in a bowl of white sugar. *(Mix white sugar 2 to 1 with colored sugar for holidays—green for St. Pat's Day, red and green for Christmas, multicolored for birthdays.)* Place on a greased cookie sheet, 12 to a standard sheet. Flatten dough balls with a greased spatula.

Bake at 325 degrees F. for 10 to 15 minutes. *(They should have a tinge of gold on the top.)* Cool on cookie sheet for 2 minutes, then remove to a rack to finish cooling. They can be decorated with frosting piped from a pastry bag for special occasions or left just as they are.

Used these for the chorale's fundraiser decorated with music notes in fudge frosting—rave reviews!

Yield: 8 to 10 dozen, depending on cookie size.

Chapter
Twenty-One

Hannah had just turned over the baking to Lisa and poured herself a cup of coffee when the phone rang. "That's got to be Mother. She's the only one who calls me this time of the morning."

"Do you want me to get it?" Lisa offered helpfully, even though her hands were covered with powdered sugar.

"No, it'll only postpone the inevitable." Hannah lifted the receiver and gave her standard greeting. "The Cookie Jar. Hannah speaking."

"I'm so glad I caught you, dear. I promised the girls I'd check. Are you booked for the second Thursday in December?"

Hannah stretched out the phone cord and walked over to her calendar, flipping the pages to December. No one booked *this* early, and Hannah knew that her mother was just fishing for information about Max Turner. "I'm free, Mother."

"Good. I joined a new group."

"That's nice." Hannah gave the appropriate response. She really should be more grateful. Delores had become a joiner since Hannah's father had died, and her groups always booked Hannah to cater their events. "What's the name of this group, Mother?"

"The Lake Eden Quilting Society, dear. They meet every other Thursday in the back room at Trudi's Fabrics."

Hannah obediently wrote down the information, but she was puzzled. As far as she knew, her mother had never picked up a needle in her life. "You're *sewing* now, Mother?"

"Good heavens, no! I managed to find them two quilting frames at an auction last month and they awarded me an honorary membership. I just go to be sociable."

"How many groups does that make now, Mother?"

"Twelve. When your father died, Ruth Pfeffer told me that I should develop outside interests. I'm just taking her advice."

"You're taking Ruth's advice seriously?" Hannah was shocked. Ruth Pfeffer, one of her mother's neighbors, had volunteered to do grief counseling at the community center after only one two-credit class at the community college. "Ruth's a dingbat—you said so yourself—and she's not qualified to counsel anyone. I'm surprised she didn't suggest suttee!"

Delores laughed. "You're right, dear. But that's illegal, even in India."

"Very good, Mother," Hannah complimented her. Occasionally Delores's sense of humor kicked in, and those were the times when Hannah liked her the best. "What kind of cookies would you like?"

"How about those Chocolate-Covered Cherry Delights? Andrea told me that they were fabulous."

Hannah jotted it down and then she realized what her mother had said. Andrea had tasted those cookies for the first time last night. If she'd mentioned them to Delores, it must have been earlier this morning. "Did you call Andrea this morning, Mother?"

"Yes, dear. We had a lovely chat. As a matter of fact, I just got off the phone with her."

Hannah's eyes widened. Her sister was *not* a morning person. "You called Andrea before eight? On a Saturday?"

"Of course I did. I wanted to make sure she was all right.

The poor dear sounded dreadful. She told me that her head was still reeling from that awful migraine."

Hannah started to grin. It wasn't surprising that Andrea's head was reeling. She'd polished off four glasses of that "impudent little wine" before Bill had come to drive her home. "I've got to run, Mother. It's late and I have to get ready to open the shop."

"You don't open until nine this morning. How about Max Turner? I heard on the radio that he was dead."

Hannah rolled her eyes at Lisa, who was trying not to look amused at her attempt to end the conversation. "That's true, Mother."

"I know it's not nice to speak ill of the dead, but Max made a lot of enemies here in Lake Eden. I don't think anyone is going to shed tears for him."

"Really?" Hannah thought she knew exactly what her mother was talking about, but she wanted to hear it from Delores. "Why is that?"

"He wasn't a nice man, Hannah. I don't want you to repeat this, but I heard that several families lost their homes because of Max Turner."

"Really?" Hannah did her best to sound as if this was the first she'd heard of it.

"He was a . . ." Delores paused, and Hannah knew that she was attempting to think of the proper word. "What's that term, Hannah? I know it has something to do with a fish."

"A loan shark?"

"That's it. You have such a good vocabulary, dear. I think it comes from all that reading you did as a child. I wonder what'll happen to those loans now?"

"I don't know," Hannah replied, making a mental note to ask Bill if he'd found any current loan papers in the stack of files he'd confiscated from Max's safe. But those files would only serve to *eliminate* suspects. If Max had been killed over a current loan, his killer would have taken the papers.

"I've already had four calls this morning about Max,"

Delores informed her. "The whole town's talking, and everybody's got a story to tell."

That gave Hannah an idea and she started to smile. Delores belonged to a dozen groups and she heard all the gossip. What if her mother heard about a loan that Max had made, a name that wasn't on any of the files that Bill had removed from the safe? That person could very well be Max's killer. "Will you do something for me, Mother?"

"Of course, dear. What is it?"

"Keep your ears open and call me if you hear anyone discussing any business dealings with Max. It's important. I really need to know."

"All right, dear. I'm sure there'll be talk—there always is. But I don't see why it's so import—" Delores stopped, and Hannah heard her gasp. "They didn't go into any details about Max's death on the radio. Was he *murdered*?"

Hannah groaned. There were times when Delores was much too perceptive to suit her. "I'm not supposed to say anything about that. It could cost Bill his promotion."

"Then I won't breathe a word. You can count on me, Hannah. I'd never do anything to hurt Bill's career. But it's just going to *kill* me not to tell Carrie!"

"I know, but the news should break any minute. Just keep listening to the radio."

"How do you know? Did Bill tell you or . . ." Delores gasped again. "Don't tell me that you discovered Max's body!"

"I really can't talk about it, Mother."

There was another lengthy pause, and then Delores sighed. "You really have to stop doing this, Hannah. You're going to scare all the eligible men off if you keep on finding murder victims. The only one who might give you a second glance would be a homicide detective!"

"I suppose you're right." Hannah started to grin. Perhaps finding bodies wasn't so bad, after all. "I really do have to run, Mother. Just remember to call me if you hear anything, okay?"

Hannah hung up and turned to Lisa. "That woman can talk longer than anyone I know."

"Mothers are like that," Lisa responded, but she looked very grave. "I couldn't help hearing your end of the conversation. Was Max murdered?"

"I'm afraid he was."

"That doesn't surprise me. He *was* a loan shark. One of our neighbors almost borrowed some money from him, but Dad looked over the papers and told him not to sign. He ended up getting a bank loan instead."

Hannah was about to ask her the neighbor's name when she realized that it didn't really matter. If the neighbor hadn't signed, he'd have no motive to kill Max.

"Why don't you sit down, Hannah? You look beat and it's only eight-thirty. And think seriously about taking the day off. You know I can handle things here."

"Thanks, Lisa. I'm really tempted." Hannah sat down on the stool at the end of the work island and thought about a day off. She could go home, brush Moishe, watch a little television, and call in a million times to find out what was happening. It was better to stay here, in the thick of things. "Thanks for offering, but I wouldn't rest anyway."

"Okay, but if you change your mind, just let me know. What do you want me to bake when I finish with the Black and Whites?"

"The Old-Fashioned Sugar Cookies," Hannah answered. "They should be chilled by then. There's only one batch of dough."

"Do you want me to roll them in white sugar, or mixed?"

"Just white. When they're cool, pick out a dozen of the best and pack them for shipping. I promised to send a sample box to the Woodleys' caterer."

Lisa looked pleased. "New business?"

"Maybe. You haven't said anything about the party. Did you have a good time?"

"It was fantastic, Hannah. I've never been to such a fancy party before. It's just too bad that we had to leave early."

"Herb was called out to the accident scene?"

"No, but he thought he should go anyway. I had him drop me off at home before he went out there. I didn't feel like staying at the party alone. He called me later and he said it was a miracle no one had been killed. Seventeen cars! Can you imagine that?"

"Unfortunately, I can. I'd better go up front, Lisa. It's almost time to open."

As she went through the swinging door, Hannah thought about the massive car pileup she'd almost joined on the interstate last year. All it took was one patch of ice, a lapse in judgment, and several drivers following too closely. She'd taken the shoulder to avoid hitting the huge Red Owl grocery truck ahead of her and she'd considered herself fortunate to wind up in a soft snowy ditch.

It was a dark morning and Hannah switched on the lights. She wasn't looking forward to the dark winter season with sunrise at nine and sunset at four. It was even worse for people like Phil Plotnik, who worked the night shift at DelRay Manufacturing. It was dark when he went to work, dark when he came home from work, and if the sun didn't shine on the weekends, he missed out completely.

A car pulled up in front of the shop and Hannah recognized Bill's old clunker. She hurried to unlock the door and scanned Bill's face in the light flooding out of the windows as he walked up to the door. He was smiling and Hannah was relieved. Bill wasn't the type to hold a grudge and it was clear that he'd forgiven her for involving his wife in her sleuthing last night.

"Hi, Hannah." Bill came in and hung up his coat on the strip of hooks near the door. "I found out about that rental car that Andrea's client saw. The name of the company is Compacts Unlimited."

Hannah ducked behind the counter to pour Bill a mug of coffee. "I've never heard of them."

"They're a small outfit. Their main office is in Minneapolis and they've got a total of fourteen lots all over the state. I talked to the woman in charge of reservations. She said their office didn't rent to anybody with a Lake Eden address, but she's sending me a printout of everyone who's rented from them in the past two weeks."

"When?"

"ASAP. She doesn't know how to gather the data from the other locations, but she said she'd call in their computer expert."

"So you'll have it today?"

"That's doubtful. The computer guy went away for the weekend, but she's trying to find him." Bill's gaze shifted toward the cookies behind the counter. "Are those Chocolate Chip Crunches?"

Hannah nodded and set out two cookies for him. This wasn't the time to remind him that he should probably watch his weight. "Did you get a chance to look at the files that were in Max's old safe?"

"Mmm." Bill swallowed. "Max made a lot of loans to a lot of people. Some of them were old, but I found about ten active ones. That's ten more suspects I'm going to have to check out."

Hannah shook her head. "I think that's a waste of time. If someone shot Max to get his loan papers, he wouldn't have left them behind."

"Good point. What do you think I should do with them?"

"Make a list of the names and then lock them up in the evidence room."

Bill looked confused. "Why should I make a list of the names when none of those people are suspects?"

"So that you can check them against any gossip we hear. If somebody talks about one of Max's active loans and it's *not* on your list, it could point to the killer."

"That's very clever, Hannah. I'll do it just as soon as I get to the station. Did you think of anything else that I should do?"

"Not really, but at least we've got a theory."

"Is it the same one you told me about the other night?"

"Absolutely. I was watching *Klute* and that's what gave me the idea. We'll know if it's right just as soon as the ballistics reports come back."

"That'll take a while, but I talked to Doc Knight this morning. He's got a good eye and he told me that it looked like the same type of bullet that killed Ron."

Hannah laughed. "I could have told him *that*!"

"Me too. Lake Eden's too small to have more than one murderer. Tell me your theory again, Hannah. I want to see if everything fits."

Hannah poured a mug of coffee for herself and sat down on the stool behind the counter. "Ron saw Max meeting with the killer at six-fifteen on Wednesday morning. After Ron left, the killer shot Max. The killer was afraid that once Max's body was found, Ron would put two and two together and identify him. That's why he tracked Ron down and shot him."

"But didn't the woman with the pink lipstick say that they weren't followed?"

"She did, but that doesn't rule anything out. Don't forget that Ron's route was posted on the wall right outside Betty's office. The killer could have checked it and caught up with him later."

"That makes sense." Bill took another bite of his cookie and chewed thoughtfully. "Then you're saying that Ron was killed just because he was in the wrong place at the wrong time?"

"That's it. If Ron hadn't gone into the dairy to pick up that extra box of Cozy Cow pens, he'd be alive today."

Bill winced. "Talk about bad luck! Are you sure that Max was killed because of a loan he made?"

"I'm not sure of anything, but it makes the most sense. The safe in the old dairy was open, but there's no way we can tell if anything is missing. I doubt that even Betty knows what was inside."

"She doesn't." Bill looked smug. "I called her this morning to ask. She told me that Max was the only one with the combination and she'd never even seen him open it. They kept all the cash from the dairy in the new safe that's in her office."

"How's Betty holding up?"

"She'll be all right. She's usually off on the weekends, but she said she's going in anyway, that someone needs to be there to answer the employees' questions and handle the phones. You got to hand it to her, Hannah. Betty was really upset when I told her about Max, but she's going to put her personal grief aside and keep on handling things just the way Max would have wanted her to, even if it means working overtime."

Hannah couldn't hide her grin. There was no way that Betty would miss this weekend at the dairy, and it wasn't for any altruistic reasons. Betty was happiest when she could hear all the gossip firsthand, and the phones would be ringing off the hook. "Did she tell you anything else?"

"She gave me the name of Max's lawyer and I checked with him to see who'd inherit. That's another good motive, you know."

"You're right, Bill. I didn't even think of that. What did the lawyer say?"

"Max left everything to his nephew in Idaho. The lawyer is going to contact him today and get his instructions."

"How about those footprints on the carpet? Were you able to tell anything about the killer from them?"

"Not really. They photographed them as part of the crime scene, but there weren't any clear impressions."

"How about the W in Max's appointment book? Do you have any leads on that?"

Bill shook his head and held out his mug for a refill. "I went through all the files, but there weren't any W names.

And we don't know if the W is a last name, a first name, or a nickname. Once we get a suspect, we can use it as part of the circumstantial evidence, but it's pretty hard to narrow down now."

The phone rang and Hannah reached out to answer it. "The Cookie Jar. This is Hannah."

"Hannah. I'm glad I caught you. This is Norman."

"Hi, Norman." Hannah frowned slightly. She didn't want to get involved in another lengthy phone conversation when this might be her only chance to talk to Bill all day. "What's up?"

"I developed the film of the party. I can bring in the prints at noon if you'll be there."

"I work here. Where else would I be?" The moment the words had left her mouth, Hannah realized that she'd been too abrupt. Norman was only trying to be nice. And if Norman came in at noon, she'd be able to give him his mother's loan papers. "Sorry, Norman. I'm really in a rush here. I'll see you at noon and I'll save a couple of my best cookies for you."

When Hannah hung up, she noticed that Bill was grinning. "What?"

"Did Norman just ask you out on another date?"

"No, he just wants to show me the pictures from the party." Hannah decided to change the subject fast. Bill's expression was a lot like her mother's when she played matchmaker. "Norman's just a friend, so get that idea right out of your head. Tell me more about this new detective from Minneapolis. I don't even know his name."

"Mike Kingston. I talked to his former partner and he says that Mike's a great cop and a really nice guy."

"You haven't met him yet?"

Bill shook his head. "No, but I saw his picture in the personnel file. He looks like a nice guy. I told you about his wife, didn't I?"

"You said she died and that's why he wanted to move here."

"Well, I found out more. She was a nurse and she was shot on her way home from Hennepin County General. Two rival gangs mixed it up and she got caught in the crossfire. But that's not the worst of it. She was four months pregnant with their first baby."

"That's awful!" Hannah shivered. "Did they catch the shooter?"

"Of course they did. They had the whole squad working on it. But the first time they tried him, he got off on a technicality. Somebody messed up with a search warrant, and the judge threw the case out of court."

"They tried him a second time?" Hannah didn't understand what Bill was saying. Wasn't that double jeopardy?

"They nailed him on a different murder. Mike and his partner worked the case themselves. They made sure that everything was done by the book and they got a conviction. The guy's doing a life sentence with no parole."

"That's good. But I bet this Mike Kingston is going to be a real stickler for police procedure."

"Sounds like it. He's going to be my new supervisor and I'm really going to have to watch it around him. Andrea's going to help me go over all my reports tonight to make sure they're perfect."

"I'll help, too, if you need me," Hannah offered quickly. "When does he start?"

"First thing Monday morning. He already rented an apartment and he drove his U-Haul down early this morning. I'm off tomorrow, and I'm going to help him move in."

Hannah couldn't resist teasing him a little. "You figure that hauling boxes and lifting a few brewskis together will help your working relationship?"

"It can't hurt. When we're through, we're going to come back to my place for dinner."

"Andrea is *cooking*?" Hannah's eyebrows shot up. Her sister was the only person she knew who couldn't even make decent instant coffee.

"No way!" Bill chuckled. "We're sending out for pizzas. Why don't you drive out and join us? You don't have anything else going for tomorrow night, do you?"

"Well, I was planning to . . ." Hannah's mind spun into overdrive, searching for an excuse.

"Come on, Hannah. Maybe you can get some insights into his character and pass them along to me."

Bill put on the look that Hannah had never been able to resist—the one she privately called begging basset hound. She gave a long sigh and then she caved in. "Okay. I'll bring dessert."

"Thanks, Hannah." Bill looked properly grateful. "Just make sure you don't mention the case. I don't want Mike to know that I recruited a civilian to help me."

"Don't worry. I won't say anything."

Bill headed toward the door. He was about to open it when he turned to grin at her. "I forgot to tell you that Delores is coming out tomorrow night. She wants to meet Mike."

Hannah's eyes narrowed as the door closed behind Bill. Things were beginning to add up. There was the remark Delores had made about how Hannah wouldn't be able to attract any man except a homicide detective if she kept on finding bodies. There was the way that Bill had told her all about Mike's background, painting him as a man with a deep sorrow that was bound to tug at any woman's heartstrings. Added to all that was the way that Bill had practically begged her to join them for pizza so that she could pass along any useful insights into Mike's character. Right. Sure.

Hannah sighed deeply and marched over to turn the "Closed" sign to "Open." Bill had set her up and he'd done it like a pro. There was only one conclusion that she could draw. Bill had been taking a crash course in matchmaking from his wife and his mother-in-law.

Chapter
Twenty-Two

Two minutes after she'd flipped the sign to "Open," Hannah's regulars began to come in. She chatted, poured coffee, and fetched cookies for two solid hours without a break. The news had leaked out and everyone she served wanted to know what she knew about Max's murder and how it related to Ron's.

"Do you think it's the same killer, Hannah?" Bertie Straub looked anxious as she munched a Molasses Crackle. She'd walked down from the Cut 'n Curl to get the latest news for her blue-haired customers, who were gossiping under the gleaming metal heads of the dryers.

"It's got to be. How could we have two killers in a town the size of Lake Eden?"

"Did *you* discover Max's body?" Bertie lowered her voice and glanced around to make sure no one was listening. "You can tell me, Hannah. I promise I won't repeat it to a soul."

Hannah had all she could do to keep a solemn expression. Telling Bertie would be tantamount to calling KCOW's talk line and broadcasting it over the radio waves. "I can't say yes or no, Bertie. All the facts are a part of the ongoing investigation."

"You did! I can tell by the look on your face!" Bertie gave a theatrical shiver and Hannah wondered if she'd joined The Lake Eden Players. "Was it terrible, Hannah?"

"It's always terrible when someone loses his life." Hannah parroted another polite phrase, the same one she'd used countless times this morning.

"They'll catch him soon, won't they? I swear I haven't slept a wink since I heard about Ron. To think that there's a killer out there among us!"

"I'm sure they will, Bertie. Bill's on the case and he's a very good detective."

Hannah was saved further questioning by the arrival of Lisa, bearing more cookies on a tray. Lisa took one look at her employer's frustrated expression and winked. "Your mother's on the phone, Hannah, and she says it's urgent. Why don't you catch the phone in back? It's quieter there. And take some coffee with you."

"I've got to run, Bertie." Hannah shot Lisa a thankful look, filled her mug with coffee, and headed off through the swinging door. She'd answered so many questions, her head was spinning, and it was only eleven in the morning.

She was about to sit down on a stool at the work island when the phone rang. Hannah grabbed it up before she could think better of it, and she heard her mother's excited voice.

"Hannah? Are you there?"

"Yes, Mother." Hannah took a slug of her coffee. "You must be psychic."

"What, dear?"

"Never mind. What can I do for you?"

"Have you seen the pictures Carrie took at the Woodleys' party yet?"

"Not yet." Hannah glanced up at the clock. "Norman said he'd bring them over at noon."

"Well, you're in for a pleasant surprise. There's one of you that's very nice. You don't look like yourself at all. Norman promised to make me an eight by ten to put in a frame."

Hannah had all she could do not to laugh. She looked nice? Not like herself at all? Leave it to a girl's mother to destroy her confidence.

"I've got to rush, dear. I'm just on my way out, but I wanted to call you first."

"Thanks, Mother. I'll talk to you later." Hannah groaned as she hung up the phone. Maybe she should accept Lisa's advice and take the rest of the day off. She'd already heard all there was to hear from her customers. She'd stick around to see that "nice" picture of her and then she'd go home and concentrate on the important things. If she really worked hard, she might be able to solve Bill's murder case before Mike Kingston came on board.

"What do you think, Hannah?" Norman watched her as she paged through the prints he'd brought. "That one on top is your mother's favorite."

Hannah sighed, staring down at the print. Her eyes were half-closed, her smile was crooked, and her hair stuck up over her left ear. "It's not exactly the best picture of me I've ever seen."

"I know," Norman sympathized. "There's a much better one of you, but my mother managed to cut off your left arm."

"Let me see." Andrea reached for the print. She'd come in, about five minutes ago, with Tracey.

Hannah watched while Andrea studied the print. She could tell, by the little line of concentration between her sister's eyes, that Andrea was trying to think of something nice to say. It must have been a struggle because it took Andrea at least thirty seconds to react. "You look a little thinner than you usually do. And your dress looks beautiful."

"I think Aunt Hannah looks pretty." Tracey smiled up at Hannah. "Maybe not as pretty as right now, but still pretty."

"Diplomatic Corps." Hannah winked at Andrea. "Tracey shows real promise."

Andrea laughed and held out her hand. "Let's see the rest."

Hannah glanced down at the next picture. It was one of Andrea and Bill, and they both looked fabulous in their formal clothing. Andrea was amazingly photogenic, while pictures of Hannah always reminded her of the "before" photos in makeup ads.

They went through the prints one by one, Hannah handing them to Andrea after she'd seen them. Thankfully, her customers were settled with their coffee and their cookies and no one rushed up to the counter to interrupt them. Hannah came to the one that Norman had mentioned and she *did* look better. She was sitting on the couch with Norman standing behind her, and it was just a pity that her left arm was out of the frame. Norman's mother had managed to center the picture so badly that almost half of the photo was taken up by the end table next to the couch.

Hannah was about to hand it to Andrea when she noticed a stack of books and papers on the table. There was a white folder on top of the stack and it had red lettering. She held it closer, squinted a little, and read the words: "Compacts Unlimited." One of the Woodleys had rented the kind of car that Mr. Harris had seen pulling out of the Cozy Cow driveway on the morning of the murders!

"What's the matter, Hannah?" Andrea caught the shocked expression that must have flitted across her face.

"Nothing, but I really like this one." Hannah turned to Norman and asked, "Can I keep it?"

"Sure. But why do you want *that* one?"

Hannah thought fast. She couldn't go wrong appealing to Norman's vanity. "It's a very good picture of you."

"It is?" Norman leaned over to examine the print. "I don't think so."

"But I do. I'd really like to have it, Norman."

Norman took the photo and examined it with a critical eye. "Let me reprint it for you. I can do some tricks with the negative in my darkroom."

"No, it's just fine." Hannah snatched the photo out of his hands. "I like it just the way it is."

Andrea stared at her. "You want to keep the one with your arm cut off?"

"If it was good enough for Venus, it's good enough for me." Hannah shot her sister a warning look.

"I could center it differently, cut off that table, and enlarge it to a head shot of the two of us," Norman suggested. "If I can do that, would you like it?"

"Of course I would. But I want to keep this one anyway."

Norman just shrugged and turned to Andrea. "How about you? Would you like copies of anything?"

"I'd love to have these." Andrea handed him two prints.

The bell over the door tinkled and Sheriff Grant walked in, followed by the most intimidating hunk of man that Hannah had ever laid eyes on. He was tall, well over six feet, and he had reddish blond hair, piercing blue eyes, and a mustache. He looked as fit as an athlete and only the deep lines in his face kept him from being classically handsome. There was a buzz of conversation from the customers at the tables and Hannah could understand why. He was the best-looking man to hit Lake Eden in a month of Sundays.

"It's him!" Andrea nudged her. "That's Mike Kingston."

"I know." Hannah grinned. Her sister had stated the obvious. Mike Kingston was with Sheriff Grant. Who else could he be?

"Hannah." Sheriff Grant strode over to the counter. "This is Mike Kingston. He'll be joining the department on Monday."

Hannah swallowed hard. She'd never been uncomfortable around men before, but Mike Kingston was an exception. The moment she'd seen him, her pulse had quickened and she found she couldn't meet his eyes. She took a deep breath, willed her voice to be steady, and said, "I'm glad to meet you Deputy Kingston."

"Mike."

His voice was deep and warm, and it matched his size. Hannah felt a purely physical reaction she hadn't experienced since her two-timing professor had invited her to his apartment. She turned quickly to perform the introductions, praying that no one would guess what effect just being in the same room with Mike Kingston was having on her. "This is my sister, Andrea Todd, and here's my niece, Tracey. And this is Norman Rhodes. He just took over his father's dental practice in town. I know you're in a hurry, so I'll just zip in back and get those cookies for you."

As Mike Kingston turned to shake hands with Andrea and Norman, Hannah made her escape to the bakery. Once she was safely behind the swinging door, she ducked into the bathroom and splashed some cold water on her face. If just meeting Mike Kingston was this much of a jolt, how was she going to handle their pizza dinner tomorrow night when she'd actually have to talk to him?

Never one to run away from a problem, Hannah decided that there was no time like the present to confront it. Mike Kingston would think that she was crazy if she ducked into a different room every time he came into The Cookie Jar. She marched out of the bathroom, picked up the box of the Black and Whites for the open house, and pushed back through the swinging door to the front of her shop.

Mike Kingston turned to smile at her and Hannah's breath caught in her throat. She hoped she wasn't staring at him like a teenage groupie who'd come face to face with her favorite rock star.

"It's really nice of you to bake these cookies for us, Hannah. Sheriff Grant said that you do it every year."

"I do." Hannah was relieved. He didn't seem to have noticed how flustered she was and that was good. "I cater your summer picnic, too. It's a bring-your-own-steak barbecue out at Eden Lake and I provide lemonade and cookies."

"That sounds good. There's nothing like a barbecue out at the lake."

"We'd better get going, Mike."

Sheriff Grant turned to his newest protégé, and Hannah could see the admiration in his eyes. He had to look up. Mike Kingston was at least six three, and Sheriff Grant was a good four inches short of the six-foot mark. The newest member of the Winnetka County Sheriff's Department made Hannah feel petite, and she'd never felt petite before in her life.

"See you later, Hannah."

Mike Kingston gave her a wave and Hannah smiled. He seemed perfectly nice. She had nothing against him personally. But she was prepared to despise him if Bill didn't get his promotion.

"Nice to meet you, Norman." Mike nodded to Norman and then he turned to Andrea. "I'm looking forward to working with your husband, Andrea."

"That's my daddy," Tracey piped up.

"I know." Mike Kingston leaned down and whispered something in Tracey's ear.

As Hannah watched, her niece's eyes widened and then she gave a delighted giggle. "Really?"

"I promise." Mike nodded. "But it's a secret until tomorrow night. I'll bring it then."

The minute the door had closed behind them, Andrea turned to Tracey. "What did he say?"

"I can't tell you." Tracey was all smiles. "You heard him say it was a secret. But you'll find out tomorrow night when we have the pizza."

Andrea exchanged a glance with Hannah. She seemed pleased that her daughter had gotten along so well with Bill's new supervisor. "I've got to run, Hannah. I'm taking a load of things out to Luanne, and Tracey's going to help me. And then we're going out to the open house at the sheriff's station."

"I've got to leave, too. I have a patient in twenty minutes." Norman reached into his pocket, pulled out a stack of business cards, and handed them to Hannah. "These are for you."

Hannah took the cards and began to smile. They were perfect, and Norman had even printed little cookies around the border. "Thanks, Norman. They're wonderful."

"I can print out more if you need them."

"Let's hope I do. Hold on just a second." Hannah opened the cash register and drew out the manila envelope with his mother's loan papers inside. "Here, Norman. This is for you."

"For me?" Norman looked puzzled as she handed it to him.

"It's something I came across the other night. Just open it when you get back to the office. There's a note inside explaining everything."

Hannah breathed a deep sigh of relief as they all left together. She had work to do and it didn't have anything to do with baking, selling, or serving cookies. She grabbed the print she'd taken from Norman and headed off to the back room to tell Lisa that she was going to take her up on her offer to stay until closing. She had people to see, calls to make, and if she got lucky, she might be able to solve Bill's double-homicide case before Monday morning.

Chapter
Twenty-Three

Hannah pushed open her condo door and caught a flash of orange out of the corner of her eye. Moishe had just jumped down from his perch on the top of the television set and he looked about as guilty as a cat could look. She glanced at the screen and realized that a nature program was on—one that was running footage of a flock of flamingos flapping their bright pink wings.

"Those birds are four times your size, Moishe." Hannah gave him a scratch under the chin to let him know that she wasn't angry. When she'd unlocked the door, her fierce feline hunter had been in the process of hanging over the top of the set to bat at the birds with his paw.

Once she'd switched off the enticing flamingos and hung up her jacket, Hannah walked out to the kitchen to fill Moishe's food bowl. Of course it was empty. It was always empty. Moishe's favorite activities when she was gone were eating and napping.

There were three messages on her answering machine. The first was from her downstairs neighbor, Sue Plotnik, asking if she could serve cookies at her Mommy and Me class next week. Hannah penciled it in on her kitchen calendar; she'd transfer it to the one at The Cookie Jar when she went in on Monday. Then she listened to her second message. It was from a man who identified himself as Robert Collins from Hideaway Resorts, who invited her to a complimentary dinner for prospective timeshare investors at a hotel in Minneapolis. Hannah didn't bother to write down his toll-free number.

The third message made Hannah perk up her ears. It was from Bill and he told her that he just wanted to keep her up to speed. The manager from Compacts Unlimited had contacted him this morning. Since she still didn't have the printout, she'd called all their other car lots and one of them had handled a rental for a customer with a Lake Eden address. Boyd Watson had rented a black compact from their St. Paul lot on Tuesday.

Naturally, Bill had checked it out. He'd called the principal, Mr. Purvis, and he'd found out that Coach Watson had been attending a statewide coaching clinic at the time. Since Boyd hadn't come back to town until noon on Wednesday, that ruled him out as a possible suspect.

Hannah's forehead furrowed as she poured herself a glass of Diet Coke and carried it into the living room. When Maryann had said that she'd driven to Minneapolis to go shopping with Boyd, she'd assumed that Maryann had picked him up and they'd gone to the Mall of America together. But Maryann had said that she'd *met* her brother at the mall. Boyd must have had his rental car by then. But why would Coach Watson go to the trouble and expense of renting a car for less than twenty-four hours when his sister was coming to meet him? It just didn't make sense.

She sighed and reached out to pet Moishe, who'd forsaken his food dish for the soft cushion of the couch and her company. Had Coach Watson been behind the wheel of the black compact that Mr. Harris had seen roaring out of the Cozy Cow driveway? The timetable was tight, but it was possible that Boyd had left before dawn, while Maryann and his mother were still asleep, and driven to Lake Eden. His last name began with a W, and he could have been the one to meet Max. If Maryann and her mother had slept until nine, Boyd might have had time to shoot both Max and Ron and get back before they woke up. But what possible motive could Coach Watson have for killing Max?

Hannah thought back to everything that she'd learned about the Watsons. Danielle's ring had cost a thousand dollars and the dress she'd worn to the Woodleys' party had sold for over five hundred. Boyd and Danielle lived in a very expensive house, and Danielle didn't work. Boyd drove a new Jeep Grand Cherokee, and Danielle had a new Lincoln. How could Coach Watson afford to maintain their expensive lifestyle on a teacher's salary?

"Boyd got a personal loan from Max!" Hannah exclaimed, causing Moishe to rear back and stare at her. "Sorry, Moishe. I didn't mean to shout, but it's the only thing that makes sense. There weren't any loan papers for him, but the safe was open and he would have taken them right after he shot Max. And then he killed Ron because Ron had seen him with Max!"

Moishe turned to give her a long, level look and then he hopped off the couch and padded into the kitchen to his food bowl. He yowled once, calling for her to get out the kitty crunchies, and Hannah went off to comply. Moishe was the most intelligent cat she'd ever met. He was waiting for her to fill up his food bowl because he knew that she had to leave again.

Danielle opened the door several inches, but no wider. "Hi, Hannah. I . . . uh . . . I'm busy right now. Could you come back a little later?"

"No." Hannah wedged her foot into the crack. "It's important, Danielle. Is Boyd home?"

"No, he's not. He's got . . . football practice . . . at the school."

"Good. That'll give us some time alone. We have to talk, Danielle."

"But I . . . I have to put on some makeup. I was just . . . uh . . . taking a nap and . . ." Danielle's voice trailed off and she gave a little sob. "Please, Hannah. I don't want you to see me like this."

Hannah made one of her instant decisions. Right or wrong, she was coming in. Never one to dither once she'd made up her mind, she simply pushed Danielle back and stepped inside.

"Oh, Hannah!" Danielle's hands flew up to her face, but not before Hannah had spotted her black eye and the red welts in the shape of a handprint across her left cheek.

"Good God, Danielle!" Hannah reached out to shut the door. "What happened to you?"

"I . . . uh . . . I—"

"Never mind," Hannah interrupted what was bound to be some sort of hastily fabricated story. "Come on. Let's get some ice on your face."

"I don't have any."

"I'll find something." Hannah took her arm and led her into the kitchen. "Are you sure he's not coming back?"

Danielle managed to look even more embarrassed. "Who? The . . . intruder?"

"Your husband." Hannah opened the freezer and rummaged around for something that would work as an ice pack. "You don't have to pretend with me, Danielle. I know he beat you up."

"How do you know that?"

One of Danielle's eyes opened wide in surprise, but the other was almost swollen shut. Hannah drew out a package of frozen peas, whacked it against the counter to loosen the contents, and handed it to her, along with the kitchen towel that was draped over the handle of the stove. "Sit down at the table. Wrap the peas in the towel and hold it up to your eye. I'll get another one for your cheek."

"Thank you, Hannah." Danielle sank down in a chair. "This is all my fault. I forgot to fill up the ice trays."

Hannah pulled out another package of frozen peas and wrapped it in a clean towel from the drawer. She held it up to Danielle's cheek and sighed deeply. "It's not your fault. Hold that with your other hand and tell me where you keep the coffee."

"I don't have any. I ran out and I forgot to buy more. That's why Boyd got so mad at me."

Hannah bristled. There had been a couple of mornings when she thought she might kill for a cup of coffee, but she hadn't really meant it literally. "How about tea?"

"I've got some instant. It's in the cupboard over the stove. And there's a hot water spigot on our Sparklettes dispenser."

Hannah found two cups, spooned in instant tea and a generous helping of sugar, and filled them with steaming water from the dispenser. She carried one over to Danielle and set hers down on the other side of the table. Hannah didn't like tea, but that didn't matter. Sharing tea gave them a common bond. "Let me look at your cheek."

"It feels better." Danielle removed the towel and managed a small smile. "I never even thought about using frozen peas before. I guess it's true when they say that vegetables are good for you."

Danielle's sad attempt at humor made Hannah see red. Danielle had said she'd never thought about using frozen peas *before*. This obviously wasn't the first time that Coach Watson had battered his wife. Hannah thought about trying to convince Danielle to press charges, or offering her advice about how she could get out of her abusive situation, but that could wait until later. Right now she had to find out if Boyd Watson was a murderer, as well as a wife beater.

"It looks a lot better," Hannah assured her. "Have some tea and then hold it there for another couple of minutes."

Danielle nodded and took a sip of her tea. "You put a lot of sugar in."

"Sugar's good for shock." Hannah retrieved the bag of Black and White cookies she'd brought in from her truck. "Have a cookie. They're chocolate."

Danielle reached for a cookie and nibbled at it. "These are good, Hannah."

"Thanks. Do you have a headache?"

"It's not a concussion, Hannah. I know the symptoms."

I'll bet you do! Hannah thought. If she remembered correctly, Danielle had been in the hospital several times in the past—once for a broken leg and other times for less serious injuries. She'd always claimed that she'd been clumsy and fallen on the ice, or broken something skiing, or been in a boat accident while she was fishing with her husband. Hannah remembered her sister's comment about Danielle's clothes and how they always covered her completely. That should have set off alarm bells in Hannah's mind, especially since Luanne had already told her that Danielle used theatrical makeup for facial blemishes. The only thing that erupted on Danielle Watson's face was her husband's bad temper!

Danielle took another sip of her tea and then held the improvised ice pack back up to her cheek. "You won't tell anyone about this, will you, Hannah?"

"You don't have to worry about that," Hannah promised, evading a direct answer. She certainly wouldn't gossip about it, and that was really what Danielle had meant. "If you ever want to talk to anyone about it, I'm here. All you have to do is call me or jump in the car and come over. I've got a guest room and you can use it anytime you need to get away."

"Thank you, Hannah."

There would never be a better opportunity and Hannah seized it. "There's something else, Danielle. If you want to press charges, I'll help you."

"No, I could never do *that*!"

It was the answer that Hannah had expected. She knew that most battered women mistakenly protected their abusers, at least until the problem got so severe that someone else noticed. Unless Danielle pressed charges, or someone actually saw Coach Watson hitting Danielle, there was nothing that the authorities could do. Hannah decided she'd give it one more try and then move on. "If you press charges, Boyd will get some help."

"What kind of help?"

"Counseling, anger-management workshops, that sort of thing." Hannah hoped the disdain she felt didn't show in her voice or on her face. To her way of thinking, mandatory sessions with a counselor were merely a slap on the wrist for chronic abusers. Anyone who caused the physical damage that Coach Watson had meted out to Danielle should have to suffer the full consequences of the law.

"Boyd's already getting counseling."

"He is?" Hannah wanted to make a crack about what a poor counselor Boyd must have, but she didn't.

"It's really a lot better now. Boyd's only hit me once since school started."

"Counting today?" Hannah couldn't resist asking.

"No, but he's under a lot of pressure with his football team. They've lost three straight."

So what does Boyd say to his team? Hannah wondered. *If you boys don't make those touchdowns, I'm going to go home and smack my wife?*

"He's always sorry, after. Really, he is. He actually broke down in tears when he saw what he did to my face. And then he went straight to the phone to put in an emergency call to his counselor. That's where he is now. I didn't want to tell you before, so I made up that excuse about football practice. Boyd drove all the way down to St. Paul because he felt so guilty."

Hannah's ears perked up. Boyd had rented the Compacts

Unlimited car in St. Paul. "Does Boyd see a counselor in St. Paul?"

"He goes to The Holland Center," Danielle pronounced the name with reverence. She looked as proud as anyone could with one black eye covered by a package of frozen peas. "It's the best in the state and he sees Dr. Frederick Holland, the head counselor and founder. You've probably seen his name in the papers. He's done some wonderful work with serial rapists."

Nothing Hannah wanted to say seemed appropriate but it didn't seem to matter. The dam had broken and Danielle wanted to talk.

"We almost got a divorce last spring. Boyd just couldn't seem to control himself, and Dr. Holland thought we'd have to split up. But Boyd said he'd just try harder, and it's worked."

Hannah glanced at Danielle's face again. If this was trying harder, she was glad she hadn't seen the results of Boyd's former abuses. Danielle was going to have a shiner the size of the Grand Canyon. "Isn't that kind of therapy expensive?"

"Yes, but Boyd's medical insurance covers eighty percent. It's the one through the teachers' union and they're very good about that. Dr. Holland bills it as occupation-related stress counseling. It would be too embarrassing for Boyd otherwise."

"I guess it would." Hannah did her best to keep the sarcasm out of her voice. God forbid that the wife beater should be embarrassed!

"When you rang the doorbell, you said you wanted to talk to me. Is it about Ron's murder again? Or what happened to Max Turner?"

Hannah assumed that Danielle wanted to change the subject, and that was fine with her. As a matter of fact, it was perfect. She needed to know more about Boyd's rental car. "I'm just clearing up some loose ends. Has Boyd rented a car lately?"

"Yes." Danielle looked surprised. "How did *you* know about that?"

Hannah thought fast. "You told me that you drove out to the casino in Boyd's Jeep Cherokee and I just assumed that he rented a car for the trip."

"But that's not exactly what happened, Hannah. Boyd rode to Minneapolis with another coach, but when he decided to stay over to see Dr. Holland, he rented a compact for a day. He had an appointment on Wednesday morning and he couldn't ask Maryann to drive him. Boyd doesn't want her to know anything about his problem."

"Of course not." Hannah gave the appropriate response.

"It was an early appointment, seven in the morning," Danielle went on. "That was the only time Dr. Holland could work him into his schedule. Boyd had to leave his mother's house at six to get there on time."

"Didn't Maryann notice that he was gone when she got up?"

"Yes, but he told her that he was going to get up early and go out for doughnuts. His mother just loves doughnuts. Boyd brought them back with him after he saw Dr. Holland."

Boyd's appointment could be verified with a phone call and Hannah decided she'd do it the minute that she got home. "Did Boyd ever borrow money from Max Turner?"

"From Max?" Danielle frowned. "I don't think so. Why?"

"I'm going to tell you something, but you have to promise not to mention it, Danielle. Not even to Boyd."

"All right," Danielle agreed, but she looked a bit uneasy. "What is it?"

"Max lent money to quite a few people in Lake Eden and one of those loans might have something to do with his death. Why did you say you didn't think Boyd had borrowed from him?"

"Because Boyd doesn't need to borrow money when he's got mine. You must know what teachers are paid, Hannah. We could never afford to live on Boyd's salary alone. We bought the cars and the house and practically everything we have with my money."

Hannah's eyebrows shot ceilingward. This was a surprise development. "What money is that?"

"The money I inherited from my uncle. I was always his favorite and he left it to me. He put it in a trust fund and I get a lump sum every year."

"And that's why you can afford all these luxuries?"

"That's right. When I get my lump sum in January, I give Boyd half and my mother invests the rest for me. We've done really well on the stock market, and Dr. Holland thinks that's part of Boyd's problem. It's very difficult for a strong male like Boyd to be married to a woman who makes a lot more money than he does."

"I suppose it is." Hannah settled for a safe comment.

"That's the reason I keep my inheritance a secret," Danielle confided. "Dr. Holland says that Boyd's ego is too fragile and he'd be tempted to strike out even more if his friends knew. You won't mention it, will you?"

"Absolutely not," Hannah agreed quickly. She could imagine the damage that Boyd would inflict on his wife if the word got out that Danielle was supporting them. He might even borrow a page from the storybook and kill the goose that laid the golden egg.

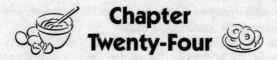

Chapter
Twenty-Four

"I know it's confusing," Hannah tried to explain as she walked back into her condo. It was clear by his startled expression that Moishe didn't know what to make of her comings and goings today. "I've come back to make a few phone calls. What do you say I keep you busy with a dish of ice cream?"

Moishe rubbed against her ankles as Hannah pulled a carton of French vanilla out of the freezer and scooped some into a dessert dish. She carried it out to the living room, set it down on the coffee table, and patted the surface. Moishe didn't need a second invitation. He approached the dish, sniffed at the mound of icy white, and then tasted it with the tip of his tongue. The cold must have surprised him because he drew back to stare at it, but that didn't stop him from going back for a second lick.

While Moishe was busy exploring this intriguing new foodstuff, Hannah flopped down on the couch and reached for the phone. She had to call Dr. Holland to confirm that Boyd Watson had kept his appointment on Wednesday morning.

Five minutes later, Hannah had her answer. She'd pretended to be a medical claims adjuster and she'd asked Dr. Holland's receptionist to verify the time of the appointment. The receptionist had told her that Mr. Watson had seen Dr. Holland at seven in the morning and that his appointment had lasted the usual fifty minutes.

"I don't know whether I should be relieved, or disappointed," Hannah confided to her feline roommate. Boyd Watson wasn't the killer and he was free to batter Danielle whenever he felt the urge.

But there was still that photo of the rental car folder in the snapshot that Norman's mother had taken. And Woodley also started with a W. Hannah went to the kitchen to fetch herself another Diet Coke and thought about the rental car that someone in the Woodley household had used. She didn't think that either Judith or Del would have rented a nondescript black compact, not when they had a whole garage full of luxury vehicles to choose from. But there was Benton and his name wouldn't have raised any red flags for the manager at Compacts Unlimited because his driver's license would still show his East Coast residence. Benton could have rented a compact car to drive from the airport to Lake Eden. He'd told Andrea and Bill that he'd taken the shuttle, but that didn't necessarily mean it was true.

Hannah picked up the phone and got the number for the shuttle service at the Minneapolis airport. There was only one shuttle that ran to Lake Eden and that made her job a little easier. She punched out the number of their airport office and rehearsed what she would say to get the information she needed. She'd picked up a new skill by listening to Andrea on the phone with the hotel clerk at the Buttermakers' Convention. It was possible to get all sorts of information if the person on the other end of the line really wanted to help you.

"On-Time Shuttle Service. This is Tammi speaking."

Hannah winced at the insipidly cheerful voice. Why did companies always hire girls who sounded as if they should be working at Disneyland? "Hi, Tammi. I really need your help. My boss, Mr. Woodley, took the shuttle to Lake Eden on Wednesday afternoon and he can't find his briefcase. He asked me to try to locate it and I'm wondering if your driver happened to find it on the shuttle bus?"

"I don't think so. Our drivers check for lost items after every run and there's no briefcase in our lost-and-found bin."

"Uh-oh," Hannah groaned, hoping that she sounded dismayed. "Is it possible that someone at your office mailed it to him and it just hasn't gotten here yet?"

"We don't usually do that, but a couple of our drivers are here right now and I can ask. Would that have been the two o'clock, four o'clock, or six o'clock shuttle?"

That stumped Hannah completely, but she recovered quickly. "I should have asked Mr. Woodley, but he just left and I didn't think of it. Is there some way that you could check for me?"

"No problem. The passenger's name was Woodley?"

"That's right," Hannah said, and spelled it out for her. "Benton Woodley."

"I'll have to put you on hold. Just a moment please." There was a brief silence and then music spewed out from the little holes on the receiver. It sounded like the chorus from "It's a Small World," and Hannah was in the process of wondering whether Tammi had chosen the song when her cheerful voice came back on the line. "Mr. Benton Woodley was our passenger on the two o'clock shuttle. I checked with the driver, but he said he didn't find anything except a pen and a monogrammed handkerchief. Maybe you should check with the airlines?"

"Good idea. Thanks, Tammi. I really appreciate your help." Hannah hung up the phone and thought about what she'd learned. Moishe jumped up on her lap and started to lick her arm with his raspy tongue. He seemed to sense that she was upset and he was doing his best to comfort her. Hannah stroked him absently and thought about the times of the murders. The fact that Benton had taken the two o'clock shuttle didn't rule him out as the killer. He could have flown in the night before, rented a car from Compacts Unlimited, and made a round-trip to Lake Eden to kill Max and Ron. If he'd returned the car to the airport location, he could have walked to the shuttle station and boarded the two o'clock bus to give himself an alibi. But why would Benton want to kill Max Turner? He hadn't visited Lake Eden in years, and as far as Hannah knew, he'd never spoken more than a few words to Max.

Her mind spinning, Hannah reached for the phone again, intending to call Compacts Unlimited to find out if Benton had rented a car. But perhaps she should leave that to Bill. He knew the manager and he could get the information much faster than she could. Hannah punched out Bill's number and reminded herself of the things she had to tell him. There was the photo of the rental folder and her suspicions about Benton. Bill didn't know anything about that. There was also Boyd Watson and she had to tell Bill that she'd eliminated him as a suspect. She wouldn't mention Danielle's painful secret right now. It would be better to wait until she had Bill's full attention. Perhaps they could think of some way to put the fear of God into The Gull's head coach.

"Bill? I've got some information that . . ." Hannah stopped short as she realized she was talking to a recorded message. Bill wasn't at his desk. When the beep sounded, she almost hung up in sheer frustration, but better sense prevailed. "Bill? It's Hannah. I eliminated Coach Watson as a suspect. He's got an alibi. But remember those pictures we took in Del Woodley's den? Norman brought them over on his lunch break and one of them showed a Compacts Unlimited rental folder. I figure that Benton must have rented it. Judith wouldn't be caught dead driving a compact and Del's got his fancy Mercedes. The W in Max's appointment book could stand for Woodley, but I don't have a motive. I'm going to nose around to see what else I can find out about the Woodleys."

Hannah sighed and hung up, picturing Bill in the sheriff station's lobby, eating dozens of the cookies she'd baked for the open house and mingling with the people who'd driven out to see their new cruisers. He was probably having the time of his life while she was sitting here agonizing over clues that didn't fit and suspects that disappeared like snowballs in the sun. She was supposed to be assisting Bill, not doing all of his legwork for him. Who was bucking for detective here, anyway?

Just then the phone rang, jolting Hannah out of her glum mood. She reached out to answer it, expecting Bill, but it was her mother.

"I'm so glad I caught you, Hannah. I have the most amazing news."

"Yes, Mother?" Hannah held the phone an inch from her ear. Her mother could deafen the person on the other end of the line when she was excited.

"I'm here at the mall with Carrie. She needed a new battery for her watch. You'll never guess what I just saw at the jeweler's! What do you think it was?"

Hannah made a face at Moishe. She was almost thirty and her mother still wanted her to play guessing games. "I'll never be able to guess, Mother. You'd better tell me."

"It was Del Woodley's ring!"

"His ring?" Hannah didn't understand what was so startling about that. Everyone she knew took rings to the jeweler's when they needed repair or resizing.

"It was for sale, Hannah. The jeweler had it displayed in a glass case and he wanted twenty thousand dollars for it."

"Twenty thousand dollars?" Hannah gasped.

"That's not unreasonable for a platinum setting and a diamond that size. Now why would Del Woodley's ring be up for sale?"

"I don't have the foggiest idea." Hannah took a moment to ponder the question, but it really didn't make any sense. "Are you sure it was Del Woodley's ring?"

"I'm positive. I admired it at their party last year and I noticed this tiny little scratch on the band. The ring I just saw at the jeweler's had the very same scratch. Do you want to know what I think?"

"Sure," Hannah agreed. It wouldn't do any good to say no. Delores would just tell her anyway.

"I think Del's in financial trouble. That's the only reason he'd part with that ring. He told me that he just adored it."

"You're right, Mother." Hannah began to smile. This opened up all sorts of intriguing possibilities. "Did you find out how long the ring has been there?"

"Of course I did. The jeweler said he'd had it for six months."

"Did he confirm that it belonged to Del?"

"No, dear. He said that whenever he accepts any expensive jewelry on consignment, he keeps the identity of the original owner confidential."

Hannah thought about that for a moment while her mother went on to describe every detail of her conversation with the jeweler. The Woodleys had spared no expense at their party, but that meant nothing. Judith was proud and she was the type to keep up appearances. If Del's business was in trouble, he could have borrowed money from Max. And if Max had called in his loan, as he'd done with Norman's parents and several other people in town, Del Woodley would have had the perfect motive to murder him.

"I'm sure I'm right, Hannah," her mother went on. "You know how good I am at noticing little details. We stopped in at the antique shop, too. Do you remember those lovely dessert dishes I gave you?"

"Yes, Mother." Hannah glanced over at the dessert dish she'd used for Moishe's ice cream.

"Be careful when you wash them. I only paid twenty dollars for the set at an auction, but they had two in the window of the antique store. They're selling for fifty dollars apiece now."

"Really?" Hannah was highly amused. She could imagine her mother's reaction if she mentioned that Moishe had just finished eating from a fifty-dollar dessert dish.

"I've got to run, Hannah. Carrie wants to shop for some new linens, and there's a line of people waiting to use this phone."

"I'm really glad you called, Mother," Hannah said. And this time she meant it.

There was a spring in Hannah's step as she walked up to the Plotniks door and rang the bell. Delores didn't know it, but she'd been a big help. Phil Plotnik was a night supervisor at DelRay and he might know if Del's business was in trouble.

The door opened and Sue Plotnik stood there, juggling a dishtowel and a crying baby. She looked surprised to see her upstairs neighbor, but she smiled. "Hi, Hannah. I hope Kevin didn't disturb you. He's got an ear infection and Phil's out getting his prescription refilled."

"I didn't even hear him," Hannah reassured her. "Did I come at a bad time?"

Sue laughed. "There isn't a good time, not with a new baby, but that doesn't matter. Come in and have a cup of coffee with me. I just made a fresh pot."

Hannah didn't really want to intrude, especially when it looked as if Sue had her hands full, but she really needed to talk to Phil. At least she could help while Sue got the coffee.

"I brought some cookies for you." Hannah walked in and placed the bag on the table. Then she held out her arms and smiled at Sue. "Let me hold the baby for you. I'll walk him around while you get the coffee."

Sue handed over the blanket-wrapped bundle with visible relief. "Thanks, Hannah. He's been crying all morning and I dropped his bottle of medicine. That's why Phil had to make a run to the drugstore. Did you get my message about catering next week at Mommy and Me?"

"Yes. Thanks for thinking of me, Sue. I've already written it on my calendar." Hannah jiggled the fussing baby a bit and then she started to pace the floor with him. Michelle had been a colicky baby, and Hannah was no stranger to crying infants. As the eldest sister, almost eleven at the time, Hannah had taken over when Delores had needed a break.

It didn't take long for the baby to quiet. Hannah paced rhythmically back and forth with a satisfied expression on her face. It was pretty obvious that she hadn't lost her touch.

Sue came in with two cups of coffee and a plate for the cookies. She set them down on the coffee table and then she stared at Kevin with openmouthed amazement. "How did you *do* that?"

"It's easy. You just have to keep your steps slow and a little bouncy. I used to pretend that I was an elephant in a circus parade. I'm going to put him down, Sue."

Sue watched while Hannah walked over to the cradle and tucked the baby inside. There was an anxious expression on her face, but it faded after several long seconds of silence. "You're a genius, Hannah."

"No, I'm not. I've just had plenty of practice, that's all. Michelle had at least four bouts of colic before her first birthday."

"You should be a mother, Hannah. All that talent going to—" Sue stopped in midthought and looked very uncomfortable. "I shouldn't have said that."

"That's okay. Just do me a favor and don't mention it to my mother. It'll give her new ammunition."

"She's still trying to fix you up with every man in town?" Sue gestured toward the couch and they both sat down.

"You could say that." Hannah took a sip of her coffee and decided to change the subject. "How's DelRay doing, Sue? That's really what I came down to ask you about."

"Everything's fine now. Phil said Del is even talking about branching out into the mail order business like Fingerhut did in St. Cloud. But it didn't look so good a couple of . . ." Sue's voice trailed off as she heard a key in the door. "Phil's coming. He can tell you all about it."

Phil opened the door, spotted Hannah, and gave her a grin. "Hi, Hannah."

"Hello, Phil."

"Hannah put Kevin to sleep for me." Sue gestured toward the crib. "She just walked like an elephant and it worked."

Phil gave his wife a glance that suggested she might be losing her marbles, but then he shrugged. "Whatever works. Is there more of that coffee?"

"Half a pot in the kitchen," Sue told him. "Get a cup and come join us, honey. Hannah came down to ask us about DelRay."

Phil poured a cup of coffee and came back to sit in the chair across from the couch. He tried a cookie, pronounced it the best he'd ever tasted, and then he asked, "What do you want to know about DelRay?"

"I just hoped there wouldn't be any big changes, now that Benton's come back," Hannah went into the opening of the speech she'd planned on her way down the stairs.

"I don't think Benton will last for long." Phil took another cookie and shrugged. "From what I hear, he was living it up on the East Coast and he just came home to make sure that the money wouldn't run out."

"Will it?" Hannah asked the obvious question.

"I don't think there's any danger of that. Sue's sister works in the accounting office and she told me that Del just landed a fat new contract on Thursday."

Hannah nodded, but it didn't really matter. Thursday was the day *after* Max had been killed. "How about before that? Was DelRay in trouble?"

"There was a problem about four years ago. It was right before Sue and I got married and I was already starting to look for a new job."

"Things were that bad at DelRay?"

Phil raised his eyebrows. "Bad? It was gruesome. We lost

five big contracts, and the front office cut the workforce in half. They did it on seniority and I'd only been there for a year. I was just lucky I survived the cut. The guy who was hired right after me got pink-slipped. But then Del got some new financing and ever since then we've been doing better."

"New financing?" Hannah's ears perked up. "You mean like a bank loan?"

Phil shook his head. "I don't know where the money came from, but it wasn't a bank loan. Sue's sister told me that the bank turned Del down. Something about being overextended."

"But there hasn't been a problem since that loan or whatever it was?" Hannah took another sip of her coffee and waited for Phil's answer.

"It wasn't so fine on Wednesday morning," Sue spoke up. "Tell her about *that,* Phil."

"Sue's right. I was a little worried when I came home from work on Wednesday morning."

"A *little* worried?" Sue laughed. "You were ready to start sending out resumes again."

"That's true. When I was leaving the plant, I saw the old man and he looked pretty grim."

"What time was that?" Hannah held her breath. The pieces were starting to fall in place.

"About six-fifteen, give or take a couple of minutes. I just got off shift and I was heading out to the parking lot when I saw him talking to the night shift supervisors."

Hannah was confused. "I thought *you* were a night shift supervisor."

"I am, but these guys are one level up from me. That's why I thought there might be trouble. The old man never comes in before nine, unless there's a real crisis."

Hannah spent another couple of minutes making conversation and then she said she had to go. As she climbed up the steps to her own unit, she tried to fit the new pieces of the puzzle into place. Del Woodley couldn't have killed Max, not if Phil had seen him at the plant. But it was certainly possible that Del had secured a loan from Max Turner four years ago. She had to check on that, and there was only one person who might know.

When she unlocked her door, no furry orange ball barreled across the room to meet her. Hannah glanced around anxiously. Where was Moishe? Then she saw him sitting on the back of the couch. The novelty of having her dash in and out had obviously worn off for him.

"Hi, Moishe." Hannah walked over to pet him anyway. "Go back to sleep. I just came home to make another phone call."

Moishe yawned and settled back down, and Hannah reached for the phone. Betty Jackson might know if Del Woodley had borrowed money from Max four years ago.

Betty's extension was busy and Hannah had to press the redial button a dozen times before she finally got through. When she said hello, Betty immediately started to tell her what was going on.

"It's been a madhouse out here!" Betty sounded even more harried than usual. "I can't get into Max's office. There's yellow tape blocking the doorway, and Bill warned me not to go in there. And everybody in town has been calling me to find out what's going to happen to the dairy."

"Do you know yet?"

"Yes. I just got off the phone with Max's nephew and he's planning to move here and take over the operation. He asked me to call an employee meeting and tell everyone on the payroll that he's not planning to make any changes. Isn't that wonderful?"

"It certainly is." Hannah did her best to sound enthusiastic. She was glad that the dairy was staying open, but she had a lot of other things on her mind. "I'm sorry to bother you, Betty, but I need to ask you a very important question. Do you know if Max ever had any business dealings with Del Woodley?"

"Just a minute and I'll get that invoice for you. Could you hold, please?"

There was a thunk as Betty set the receiver down on her desk, and Hannah heard her tell several people to leave her office because she had an important supplier on the line. A few seconds later, there was the sound of a door closing and then Hannah heard heavy footsteps as Betty returned to her desk.

"Sorry, Hannah. I didn't want to say anything while there were people in the office, but Max did have dealings with Del Woodley. I'm not supposed to know anything about it, but I just happened to pick up the extension while Max was talking to Del."

Hannah grinned. It sounded as if Betty spent most of her working hours listening in on conversations that she wasn't supposed to hear.

"Del called a few months ago," Betty continued. "It was about a personal loan. He was complaining about the high interest rates, and Max wasn't very nice to him."

"Really?" Hannah feigned surprise.

"As a matter of fact, he was very nasty. Max told Del that if he didn't like the interest rates, he could just come up with the money and pay off the loan."

"Did Del pay off the loan?"

"I don't know, Hannah. Del didn't call again and that's the last I ever heard about it."

"Thanks, Betty." Hannah hung up the phone and dropped her face in her hands. This was all very confusing. Perhaps she should take a run out to the dairy and look at the crime scene again. It was possible that Bill might have missed something that pertained to the loan that Del had taken out with Max.

"I'm leaving again, Moishe," Hannah announced as she stood up and felt around in her pocket to make sure she had her keys. But Moishe didn't rush to the food bowl as he usually did. He just opened his good eye and gave her what amounted to an extremely bored kitty shrug.

Chapter
Twenty-Five

Hannah zipped down Old Lake Road at seventy miles an hour, just about as fast as her Suburban would go. She had almost reached the intersection at Dairy Avenue when she began to reconsider her destination. It would be a waste of time to go over the crime scene. The killer had planned everything carefully, making a private appointment with Max and tricking him into opening the old safe in the original dairy. There was no way such an organized killer would have left any incriminating evidence behind.

So what should she do? Hannah took her foot off the gas pedal and let her Suburban slow to the legal limit. Perhaps she should run out to the sheriff's station to find Bill. She had more facts for him, information that she hadn't yet learned when she'd left her voice mail message. She could pull Bill aside and tell him everything. Between the two of them, they could figure out what to do next.

Hannah glanced in her rearview mirror and saw that the road was clear behind her. She slowed her truck to a crawl and did something she'd never done before in her life. She hung a U-turn right across the double yellow line and headed for the Winnetka County Sheriff's Station.

As she pushed the speedometer up to seventy again, Hannah thought about Del Woodley. He couldn't have killed Max. The laws of physics were absolute and he couldn't have been in two places at the same time. Even if Phil had been wrong by five minutes and Danielle's watch had been off by the same amount, it still wasn't possible to drive from DelRay Manufacturing, out on the interstate, to the Cozy Cow Dairy in that length of time.

But Benton could have killed Max. Hannah's hands tightened on the wheel as that thought occurred to her. Phil had said he'd come home because he was worried that the family money would run out. If Max had called in his loan and Del had told Benton about it, Benton could have decided to protect his inheritance by shooting Max and stealing the paperwork.

Hannah thought about Benton as she raced down the highway. He'd always enjoyed having money. From first grade on, Andrea had come home from school talking about Benton's new leather backpack, or the complete set of Disney movies that Benton's parents had bought for him, or the souvenirs that he'd brought back from his summer vacations. Benton had been the most popular boy in the class because he'd treated his classmates to the luxuries their parents couldn't afford. "Give them things and make them friends" had been his motto.

Benton's family wealth had been even more apparent in high school. Then Benton had dazzled the girls, Andrea included, by picking them up in his shiny new convertible and showering them with expensive gifts. The huge bottle of perfume that he'd given Andrea for Christmas had been just one example. Delores had priced it and she'd told Hannah that it had cost over two hundred dollars.

Hannah doubted that Benton's habits had changed in the years since he'd been gone. She was sure that he was still buying friendship with his money. What if all the cash that he used to impress people suddenly started to dry up? Would that be a strong enough motive to kill the person who'd threatened Benton's whole way of life?

There was a slow truck ahead and Hannah pulled out to whiz past him. Yes, Benton could be the killer. He was smart enough to have arranged the whole thing, and people had murdered for a lot less. And Benton didn't really have an alibi for the times of the murders. Unless he could come up with a plane ticket that proved he hadn't landed at the airport until *after* Max and Ron had been murdered, Benton Woodley was the number one suspect on Hannah's list.

Actually, Benton was her only suspect. Hannah sighed deeply and tromped even harder on the accelerator. She had to find Bill at the open house and tell him her new theory. Bill didn't know that Del Woodley had put up his ring for sale and he'd never guess that Del had borrowed money from Max. She couldn't expect him to solve the case unless he had all the facts.

Hannah's foot lifted from the gas pedal again as another thought occurred to her. Exactly how would she manage to get Bill alone? Mike Kingston would be there and he was Bill's new supervisor. And Bill had warned her not to let on that she was helping with the investigation. It was true that Mike didn't start until Monday, but he'd be there at the open house. She couldn't just barge in and announce to Bill *and* Mike that she'd solved the case.

The truck had turned off and now there was no one behind her. Hannah hit the brakes and peeled another U-turn. Going out to the sheriff's station had been a bad idea. She'd have to wait until Bill got home tonight before she could tell him that she knew who the killer was. But what should she do now? It was only three-thirty and the rest of the afternoon stretched out ahead of her.

The moment she thought of it, Hannah began to smile. She'd go out to DelRay Manufacturing to talk to Benton. She'd make polite conversation and ask him about his flight. She could always say that a friend of hers, a fictional friend who lived on the East Coast, was planning to come out for a visit. That would be a perfect excuse to ask him which airline he'd used, how long his flight had taken, and whether he'd had to wait long at the airport for the shuttle. Thanks to Andrea, she had the advantage of knowing that Benton always flicked his fingernail with his thumb when he was lying. She'd watch Benton carefully to weed out the truth from the lies. . . .

No, she couldn't talk to Benton. It wouldn't look good if she interrogated a murder suspect without Bill. Hannah eased up on the accelerator again, preparing for another U-turn. Her last instinct had been right. She'd drive straight out to the sheriff's station and give some excuse for needing to see Bill alone. It could be a family emergency, something to do with Delores. Then Mike would leave them alone and she could . . .

She was running in circles and she had to stop it. Hannah pulled over to the shoulder of the road and shut off her engine. Three consecutive U-turns was quite enough and she'd been about to make the fourth. What was wrong with her today? Why couldn't she think logically? It felt as if she'd been trying to assemble a complicated jigsaw puzzle with a blindfold on, and someone kept slipping in a piece from a totally different puzzle to confuse her.

"Think," Hannah muttered to herself. "Just sit here and think. You're smart. You can figure out what to do."

She'd already eliminated a ton of suspects until all she had left was Benton. Hannah was sure that he was the killer, but how could she help Bill to prove it? She had to take a giant step back and think about what had led her to suspect Benton in the first place. And that took her back to the Compacts Unlimited folder in Del Woodley's den. She had to prove that Benton had rented the black compact car that Mr. Harris had seen speeding out of the driveway at the dairy. Hannah supposed she could wait for the list of customers that the manager had promised to send to Bill, but it meant that a whole day, perhaps two, would be wasted. There was another way for her to find out, a way that should have occurred to her immediately if she'd just taken the time to think about it.

Hannah smiled as she started her engine and pulled back out on the road. She was going to drop in for a nice neighborly visit at the Woodley Mansion. She'd bring Judith Woodley some cookies as a thank-you for the lovely party, and then she'd ask her a few polite questions about Benton. She'd mention that her mother had left her handkerchief in the den when they'd used it as a setting for the photos, and Judith would give her permission to search for it. If Hannah could just get a second look at that folder from Compacts Unlimited, she'd be able to confirm that Benton had rented the car.

"Good afternoon, Hannah." Hannah could tell that Judith was surprised to see her, but good breeding didn't allow her to turn a gift-bearing visitor away. "Del and Benton are still at work, but you're welcome to come in and take tea with me."

"Thank you. I'd love to have tea with you," Hannah said quickly and she gave a triumphant smile as Judith led the way down the hall. Judith had sounded very reluctant. A truly polite guest would have made some excuse to decline. But Hannah was only masquerading as a guest and she figured that a halfhearted invitation to stay for tea was better than no invitation at all.

As they passed the den, Hannah glanced in at the table by the couch. The rental car folder was gone. She frowned and decided to skip the bit about her mother's lost handkerchief. It wouldn't serve any purpose now.

"This is my little sitting room," Judith announced as she paused at an open door. "Please go in and make yourself at home. I have a phone call to return, but my housekeeper will bring in the tea tray, and I'll be with you in just a few moments."

Hannah nodded and kept the smile on her face until Judith had left. There was nothing "little" about Judith's little sitting room. Hannah's whole condo could have been plunked down in the center, with plenty of room to spare.

As she gazed around her, Hannah conceded that it was a lovely room. It was tastefully decorated in silks and satin and it had an incredible view of the garden. While most gardens looked brown and dead this time of year, Judith's was lush and green. Her gardener had planted rows of small ornamental spruces in an intricate design that zigzagged around the beautiful statuary and nestled up against pretty little wrought-iron benches.

"Excuse me, ma'am." A housekeeper in a black silk dress with a white lace collar came into the room. She was carrying a tray containing an antique tea set that Delores would have killed for. Hannah had learned a bit about fine china and porcelain on her forays to estate sales and auctions with her mother and she recognized the pattern. It was a rare and beautifully rendered set that Wedgwood had offered for a limited time in the eighteen hundreds.

The housekeeper walked over to the antique piecrust table at the far end of the room and arranged the tea set carefully on its polished surface. She also set out a platter of dainty finger sandwiches. "Mrs. Woodley asks that you begin without her, ma'am. Shall I pour?"

"Yes, please." Hannah took a seat in one of the two chairs that flanked the table. Both chairs had a lovely view of the garden, but Hannah was much more interested in watching how the housekeeper poured the tea. It was done efficiently and very carefully, golden tea streaming from the spout to fill the lovely china cup without a splash. As the housekeeper blotted the lip of the teapot with an impeccably clean white linen napkin, Hannah couldn't help wondering whether knowledge of correct tea-pouring etiquette was one of the prerequisites for employment at the Woodley estate.

"Lemon or sugar, ma'am?"

"Neither, thank you," Hannah responded with a smile. "I'm really glad you poured that. I would have been petrified that I'd drop the pot."

The housekeeper gave a startled smile, but she immediately regained her composure. "Yes, ma'am. Will there be anything else?"

"I don't think so." Hannah had the urge to do something totally inappropriate. All this formality was getting to her. "Actually I hate tea, but don't tell Queen Judith that I said that."

"No, ma'am. I shan't."

The housekeeper beat a hasty retreat, but Hannah heard the sound of stifled laughter as the door closed behind her. That made her feel good. She doubted that Judith's domestic staff got many laughs from her guests.

Once the sound of housekeeper's footsteps had faded off down the hallway, Hannah lifted the other teacup and took a peek at the mark on the bottom. She was right. It was Wedgwood. She could hardly wait to tell Delores that she'd actually sipped tea from such a rare and expensive cup.

There was nothing to do but wait for Judith, and Hannah took stock of her surroundings. There was a secretariat of French extraction in a corner. It was probably from the time of Louis XIV, but she wasn't entirely sure. Somehow she doubted that Judith would ever buy copies, regardless of how cleverly they'd been crafted.

The wing chairs were antiques from the mid-eighteen hundreds, undoubtedly English and most certainly expensive. Mentally Hannah added up the items of furniture that surrounded her and came up with a staggering amount. No wonder Del Woodley had needed to borrow money. His wife had spent close to a hundred thousand dollars decorating her sitting room!

All that adding made her hungry and Hannah eyed the platter of sandwiches, little rectangles of bread with the crusts removed. Why did people who wanted to be sophisticated cut the crusts off slices of bread? As far as Hannah was concerned, the crusts were the best part. The filling in the sandwiches was green and since she didn't think that there was any moldy bologna in the Woodleys' refrigerator, Hannah assumed that it must be watercress or cucumber. A vegetable sandwich on white bread with the crusts missing wasn't exactly Hannah's idea of haute cuisine. She was just wondering if they might taste better than they looked when she heard footsteps approaching. Judith was coming and Hannah pasted a perfectly polite expression on her face. It was showtime.

Chapter Twenty-Six

"Hannah dear. I'm terribly sorry to have kept you waiting," Judith greeted her as she walked over to take the other chair. "I see that Mrs. Lawson has poured your tea."

Hannah raised her cup to take a hasty sip. The tea was lukewarm since she'd left it standing for too long, but she managed a smile. "It's delicious."

"I do prefer oolong, but most of my guests are partial to Darjeeling."

Hannah wasn't sure whether the tea she'd just sipped was oolong or Darjeeling, but it didn't really matter. "I came to compliment you on your party, Judith. It was perfect, as always."

"Thank you, dear."

Judith poured herself a cup of tea and Hannah noticed that it was steaming as it flowed from the spout of the antique teapot. There were no cracks in Judith's rare Wedgwood, though the tea set was almost two hundred years old. Delores had mentioned that even hairline cracks diffused the heat and cooled the tea.

Judith was perfectly silent as she sipped her tea, and Hannah knew she had to say something. Her hostess wasn't making it easy and Hannah had never been any good at polite small talk. "It was so nice to see Benton again," Hannah began. "Will he be here for long?"

"I'm really not sure. We haven't had time to discuss his plans."

Nothing useful there, Hannah thought to herself and decided to try a more direct method. "I was wondering if Benton was satisfied with the car that he rented."

Hannah was rewarded for her efforts by a raised, perfectly shaped eyebrow and total silence. Judith was the master of the noncommittal.

"I'm talking about the car from Compacts Unlimited," Hannah explained. "I noticed the folder when your husband gave us permission to take pictures in his den."

"Oh, that wasn't Benton's car," Judith corrected her. "The party people rented from Compacts Unlimited."

Hannah kicked herself mentally for not thinking of that possibility. The maid at the party had told her that Judith had paid for transportation. But just because Benton hadn't rented the car didn't mean that he hadn't used it while it was here. And it had been here on Wednesday morning.

"Why are you so interested in rental cars?"

Judith's question pulled Hannah back from her thoughts with a jolt. She was getting nowhere, fishing for information, and Judith had given her the perfect opportunity. She might as well come right out and ask.

"Look, Judith." Hannah raised her gaze to Judith's perfectly calm green eyes. "I probably shouldn't say anything, but a black rental car from Compacts Unlimited was spotted leaving the dairy on the morning that Max Turner was shot. I certainly don't believe that Benton had anything to do with Max's murder, but my brother-in-law is in charge of the investigation and he'll probably be by to ask questions. I just wanted to warn you."

"Warn me? Why would you want to warn me?"

Hannah sighed. "I guess *warn* was the wrong word. I should have said that I came to *alert* you. Benton does have an alibi for the time of Max's murder, doesn't he?"

"Of course he does!" Judith's voice dripped ice. "Benton wasn't even in town at the time!"

"That's what I thought. If Benton still has his airline tickets, don't let him throw them away. They could prove his innocence."

Judith's eyes narrowed. "Are you telling me that your brother-in-law suspects Benton of murdering Max Turner?"

"No. This is just between you and me. If you can find Benton's airline tickets and show them to me, I won't need to mention it to Bill. You've always been nice to me and I'd really like to save your family from the embarrassment of a police visit."

"Thank you for your concern, Hannah." Judith gave her a small, cold smile. "If you'll give me a moment, I'll locate those tickets for you. They're probably in Benton's suite. Just wait right here and I'll find them."

Hannah gave a big sigh of relief when Judith left the room. That comment she'd made about saving the family from embarrassment had worked. She'd also saved Bill from embarrassment. Judith wasn't the type to be intimidated by the authorities and she might have sued the Winnetka County Sheriff's Department for harassment if Bill had dragged Benton in to interrogate him.

The seconds ticked by and Hannah reached for a sandwich. She'd skipped lunch and her stomach was rumbling. The sandwiches weren't bad, definitely watercress, but they weren't what she'd call substantial. She could scarf up the whole tray and they still wouldn't make a decent meal. Hannah was just lifting the top off another—perhaps there were some with chicken or tuna mixed in somewhere—when she heard Judith's footsteps approaching in the hallway. She replaced the bread just in time and pasted a smile on her face.

"Here they are." Judith was carrying a silk shawl over her

right arm and her voice was trembling slightly. It certainly wasn't cold in the room, but perhaps just knowing that Benton was a suspect in a homicide had given her a chill. She sat down in her chair with the shawl on her lap and handed Hannah the tickets with her left hand. "If you'll open the folder, you'll see that Benton's plane didn't land until twelve-seventeen. I assume that this will clear him as a suspect?"

Hannah examined the tickets. "Yes, it will. I'm really sorry that I had to bring it up and I hope that I didn't upset you too much. It was just that the circumstantial evidence against Benton seemed overwhelming."

"Overwhelming?" Judith's eyebrows shot up. "How can that be? A killer requires a motive. What possible motive could Benton have for killing Max Turner?"

"Actually," Hannah hesitated, choosing her words carefully, "it concerns the personal loan that your husband had with Max Turner."

"What are you talking about, Hannah?"

Judith looked flustered, not at all like her usual poised self and Hannah wondered if she should backpedal. But Judith had been very forthcoming and she deserved the truth. "I'm sorry I have to tell you, Judith, but Del secured a personal loan from Max Turner. I just learned about it this afternoon. And I know that Del was having some problems making the payments. You can see how this all fits together, can't you?"

"Yes, I can." Judith's voice was hard and Hannah assumed that she was embarrassed. "You thought that Benton shot Max so that Del wouldn't have to honor the loan. Is that right?"

"That's it. I'm really sorry, Judith, but it did make sense. You've got to admit that."

Judith dipped her head in a nod. "You're right, Hannah. It did make sense. Does your brother-in-law know about the loan?"

"No. There's no record of it and I can't see any reason to tell him, now that Benton's been cleared. And Del has an air-tight alibi for the time of Max's murder. He was meeting with his night supervisors at DelRay and there's no way he could have been in two places at once. The only other person who would care about the loan is you, and . . ."

"Brava, Hannah." Judith smiled an icy smile and pulled a gun from beneath the folds of her silk shawl. "It's unfortunate that you put the pieces together, but now that you have, I can't let you tell your brother-in-law."

"*You* killed Max?" Hannah gulped. She'd never stared into the barrel of a gun before and it wasn't an experience she'd care to repeat. And if the cold, calculating expression on Judith's face was any indication, Hannah suspected that she might not get a chance to repeat anything ever again.

"You were asking too many questions, Hannah. And you were skirting much too close to the truth. I knew it was only a matter of time before you arrived at the accurate conclusion and conveyed it to your brother-in-law. I couldn't let you do that, now could I?"

Judith was going to kill her. Hannah knew that with heart-sinking certainty. She also knew that she had to keep Judith talking, to buy herself some time until the reinforcements came.

But there weren't any reinforcements, Hannah reminded herself. She hadn't told Bill that she was going to see Judith and he didn't know anything about Del's loan with Max. To make matters worse, Bill wasn't even a detective yet. He'd never figure it out in time!

"Nervous, dear?"

Judith's voice was taunting and Hannah shuddered. The polite socialite had turned into a cold-blooded killer and she was a goner unless she could keep Judith talking. "Of course I'm nervous! When did you get the gun? Or did you have it with you when I walked in the door?"

"Do you honestly think that I'd carry a gun around in my own home?" Judith laughed lightly.

Of course you wouldn't. Even a shoulder holster would ruin the lines of your dress, Hannah thought. And then she wondered how she could think flippant thoughts when Judith was about to kill her. Either she was much braver than she'd ever imagined, or she still expected the cavalry to ride in at the last minute.

Hannah's mind spun at top speed, searching for questions that Judith might want to answer. The killers in her favorite movies seemed to like to explain why they'd murdered their victims. All she had to do was keep Judith's mind off shooting her until she could figure out what to do. "When did you go to get the gun? I'm curious."

"Why?"

"I don't know. That's just the way my mind works. You're going to shoot me anyway. You might as well do me a favor and satisfy my curiosity first."

"And why should I do any favors for you?"

"Because I brought you cookies," Hannah answered. "They're some of my best, Pecan Chews. You're going to love them."

Judith laughed. She seemed to think that Hannah's comment was funny. Maybe it was, but it was difficult for Hannah to see the humor past the gun barrel right now.

"Come on, Judith," Hannah tried again. "What harm can it do to tell me? You were smart to get the gun. I just want to know when you realized that you needed it."

"I had the gun when I came back with the plane tickets. It was under my shawl."

Hannah sighed. She should have noticed that Judith's silk shawl didn't complement the dress she was wearing. If she'd been thinking straight, she would have realized that something was up. "You were planning to shoot me then?"

"Not then. I brought the gun as a precaution, but I hoped that I wouldn't have to use it. Unfortunately you forced my hand by mentioning the loan."

"Me and my big mouth," Hannah blurted out. Then she sighed. "If I hadn't said anything about the loan, you would have let me leave?"

"Yes. But you *did* say something, and now it's too late."

Hannah thought of another question as fast as she could. "I know about some of Max's other loans and how he forced people to sign over their property as collateral. Is that what he did to you?"

"Yes. DelRay suffered a setback and when Del needed more capital, he signed over my home. He was a fool to do it. I advised him against it, but he wouldn't listen. Del was never very bright."

The gun barrel wavered slightly and Hannah wondered if she should make a grab for it. In one of the detective shows she'd watched, the main character had jammed his finger somewhere or other to keep the gun from firing. But that gun hadn't looked like the one that Judith held. If she got out of this alive, she was going to find out everything she could about guns and how they operated.

"You're very quiet, Hannah." Judith's lips twisted up in a parody of a smile. "Aren't you going to ask me any more questions?"

Hannah shook off all thoughts that weren't useful and latched on to another question. It was good that Judith wanted to talk about Max and what she'd done to him. "Why didn't Del get a loan from the bank? It would have been a lot safer than going to Max."

"The bank refused him. They said that he was over-extended and they were right. I advised Del to close the doors, but all he could think about was how it would affect his work force. Those people would have found other jobs. And even if they hadn't, it wouldn't have mattered to me!"

Hannah tried not to let her emotions show. Judith was totally self-centered. Her only concern was for her home, not for the hundreds of Lake Eden workers who would have lost their jobs. "I assume that Max called in Del's loan and that's why you felt you had to . . . to act."

"That's exactly right. I warned Del to be careful about hidden clauses when he signed the loan papers, but he's never been proficient at reading legal documents. Max took advantage of his naivete."

"He didn't have a lawyer read over the loan papers?"

"There wasn't time. Max told him that the deal was off if he didn't sign right away. Del was desperate and that made him vulnerable. Max counted on that. The man had no scruples!"

Hannah took a deep breath. From what she'd learned about Max, she could agree with Judith completely on that point. "You're right, Judith. And you're not the first person that Max tried to ruin. Was he really going to foreclose on your home?"

"Yes, and I couldn't let that happen. Del built this house for me. It was a condition of our marriage. I had the architect follow the blueprints for my father's house. This is an exact replica and I couldn't bear to lose it. Surely you can appreciate that."

"Your home means that much to you?"

"It's my life!" Judith looked fiercely protective. "How could I stand by and do nothing while Max Turner was threatening to take my *life* away?"

Hannah bit back the urge to remind Judith that she had taken Max's life away in a much more tangible and permanent fashion. "Is that the reason you called Benton home?"

"Of course it is. But Benton doesn't love this house the way I do. He actually told me that I had to accept it, that his father had signed those loan papers voluntarily and there was no recourse we could take."

"So you decided to kill Max and get the loan papers back?"

"What other choice did I have? I couldn't stand by and let Max Turner evict me from my lovely home!"

"No, I guess not." Hannah saw that Judith's hand was trembling slightly and she asked another question to calm her down. "Wasn't Max suspicious when you called and said you wanted to see him?"

Judith gave a cold little laugh. "Max wasn't bright enough to be suspicious. I told him I'd sold some family heirlooms and that I was prepared to pay off Del's debt. When I arrived at his office, I demanded to see the loan papers before I gave him the money."

"So he took you into the old dairy and got them out of the safe?"

"Yes, but I had to show him the money first. You should have seen the greed on his face. It was appalling!"

Hannah was confused. "Then you had enough money to pay off the loan?"

"Of course not. I simply let him glimpse a sheaf of thousand dollar bills. Max was too stupid to realize that only the top five were authentic. And after he handed me the loan papers, I took a great deal of pleasure in ridding the world of Maxwell Turner!"

Judith's eyes turned hard and Hannah knew she should do something to appease her anger. "There are a lot of people who'd thank you, Judith. If the other people that Max tried to ruin knew what I know, they'd probably erect a statue of you in Lake Eden park."

"But they don't know." Judith wasn't so easily taken in. "And they *won't* know."

"Of course they won't. Nobody will ever figure it out. But why did you kill Ron?"

"He saw me with Max." Judith sounded sad. "I didn't want to do it, Hannah. It was nothing personal and I do feel a great deal of remorse about ending his life. It's important that you believe that."

"Then Ron's only fault was being in the wrong place at the wrong time?"

Judith sighed. "That's right. I do wish that he hadn't come

into the dairy, but once he saw me, I had to act. When Max's body was discovered, he would have mentioned seeing me there. It wasn't pleasant, Hannah. I liked Ron. He didn't deserve to die."

"Do I deserve to die?" Hannah held her breath, waiting for Judith's answer. Perhaps, if Judith felt guilty enough, she might reconsider.

"No. I like you, Hannah. Your candor is refreshing. And that's precisely why this whole situation is so difficult. At least it'll be over quickly. I wouldn't want you to suffer. I have everything all planned out."

"Really?" Hannah attempted to sound interested, but talking about her impending death was frightening. "What have you planned? You won't want to slip up now, when you're so close to getting away with the perfect murders."

"I won't slip up," Judith sounded very confident. "It's simple, Hannah. I'm going to walk you outside, shoot you in the back of your truck, and drive it down to the lake on the back of our property. Once I release the brake and push your truck down the hill, it'll sink without a trace."

Hannah shivered and picked up her teacup to take another sip. Hearing about the disposal of her very alive body in such a cold-blooded way made her mouth go dry. "That's very clever. But how about your housekeeper? She knows I'm here and she'll hear the shot."

"She's gone. I dismissed her for the remainder of the day. We're quite alone, Hannah, and Benton and Del won't be home for hours. They have a late meeting at the plant." Judith motioned with the gun barrel. "That's enough talking. Put down your teacup, Hannah. This tea set is a priceless family heirloom. It's been in my family for almost two hundred years. It was a gift from King George the Third, and my paternal grandmother brought it here from England. I'm really quite fond of it."

Hannah thought fast, still holding the teacup. "My mother's a collector. This is Wedgwood, isn't it?"

"Of course." Judith gave an amused laugh. "Even an amateur collector would recognize its value immediately. Do you know that I've been offered over a hundred thousand dollars for the set?"

"You should have taken it," Hannah blurted out, an idea beginning to form in her head. "It's a fake."

"What?" Judith gasped, staring at her in disbelief.

"Here, I'll show you." Hannah put down her teacup and lifted the lid of the pot to examine the mark that was stamped on the underside. "A lot of people don't know it, but I made a study of Wedgwood for my mother. This tea set is very rare and Wedgwood put a double maker's mark right here. Yours has only one maker's mark and that proves it's not authentic Wedgwood. See what I mean?"

Hannah transferred the lid to her left hand and the gun barrel dropped an inch or so as Judith leaned over to look at the mark. This was it. Hannah knew she'd never have a better chance. She grabbed the teapot with her right hand and threw the steaming tea directly at Judith's face. Judith reacted by jumping back and Hannah tackled her before she could catch her balance. The gun went flying out of Judith's hand, and Hannah knocked her to the floor as hard as she could, grinding her down into the nap of the expensive Aubusson carpet.

Judith flailed out with long manicured nails, but she was no match for Hannah's adrenaline rush. It also helped that Hannah outweighed her by a good thirty pounds. In no time at all, she had flipped Judith over on her stomach, twisted her hands behind her back, and bound them firmly with the Hermès silk scarf that Judith had been wearing around her neck.

Hannah's hands were shaking as she picked up the gun and trained it on the back of Judith's head. "One move and you're dead. You got that, Judith?"

There was no reply from the quaking socialite on the floor, but Hannah hadn't expected one. She marched to the phone, intending to tell the secretary at the sheriff's station to get Bill on the line, when the very brother-in-law that she was about to call rushed into the room.

"I'll take over now, Hannah." Bill sounded proud of her, but Hannah was a bit too rattled to react. "You can give me the gun."

Hannah shook her head. She wasn't about to take any chances with the woman who'd almost killed her. "Cuff her first, Bill. She's tricky and that silk scarf might not hold."

"Okay." Bill started to grin as he walked over to Judith and slipped on the cuffs. "She killed Max and Ron?"

"That's right. Read her her rights, Bill. I sure don't want this case dismissed on a technicality."

For a moment Hannah thought she'd blown it, because Bill gave her one of those "Just who do you think you are?" looks. But he must have decided to cut her some slack because he proceeded to read Judith her rights.

"How did you know I was here?" Hannah asked when Bill had finished with the legalities.

"I got your message about the rental car folder and I drove out to DelRay to talk to Del. He said he hadn't seen you and I figured that you must be here. I'm sorry I didn't get here sooner, but it looks like you handled it just fine. Maybe I can take a few lessons from you."

"Whatever," Hannah said modestly. She wasn't about to admit that she'd been saved by a combination of serendipity, fortuity, and blind dumb luck.

The next few minutes seemed to fly by in a rush. Backup arrived to take Judith into custody, Bill took Hannah's statement in the Woodleys' massive kitchen, and Judith's sitting room was roped off with yellow crime-scene tape. Hannah warned Bill to tell the deputies to be careful with the tea set; it actually *was* a priceless antique. Then Bill walked her out into the crisp night air she'd never thought she'd enjoy again.

The night was incredibly peaceful. Gentle snowflakes were falling and it seemed a fitting end to a day that had been filled with confusion, frustration, fear, and finally a sense of a job well done. Hannah was about to climb into her Suburban when she remembered what she'd seen on the counter in the Woodleys' kitchen. "I forgot something, Bill. I'll be right back."

Hannah raced back into the house and headed straight for the kitchen. There it was: her white bakery bag with the red plastic handles and "The Cookie Jar" printed on the side in gold letters. She snatched it up and ran back outside again.

"These are for you." Hannah was breathless as she handed the bag to Bill. "They're my best cookies, Pecan Chews."

Bill looked both surprised and pleased. "Thanks, Hannah. Why did you leave them inside?"

"I used them as an excuse to see Judith." Hannah laughed and the echo of her own laughter sounded wonderful to her ears. "I gave them to her as a hostess gift, but I don't think she's going to be doing much entertaining where she's going to end up."

Epilogue

It wasn't bad as family parties went and Hannah was pleasantly surprised. Norman had gone out to the sheriff's department open house and he'd offered to help Bill move Mike Kingston into his new apartment. Naturally, Bill had asked him to come back to the house for pizza with them and now they were all sitting around Andrea and Bill's dining room table, munching pizza, the salad Delores had brought, and Hannah's contribution, two pans of her Lovely Lemon Bar Cookies. She'd told everyone she thought it was appropriate to bring bars because Judith Woodley was behind them at last.

Something else had happened that made this night into a celebration. Sheriff Grant had promoted Bill to detective and he'd decided that Bill should be Mike's partner. Mike was still Bill's supervisor, but they would be working together on cases. Of course Sheriff Grant didn't know anything about Hannah's part in solving the double-homicide, and neither did Mike. Hannah had told Bill that she wanted all of the credit to go to him.

There was another thing to celebrate and it concerned Andrea's career. Bill had decided that since Tracey loved preschool so much, it would be a shame to take her away from the friends she'd made. And since Tracey would be spending her days at Kiddie Korner, Andrea could keep right on selling real estate.

"Time for bed, Tracey." Andrea sounded relaxed and happy as she turned to her daughter. "You've got school tomorrow."

"Okay, Mommy. I can take the detective bear that Mike gave me, can't I?"

"Sure, you can," Bill answered her.

"But it's a collectible," Delores objected. "What if one of Tracey's friends gets it dirty?"

Mike shrugged. "Then it'll get dirty. Let her take it, Andrea. It's not much of a present for Tracey if she can't play with it."

"You're right." Andrea smiled at him and then she turned to Tracey. "You can take it, honey. It's okay."

Hannah watched the exchange and it made her feel good. Perhaps Andrea was becoming a little less materialistic. She certainly was becoming more maternal. Tracey had called her "Mommy," and Andrea hadn't objected to the label.

After Tracey had kissed everyone good night and left to go upstairs with Andrea, Delores motioned to Hannah. "Could you help me dress another salad, dear? We're running out."

"Sure." Hannah followed Delores into the kitchen, but the moment they were out of earshot, she took her mother's arm. "Spill it, Mother."

"Spill *what,* dear?"

"The reason you wanted to get me alone. We weren't running out of salad. The bowl was half full."

"You always were the smart one." Delores laughed. "I just wanted to know how you felt with two men competing for you."

Hannah reared back on her heels and gave her mother a

look that would wither baby grapes on the vine. "Are you crazy, Mother? Norman isn't interested in me that way. We're friends, but that's as far as it goes. And Mike Kingston certainly isn't. He's just being polite to his new partner's sister-in-law."

"I don't think so." Delores didn't seem at all swayed by that argument. "Norman told Carrie that you're the first girl he's felt comfortable with in years."

"That's nice, but it doesn't spell romance. Norman's just as comfortable around Andrea. As a matter of fact, I think he's even *more* comfortable around her. They were huddled together in the living room for a long time, discussing what color Andrea should choose for her new carpet."

"But Andrea's married," Delores pointed out, "and you're not."

Hannah couldn't resist teasing her mother. "That's true. Do you think that Norman would feel even more comfortable around me if I got married?"

"That's not what I mean and you know it!" Delores sounded as outraged as she could, given the fact she had to keep her voice down.

"Sorry, Mother. It's just that you're always trying to push me into marriage. I've told you before, I'm perfectly happy being single."

"That'll change when you meet the right man." Delores seemed very certain. "I think you've already met him and you just haven't realized it yet. Norman's a very good catch."

"You make him sound like a trout."

"It fits, dear." Delores looked highly amused. "Norman's swallowed the bait. Now all you have to do is reel him in."

Hannah laughed at the mental picture that popped into her head, and Delores joined in. When they stopped laughing, Hannah gently admonished her. "If you stop trying to set me up with every man in town, we'll get along much better. You've already got a grandchild and she's perfect. And your son-in-law just solved a double homicide and got promoted to detective. Let's just have a good time tonight and celebrate all the good things that have happened."

"You're right, Hannah," Delores agreed. "But I still think both of those men are competing for you."

There was no stopping Delores, and Hannah was almost ready to give up the fight, but not before she fired a parting shot. "If they're competing for me, why hasn't either one of them asked me out?"

"Oh, they will." Delores sounded very confident. "Before the night's over, you'll have two dates."

"You think so?"

"Want to bet?"

"I don't know. What's in it for me when I win?"

"If you win," Delores corrected her.

"All right, *if* I win."

"I'll buy you a new outfit. Claire has a stunning green silk suit that'll look just lovely on you."

Hannah had seen the green silk in Claire's window and Delores was right: It was stunning. "You'll never win this bet, Mother, but just for form's sake, what do you want if *you* win?"

"I want you to stop wearing those awful old tennis shoes. They're disgusting!"

"But I love them." Hannah glanced down at her old Nikes, the most comfortable shoes she owned.

"You've loved them for the past five years and it's time to give them a decent burial." Delores gave her a challenging smile. "What are you so worried about? You just told me that I couldn't win."

Hannah thought about it. The probability that both Norman and Mike would ask her for a date before the night was over was too astronomical for her to calculate without using numbers with strange names like googol and googolplex. "Okay, Mother. You've got a bet."

"Good." Delores beamed at her. "Let's put that salad together before someone comes in to ask what we're talking about."

When the salad was ready, Hannah carried it out to the table. Delores started bending Mike's ear about collectible toys, and Norman and Andrea got into a discussion about textured walls and the sponge method of applying paint. That left Hannah with Bill and she knew she'd never have a better opportunity to talk to him about Coach Watson.

"Will you show me where you keep the recycle bin?" Hannah picked up her Diet Coke can.

"You know where it is. It's that yellow box in the kitchen, under the sink."

Hannah glanced around. No one was paying any attention to them, so she grabbed Bill's arm and leaned close. "I need to talk to you alone."

"Oh," Bill whispered. "Sorry, Hannah. Let's duck into the living room."

Once they were out of earshot, Hannah turned to him. "I need a favor, but it's tricky."

"Okay. What is it?"

"This isn't official, Bill. And you can't let anyone know that I told you."

"I won't say anything."

"I know that Coach Watson has been battering Danielle. I talked to her about it, but she won't press charges."

"There's nothing I can do if she won't file a report." Bill sighed deeply. "It's really a shame, but my hands are tied."

"I know. Boyd's in therapy, but I'm still worried. I just wondered if you could keep an eye on him unofficially."

"I can do that."

"You can't say anything to him. If he thinks that Danielle told anyone, he might just snap."

"That's been known to happen. Can I ask Mike for some advice on this?"

"Good idea." Hannah smiled. "He must have dealt with this type of situation before. But don't mention Boyd or Danielle by name."

"I won't. It's a good thing you told me now, just in case something happens."

Hannah shivered as she walked back into the dining room with Bill. She hadn't known Danielle very well before Ron had been killed, but she did now, and she liked her a lot. She wished that she'd been able to do more to protect her, but Danielle was in denial and the system couldn't work if she wouldn't let it.

Hannah's mood improved as they rejoined the group around the table. The conversation was lively and there was a lot of good-natured ribbing. It was one of the best parties they'd ever had, and Hannah wondered if they should always invite some extra guests to their family affairs.

Several times, as they were eating dessert and drinking coffee, Delores winked at her. Hannah winked back. Her favorite old Nikes didn't seem to be in any danger.

Dating was the furthest thing from Hannah's mind when she went into the kitchen to fetch the extra pan of bar cookies she'd brought and found Norman already there, waiting for her. "Hi, Norman. Are you sneaking bar cookies behind our backs?"

"No." Norman looked very serious as he shook his head. "I was waiting for a chance to talk to you alone, Hannah. I wanted to thank you for those loan papers. My mother would thank you, too, if she knew."

"That's okay, Norman. I didn't want anyone else to see them, so I just . . . uh . . ."

"Appropriated them?" Norman grinned as he supplied the word.

Hannah grinned back. "That's right."

"Will you have dinner with me next Friday night? We could drive to that steak place out by the lake. I really need to talk to you in private, Hannah. It's about my mother."

"Sure," Hannah agreed without a second thought. "That'd be really nice, Norman."

It wasn't until Hannah was back in her chair that she realized Delores had won fifty percent of the bet. Norman had asked her to dinner and that counted as a date. She glanced at Mike. There was no way he'd ask her out. Her favorite shoes were secure.

The party broke up about ten. Bill and Mike had to report in at eight and Norman had an early appointment. They walked Delores out to her car, and Hannah lingered to help Andrea toss the paper plates and pizza boxes in the trash. When the cleanup was finished and Bill had set out the garbage cans for pickup the next morning, she slipped into her boots, said good night to her sister and brother-in-law, and walked through the soft white snow to her truck.

"Hannah?"

"Hi, Mike." Hannah was surprised to see Mike Kingston leaning up against the hood of her truck. "I thought you'd left."

"Not yet. I wanted to talk to you, Hannah."

His voice sounded stressed and Hannah began to frown. "Sure. What is it?"

"I like you, Hannah."

Hannah was confused. What did liking her have to do with anything? "I like you, too, Mike."

"And I'd like to get to know you better."

Hannah began to suspect that something she hadn't thought would happen was happening. "I'd like to know you better, too."

Mike grinned and his whole face lit up. "That's a relief. I just moved here, so I don't know what there is to do on the weekends, but if I can come up with something good, how about going out with me on Saturday night?"

Hannah was so stunned her mouth dropped open. "You're asking me to go out this Saturday night?"

"That's right. We can find something to do in Lake Eden, can't we?"

"Sure, we can." Visions of satin sheets and feather pillows flitted through Hannah's head for a split second, but she pushed them firmly out of her mind. It was just that Mike was so handsome and sexy. And she was so . . . available.

Mike grinned again. ''I guess I'd better hit the road. Six o'clock comes pretty early."

"Six?" Hannah's eyebrows shot up. "I thought you didn't have to be at the station until eight."

"I don't, but my new place has a gym and I like to work out in the mornings. Do you want me to follow you home?"

Hannah pushed another image from her mind. She didn't think Mike had meant *that*. "Why would you want to follow me home?"

"I can think of several reasons, but we'd better not get into that now. I just meant that I was concerned for your safety. You're all alone and it's dark."

"I'll be perfectly safe, Mike. This is Lake Eden. We don't have any crime here."

"You don't count a double homicide as a crime?" Mike started to laugh.

Hannah laughed too, even though the joke was on her. "You've got a good point, but that was the exception rather than the rule. I'll be just fine. You should go home and get some sleep."

"I will." Mike turned to walk to his car. He climbed in, started the engine, and then rolled down the window. "I'll call you at work tomorrow and we'll set a time for our date."

"I'll be there all day." Hannah waved as he drove off. She was sliding in, behind the wheel of her Suburban, when his last words sank in. She'd just accepted a date with Mike Kingston.

"Uh-oh!" Hannah frowned as she reached out and grabbed the sneakers that she'd tossed on the passenger seat. She got out of her truck, marched over to one of the garbage cans that Bill had set out for the morning pickup, and hoped that Delores would appreciate what she was about to do. She had a date with Norman, and she had a date with Mike. They'd both asked her out before the night was over, and she'd never welshed on a bet in her life.

Two dates in one night—not bad at all! Hannah's frown changed to a grin as she lifted the lid and dropped her very favorite five-year-old pair of Nikes inside.

LOVELY LEMON BAR COOKIES

Preheat oven to 350° F.,
rack in the middle position.

2 cups flour *(no need to sift)*
1 cup cold butter *(2 sticks, ½ pound)*
½ cup powdered *(confectioners')* sugar *(no need to
    sift, unless it's got big lumps)*

4 beaten eggs *(just whip them up with a fork)*
2 cups white *(granulated)* sugar
8 tablepoons lemon juice *(½ cup)*
1 teaspoon or so of zest *(optional) (zest is finely
    grated lemon peel)*
½ teaspoon salt
1 teaspoon baking powder
4 Tablespoons flour *(that's ¼ cup—don't bother to
    sift)*

Cut each stick of butter into eight pieces. Zoop it
up with the flour and the powdered sugar in a food
processor until it looks like coarse cornmeal *(just like
the first step in making a piecrust)*. Spread it out in a
greased 9 x 13 inch pan *(that's a standard sheet cake
pan)* and pat it down with your hands.

Bake at 350 degrees for 15 to 20 minutes, or until golden around the edges. Remove from oven. *(Don't turn off oven!)*

Mix eggs with white sugar. Add lemon juice *(and zest, if you want to use it)*. Add salt and baking powder and mix. Then add flour and mix thoroughly. *(This will be runny—it's supposed to be.)*

Pour this mixture on top of the pan you just baked and stick it back into the oven. Bake at 350 degrees F. for another 30 to 35 minutes. Then remove from the oven and sprinkle on additional powdered sugar.

Let cool thoroughly and cut into brownie-sized bars.

Brought these to the pizza party following Mike Kingston's move, the day after Bill solved the double-homicide case and got his promotion. (I'm a good sister-in-law. I gave him every speck of the credit.)

Index of
Cookie Recipes

Baking Conversion Chart

These conversions are approximate, but they'll work just fine for Hannah Swensen's recipes.

VOLUME:

U.S.	Metric
½ teaspoon	2 milliliters
1 teaspoon	5 milliliters
1 Tablespoon	15 milliliters
¼ cup	50 milliliters
⅓ cup	75 milliliters
½ cup	125 milliliters
¾ cup	175 milliliters
1 cup	¼ liter

WEIGHT:

U.S.	Metric
1 ounce	28 grams
1 pound	454 grams

OVEN TEMPERATURE:

Degrees Fahrenheit	Degrees Centigrade	British (Regulo) Gas Mark
325 degrees F.	165 degrees C.	3
350 degrees F.	175 degrees C.	4
375 degrees F.	190 degrees C.	5

Note: Hannah's rectangular sheet cake pan, 9 inches by 13 inches, is approximately 23 centimeters by 32.5 centimeters.

Please turn the page for an exciting bonus novella and additional recipes from Joanne Fluke!

The Cookie Jar
Lake Eden, MN

Joanne Fluke
Hannah Swensen Mystery Series
Kensington Publishing Corporation
New York, NY

Dear Joanne,

It seems like forever since I've seen you, now that you've packed up and moved to Southern California. When are you coming back to Lake Eden for a visit? You have friends here, you know. And I really miss our morning coffee at The Cookie Jar.

I'm so glad you're finally telling Candy's story! I was surprised you didn't write about it when it actually happened, only two weeks after I helped Bill solve his first double homicide case, but I guess you were busy writing the other books in my biography.

Now that I think about it, I believe I know why you waited so long to write Candy's story. It's because there's no murder. Just think about it, Jo . . . you've written about murder in every single book. It's even in every title! There's this one, *Chocolate Chip Cookie Murder*, and *Strawberry Short-cake Murder*, *Blueberry Muffin Murder*, *Lemon Meringue Pie Murder*, *Fudge Cupcake Murder*, *Sugar Cookie Murder*, *Peach Cobbler Murder*, *Cherry Cheesecake Murder*, and *Key Lime Pie Murder*. It doesn't take an advanced degree in clinical psychology to realize that you're obsessing about homicide. Even Mayor Bascomb noticed. Now, both of us know that Lake Eden is a very nice place to live. And while it's true that we have a lot of homicides for such a small town, we don't want people to get the idea that it's the murder capital of the world, do we? One other thing . . . could you make it perfectly clear that I don't enjoy finding dead bodies, despite what Mother thinks?

Thank you for doing such a good job of chronicling my life, and thanks again for writing about Candy. I'm just glad that we could solve the puzzle of her identity. Now I've got to run. Moishe is yowling for me to fill his food bowl, the phone is ringing off the hook (it's probably Mother,) and I'm late for work at The Cookie Jar. You lived here long enough to know that time never slows down in Lake Eden, unless you happen to be on Old Lake Road stuck behind a snow-plow.

Hannah Swensen

P.S. How about making me ten pounds thinner in the next book? I'd really appreciate it!

CANDY FOR CHRISTMAS

JOANNE FLUKE

Chapter One

"Bye, Moishe." Hannah Swensen tossed a few salmon-flavored treats that were shaped like little fish to her twenty-five-pound feline roommate. It was the same leave-taking ritual they'd gone through every morning for the past year, but on this particular morning, as she locked the condo door behind her and started down the covered stairs that led to the basement garage, Hannah had a startling thought. If the salmon-flavored treats were shaped like little fish, what shape were the liver-flavored treats? The only thing she could think of that was shaped like a liver was . . . somebody's liver. And what shape was that, anyway?

Ten minutes later, Hannah was on the road, driving the familiar route to her shop in Lake Eden, Minnesota. The winter landscape at four-thirty in the morning was gorgeous. Her headlights sparkled on the freshly fallen snow and sent what looked like diamonds skittering across the road. The lazy flakes that fell from the sky served as a curtain, muffling sound until all she could hear was the soft rumbling of her motor and the rhythmic swish of her tires. There was no other traffic. Nothing else was moving in the bitter-cold Minnesota predawn. Hannah felt like the only woman left on

Earth, traveling smoothly into the night in a magical candy apple red coach with four-wheel drive that was filled with the aroma of vanilla, cinnamon, and chocolate.

It would have been a perfect fantasy, except for one jarring note. The heater in Hannah's truck was failing, and her teeth were chattering in a lengthy drum roll that would have been the envy of the rhythm section of the Jordan High marching band. As she had on every other morning this week, she promised herself that as soon as she got a little ahead, she'd have it fixed. In the meantime, her warmest parka and gloves would have to do.

Almost there, Hannah told herself as she stopped for the red light at the intersection of Old Lake Road and Carter Avenue. Old Lake Road was fairly busy at peak traffic hours, but Carter Avenue led to only one sprawling showplace home in the center of a private pine forest. That home belonged to Mayor Bascomb's in-laws and everyone knew that he'd installed the stoplight to please his wife, Stephanie.

Since the light had a reputation for taking a while, Hannah wiggled her toes inside her boots in an effort to restore warmth and mobility. Then she counted to a hundred. And then two hundred. She had reached five hundred and was mentally composing a letter to the editor of the *Lake Eden Journal*, expressing the need for a sensor on the stoplight, when it finally clicked to green and she could drive forward again.

Another five minutes and she was turning in at the city limits, driving down the quiet streets with their darkened houses. Everyone was asleep, and she would be too, if she didn't have to bake the day's cookies before she opened her coffee shop and bakery, The Cookie Jar.

The Lake Eden business district was deserted at this time of morning. All the stores had dim lights inside, the result of an article Sheriff Grant had written for the *Lake Eden Journal* on burglary prevention, but nothing was moving inside. It would be another hour before Hal unlocked the front door at the café for the workers on the morning shift at DelRay Manufacturing.

Hannah drove down Main Street and was about to turn on Fourth, when she noticed that the twinkle lights around the inside of the window of her coffee shop were still on. She thought she remembered turning them off, but perhaps she'd forgotten. She had been in a rush to get home last night. Hannah just hoped her power bill wouldn't be sky high for this one infraction. After all, how much current could a hundred-bulb string of minilights draw? Perhaps she wouldn't even see an increase. She was usually very careful when it came to turning off the lights and locking up.

As she pulled into the alley, Hannah slowed her truck to a crawl to navigate the icy ruts that a truck had made, delivering donations to the Helping Hands Thrift Shop. A hundred yards and a dozen or so jarring thumps later, she was turning into her own lot and parking in her spot by the back door.

To plug in, or not to plug in. That was the question. Rayne Phillips, the weatherman on KCOW radio, had promised the day would warm to the high twenties. As Hannah climbed out of her truck and eyed the strip of outlets installed at bumper level at the back of her building, she added that bit of information to the mix. If Rayne had it right, she wouldn't need to use her heater. But if Rayne was wrong, her oil would chill to the consistency of chewing gum and her truck wouldn't start when it was time to drive home.

Hannah stood still, debating with herself for a moment, and then she laughed. Rayne Phillips had been wrong about the weather more times than he'd been right, and it would be wise to play the percentages. Plugging in her car might be unnecessary, but *not* plugging in her car could mean she'd have to call Cyril Murphy at the garage.

Once plugged in, Hannah headed for the back door of the white stucco building. She was about to insert her key in the lock when she stopped short and frowned. The knob was a bit icy, as if a warm hand had recently gripped it. That was odd. Her assistant, Lisa Herman, wasn't scheduled to come in this early. If, for some reason, Lisa had arrived first, her old car would be here. Unless, of course, her car had failed to start and she'd caught a ride to work with one of her neighbors.

Hannah stood dithering for a moment. If Lisa was here, it would account for the lights she'd seen. She always turned them on and propped open the swinging door to the coffee shop, so that she could enjoy them while she helped with the early morning baking.

Standing here wondering was not only silly, it was cold! All she had to do was go inside and see. Chiding herself for her chilly mental debate, Hannah unlocked the door and flicked on the lights. And then she blinked. And blinked again. Several times.

Lisa had been here and the proof was right in front of her eyes. The dirty dishes they'd left in the sink were gone, and the floor had been freshly mopped. Normally, Hannah and Lisa did these things before they left for the night, but Hannah had been in a hurry to get home, and Lisa had invited two of her dad's friends for dinner. Unless the elves had left the shoemaker's shop and taken up residence at The Cookie Jar, Lisa must have come in sometime during the night to wash the dishes and mop the floor!

Perhaps she'd put on the coffee, too? Hannah glanced at the kitchen pot, but the little red light wasn't glowing. No coffee there. She went through the swinging door to check the big thirty-cup percolator, but it was still tipped upside down on a towel, the way they always left it after they washed and dried it. Lisa loved coffee as much as Hannah did. It would be ready if she'd come in early.

Hannah felt a chill that had nothing to do with the winter weather as she noticed that the multicolored lights were off. They'd been on when she'd driven past only minutes ago. Her early morning cleaner must have vamoosed only moments before she pulled up in her parking space. If she'd hurried just a little, she could have caught her, or him, or perhaps several elfin thems!

Remembering the thin sheen of ice on the doorknob made Hannah discard her theory of helpful storybook creatures who could sneak in and accomplish great quantities of work in the blink of an eye. Her benefactor had been a real live person, one who could reach the doorknob and who didn't drink coffee. But who had cleaned up the kitchen on one of the coldest mornings of the year? And why?

Lisa came in the back door at a quarter to seven, fifteen minutes before she was expected. She found Hannah sitting at the work island in the center of the room, sipping a cup of coffee.

"Hi, Hannah," she said, hanging her coat on the rack by the back door and slipping out of her boots and into her work shoes. "You cleaned up the kitchen and did all the baking without me?"

Hannah shook her head. "I did the baking, but I didn't clean the kitchen. That was all done when I came in at a little before five this morning. I thought maybe you couldn't sleep and you'd done it."

"No way. And I don't sleepwalk, either. I wonder who . . ." Lisa stopped in midthought and began to frown. "Is anything missing?"

"Nothing I can see. Besides, our mystery cleaner left us a gift, and people who come in to steal things don't usually do that."

"What gift?"

Hannah pointed. "Candy. The note said they're called Brown Sugar Drops and they're on a plate right next to the coffee pot."

"Did you try one?"

"Of course. They're wonderful."

"Okay. I'll try one, too."

"You'll try one now that I've acted as official poison taster and I haven't keeled over yet?"

"That's right." Lisa laughed as she walked over to get a piece of candy. She popped it into her mouth, chewed, and headed for the pot to pour herself a cup of coffee. "This is good candy. It reminds me of the maple sugar candy my dad used to buy, except that was a little different. I just wish we had the recipe."

"We do," Hannah told her, pulling out a stool so that Lisa could sit at the workstation, and handing her the handwritten recipe their early morning visitor had left.

Lisa glanced down at the recipe. "This is great. I'm really glad she left it for us."

"She?"

"I think so. The writing looks feminine."

Hannah began to grin. "Because it's neat?"

"That could be part of it. But it's also small. The letters are delicate and all the men I know write a lot larger."

"I don't think that proves anything. My dad had small handwriting. He could fit things on drawer labels that I had to abbreviate. I think it depends on how you were taught. People used to take great pride in their handwriting. If you look at documents from the eighteen hundreds, you'll find some notable men with perfect penmanship. And how about the illuminated manuscripts all those monks wrote in the Middle Ages?"

"You're right," Lisa admitted. "I guees I made a sexist remark."

"You certainly did. And I totally agree with you."

"You do?"

"Absolutely. I'm convinced that a woman wrote that recipe."

"Why?"

"Because men don't usually use turquoise ink."

Lisa took a huge swig of her coffee. "I'm not awake enough for this yet." She took another swig and then she looked at Hannah again. "If you agreed with me in the first place, why did you argue?"

"Because I like to argue. It gets my brain cells firing and we need all the brainpower we can get today."

"You mean because we have to figure out who broke in and cleaned our kitchen for us?"

"That's right. And we have to figure out something else, too."

"What's that?"

"The next time it happens, we have to figure out how to get her to put on the coffee before she leaves."

BROWN SUGAR DROPS

Hannah's 1st Note: Candy told us that the original name of this recipe was "Browned" Sugar Drops. Over the years, it got shortened to Brown Sugar Drops, even though there's no brown sugar in the candy.

To make this candy, you will need a candy thermometer. I use the kind with a glass tube and a sliding metal clamp that attaches to the side of a saucepan. And even though the recipe calls for a 3-quart saucepan, I always use my 4-quart pan. That way I don't have to worry about the candy foaming up over the sides.

> 1 cup buttermilk
> 2½ cups white *(granulated)* sugar
> 1 teaspoon baking soda
> 2 Tablespoons *(⅛ cup)* white Karo syrup
> ½ cup butter, room temperature *(1 stick, ¼ pound)*

Before you start, get out a 3-quart saucepan and your candy thermometer. Place the thermometer inside the saucepan with the sliding clamp on the outside. Slide the thermometer through the clamp until it's approximately ½ inch from the bottom of the pan.

(If the bulb touches the bottom of the pan, your reading will be wildly off.)

On a cold burner, combine the buttermilk, sugar, baking soda, and white Karo syrup in the saucepan. Stir the mixture until it's smooth.

Turn your burner on medium high heat. STIR the candy mixture CONSTANTLY until it boils. *(This will take about 10 minutes, so pull up a stool and get comfortable while you stir.)*

Move the saucepan to a cold burner, but don't turn off the hot burner. You'll be getting right back to it.

Drop the butter into the candy mixture and stir it in. *(This could sputter a bit, so be careful.)* Slide the saucepan back on the hot burner and watch it cook. STIRRING IS NOT NECESSARY FROM THIS POINT ON. Just give it a little mix when you feel like it. Enjoy a cup of Swedish Plasma and one of those yummy cookies you baked last night while you wait for the candy thermometer to come up to the 240 degree F. mark.

When your thermometer reaches 240 degrees F., give the pan a final stir, turn off the burner, and take your candy from the heat. Let it cool on a wire rack or a cold burner until it returns to almost room temperature. Then stir it with a wooden spoon until it looks creamy.

Lay out sheets of wax paper. Drop the Brown Sugar Drops by a spoon onto the paper. Don't worry if your "drops" aren't of uniform size. Once your guests taste them, they'll be hunting for the bigger pieces.

Hannah's 2nd Note: If the time gets away from you and your candy hardens too much in the pan, you can stick it back on the burner over very low heat and stir it constantly until it's the proper creamy texture again.

Lisa's Note: This candy reminds me of the kind that's shaped like maple leaves. Dad used to bring it back from Vermont when he went back to visit Uncle Fritz and I loved it. Just for fun, I tried adding a teaspoon of maple extract and it was really good that way!

Yield: 3-dozen bon-bon size pieces of delicious candy.

Chapter Two

Candice Roberts arranged her sleeping bag under the lights by the front window of The Cookie Jar. The heater in the coffee shop blew out warm air that smelled like cookies, and Candy's stomach growled even though there was no way that she could be hungry. She'd eaten the ham and cheese sandwich that the red-haired owner had left for her, along with the bag of potato chips and the sour dill pickle that had reminded her of the kind Granny Roberts used to make. And then, for dessert, she'd polished off six of a dozen cookies that had been left on a plate for her, and she'd washed them down with a full glass of milk from the walk-in refrigerator.

Once the sleeping bag was arranged to her satisfaction, Candy snuggled in and thanked her lucky stars that she wasn't outside in the bitter cold. Her sleeping bag was rated for twenty below, but a glance at the thermometer in the kitchen window had told her that it was twenty-three below zero tonight, and it would probably get even colder before the sun came up in the morning.

A tear rolled down Candy's cheek and dripped onto the fabric of her sleeping bag. It had been her dad's last Christmas present to her, along with the down-filled, quilted field jacket that was getting just a bit too tight across the shoulders, and the buckskin mittens he'd called "choppers" that were lined with real fur. Dad had grown up in Minnesota, and they'd planned to go winter camping at the campground he remembered on the shores of Eden Lake.

Another tear joined the first, and then another. Now she'd never go camping with her dad again. A year ago, Dad had gone down to the clinic for an emergency. On his way home, a drunk driver had hit him and he'd died on the way to the hospital.

For a long while, Candy hadn't thought she'd ever be happy again. She missed him so much. But she'd talked a lot with Mom, and that had helped. She was just starting to feel as if things might actually be okay when disaster struck again.

Just thinking about it caused another tear to fall, and then the dam broke. Candy cried until there were no more tears left, and then she closed her swollen eyes. She missed her dad, but missing him couldn't bring him back again. And she missed her mom, but she wouldn't see her again for a long, long time.

"You really wouldn't mind driving past my shop?" Hannah asked, turning to Norman to make sure he was serious. They'd just finished dinner at the Lake Eden Inn where they'd had several new appetizers that Sally Laughlin, the co-owner and chef, would be featuring at her huge Christmas party next Friday night. It was a straight shot from the Lake Eden Inn to Hannah's condo, but driving into town, where Hannah's cookie shop was located, amounted to a twenty-six-mile detour.

"Why would I mind?" Norman answered her question with a question, something that Hannah's mother frequently accused her of doing. "It gives me more time with you."

The smile Norman gave her looked perfectly genuine in the dim light coming from his dashboard. Hannah smiled back and they were off, heading to Lake Eden on a wintry night that suddenly seemed much warmer to Hannah. "Would you like to hear about the night visitor I had this morning?" she asked.

"A night visitor in the *morning*?" Norman turned on the windshield wipers to handle the light sprinkling of snow that was falling. "Isn't that a contradiction in terms?"

"No. Do you want to hear about it?"

"Yes, I want to hear about it."

"All right then. The lights in the window were on when I drove past the front of the shop this morning. And then, when I unlocked the back door, I noticed that there was ice on the knob, as if a warm hand had gripped it just moments before."

"You thought someone might be inside your shop and you went in anyway?" Norman glanced at her sharply.

"Of course I did. This is Lake Eden. We don't have any crime to speak of."

Norman didn't say anything. He didn't have to. He just ran his finger across his throat in a slashing motion.

"Okay, okay. I get your point. Maybe we do have a *little* crime. But it was only one double-homicide, and I don't think we've ever had one before. Lake Eden's a really safe place to live in the winter, at least as far as break-ins go."

"It's too cold for crime?" Norman guessed.

"That's part of it. Everybody's so busy concentrating on keeping warm, they don't have time to commit petty theft. I never double-lock the back door to The Cookie Jar in the winter. What if some homeless person is freezing outside and needs to get in out of the cold?"

Norman turned to give her a smile. "You're a kind woman, Hannah. Foolish, but kind."

"Well, I've never had any trouble, and I didn't have any trouble this morning. As a matter of fact, whoever slept at

The Cookie Jar last night got up early, did all the dishes, and mopped the floor."

"As a thank-you for the warm place to sleep?"

"I think so. She also made us a batch of really great candy and left us the recipe. That's what gave us the idea to offer candy over the holidays. Homemade candy is so much better than anything you can buy in the stores. And a lot of people don't have time to make their own."

"Good idea. If you can make English Toffee, I'll get some for my mother for Christmas. It's her favorite, and she's always complaining that the kind you buy isn't as good as the kind her mother used to make."

"Ibby used to make English Toffee. It was really good, and she gave me a copy of her recipe."

"Who's Ibby?"

"A teaching assistant in the English Department. I met her when I took a graduate seminar in college. Ibby was an expert on Seventeenth-Century English Metaphysical Poets."

"Like Donne?"

Hannah gave him a thumbs-up. "That's right."

"And . . . Traherne?"

"Right again." Hannah was impressed. Most people had no idea who the metaphysical poets were and certainly wouldn't be able to name two of them. "How did you know that?"

"Mother."

"Your mother liked the metaphysical poets?"

"No, she liked 'A Visit from Saint Nicholas.' "

"So does Mother. But what does that have to do with Donne and Traherne?"

"We had a big family Christmas every year with all the uncles, aunts, and cousins. I made the mistake of memorizing it when I was four, and every year from then on, my mother asked me to recite it."

"That can be embarrassing, especially if you don't want to do it," Hannah sympathized.

"Not to mention 'dangerous.' "

"Dangerous?"

"That's right. My cousins didn't like it when I was in the spotlight, and they used to give me a hard time after we were excused from dinner. I told my mother and she said to ignore them, that they were just jealous."

"So what did you do?"

"A week before the next Christmas, I memorized four pieces from the metaphysical poets, the longest ones I could find."

"And it worked?"

"Like a charm. My mother never asked me to recite again."

"How about your cousins?"

"The oldest one caught on to what I was doing and told the others. We were pretty good friends after that." Norman began to frown. "I can't imagine anyone choosing to become an expert on the metaphysical poets."

"I couldn't imagine it either. But I asked Ibby and she said she chose them because there were only seven. She figured she could handle that."

"But John Donne was prolific."

"That's true. And he's not what anyone would call a 'fun read.' A lot of his poetry is about depressing subjects."

"Really?" Norman gave a little grin. "You don't think that 'So doth each tear, Which thee doth wear, A globe, yea world, by that impression grow, Till thy tears mix'd with mine do overflow. This world, by waters sent from thee, my heaven dissolved so,' is cheerful?"

"The imagery's nice, but it's about crying and that's not a very cheerful subject."

"You've got a point. So how does Ibby's English Toffee fit into metaphysical poetry? Or does it?"

"Ibby used to bring her toffee to our study groups to make sure we all showed up. And the department loved her because nobody ever missed her sessions."

"They should have done that in dental school. I had to force myself to go to my class in Billing and Business Management Models." Norman pulled up in back of The Cookie Jar and took Hannah's parking spot. "If you can find that toffee recipe, I'll take thirty half-pound boxes."

"For your *mother?*"

"Just one box for my mother. I'll give the other twenty-nine to my patients for the holidays."

"That's nice of you, but . . ." Hannah stopped and began to frown.

"But what?"

"I don't want to talk myself out of a big sale here, but isn't that sending the wrong message?"

"What do you mean?"

"You're giving them candy. And candy is practically solid sugar. I thought dentists wanted their patients to avoid a lot of sugar."

"Not necessarily. We encourage our patients to brush and floss after eating sweets, but we don't tell them not to eat candy. If everyone ate correctly and practiced impeccable dental hygiene, there wouldn't be any need for dentists. And then I'd be out of a job!"

Hannah turned to stare at him. She thought he was joking, but she wasn't completely sure. Then she saw the corner on his mouth twitch slightly and she knew he was pulling her leg. "I've never thought of it from that perspective before. And it seems we're in the same boat."

"We are?"

"If everyone ate exactly what they should and never treated themselves to sinful desserts, I'd be out of business, too!"

Chapter
Three

Hannah stood staring at the back door of her building for a moment and then she sighed. "I wonder what she'll do when we come in."

"She'll run."

"You think?"

"I'm positive. From what you said, she sounds like an intelligent girl. She knows it's illegal to break into a locked store."

"But she only broke in because it was cold outside."

"I know."

"And she tried to pay me for staying overnight by making candy and cleaning my kitchen."

"That's true, but she still broke in twice that you know of."

"Once," Hannah corrected him.

"But the lights in the window are on. Doesn't that mean she's here tonight?"

"Oh, she's here. But I gave her tacit permission to stay."

"You left her a note?"

"No, I left her a sandwich and a plate of cookies. I wouldn't have done that if I didn't want her in my shop."

"All right. Let's say she figured out that the sandwich and the cookies were for her and she ate them. And she's all bedded down inside for the night. I still think she'll run when you come in."

Hannah thought about that. Norman could be right. Someone desperate enough to break into a shop and sleep on the floor might think the sandwich and cookies were a trap to catch her. "So do you think that I ought to just leave her alone?"

"Absolutely not. For all you know she's underage and her family is worried sick about her. What we should do is talk to her, find out her story and see if we can do something to help."

"You said *we*," Hannah pointed out. "Does that mean you want to get involved?"

"I'm already involved. I got involved when I agreed to drive you to the shop. There may be something I can do to help her. For instance . . . what if she has a crippling overbite?"

Hannah burst out laughing and immediately clamped a gloved hand over her mouth. They had to be quiet, and that was difficult when Norman was so funny. She wanted to reach out and give him a hug, but she resisted the impulse. Although she didn't think he'd misinterpret it, she couldn't be a hundred percent sure. "I know we should talk to her," she told him, "but what if you're right and the minute she sees us, she bolts?"

"That's where I come in. You go in the back door and I'll walk around to the front. If she takes one look at you and tries to run out the front, I'll nab her and bring her back."

"Okay," Hannah agreed, giving in to her impulse and hugging Norman anyway. He really was a nice guy. "I'm ready if you are."

All was quiet as they climbed out of Norman's sedan. They closed the doors silently and then they headed for the back door of The Cookie Jar.

"Wait for a minute before you go in," Norman whispered. "I'll give a low whistle when I get to the front of the building."

"How about a bird song? That's what the Indians used to do, at least in the movies."

"The only bird call I know is the Minnesota state bird."

"The loon?" Hannah was so surprised, she almost forgot to whisper. "Why did you learn that?"

"You don't want to know."

"Yes, I do. Why?"

Norman looked a little embarrassed. "So I could do it at parties when I was in dental school, but there's no way I'm going to do it now. It sounds like an insane woman laughing, and I'd probably scare both of you to death. Just listen for my whistle, okay?"

"Okay." Hannah took up her position at the back door and waited. It seemed to take forever for Norman to get around to the front of the building, but at last she heard his signal. She unlocked the back door, stepped in quietly, and threw the deadbolt from the inside. It would take her nocturnal visitor precious seconds to figure out the old-fashioned lock and that would give Hannah time to catch her if she tried to leave the back way.

Hannah tiptoed through her silent kitchen, checking every nook and cranny. No one was hiding in any of the corners, or in the pantry. The bathroom was deserted, but someone had used the shower within the last few hours. There were still a few beads of water on the walls of the enclosure, and the towels were damp to the touch. She came out the door and headed for the front. There was only one place left to check, and that was the coffee shop.

Careful not to make a sound, Hannah pushed open the swinging door to the coffee shop. Her eyes were immediately drawn to the front window and the lights that were on for the second night in a row. Her elfin visitor was here. Now all she had to do was find her.

Hannah moved closer as she noticed a bulky pile of bedding that hadn't been there when she'd closed up her shop. It was a sleeping bag stretched out under the lights in the window. Hannah was reminded of all those times as a child when she'd fallen asleep under the tree, half-listening to the adults talking, comforted by the twinkling lights and familiar ornaments, and knowing that Christmas was only a week or two away.

The girl was turned toward the lights, rosy in sleep and glowing from the red bulb that was directly above her face. With her long eyelashes and slightly parted lips, she looked like a porcelain doll with rouge-painted cheeks. In the silence of the shop, with only the hum of the cooler behind the counter, Hannah could hear her breathing softly in slumber.

Hannah admired the picture she made for a moment, and then she put her investigational skills to work. The girl's fingernails were clean and so were her clothes and her sleeping bag. That meant she hadn't been on the streets for long. She wasn't starving, either. Her left arm, the one that wasn't covered by the sleeping bag, was nicely rounded. On the whole she looked healthy and younger than Hannah had expected.

People usually looked younger while they slept. The cares and worries of the day were erased by peaceful oblivion, and a stress-free persona emerged. Perhaps this girl wasn't as young as she looked, but Hannah had her doubts. She seemed innocent, almost untried, on the brink of discovery but not yet comfortable with her newly adult form.

Hannah began to frown. She really hated to wake her uninvited boarder just to tell her that she could sleep in the coffee shop. It was almost the same as a nurse waking a patient in the hospital because it was time for a sleeping pill. If the girl was a runaway, there was little joy in her life. And right now she appeared to be dreaming about something pleasant, judging by the half-smile on her face. It seemed a shame to shatter her happiness, but it had to be done and the sooner

the better. There was no way Hannah was going to let someone who appeared to be far younger than her youngest sister
go back on the streets again! Besides, Norman was standing
outside the front door shivering, and it was time to let him in.

"Wake up," Hannah said softly, hoping she wouldn't
cause the girl to panic. "I need to talk to you."

The girl groaned an inarticulate protest and made a little
moue of distaste. "Not yet. Go 'way, Mom."

She had a mother. Hannah added that to the mental list of
facts and suppositions she'd gathered. "Come on, now. Wake
up. You can go back to sleep right after you talk to me."

The girl looked as though she was going to roll over and
ignore the intrusion, but then some internal sense of preser-
vation must have kicked in. She sat up with a jolt, her eyes
flew open, and she stared hard at Hannah. "Who are you?"

"Hannah Swensen. This is my coffee shop. Who are
you?"

"I'm Candy."

"Candy who?"

"Candy R . . . never mind. You don't need to know my
name." The girl wiggled from her sleeping bag and got to her
feet. "Please don't call the cops. I'm leaving right now."

And before Hannah could open her mouth to say that
there was no need to run, the girl grabbed her sleeping bag
and raced for the front door, unlocking it in a flash and dashing out.

"Good grief!" Hannah gasped, hardly believing her eyes.
She'd never seen anyone move that fast. It was obvious that
the girl had been prepared for rude awakenings. She'd slept
in her clothes and she must have hidden her other belongings in the bottom of her sleeping bag. All that was left to
prove she'd been there in the first place was a bare spot on
the floor where she'd moved a table and two chairs so she
could stretch out.

"Let me go! Come on, Mister! Please? I wasn't hurting
anything, really I wasn't!"

Hannah hurried to the door to help Norman, who'd caught the fleeing runaway as she'd rushed out into the night. "It's okay, Candy. We didn't call the police and we're not going to. You've got my permission to stay here for the night."

"I do?" Candy still looked frightened, but her struggles diminished noticeably. She gave another twist to try to get away from Norman's grasp, but it was clear her heart wasn't in it.

"How about some hot chocolate?" Hannah suggested, motioning for Norman to escort her to the kitchen. "You don't want to catch a cold, dashing outside like that without your coat."

Candy gave a little nod. "That would be great, but being outside in the cold doesn't give you a cold. My dad said that when people tell you that, it's just an old wives' tale."

"But I'm not married and I'm not that old," Hannah shot back, and she was gratified when Candy laughed. For someone who'd been jolted out of sleep by a stranger and had fled into the bitterly cold night with all her belongings, she had managed to maintain her sense of humor. "Is your dad a doctor?"

"My dad was a vet. He's dead now. You're sure you didn't call the cops on me?"

"Of course I didn't. This is a small town. If I'd called them, they'd be here by now."

Candy turned to Norman. "How about you? Did you call them?"

"Not me. My cell phone's still in the car." Norman glanced down at Candy's feet. "Isn't it hard to climb into a sleeping bag when you're wearing tennis shoes?"

"Not if you unzip it all the way. Getting out is the hard part. The soles stick to the lining of the bag and you have to keep tugging it down."

"Maybe you should think about wearing two pairs of

socks. Then your feet would be warm and you wouldn't have to bother with shoes."

Candy shook her head. "I don't do it to keep my feet warm. I have to be prepared in case I need to run."

Hannah stood at the stovetop, stirring the hot chocolate and listening to Norman and Candy. He'd only been talking to her for a few moments, but already she seemed comfortable with him.

"You don't have to worry about that anymore," Norman told her. "Hannah's going to let you stay."

"Why would she do that?"

Hannah jumped in, right on cue. Norman had given her the perfect opening for the plan she'd been hatching. "Because I could use some help around here. Have you ever worked as a waitress?"

"Sure," Candy replied quickly, and then she gave a little sigh, "but not the way you mean. I could do it, though. I know I could. I mean, I know how to set a table, and pour coffee for people, and dish up food and stuff like that. And I can make candy for your shop. I've been making candy for a couple of years now, ever since I turned thir . . ."—Candy stopped abruptly and swallowed hard—". . . ever since I was really young."

Hannah smiled. Getting information from a chilled, tired teenager wasn't at all difficult. She'd already learned that Candy's last name started with *R*, she had a mother and a deceased father who'd been a veterinarian, and a couple of years had passed since she'd been thirteen. If this kept up, they'd have the story of Candy's life before they'd finished their hot chocolate.

"Here you go," Hannah said, carrying Candy's mug to the workstation and setting it down in front of her. She poured a mug for Norman, filled one for herself, and delivered those, too. "I don't know if you're still hungry, but would you like a cookie?"

Candy looked delighted. "You bet! I mean . . . yes, please. You make really good cookies."

"Thanks." Hannah hid a grin as she carried a plate of her newest creation to the table. Obviously, Candy had been taught to be polite and that was another fact to add to the mix. "You two can be my taste testers," she told them. "I'm trying out a new cookie and I'm not sure what I'm going to call it. Maybe you can help me come up with a name."

"They're good," Norman said, after the first bite. "That's raspberry I taste, isn't it?"

"Yes. I made them with seedless raspberry jam."

Candy finished her first cookie and started to reach for a second. Then she drew her hand back and looked at Hannah. "Could I please have another?"

"Of course. Help yourself."

"I like the way the outside crunches and the inside is chewy." Candy took another bite and then she looked over at Hannah again. "Could you make them with other jams, like blackberry? Or strawberry, or mixed berry?"

"I don't see why not. They might not be as attractive if you used blueberry, but any other berry should be fine."

"That's perfect, then. How about if you call them Merry Berry Cookies? It rhymes and everything, and that means it'll be easy to remember. And eating them makes you happy so that's where the 'merry' part comes in."

"What a great idea!" Norman praised her. " 'Merry Berry Cookies' sounds perfect to me. Are you sure you don't have an advanced degree in marketing?"

Candy giggled and Hannah felt like beaming. Norman was helping to relax her, and perhaps she'd tell them more about her background and what she was doing here in Lake Eden.

"I don't have an advanced degree in anything. I haven't even finished . . ." Candy halted and cleared her throat. "I haven't even declared my major yet."

Hannah glanced quickly at Norman. They both knew

what Candy had been about to say. *I haven't even finished high school,* would be a fairly safe guess.

"How old are you, Candy?" Norman asked the question that was on the tip of Hannah's tongue. It would be interesting to see how many fictional years Candy would add to her young life.

"Twenty," Candy said, without batting an eyelash, and Hannah got the impression she'd told that particular lie before. "I'll be twenty-one next month."

Hannah and Norman locked eyes. Even though they didn't say a word, Hannah got the feeling that Norman could read her mind and he agreed with what she was thinking. More questions would serve no purpose other than to elicit more lies from Candy. It was time to call it a night and let her think they'd believed her.

Norman gave a yawn that Hannah suspected was purely theatrical, and finished his mug of hot chocolate. "We'd better hit the road, Hannah. Tomorrow's a workday and you have to get up early."

"Right," Hannah agreed, and then she turned to Candy. "You'll be perfectly safe here if you lock the door behind us. I'll be back around five tomorrow morning to start the baking."

"I'll help you. I like to get up early. Is there anything I can do before you come in?"

"Only if you get up before five."

"Oh, I will. I'll be up by four-thirty."

"Then you can put on the coffee." Hannah motioned toward the kitchen pot. "The grounds and filters are in the cupboard to the left of the sink."

"Okay. It's just like the pot Dad had at the clinic, so I know how to do it. How strong do you like it?"

"As strong as it gets."

Candy nodded quickly. "You want me to fill the basket almost all the way to the top with grounds?"

"That'd be perfect. Thanks, Candy." Hannah slipped into

her coat and pulled on her gloves. "I'll see you in the morning, then."

Hannah and Norman made their exit. They stopped outside the door, and by unspoken agreement they waited until they heard Candy lock the door behind them. Then they hurried to Norman's car and climbed in, shivering.

"I'll get the heater going right away," Norman promised, firing up the engine and turning the heater to high.

Hannah shivered as he backed up the car. She shivered some more as he drove out of the parking lot and down the alley. But when Norman stopped at the end of the alley, she realized that she'd stopped shivering. As a matter of fact, she had to slip off her gloves and unzip her parka a bit because she was too warm. Norman's heater was pouring out waves of hot air that felt positively tropical.

One glance at the windshield and Hannah was even more impressed. Instead of the patches of frost that clung to the inside of her windshield for the first five or six miles of winter driving, Norman's windshield was already picture window clear and they'd been driving less than a block!

Just to make sure, Hannah reached out to touch one of the buttons on the radio. It was warm instead of icy cold. "I love it," she breathed.

"You love what?"

"Your heater. If I knew how to hook it up, I'd steal it and put it in my truck."

"But then *I'd* freeze. Maybe we'd better work out a compromise that'll make both of us happy."

"What did you have in mind?"

"I could drive you to work every morning and back home every night. Then both of us would stay warm."

Hannah had a feeling she knew what was coming, but she decided she'd bite anyway. "But you live in town, and I live out of town. Would you really be willing to make two round-trips a day?"

"I'd only have to make one round-trip if I stayed at your

condo." Norman gave her a grin that looked positively devil-ish, and then he waggled his eyebrows up and down to add to the illusion.

Hannah laughed at his antics. "Only in your dreams, Nor-man!" she retorted. But she had to admit that Norman's compromise did have a certain appeal that wasn't entirely due to the cold winter weather.

MERRY BERRY COOKIES

Don't preheat the oven yet—this cookie dough has to chill before baking.

1½ cups melted butter *(3 sticks, ¾ pound)*
2 cups white *(granulated)* sugar
½ cup melted raspberry, blackberry, strawberry, or
    any berry jam *(I used Knott's seedless
    raspberry)*
2 beaten eggs
½ teaspoon baking soda
1 teaspoon salt
4 cups flour *(pack it down in the cup—don't sift it)*
⅓ cup white *(granulated)* sugar for later
⅓ cup berry jam for later

Melt the butter in a large microwave-safe bowl. Add the white sugar and mix it in thoroughly. Let the bowl sit on the counter while you do the next step.

Melt the jam in the microwave or in a saucepan over low heat. Once it's the consistency of syrup, mix it in with the butter and sugar.

Add the eggs, baking soda, and salt, stirring after each addition.

Add the flour and mix thoroughly. Cover the bowl and refrigerate the dough for at least 2 hours. *(Overnight's even better.)*

When you're ready to bake, preheat the oven to 350 degrees F., rack in the middle position.

Roll the chilled dough into small walnut-sized balls with your hands. Put 1/3 cup white sugar in a small bowl and roll the balls in it. Place them on a greased standard-sized cookie sheet, 12 cookies to a sheet. Flatten the dough balls with a greased spatula. Make a small indentation with your thumb or index finger in the center of each cookie. Fill the indentation with a small bit of jam *(about $1/8$ teaspoon.)*

Bake the cookies for 10 to 12 minutes at 350 degrees F. Let them cool for 2 minutes on the cookie sheet, and then transfer them to a wire rack to finish cooling.

These cookies freeze well. Roll them up in foil, put them in a freezer bag, and be sneaky about how you label them or the kids will find them and eat them frozen.

Yield: 8 to 10 dozen, depending on cookie size.

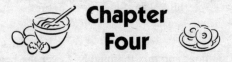

Chapter
Four

Perhaps a more imaginative person could have seen mythical figures in the irregular swatches of plaster on her bedroom ceiling, but Hannah wasn't in the mood. She also wasn't keen on counting sheep, reciting her times tables all the way through the dreaded sevens, or mentally cataloguing her cookie recipes. Her never-fail sleep aid, reading the statutes of the Winnetka County Health Board, hadn't even made her eyelids heavy, and there was no way she was going to take any over-the-counter remedies when she had to get up in less than five hours.

Hannah switched on the light, causing her bedmate to blink and then stare at her with startled yellow eyes. She'd been tired when Norman had left, so tired that she'd barely been able to get ready for bed and climb under the covers. The pillow had been perfectly supportive, cradling her head just so, and the quilt had formed a warm and comforting cocoon. Moishe had purred softly beside her, actually letting her cuddle him close for ten seconds or so before he'd padded down to sleep on her feet, and the rhythmic whoosh of warm air from the heat vents had been positively soporific. Unfortunately, it had all gone downhill from there.

She'd started thinking about Candy and how frantic her family must be, and that had made her eyes open wide and her mind kick into high gear. She had to figure out where Candy came from, discover why she'd run away, and try to get her to go back home where she belonged.

There was no way she could sleep with a problem this weighty on her mind. Hannah put on her slippers and shrugged into her robe, knotting the sash around her waist. She always thought best when she was cooking, and since she was wide awake anyway, she might as well look for Ibby's toffee recipe and make it tonight. She could take some to work tomorrow morning so Norman could taste it.

"Coming?" Hannah asked, turning to look at her feline roommate. But Moishe had commandeered her pillow the moment she'd left it and he was stretched out on top like a sphinx, his front paws aligned in front of him, his head held perfectly erect, and his expression regal.

"Guess not," Hannah said, answering her own question as she walked out of the room.

To Hannah's sleep-deprived eyes, the kitchen appeared glaringly bright with its white walls and appliances. She had the urge to fetch her sunglasses as she got out her box of recipes marked "TO TRY" in big red letters. She lifted the lid, frowned at the pieces of multicolored and mismatched paper that were stuffed haphazardly into the interior, and set it down on the kitchen table with a clunk. Then she put on the coffee, snatched the carafe aside, and stuck her mug directly under the stream of fresh coffee dripping through the grounds. When her mug was full, she completed her juggling act by removing her mug and replacing the carafe.

Going through recipes without reading them was like eating a cream puff before it was filled. Even though Hannah did her best to page quickly through them, she found herself pulling out several she wanted to try immediately, some she needed to make for Christmas, and even more she intended to try within the next few months.

Her mug was empty by the time she finished sorting all the papers in the box, and Hannah got up to refill it. She hadn't found Ibby's toffee recipe, but she was sure she had it.

There was another place she could look. Hannah headed for the bookshelf in the living room where she kept her collection of cookbooks. One was from her father's mother, Grandma Ingrid, and it had an envelope for recipes on the inside of the front cover. She might have slipped it in there.

By the time she'd finished going through the envelope, Hannah had a fistful of recipes to add to her piles on the kitchen table. Unfortunately, Ibby's toffee recipe wasn't among them. That meant there was only one more place to look and the moment Hannah thought of it, she was off and running to the guest room closet, where she was almost certain she'd stashed her old college backpack.

It took some doing. The closet was stuffed with cast-off clothing and other useless items she hadn't been able to throw away, but eventually Hannah emerged from the depths, her search complete. Her naturally unruly red hair had been made even more unruly by an intimate encounter with a black plush coat that had belonged to her maternal grandmother, but she was clutching a bright red backpack covered with sewn-on patches from exotic places she'd never been.

"I found it!" she said, as she switched off the lights and carried it down the hall to the kitchen. That was another advantage of living alone. There was no one to think you were crazy if you talked to yourself. And on the off-chance that someone dropped by and caught her at it, Hannah could always pretend she'd been talking to Moishe and she hadn't realized he'd left the room.

Hannah sat down, took another sip of coffee, and eyed the backpack. Without books it seemed oddly deflated, like a beach ball that had been left out all winter. It didn't look promising, but it was the only place she had left to look.

"Here goes nothing," Hannah said to the cat that wasn't there, and plunged her hand down into the bottom of the backpack. The first thing she encountered was her old lunch sack with something in the bottom. Whatever it was, or had been, it was light years past the expiration date. Hannah also found a pair of sunglasses, a handful of assorted pens, and a combination lock to which she'd forgotten the combination. Eventually her fingers touched paper, stiff paper the size of an index card.

Heart beating hard, Hannah drew her hand from the backpack and took a look. It was Ibby's recipe for Metaphysical English Toffee. She could hardly wait to taste it again!

A quick glance at the list of ingredients and Hannah realized that she was in luck. She had everything, even a package of Club Crackers. They were her mother's favorite cracker and Hannah had stocked up for the holidays.

It didn't take long to line a pan with foil and spray it with nonstick cooking spray. Hannah covered the foil with crackers and mixed the toffee ingredients together in a saucepan. As she was stirring the boiling toffee mixture, waiting for five minutes to elapse, she thought about Candy again. It certainly couldn't hurt to ask an expert some questions, and she had an expert right in the family. Her brother-in-law, Bill, was a sheriff's deputy.

Hannah glanced at the clock. It was eleven-thirty, but Bill always stayed up until midnight. If she were in luck, he'd answer the phone before it woke her sister, Andrea. Hannah reached for the phone, punched in the number, and kept right on stirring while it rang.

"It's right here on the table by the front door. You must have set it down while you were looking for your car keys. I'll drive it out there right now if you want me to, but that means I have to wake Tracey and . . ."

"It's me, Andrea," Hannah said, interrupting what was obviously an explanation meant for her brother-in-law. "Bill left for work and he forgot his lunch?"

"Yes, and he's pulling a double. One of the guys called in sick."

"Do you want me to take something out to him?"

"That's nice of you, Hannah, but you don't have to. He can just call out for pizza again. He's done this same thing a couple of times before, and that's what he did then." There was a pause, and when Andrea came back on the line she sounded puzzled. "Come to think about it, it's usually when I make bologna and pimento cheese sandwiches. If I didn't know better, I'd think he didn't like them."

Hannah didn't join in as her sister gave a little laugh at what she assumed was an absurdity. Hannah had tasted Andrea's bologna and pimento cheese sandwiches. Once. On a scale of one to ten, they were a minus six.

"What are you doing up so late?" Andrea asked.

"Making toffee. If it's good, I'll save some for you."

"Anything you make is good. And I love toffee. Is it the kind with the chocolate and nuts on top?"

"That's right."

"Oh, good! That's Bill's favorite, too. Maybe you can teach me how to make it."

When cows do calculus, Hannah thought, but she didn't say it. Andrea was a disaster in the kitchen. There was no way a mere mortal could teach her to cook.

"So did you need something?" Andrea asked, erasing Hannah's mental image of bovines standing on their hind legs to write complicated mathematical formulas on a chalkboard.

"Not really. I just wanted to ask Bill a question."

"About Mike Kingston, I'll bet." Andrea named the newest detective on the squad. "Well, I can save you the trouble. Mike told Bill he had a great time going bowling with you. And he's going to ask you out again for this weekend."

"That's . . . great," Hannah said. She wasn't sure she liked the early date-warning system, but it was probably unavoidable since Bill was working with Mike.

"Anyway, if there's nothing else, I've got to get to bed. I've got an early day tomorrow."

"You're getting up early?" Hannah hoped she didn't sound as shocked as she felt. Andrea set her own hours at Lake Eden Realty. She usually slept until nine or so and then took another hour to get ready for work. Since most people didn't go out house hunting until noon or later, that worked out just fine.

"I've got a showing at one," Andrea explained. "And that means I have to get up at seven."

"It takes you six hours to get ready for a showing?"

"Of course not! It's just that tomorrow afternoon is the Dorcas Circle Luncheon and the Cut 'n Curl is booked solid. The only time Bertie can squeeze me in is at eight in the morning. And that reminds me . . ."

"I'll be glad to," Hannah interrupted, knowing exactly what her sister was going to ask. "Just bring Tracey in before you go to Bertie's, and I'll make sure she gets to Kiddie Korner on time."

"Thanks, Hannah. You're a doll, you know that?"

"I know. That's why Mike wants to take me out again."

"Actually . . . that's *not* why," Andrea said, taking Hannah literally. "He told Bill you were the funniest woman he'd ever met."

Hannah tried to think of something to say, but it was difficult. She wasn't sure if being funny was more important than being a doll. She also wasn't sure if what Mike had said was a compliment or not. After all, clowns were funny, but you wouldn't necessarily want to date one.

The timer dinged, saving her from analyzing the problem further, and Hannah pulled her pan of toffee off the heat. "I've got to go. My toffee needs me. I'll see you in the morning, Andrea."

Pouring the hot candy mixture over the crackers wasn't difficult and neither was slipping the pan into the oven. Hannah set the timer for ten minutes and sat down at the kitchen table to wait. If the toffee turned out well, she'd drop some off for Bill on her way in to work tomorrow morning. He'd probably ask her to join him for some perfectly dreadful squad room brew that resembled coffee about as much as a tractor resembled a high-performance sports car, but it would give her a chance to ask him some theoretical questions about police procedure and runaways.

When the timer rang again, Hannah took the pan out of the oven and sprinkled on the milk chocolate chips. She waited until the chips started to melt, and then she spread them out with her spatula. Once she'd scattered chopped pecans over the top and put the pan in the refrigerator, she cleaned up the kitchen and headed off to bed for a second attempt at sleep.

Just as she'd expected, Moishe was still spread out on her pillow. Hannah climbed into bed on the other side and grabbed Moishe's pillow. It was foam and she hated foam pillows. Not only that; it was lumpy foam that was starting to crumble and smell. It was almost worse than no pillow at all, but she was simply too tired to get into a turf war with her cat over the expensive goose-down pillow she'd bought at the Tri-County Mall. She bunched the foam up, shoved it under her neck, and hoped that she wouldn't be as stiff as a board in the morning. And then, even though she wasn't used to sleeping on that side of the bed, and the foam pillow felt like a giant bag of petrified miniature marshmallows, and she'd forgotten to take off her slippers, she fell asleep almost instantly.

IBBY'S METAPHYSICAL
ENGLISH TOFFEE

Preheat oven to 350 degrees, rack in the middle position.

16-ounce box Club Crackers*** *(Mine were made by Keebler)*
1 cup butter *(2 sticks, ½ pound)*
1 cup brown sugar *(tightly packed)*
2 cups milk chocolate chips *(12-ounce bag)*
2 cups chopped pecans *(salted or unsalted, it really doesn't matter)*

*** *There are three packets in a 16-ounce box of Club Crackers. You'll use only one packet. You can buy a smaller box if you can find it, but you can always use extra crackers, right? If you can't find Club Crackers at your store, you can use any brand of salted soda crackers. Your goal is to cover the bottom of the pan as completely as you can with something both crispy and salty.*

Line a 10-inch by 15-inch cookie sheet with foil. If you have a jellyroll pan, that's perfect. If you don't, turn up the edges of the foil to form sides.

Spray the foil with Pam or other nonstick cooking spray. *(You want to be able to peel it off later, after the candy hardens.)*

Line the pan completely with Club Crackers, salt side up. Cover the whole bottom. *(You can break the crackers in pieces to make them fit if you have to.)* Set the cracker-lined jellyroll pan or cookie sheet aside while you cook the toffee mixture.

Hannah's 1st Note: You don't need a candy thermometer to make this candy.

Combine the butter with the brown sugar in a saucepan. Bring it to a boil over medium high heat on the stovetop, stirring constantly. Boil it for exactly five minutes, stirring it constantly. If it sputters too much, you can reduce the heat. If it starts to lose the boil, you can increase the heat. Just don't stop stirring.

Pour the mixture over the crackers as evenly as you can.

Hannah's 2nd Note: I start by pouring the mixture in lines from top to bottom over the length of the pan. Then I turn it and pour more lines over the width of the pan. Once the whole pan is cross-

hatched with the hot toffee mixture, I pour any that's left where it's needed. If it doesn't cover the crackers completely, don't worry—it'll spread out quite a bit in the oven.

Slide the pan into the oven and bake the toffee at 350 degrees F. for 10 minutes.

Remove the pan from the oven and sprinkle the milk chocolate chips over the top. Give the chips a minute or two to melt and then spread them out as evenly as you can with a heat-resistant spatula, a wooden paddle, or a frosting knife.

Sprinkle the chopped pecans over the top of the chocolate and refrigerate the pan.

When the toffee has thoroughly chilled, peel it from the foil and break it into random-sized pieces.

Hannah's 3rd Note: Ibby used her toffee as a reward for high quiz scores. Once you taste it, you'll know why I can still recite at least one stanza from each of the Metaphysical Poets.

Chapter
Five

The headlights of Hannah's cookie truck glared against the row of single-pane windows marching across the front of the squat red brick building that housed the Winnetka County Sheriff's Department. It was a fairly new structure, built with county money, and the windows, one to each office, didn't open. This made it more energy efficient, according to county government guidelines. Regardless of the season or the outdoor temperature, the inside was maintained at a politically correct sixty-eight degrees.

There were eight head-in parking spots that were earmarked for visitors, and Hannah had her pick of all eight of them. Since her mother hadn't raised a fool, she took the one closest to the front door. Grabbing the sample box of toffee she'd prepared before she'd left her condo, and armed with three bags of day-old cookies that would be speedily devoured by anyone on duty inside, she made a hasty exit from her truck and hurried to the front door.

Hannah pushed open the first door and stepped into the enclosure that served as a cloakroom. It was narrow, more like a hallway than a room, and it contained a rack for boots and a series of hooks for hanging parkas and scarves. The door to the inside of the sheriff's station was at the end, and the enclosure also served as a buffer between the frigid winter air and the deputy who manned the front desk.

Hannah couldn't help grinning as she slipped out of her boots and hung her parka on a hook. The county board had spent thousands of dollars to research the energy-saving inner door and outer door plan, something any Minnesotan who had an enclosed front or back porch could have told them for free.

Just as Hannah was reaching for the inner door to let herself in, it opened and Bill appeared. "Come on in, Hannah. I was in the office and I saw you pull up."

"Hi, Bill," Hannah greeted him, handing over the plate of toffee.

"What's this?"

"English Toffee. I made it last night. And I brought cookies, too. Do you have time for coffee? I need to talk to you about something."

"I've got nothing *but* time. It's been dead as a doornail all night." Bill stopped and frowned slightly. "I wonder what that means anyway."

"What *what* means?"

" 'Dead as a doornail.' I've been saying it all my life and I don't know what it means."

"It dates back to the thirteen hundreds. Shakespeare even used it in *Henry IV*. Most scholars think it came from clinching a nail."

"What's that?"

"Driving in a long nail and hammering the end over on the inside, so it can't be removed. That's what they used to do before they had screws to lend extra strength to things like doors. The doornails were called 'dead' because they were bent and they couldn't be pulled out and used again." Hannah stopped talking when she noticed that Bill was staring at her in amazement. "What?" Hannah said.

"I was just wondering how you know all that."

Hannah shrugged. "I read it somewhere and it just stuck in my mind. Things do that sometimes."

"Okay, I'll take your word for it. Go on down to my office and I'll get you some coffee from the break room. It's fresher than what's in the vending machine."

"But is it *better*?" Hannah asked, and then she headed for his office. She'd find out soon enough.

Hannah walked down the hallway and opened the door with the fake brass plate that said, "William Todd, Detective" in stamped letters designed to look like engraving. She stepped inside the room that was more cubicle than office, and took one of the chairs in front of the desk. Regular deputies had desks in a type of squad room. Each desk was enclosed by chest-high walls that created a feeling of privacy if you were seated. That illusion was quickly shattered by standing up, and deputies practiced what they called the "over the back fence" communication all the time. When you needed to talk to another deputy, you simply stood up, peered over the walls, and shouted.

When Bill had made detective, one of the perks was an office with real walls, an actual door that locked, and a nonfunctioning window that looked over the guest parking spaces. As she waited, Hannah turned to look out Bill's window. Her cookie truck was in plain sight, appearing more wine-colored than red in the wash of bluish light from the spotlights mounted on the front of the building. No other "guests" had arrived. Her truck was the only vehicle to break the profile of the flat, white snow stretching across the treeless expanse of county land that ended abruptly at the road.

Hannah heard footfalls outside in the hallway. It must be Bill with the coffee. She quickly stuck a smile on her face and took a deep breath to steady herself. It wasn't in her nature to be duplicitous. Most people could tell when she was feeding them a line simply to get information. But Bill had been at work for over five hours already, and he was bound to be tired. Perhaps he wouldn't tumble to the fact that this was far more than a social call.

"Look who I found in the break room," Bill said, stepping in with the coffee. "I told him you brought cookies and he insisted on coming along."

Hannah turned, expecting to see Rick Murphy or one of the other deputies she knew, but instead she found herself staring at Mike Kingston. What was *he* doing here so early? As head detective, he worked regular hours and never drew a double unless there was a big case or . . .

"Hi, Mike," she said, interrupting her own train of thought.

"Hannah." Mike took the other chair in front of Bill's desk and reached out to touch her hand. "You're up early."

"I'm always up early. I have to bake before we open." Hannah met his friendly blue eyes and fought the urge to lean closer. The man was charismatic, not to mention incredibly attractive. "I didn't know you worked graveyards."

It wasn't until Mike laughed that Hannah realized she'd made a joke. A homicide detective working graveyards. Very funny. "Sorry about that," she apologized. "I was just surprised to see you here this time of the morning."

"I'm a morning person. I like to come in when it's quiet and ease into the day. Bill said you wanted to talk to him. I can leave if it's personal."

"No! I mean . . . it's not personal at all. It's theoretical. At least I *hope* it's theoretical." Hannah took a deep breath and went into the speech she'd rehearsed during her drive from the condo.

"Lisa's cousin ran away from home, and she's only fifteen. Her mom thinks she's bunking in with a friend and she'll come back when she gets tired of sharing a bathroom, but she asked Lisa what would happen if the girl got picked up by the police."

Bill smiled as he reached for a cookie. "That's easy, Hannah. She's underage, so the authorities would return her to the custody of her parents."

"But what if she won't tell the authorities who her parents are or where they live?"

"That makes it a little harder." Bill handed the sack of cookies to Mike, who took one and passed it back. "Then the authorities will remand her to the custody of Child Protective Services until the parents can be located. What kind of cookies are these, Hannah? They're great!"

"Butter-Scotchies. They're made with butterscotch chips and rolled oats." Hannah did her best to curb her impatience. She needed more information, and she had to be careful neither man suspected that she was describing Candy and her own situation at The Cookie Jar.

"These are perfect for breakfast," Mike said, reaching for another, "especially because they've got oatmeal. My mother used to try to get me to eat it every morning, and I would have if she'd baked it in cookies like these."

Hannah smiled to acknowledge the compliment, but it was time to get down to business. "Let's say this runaway turns up right here in Lake Eden, and she refuses to cooperate with you. She won't give her last name, or her hometown, or even her home state. She claims she's over eighteen, but she doesn't look it and she can't prove it. What steps will you take?"

"I'll contact Lisa and tell her to call her aunt. The girl can stay with Lisa and her father until her mother comes to get her."

Hannah came close to groaning. Mike was taking her literally. Perhaps she was better off asking Bill. "Okay, forget I mentioned Lisa. I'm curious and I want to go back to the theoretical. Let's pretend that you don't know the girl and you don't know the parents. What will you do, Bill?"

"After we interview her, we'll call Child Protective Services to come and get her. They'll take custody and make sure she's cared for. Then we'll concentrate on finding out where she came from."

"How will you do that?"

"We'll check the missing persons reports," Mike stepped in, "and compare the picture we took of her to the pictures on file. And we'll file our own report with her picture, saying we found her and listing anything we know about her. Then we'll run her prints to see if she's in the juvie system. If she's run away from home before, she could be there."

"And that's it?" Hannah asked, gazing at the two men in surprise. "That's all you'll do?"

"That's all we *can* do," Mike corrected her.

"So she'll just stay in the Winnetka County Children's Home until they decide she's eighteen?"

Mike shrugged. "That's the way it happens sometimes. But don't forget that there's a reason she ran away from home in the first place. Maybe she's better off in the county home."

Hannah had done volunteer work at the Winnetka County Children's Home. The children were well cared for and the staff tried their best to make it cheerful, but the old granite building was an institution, not a real home.

"Gotta run," Mike said, standing up and reaching out for Hannah's hand. "How about Saturday night? Do you want to go have a burger and take in a movie or something?"

"I'd love to," Hannah said, glad that her voice hadn't squeaked, or quavered, or done anything to show how excited she was that he'd asked her for another date.

"See you at six, then. If you're ready to leave now, I'll walk you to the front door."

"We'll both walk her to the front door," Bill said, getting to his feet. "It's the least we can do for all those cookies."

Hannah felt a little strange as Bill took her left arm and Mike took her right. And she felt even stranger as they walked down the hallway toward the desk at the entrance. If anyone had been waiting in the plastic chairs in the lobby, she might have felt the need to explain that she wasn't under arrest, that the detective on her left was her brother-in-law and the man on her right was her date for Saturday night.

BUTTER-SCOTCHIES

Preheat oven to 350 degrees F., rack in the middle position.

1 cup butter *(2 sticks, ¹⁄₂ pound—melted)*
1 cup brown sugar
1 cup white *(granulated)* sugar
2 eggs—beaten (just beat them up in a glass with a fork)
1 teaspoon baking powder
¹⁄₂ teaspoon baking soda
¹⁄₂ teaspoon salt
1 teaspoon vanilla extract
2 cups flour *(don't sift—pack it down in the cup)*
2 cups butterscotch chips *(an 11-ounce package will do just fine)*
1¹⁄₂ cups rolled oats *(uncooked oatmeal—I used Quaker's Quick 1-Minute rolled oats)*

Melt the butter in large microwave-safe bowl. *(About 90 seconds on HIGH.)* Add the sugars and let it cool a bit. Then add the beaten eggs, baking powder, baking soda, salt, and vanilla extract.

Mix in the flour and then the butterscotch chips. Add the rolled oats and mix in thoroughly. Let the dough rest, uncovered, for 10 minutes to allow the butter to solidify.

You can either drop this dough by rounded tea-spoon onto a greased cookie sheet, 12 to a sheet, or roll the dough in balls with your hands and place them on the cookie sheet, pushing them down just a bit so they won't roll off on their way to the oven. *(I prefer rolling the dough balls—the cookies turn out nice and round.)*

Bake at 350 degrees for 12 to 15 minutes. Cool on the cookie sheet for 2 minutes and then remove them to a wire rack to cool completely.

These freeze really well if you roll them in foil and put them in a freezer bag.

Yield: This recipe makes approximately 8 to 9 dozen cookies, depending on cookie size.

Hannah's Note: Mother's friend Carrie just loves these when I use one cup of butterscotch chips and one cup of milk chocolate chips.

Chapter Six

"Okay, so what's going on with Lisa's aunt?"

"Andrea?"

"That's right. Bill just called and told me you brought him some goodies. And while you were there, you told him that Lisa's cousin ran away from home. Is that true?"

"Well, actually…"

"I didn't think so, especially when Bill said you asked him some questions about underage runaways. So where are you keeping her?"

Hannah glanced over at Candy, who was helping Lisa transfer several pans of freshly baked cookies to the glass jars they used for display. When the phone had rung at seven-thirty in the morning, she'd answered it assuming that it was her mother. Instead it was Andrea with a mouthful of questions.

"Right here." Hannah gave a little sigh. She thought she'd done a fine job of convincing Bill and Mike that her questions were purely theoretical. "Bill's on to me?"

"No, Bill's not on to you. *I'm* the one who's on to you. You never could fool me, Hannah."

"Not even second-hand?"

"Not even then. So what gives?"

Hannah sighed and stretched the phone cord out so that she could step into the coffee shop for more privacy. Even at a young age, Andrea had always known when Hannah was trying to pull the wool over her eyes. At the same time, Andrea was fiercely loyal to her family. If Hannah told her about Candy and asked her to keep it a secret, Andrea wouldn't say a word to anyone.

"Two nights ago, a homeless girl broke into my shop to get out of the cold. I left her some food last night and managed to catch her. I told her she could stay here and I promised that I wouldn't call the cops. I'm pretty sure she ran away from home."

"And she's underage?" Andrea asked.

"Norman and I both think so."

"Norman saw her?"

"We had a date last night and he helped me catch her."

"Some date!"

Hannah chuckled. "Well, that wasn't *all* we did. We went out to dinner first."

"Good. At least it wasn't a total waste. So what are you planning to do with her?"

"Keep her and try to find her mother. She said her father's dead and that rang true."

"You're going to try to do it by yourself?"

"Yes. If I turn her over to the authorities, they'll just put her in the county home."

"That's true." Andrea gave a little sigh that smacked of resignation to Hannah. "Okay, I'll help you. It's almost like a murder and we already know we're good at solving those."

"How is it like a murder?" Hannah asked, torn between wanting a peek into her sister's thought processes, and believing that she was better off not knowing.

"Instead of looking for a killer, we'll be looking for a mother."

"Right," Hannah said, wishing she hadn't asked. "Don't

forget that you're married to a sheriff's detective and I'm harboring a runaway. Are you sure you want to get involved?"

"Of course I do! I have to save you from yourself. There's no way you can get any information because you can't lie. You've never been any good at it."

Hannah didn't bother to deny it, since her sister was right.

"I, on the other hand, am an expert liar!"

Again, Hannah was mute. She didn't want to get into an argument about whether expertise in something that was morally reprehensible should give Andrea bragging rights.

"Just let me take care of everything. I'll stop by to see the girl after I get my hair done. And you should watch her around Tracey."

"She's a nice girl, Andrea. She wouldn't hurt Tracey."

"You underestimate me, Hannah. That isn't why I said you should watch her. If she's really good with Tracey, it might mean she's used to being around kids that age. And that might mean she's got a younger brother or sister."

"You're absolutely right." Hannah knew it was time to eat a little crow. "Good thinking."

"Thank you. I'm good at these things."

"You certainly are." Hannah decided that constituted her last bite of crow. "Don't forget to be careful what you say when you meet her. You can't let on that you know she's a runaway, or she'll bolt and we'll never see her again."

"Right. What cover story are you going to use about why she's there at The Cookie Jar?"

"I haven't come up with one yet."

"Then you should let me do it. I'm better at cover stories than you are. Let's say she's Ellen's youngest sister."

"Ellen?"

"Ellen Wagner, your old college roommate. You introduced me when we drove up for your graduation."

"You're right. I'm surprised you remember her."

"I remember the dress more than her. Girls that big

shouldn't wear large prints, especially in bright colors. She came from a big family, didn't she?"

"Yes, in North Dakota."

"That'll work. A grain of truth always helps in a cover story. Anyway, Ellen called you and asked you to hire her sister for your busy time over the holidays. And the reason she wanted you to hire her is because . . . What's your runaway's first name? Do you know it?"

"It's Candy."

"Okay." Andrea took a deep breath that Hannah could hear over the phone as she picked up the threads of her fabrication again. "Ellen asked you to hire Candy over the holidays because Candy's boyfriend broke up with her and he started dating her best friend. And Candy couldn't stand to be in the same small town with them."

"That sounds good to me. And it gives us another grain of truth for your cover story."

"What's that?"

"Everyone in Lake Eden knows I could use some help over the holidays. Lisa and I are so busy, we have to make an appointment with the Kleenex box to sneeze."

Baking at The Cookie Jar was a dream come true. Hannah was nice and she said funny things that made Lisa and Candy giggle. Candy hadn't felt this good since she'd grabbed her things and hit the road, and she found herself smiling as she shaped a pan of Candy Cane Cookies the way Lisa had taught her. It was easy. All you had to do was roll out a spoonful of white dough and another of pink dough, twist the two rolls together, and shape it into a cane with a crook on top.

"We bake these only nine minutes," Hannah told her. "Any longer and the white part will turn brown."

"Wouldn't that be *golden* instead of *brown*?" Candy

quipped, remembering how her mother had described the cake they'd left in the oven too long.

Hannah laughed and turned to Lisa. "She's a natural. She's already read the baker's excuse book."

Candy finished the last sheet of cookies and slipped them into the oven. They were flavored with almond and her mother would have loved them. There was a bakery only three blocks from their house and she used to walk down there every Saturday morning and buy Mom a chocolate-covered stick of marzipan.

Tears sprang to Candy's eyes. She really missed her mother. To keep from thinking about her too much, she concentrated on the cookies baking in the oven.

"You don't have to watch them every second," Lisa told her. "You set the timer, didn't you?"

"Sure, I did. For nine minutes. And I wasn't really watching the cookies." Candy blinked the moisture from her eyes and turned to face Lisa. "Do you want another candy recipe? I just remembered one."

"You memorized recipes?"

Candy nodded. "I've got one of those weird memories. I can see the recipe in my mind and all I have to do is read it out loud. I forget what it's called."

"Photographic memory," Hannah supplied the term. She was standing at the counter, her back to Candy and Lisa, crushing peppermint candy for the topping on the Candy Cane Cookies. "It's like your mind takes a picture with a camera. There are times I wish that I had a photographic memory, but I understand there's a drawback."

"What's that?" Candy asked.

"Photographic memories aren't very selective. Memorizing recipes is a skill that could come in really handy, but I'll bet you find yourself memorizing a lot of useless things, too."

"You're right!" Candy said with a giggle. "I still remember the license plate on our old van. It was personalized and it said, *critters*. Mom got it for Dad when he opened the clinic."

Lisa laughed. "That's cute. How about your driver's license number? Did you memorize that?"

"I don't have…" Candy stopped in mid-sentence. She'd told Hannah that she was twenty and that meant she should have a driver's license. "I don't have that one memorized. I can name all the books of the Bible in order, though. I memorized them right before we went to visit Grandpa Samuel. He's a Methodist minister."

"I'll bet he was impressed," Hannah said, turning to smile at her.

Candy nodded. "So was Mom. And after that, she used to ask me to memorize things for her."

"What things?"

"The grocery list when we went to the store. That was just in case she forgot it. And Dad's number at the clinic. She could never remember it. I tried to teach her, you know? I told her it was all ones, fours, and eights. I mean, how hard is eight-one-four, eight-four-four-one? But she kept getting it mixed up."

Candy stopped speaking and frowned slightly. It was time to change the subject. She was talking too much about herself and she didn't want Hannah or Lisa to guess where she came from. "When we're through with the cookies, do you want me to make you a chocolate pecan roll? You could sell it in slices."

"That sounds fabulous," Lisa said. "How about it, Hannah?"

"Absolutely. If there's anything you need that we don't have, I'll give you some money and you can run down to the Red Owl."

Candy thought about that for a minute and then she shook her head. She'd taken a good look at the contents of Hannah's pantry the first night she'd stayed in The Cookie Jar, and she'd spotted almost everything she needed. "Do you have butter?"

"We've always got butter," Hannah told her. "My Grandma Ingrid used to always say that there's nothing that doesn't taste better with more cream, more sugar, and more butter."

Candy laughed. It was a funny line and she had to remember it so she could use it on Mom. But she wouldn't see Mom again, at least not for a very long time.

"Anything else?" Lisa prompted her, and Candy was glad. She was getting sad again, thinking about Mom and home.

"Chocolate in squares, the kind that's wrapped in white paper. I need two of them."

"Unsweetened, semi-sweet, or German's?" Hannah gave her three choices.

For a second, Candy was stymied. She hadn't known there was more than one kind of chocolate that was wrapped in white paper. The one she needed smelled good and tasted awful, but they might not know that. "Just a second, and I'll tell you what the package says," she said.

Candy shut her eyes and thought about the package they kept in the cupboard at home. "It comes in an orange and brown box and it says *Baker's* in big yellow letters. And there's a picture of a lady in an apron right before the name. That's at the top on the brown part. And then on the orange part it says, *Unsweetened Baking Chocolate Squares*." Candy opened her eyes and blinked.

"You were visualizing it, right?" Hannah asked.

"Right. Do you have it?"

"Yes, we do. Anything else?"

"Just stuff you already have. Do you want me to write out the recipe to make sure?"

"Good idea," Hannah said, handing her a pen and one of the notebooks that secretaries used to carry in the old black-and-white movies Mom and Dad used to watch. "It never hurts to double-check. If we like it, I'll add it to our recipe file. Put your name on top so we can give you credit if we use it in the shop."

Candy took the notebook and began to write, feeling a bit like an old-fashioned secretary taking a letter in shorthand for her boss. Once she'd finished, she put her first name at the top of the page, just like they'd done in English class, and sheer force of habit almost caused her pen to keep going. She caught herself just in time and drew a little doodle instead.

CANDY CANE COOKIES

Preheat oven to 375 degrees F., rack in the middle position.

THE TOPPING:
½ cup hard peppermint candy, crushed***
½ cup white *(granulated)* sugar

THE COOKIE DOUGH:
1 cup softened butter *(2 sticks, ½ pound)*
1 cup powdered *(confectioner's)* sugar
1 beaten egg *(just mix it up in a cup with a fork)*
1 teaspoon salt
1½ teaspoons almond extract
1 teaspoon vanilla extract
2½ cups flour *(pack it down in the cup when you measure it)*
½ teaspoon red food coloring

*** *You can use round red-and-white peppermint candies that look like buttons, regular candy canes, or any other peppermint candy that you can crush into small separate pieces. You could even use pastel mints, the tiny little "pillows" you'll find in a pretty bowl right next to the mixed nuts at almost every Lake Eden wedding reception.*

Hannah's 1st Note: Lisa and I prefer to use the big round peppermint candies that practically melt in your mouth because they're a lot easier to crush.

To make the topping, place the peppermint candies in a sturdy plastic bag and crush them with a rolling pin, or a mallet. You'll need ½ cup to top your cookies.

In a small bowl, mix the ½ cup crushed peppermint candies with the ½ cup white sugar. Set the bowl aside for now.

To make the dough, you'll need two bowls, a small and a medium-sized.

In the medium-sized bowl, combine the softened butter, powdered sugar, beaten egg, salt, and extracts. Stir until they're well combined. Then add the flour in half-cup increments, stirring after each addition.

Round up the dough and divide it in half. Put one half in the small bowl and cover it with plastic wrap so it won't dry out. This will be the white part of your Candy Cane Cookies.

Blend the red food coloring into the other half *(the dough in the medium-sized bowl.)* Mix it until it's a

368

uniform color. This will be the red part of your Candy Cane Cookies.

Lightly flour a breadboard or rectangular cutting board and place it on your counter. You'll use this surface to roll the dough.

Remove a teaspoon of white dough from the small bowl and roll it into a four-inch-long roll by pushing it back and forth with the palms of your impeccably clean hands.

Remove a teaspoon of red dough from the bowl and form a similar four-inch-long roll.

Place the two rolls side by side on the board, hold them together, and twist them like a rope so that the resulting cookie resembles a candy cane. Pinch the ends together slightly so they won't separate.

Place the cookie on an UNGREASED standard-size cookie sheet and bend down the top to make a crook. You should be able to get four Candy Cane Cookies in a row and three rows to a cookie sheet.

Hannah's 2nd Note: The first time we made these, we rolled out a dozen white parts first and

then we rolled out a dozen red parts. Our dough got too dry sitting on the board and the red and white twists we formed came apart. Now we shape these cookies one at a time and keep the dough bowls covered with plastic wrap when we're not rolling. I'd really recommend forming these cookies one at a time.

Once you've completed twelve cookies, cover your bowls of dough with plastic wrap. You don't want them to dry out between batches.

Before you put your first pan of cookies in the oven to bake, spread out a length of foil and place a wire rack on top of it. This will hold your hot cookies when you decorate them with the peppermint candy and sugar topping. Once the cookies are completely cool, they can be transferred to a foil-lined box or a platter and you can round up any topping that's fallen through the rack to use again.

Bake your cookies at 375 degrees F. for 9 minutes. *(They should be just beginning to turn golden when you remove them from the oven.)*

Immediately remove the cookies from the baking sheet and place them on the wire rack. Sprinkle them with the mixture of candy and sugar while they are still very hot.

Continue to roll, shape, bake, and top your cookies until you run out of dough.

Yield: Approximately 4 dozen cookies, depending on cookie size.

CHOCOLATE PECAN ROLL

Hannah's 1st Note: You don't need a candy thermometer to make this candy.

14-ounce can sweetened condensed milk *(NOT evaporated milk)*
2 one-ounce squares of unsweetened chocolate *(I used Baker's)*
2½ cups semi-sweet chocolate chips *(15 ounces)*
1 teaspoon butter
1 teaspoon vanilla extract ***
pinch of salt
8-ounce package dried apricots *(or pineapple, or cherries, or whatever)*
1½ cups roughly chopped pecans *(measure after chopping)*

Hannah's 2nd Note: You don't absolutely positively have to use unsweetened chocolate squares. If you don't have them on hand, just use three cups of semi-sweet chocolate chips instead of 2 ½ cups and it'll work out just fine.

*** *You can use almost any dried fruit in this candy. Lisa tried it with dried sweetened pineapple and*

pineapple extract, and it was delicious. If there's an extract that matches your fruit, you can use it instead of the vanilla.

Chop the dried fruit into pea-sized pieces. Then chop the pecans and measure out one and a half cups. *(This is easy to do if you have a food processor, but a knife and chopping board will work also.)*

Chop the squares of unsweetened chocolate into chip-sized pieces. *(They'll melt faster that way.)* Empty the can of sweetened condensed milk into a 2-quart saucepan. Add the unsweetened chocolate pieces and the semi-sweet chocolate chips.

Stir the mixture over low heat until the chocolate has melted. Give a final stir and take the pan from the heat.

Mix in the butter, flavor extract, salt, and the dried fruit. *(Don't add the nuts yet—they're for later when you make the rolls.)*

Put the saucepan in the refrigerator and chill the candy for 30 to 40 minutes.

Take the pan out of the refrigerator and divide the candy in half. Place each half on a two-foot-long piece of waxed paper.

Shape each half into a roll that's approximately a foot and a half long and about 1½ inches in diameter.

Roll the candy logs in the chopped nuts, coating them as evenly as you can. Press the nuts in slightly so they'll stick to the outside of the roll.

Roll the finished logs in clean waxed paper, twist the ends closed, and place them in the refrigerator for at least two hours to harden.

Cut the candy rolls into half-inch slices with a sharp knife.

Yield: Makes about 48 slices of delicious candy.

Chapter Seven

"Goodbye, Aunt Hannah. See you later!" Tracey gave her a kiss that landed on her chin, and then she ran over to hug Lisa. Once that was done, she gave a little wave in Candy's direction. "'Bye, Candy. It was nice meeting you."

"Nice meeting you, too," Candy said, giving Tracey a friendly smile. "Sorry about that fraction thing."

"That's okay. You didn't know. And I didn't know either!"

Both Candy and Tracey laughed at that, and Hannah watched her niece as she went out the back door with Janice Cox, her preschool teacher. Janice had come in to pick up some cookies she'd ordered, and she'd offered to give Tracey a ride to Kiddie Korner.

"Come on, Candy. You can help me set up the tables," Lisa said, herding the young teenager, who claimed to be twenty, into the coffee shop. "Once that's done, we'll open and I'll teach you how to go around with the coffee."

Once they'd left, Hannah reached for the steno pad that contained the information she'd gathered about Candy, and took out her pen to make another entry. *Only child?* she wrote. It was clear that Candy hadn't had much experience with preschoolers. When Tracey had offered to help Candy mix up the dough for the Chocolate Mint Softies they were serving for the Lake Eden Quilting Club's Christmas party, Candy had handed her the recipe and asked her to measure the brown sugar.

If Hannah had heard the exchange, she would have told Tracey how much was called for in the recipe and given her the correct measuring cup. Her niece knew how to measure brown sugar. She'd helped Hannah and Lisa bake before. She could even identify the line that called for brown sugar in the list of ingredients because she could read the words *brown* and *sugar*. But the Chocolate Mint Softies called for two-thirds of a cup of brown sugar. And while Tracey knew her whole numbers up to twenty, she didn't know her fractions yet. If Candy'd had a little sister or brother, or if she'd spent time with kids Tracey's age, she would have known that most five-year-olds couldn't even read yet, and it would be several more years before they understood fractions.

Once she'd stuffed the list of clues to Candy's identity back in the bottom of her purse, Hannah began to fill the display jars. She'd just finished helping Lisa and Candy carry them out into the coffee shop when Andrea came in the back door.

"Well?" Andrea asked, breezing in without knocking. She shut the door, took several steps forward, and turned around smoothly like a model. "What do you think?"

"Gorgeous," Hannah replied. Her comment referred to her sister's hairstyle, an elaborate twist with feathered curls softly framing her face, and also to her outfit. Andrea was wearing a bright coral wool suit with fur around the collar. It was a color that Hannah would wear only if she wanted to help Jon Walker, the owner of the Lake Eden Neighborhood Pharmacy, sell his entire stock of sunglasses. Redheads couldn't wear coral. It was a law. Or if it wasn't a law, it should be.

"I think the butterscotch is good, don't you?"

For a moment Hannah thought her sister was referring to the batch of cookies she'd taken to Bill and Mike at the sheriff's station. Then she noticed that Andrea was holding out one foot to show off her high-heeled boots that were made from butterscotch-colored leather.

"Very nice," Hannah said, wondering how Andrea could possibly walk in heels that high. "I hope you're not showing a farm."

"I'm not, but why?"

"Those heels are pretty high for the country, especially if you have to walk up banks of snow."

"High heels are better than flat heels. I can dig in with these and I don't slip."

Hannah's mind flashed back to a documentary she'd seen about mountain climbing and the pitons they used as footholds to scale steep slopes. She could visualize her sister in the Himalayas, digging in with her heels and walking right up to the top of the mountain, passing veteran climbers and their Sherpas alike.

"Why are you smiling like that?"

Hannah knew Andrea wouldn't think her mental image was funny, so she made up something on the spot. "I couldn't even walk in those things, much less climb snowbanks."

"I know you couldn't. You never bothered to practice. Remember how I used to walk up and down on the living room rug in my heels?"

Hannah remembered, and the memory brought on another smile. Andrea had clocked miles on their lime-green living room carpet wearing heels and whatever old clothes she'd put on after school. Sometimes it was jeans and high heels. In the summer, it was shorts and high heels. Occasionally it was pajamas and high heels.

"If you'd practiced as much as I did, you'd be comfortable in high heels."

"No, I wouldn't. I have lousy balance and no inclination to break my neck."

"Well, whatever." Andrea patted her shoulder bag purse. "This purse wasn't made by the same manufacturer, but I think it's a good match with my boots."

"Looks good to me," Hannah said. She'd never bothered having shoes and purses that matched, but both her mother and Andrea insisted that mismatched accessories were a fashion no-no.

"Bill called me a couple of minutes ago and said he might drop by. You clued in Lisa, didn't you?"

"Yes, if you're talking about her fictional aunt. And she knows that Candy is a runaway who's supposed to be my college roommate's younger sister."

"How about Candy? Does she know who she's supposed to be?"

"Not yet. I thought I'd let you tell her. You're the one who made up her cover story."

"All right. Where is she?"

"In the front helping Lisa. I'll go get her and introduce you. Be really careful. She's still a little nervous, and she might run if you say the wrong . . ."

Hannah stopped speaking as the swinging door between the coffee shop and the kitchen barged open and Candy rushed in. She didn't look to the right or the left. She just made a beeline for the back door, jerked it open, and rushed out.

"Uh-oh!" Hannah gasped. "I'd better go catch . . ."

For the second time in a row, she stopped speaking in midsentence, but this time it was from sheer relief. Norman was coming in the back door, and he had Candy by the arm.

"We've got to stop meeting this way," he said, grinning down at her. "Why were you running like that? I thought you and Hannah worked things out."

"She called the cops!" Candy gasped. "She promised me she wouldn't but she . . ."

"No, I didn't," Hannah interrupted.

"Well, one just came in the door. And Lisa must have

known what you were going to do, because she said 'Hi' to him!"

"Bill?" Hannah guessed, turning to Andrea.

"Bill," Andrea concurred, getting up from her stool. "I'd better go out there before he comes back here." She turned to Candy. "Nice to meet you, Candy. Bill's my husband and he won't bother you. I'm going to tell him that you're Hannah's college roommate's sister."

"What was that again?" Candy asked, looking perplexed.

"Hannah will explain everything. But I want you to know that you don't have to worry about a thing. There's no way we're going to let you spend Christmas at the county children's home."

CHOCOLATE MINT SOFTIES

Preheat oven to 350 degrees F., rack in the middle position

2 one-ounce squares unsweetened baking chocolate
½ cup *(1 stick, ¼ pound)* butter at room temperature
⅔ cup brown sugar, firmly packed
⅓ cup white *(granulated)* sugar
½ teaspoon baking soda
½ teaspoon salt
1 large egg
1 teaspoon peppermint extract
½ teaspoon chocolate extract *(if you can't find it,
   just use vanilla)*
¾ cup sour cream
2 cups flour *(pack it down in the cup when you
   measure it)*
¾ cup very coarsely chopped pecan pieces *(you'll
   want some big pieces)*

Line your cookie sheets with foil and spray with
non-stick cooking spray. Leave little "ears" of foil
sticking up on the side, large enough to grab later.
*(This is so you can slide the cookies and the foil right
off the sheet when they're baked.)*

Unwrap the squares of chocolate and break them apart. Put them in a small microwave-safe bowl. *(I use a 16-ounce measuring cup.)* Melt them for 90 seconds on HIGH. Stir them until they're smooth and set them aside to cool while you mix up your cookie dough.

Hannah's 1st Note: Mixing this dough is a lot easier with an electric mixer. You can do it by hand, but it'll take some muscle.

Combine the butter and sugars together in the bowl of an electric mixer. Beat them on medium speed until they're smooth. This should take less than a minute.

Add the baking soda and salt, and resume beating on medium again for another minute, or until they're incorporated.

Add the egg and beat on medium until the batter is smooth *(an additional minute should do it.)* Add the peppermint and chocolate extracts, and mix for about 30 seconds.

Shut off the mixer and scrape down the bowl. Then add the melted chocolate and mix again for another minute on medium speed.

Shut off the mixer and scrape down the bowl again. At low speed, mix in half of the flour. When that's incorporated, mix in the sour cream.

Scrape down the bowl again and add the rest of the flour. Beat until it's fully incorporated.

Remove the bowl from the mixer and give it a stir with a spoon. Mix in the pecan pieces by hand. *(A firm rubber spatula works nicely.)*

Use a teaspoon to spoon the dough onto the foil-lined cookie sheets, 12 cookies to a standard-sized sheet. *(If the dough is too sticky for you to work with, chill it for a half-hour or so, and try again.)* Bake the cookies at 350 degrees F., for 10 to 12 minutes, or until they rise and become firm.

Slide the foil from the cookie sheets and onto a wire rack. Let the cookies cool on the rack while the next sheet of cookies is baking. When the next sheet of cookies is ready, pull the cooled cookies onto the counter or table and slide the foil with the hot cookies onto the rack. Keep alternating until all the dough has been baked.

When all the cookies are cool, set them out on waxed paper for frosting.

Chocolate Butter Frosting:
2 one-ounce squares unsweetened baking chocolate, melted
⅓ cup butter, room temperature
2 cups powdered *(confectioners')* sugar
1½ teaspoons vanilla extract
Approximately 2 Tablespoons cream *(or milk)*

Unwrap the squares of chocolate and break them apart. Put them in a small microwave-safe bowl. *(I use a 16-ounce measuring cup.)* Melt them for 90 seconds on HIGH. Stir them until they're smooth and set them aside to cool.

When the chocolate is cool, mix in the butter. Then stir in the powdered sugar. *(There's no need to sift unless it has big lumps.)*

Mix in the vanilla extract and the cream. Beat the frosting until it's of spreading consistency.

Hannah's 2nd Note: This frosting is the no-fail type. If it's too thick, add a bit more cream. If it's too thin, add a bit more powdered sugar.

Frost your cookies and leave them on the waxed paper until the frosting has hardened. *(If you're like me, you'll sneak one while the frosting is still soft, just to test it, of course.)*

When the frosting has hardened, arrange the cookies on a pretty platter and enjoy. They store well in a covered container if you separate the layers with wax paper.

Hannah's 3rd Note: Lisa says that when she's in a hurry and doesn't have time to make a frosting, she just sprinkles the cookies with a little powdered sugar while they're still warm. She does a second sprinkling when they're cool and calls it a day.

Yield: Approximately 6 dozen cookies.

Chapter Eight

It was four days before Christmas and Hal & Rose's Café was decorated for the season. There was a silver metal Christmas tree in the corner that was illuminated by a spotlight with a slowly revolving color wheel. The tree was red for ten seconds, blue for ten seconds, green for ten seconds, and yellow for ten seconds. Then the cycle started all over again. Hal had purchased the tree from Hannah's father at Lake Eden Hardware in the seventies, and it was still going strong.

Hannah, Andrea, and Norman sat in the back booth under several strings of multicolored tinsel garlands that had been looped over the ceiling light fixtures in a crisscross pattern. A small fake poinsettia sat in the exact center of each table, and brightly colored cardboard cutouts of wreaths, snowmen, and sleighs were taped to the backs of the booths.

Except for the perpetual poker game that Hal hosted in the private banquet room in the back, the restaurant was deserted. It was two-fifteen in the afternoon, too late for lunch, and too early for the students at Jordan High to order after-school hamburgers and french fries. Even Rose had defected. She'd refilled their mugs, plunked the coffee carafe down on the table, told them to help themselves, and headed upstairs to the apartment over the restaurant to wrap a few Christmas presents.

"So what do we have so far?" Andrea asked, blowing on her coffee to cool it before she took a tentative sip.

Hannah got out her steno pad and prepared to read her notes aloud. She was taking a breather from work so that they could have a strategy meeting. Lisa and Candy were handling everything, and after a week at The Cookie Jar, Candy was fitting right in. Everyone appeared to believe Andrea's cover story, although Hannah thought Bill might be a bit suspicious. He was letting it slide, though. Bill wasn't about to haul Candy off to the county home right before Christmas, especially since she was now staying in the guest room at Hannah's condo.

"She's approximately fifteen, she doesn't have a driver's license yet, and she lives with her mother. Her father was a veterinarian, and he's dead."

Andrea shook her head. "We don't know that for sure."

"We don't know *what* for sure?" Hannah asked with a frown.

"We don't know her father's dead."

"Why would Candy lie about something like that?" Norman wanted to know.

"Divorce. I heard all about it on a talk show. Some kids don't want to admit their parents have broken up. They'd rather say that one of them is dead."

Norman looked puzzled. "But why?"

"It ends the discussion. If someone says, *My dad is dead*, you say, *I'm sorry*. And then you change the subject. If someone says, *My parents are divorced*, you might ask questions about which one they live with, and how often they see the other one, and things like that."

Norman nodded. "That makes some kind of sense, but I still think he's dead."

"So do I." Hannah glanced down at her notebook again.

"I'm almost positive her name really is Candy. She answers to it even when she's distracted, and it sounds natural when she says it. And I'm pretty sure her last name starts with an *R*."

"She told you that?" Andrea asked.

"In a way, but she didn't mean to. That first night when I woke her up, I asked her name. She said *Candy,* and then she began to say something that started with an *R*. When she realized what she was doing, she stopped cold and told me that I didn't need to know her last name."

"It's probably an *R*, then," Norman decided. "What else?"

"She has a photographic memory, although I'm not sure if that's a clue or not. And when she was demonstrating it for me, she said she remembered the personalized license plate her mom gave her dad for his van. It said *critters*. And she told us her dad's phone number at his clinic. It was eight-one-four, eight-four-four-one."

"That's a great clue!" Andrea exclaimed, giving her a thumbs-up.

"Only if her father's not dead and the clinic she was talking about is still open."

"Chances are, it's still open even if he's dead," Norman told her. "Most clinics don't go out of business when the doctor dies. Look at my father's practice. If I hadn't come back to run it, my mother would have sold it to another dentist. And you can bet he wouldn't have changed the number, since all the patients already have it. You see medical practices for sale all the time. What you're buying is the equipment and the existing patient list."

Andrea gave him a bright smile. "Norman's right, Hannah. Just look at Bertie. She didn't start the Cut 'n Curl from scratch. She bought the former owner's equipment and her client list. And I know for a fact that she kept the same phone number."

"Maybe the vet clinic still has the same phone number, but unfortunately, there's a hitch." Hannah didn't bother to point out that buying a medical practice wasn't exactly the same as purchasing a beauty shop, and that Andrea was guilty of trying to add apples and oranges.

"What's the hitch?" Norman asked.

"Candy didn't give me the area code."

Andrea waved off that concern. "We ought to be able to get around that. I mean, how many area codes can there be?"

"Over two hundred sixty, and that's not counting Canada. I looked it up in the phone book. It would take hours to dial all those numbers."

"I'll do it," Andrea volunteered. "It won't take me that long since I've got programmable one-button dialing. All I have to do is punch in the area code and my phone will put in the rest."

Hannah just shook her head. "Okay, if you think you can do it, but I don't even want to think about what Bill will say when you get your next phone bill."

"He won't say anything, because it'll be the same as this month's phone bill."

"You have a cell phone with unlimited minutes and no roaming charges?" Norman guessed.

"That's right. I'll start calling the minute I get home and work until Bill comes in the door. I'll do what it takes, Hannah. If I have to, I'll wait until he goes to sleep and I'll call all night."

"They might not be open all night," Hannah pointed out.

"I know that. But since it's a clinic, there's bound to be an answering service. Is there anything else I should know about Candy's family?"

Hannah glanced back down at her notes. "Her mother taught her how to make candy, but you already knew that. And here's something, but it doesn't do us a whole lot of good." Hannah pointed to a note she'd made. "She said her Grandfather Samuel is a Methodist minister, but I don't know what side of the family he's on."

"So far the phone number's our best bet," Norman said.

"I'll hop on the Internet to see if I can track down that license plate, but it's a long shot since she didn't say exactly how they spelled it and we don't know the state. And if her father's dead and her mother sold the van or something like that, the plate could have gone back into circulation."

"I've got a theory about her home state," Hannah told them. "My guess is, it's not Minnesota. We watched the news last night right before she went to bed, and she wasn't a bit jumpy."

Norman gave a nod. "And she would have been jumpy if she was afraid her mother had reported her missing? And they might show her picture on television?"

"Exactly. Not only that; they did a sound bite from the governor's last speech, and Candy asked me who he was."

"Then she's not from Minnesota. Where do you think she came from?" Andrea asked.

"Somewhere in the Midwest, probably no more than a day or two away from Lake Eden on the bus, or by hitchhiking. I could be wrong, but the night we found her, I noticed that her clothes were still clean and her sleeping bag looked almost new."

"That all makes sense to me," Andrea told them, finishing her coffee and sliding out of the booth. "I think your idea about the Midwest is right, especially since she doesn't have an accent. I'll try the Dakotas first and work my way around in a circle. Where will you be if I get a hit, Hannah?"

"I'm at the shop until six. We're closing at five, but I want to mix up a double batch of Fudge-Aroons to take to Sally's Christmas party on Friday night. You're going aren't you, Norman?"

"Yes. Will you save me a dance?"

"Absolutely," Hannah said, hoping her smile wasn't slipping. Norman was a great guy, but he wasn't what anyone without steel-toed boots might call an accomplished dancer.

"How about Candy? Is she going?" Andrea wanted to know.

"Of course. I told her it was one of the biggest parties of the year and she's all excited about it."

"Does she have a dress?"

"Not yet, but I talked to Claire and I'm taking her over to Beau Monde tomorrow."

"Don't forget shoes. She can't wear tennis shoes with a fancy party dress."

"I won't forget." Hannah was grateful for the reminder, but she wasn't about to let her sister know that she hadn't even thought about shoes.

"So you'll be home at . . . what? Six-thirty?"

"That's about right."

"Okay." Andrea turned to go, but then she turned back. "What do you want me to say when I find Candy's mother?"

Hannah thought about that for a moment, and she remembered what Mike had said. Some runaways had a very good reason for leaving home. "If the mother's not too far away, see if you can get her to come here. Tell her that if I bring Candy back without resolving anything, she'll just run away again. And the next time she could get into big trouble."

"Okay, but what if she won't come here?"

"Then I'll go there, wherever it is." Hannah felt the same surge of fierce protectiveness she experienced when she held small kittens and puppies. "Just make it clear that I'm not letting Candy out of my sight until I know she's going to be okay."

FUDGE-AROONS

Do not preheat oven—this dough must chill before baking.

> 1 cup chocolate chips (6-ounce package)
> 1 cup butter *(2 sticks, ½ pound)*
> ½ cup brown sugar
> 1½ cups white *(granulated)* sugar
> 2 teaspoons vanilla extract
> ½ teaspoon salt
> 1 teaspoon baking soda
> 2 beaten eggs *(just whip them up with a fork)*
> 3½ cups flour *(not sifted—pack it down when you measure it)*

Put the cup of chocolate chips and the cup of butter in a 4-cup bowl and microwave on high for 2 minutes. Stir until smooth and let the mixture cool while you do the next step.

Combine the brown sugar and white sugar in a large mixing bowl. Add the vanilla, salt, and baking soda. Mix in the two beaten eggs.

Check the chocolate chip and butter mixture. If it's cool enough to touch, add it to the sugar mixture and stir thoroughly.

Add the flour in half-cup increments, stirring after each addition.

Cover your bowl and refrigerate it. This dough must chill for at least an hour. *(Overnight is fine, too.)*

The coconut *("aroon")* filling must also chill. Mix it up now.

COCONUT FILLING:
2 cups shredded coconut
1 cup white *(granulated)* sugar
1 cup flour *(not sifted—pack it down when you measure it)*
½ stick cold butter *(¼ cup, ⅛ pound)*
2 beaten eggs

In a food processor with the steel blade, zoop up the coconut with the sugar and flour. Pulse it several times so that the coconut flakes are no longer than a quarter inch.

Cut the butter into four pieces and add them to your work bowl. Pulse again, until the mixture looks like coarse meal.

Crack the eggs into a small bowl or a cup and whisk them up with a fork. Add them to your work bowl and pulse until they're incorporated into the mixture.

(If you don't have a food processor, you don't have to buy one to make this cookie—it's just a little messier when the coconut flakes are longer. To make this cookie without a food processor, just add all of the ingredients except the butter to a small bowl and stir them up. Then melt the butter and mix it in.)

Cover and chill the coconut mixture for at least an hour. *(Overnight is fine, too.)*

When you're ready to bake, preheat the oven to 350 degrees F., rack in the middle position.

Form balls of chocolate dough, 1 inch in diameter, with your hands. Place them on a greased cookie sheet, 12 to a standard-sized sheet. Press them down with the heel of your impeccably clean hand.

Form balls of coconut just a bit smaller than the chocolate balls you made. Place them on top of each squashed chocolate ball. Now squish those down.

Make 12 more chocolate balls, the same size as the first ones, and put them on top of the squashed coconut balls. Press them down slightly to make little "sandwiches."

Bake at 350 degrees F. for 9 to 11 minutes. Let the cookies cool on the sheet for at least two minutes. When they're cool enough to remove, use a spatula to move them to a wire rack to complete cooling.

Yield: 5 to 6 dozen yummy cookies.

If you have any coconut mixture left over, form coconut balls, 12 to a baking sheet, put a milk chocolate chip on top of each ball and press it down slightly, and bake at 350 degrees F. for 10 minutes.

Norman wants me to make these cookies even chewier—he says it'll provide more revenue for his dental clinic. (He's kidding . . . I think.)

Chapter Nine

When the phone rang at seven in the morning, Hannah grabbed it. She'd been on pins and needles all night, wondering if Andrea would be successful in her phone search for Candy's mother.

"The Cookie Jar. This is Hannah speaking," she said, hoping it was her sister and not another customer with a big cookie catering order they couldn't possibly fill before Christmas.

"She's there, right?"

It was Andrea and it didn't take sisterly telepathy to know that she was talking about Candy. "That's right."

"Meet me in the back booth at Hal and Rose's in fifteen minutes. Say you have to deliver some cookies or something. I've got big news!"

Hannah frowned as the line went dead. Andrea was prone to play drama queen, but if she'd managed to find Candy's mother, Hannah would be the first to applaud her performance.

"Is something wrong?" Lisa asked, noticing Hannah's frown.

"Just another emergency cookie order. I have to run out

with three dozen, but I'll be back before we open. Will you bag them up for me, Candy?"

"Sure." Candy grabbed one of their distinctive bags, snapped it open, and slipped on a food service glove. "What kind do you want?"

"Anything we can spare. You must have heard that old saying: "Baggers can't be choosers.""

"I love these cookies! What do you call them again?" Andrea rooted around in the bag to find a sibling to the three she'd just eaten.

"Fudge-Aroons. Are you going to tell me, or not?"

"I'm getting to it." Andrea glanced around, but no one was paying the slightest attention to them. The regulars were at the counter, downing mug after mug of Rose's strong coffee, and there were faint sounds of sweeping as Hal prepared the banquet room for the day's poker game. Only one other booth was filled, and it wasn't within earshot. Cyril Murphy and Father Coultas were eating fried eggs and double orders of bacon for breakfast, something Cyril's wife and Father's housekeeper wouldn't let them have because they were supposed to watch their cholesterol.

"So you found the vet clinic?" Hannah prompted.

"Of course I did. It's in Des Moines, Iowa. I left my number with the answering service, but the vet didn't get back to me until eight last night."

"And he gave you Candy's home phone number?"

"No, he didn't have it. But he told me the name of the last vet. Candy's dad was Dr. Allen Roberts. He died last year, so Candy didn't lie about that."

"I didn't think she was lying." Hannah shook her head when Rose held up the coffee pot. Her mug was almost empty, but now that Andrea had finally started to tell her about the phone calls, she didn't want anything to interrupt her. "So Candy's last name really does start with an *R*."

"That's right. I called information for her home phone number, but there was no listing for Allen Roberts. I figured that Candy's mother must have put it in her name after her husband died, so I got a list of every Roberts in Des Moines."

"Were there a lot of them?"

"I'll say! I never thought of Roberts as a common name before, but the operator gave me dozens of numbers. I started calling right away, but I had to stop when Bill came home."

"But you managed to find Candy's mother?" Hannah asked, cutting to the chase.

"Right before I called you this morning. She cried on the phone, Hannah. She's been worried sick about Candy and she was so happy to hear that she's all right."

Hannah couldn't even begin to imagine the stress Candy's mother had been under. "Did you ask her to come here so we could help work things out with Candy?"

"Yes, and she agreed. I put her on hold and called Sally at the inn to see if there were any vacancies. When Sally said there were, Deana told me she'd throw some things in a suitcase and they'd get on the road right away."

"*They'd* get on the road?" Hannah picked up on the plural.

"The three of them. Deana is Candy's mother. I told you that already. And then there's Deana's new husband, Larry. And his daughter Allison."

Hannah looked thoughtful. "When did Candy's mother get married again?"

"The day before Candy ran away. And I know what you're thinking, Hannah. I'm pretty sure that has a lot to do with it, too."

Hannah sighed, her heart going out to the teenager whose life had changed so drastically in the past year. "A death in the family, a new stepdad, and a new stepsister. That's bound to upset anybody. Did Candy leave a note?"

"Yes, and Deana's bringing it with her. She said she cries every time she reads it."

Mommy,

I love you so much, and I just want you to be happy. I know you love Larry and he makes you laugh the way Dad used to do. I'm really glad you married him. He's been good about not trying to take Dad's place and I know he doesn't mind it if I call him Larry instead of Dad. If it was just you and Larry, I think we'd be okay. But it isn't.

I can't compete with Allison. Larry says she's perfect and she's won all those awards. He told me that she's beautiful, and she sings better than anyone on television, and she makes the honor roll all the time. She's totally different than I am. And Larry is going to compare me to her even if he tries not to.

It's not going to work, Mom. I'm never going to be able to sing, and play the flute, and make the honor roll every time. That's why I have to leave. Allison is going to hate me because I'm not like her. And then we'll fight and you'll stick up for me. That's going to cause trouble between you and Larry, and I don't want you to have to choose between us.

Don't worry about me. I'll find a job and be okay. I look older than I am and I'm not afraid of hard work. When Allison graduates and goes off to college, I'll come back for a visit. And every once in a while, I'll write to you to let you know that I'm all right.

Please don't try to find me, Mom. It'll ruin everything.

I love you, Candy

Hannah looked up to find three people staring at her over the coffee table in what Sally had named The Sunflower Suite by virtue of the pattern in the living room wallpaper. The three pairs of concerned eyes belonged to Deana, Larry, and Allison.

"It's my fault," Larry said, frowning. He was an attractive

man with glasses and a neat little beard. "I wanted her to like Allison and I guess I went overboard when it came to describing her."

The woman who looked like an older version of Candy shook her head. "It's more my fault than yours. I should have realized that Candy would be upset about sharing with another teenager her age. It's a real adjustment. From the time she was a little girl, she's always had all my attention."

Hannah glanced at Allison, who sat with downcast eyes. She was nice looking, a bit overweight, but well dressed in designer sportswear. She wasn't the beautiful girl that Candy had written about in her note, and Hannah was willing to bet the farm that she wasn't a great singer or an academic genius either.

"What do you think about this whole thing, Allison?"

"I wish she hadn't run away," Allison said, and Hannah could hear the hurt in her voice. "Dad always makes me out to be better than I am. That's because he loves me and he can't see my faults. But I'm a real person, and Candy would have seen that if she'd stuck around long enough to meet me. We could have been friends if she'd given me a chance."

That was what Hannah was waiting to hear and she jumped in with both feet. "I'm going to give you the chance."

"How are you going to do that?"

"You're going to meet Candy in a neutral place and see if you can get along."

"That won't work," Allison shook her head. "She's already decided she doesn't want anything to do with me."

Hannah smiled as her plan crystalized. The idea had begun to take form when Allison had said the two girls had never met. "Candy won't know who you are. You've never met, right?"

"That's right. She ran away the day before I got to Des Moines."

"Has she ever seen a picture of you?"

"I don't think so. And if she has, it's an old one. I didn't like my school pictures this year, and they were even worse last year. When I got them, I tore them up and didn't give them out to anybody, not even Dad."

"Perfect." Hannah turned to Larry. Can you stay over until Saturday morning?"

"Of course we can. We'll stay as long as it takes to convince Candy to come back to Des Moines with us."

"I want to see my daughter," Deana said, and Hannah could tell she was on the verge of tears.

"I know you do, but it's not going to work if you just walk in on her. She might bolt and then none of us would ever find her again. I've got a plan, but you'll have to be a little patient while I arrange some things."

"How long do I have to be patient?"

"Twenty-four hours. Tomorrow night is Sally's big Christmas party. She has one every year. Everybody who's staying at the inn is invited, and so are a lot of locals from Lake Eden. I'm bringing Candy." Hannah leaned forward and lowered her voice. "Now here's what I think we should do . . ."

Candy loved to shop and she couldn't seem to stop smiling. They'd gone out the front door of The Cookie Jar and into the next building over. There were party dresses on the mannequins in the window, and Hannah had said they were going to buy something for her to wear to the party tomorrow night.

Mom would love this place! Candy thought, looking around at the thick carpet, the soft lighting, and the closets filled with clothing. There were no racks crowded together and stuffed with clothes that were half off their hangers. Everything was in its own closet, and each closet was marked with a little gold number that told you the size. And instead of just going through the closets by yourself, you told the owner what you needed and asked her to help you choose it.

There were chairs in a conversational grouping in the center of the room, and Candy supposed they were for husbands or friends who wanted to wait while you tried on something and then walked out to model it. Candy was sitting in a pink satin chair while Hannah sat across from her in a pale green chair. The owner was standing at one of the closets, making a selection, and as Candy watched, she chose a dress and carried it over to them.

"This should be nice on you, Candy." The owner was holding the most beautiful dress Candy had ever seen. "I think wine is your color. You need a deep, rich color with your skin and hair, don't you think?"

"Oh, yes," Candy breathed. One glance at the dress and she was in love. She would have agreed that the world was flat as long as she got the chance to try it on.

"Do you need any help?" Hannah asked her.

"No, thanks. I can manage." Candy held out her arms for the dress and tried to keep from skipping as she walked back to the fitting rooms. It was as light as a feather and it shimmered in her hands.

It took only a second to peel off her jeans and sweater. And then carefully, oh, so carefully, Candy unzipped the dress and lowered it over her head. As it settled into place, she thought she could hear strains of beautiful music. She zipped it up, twirled around on the balls of her feet, and gave a delighted little laugh as she saw her reflection in the mirror. She looked gorgeous, not like herself at all. And she looked older, at least seventeen, and maybe even the twenty she'd told Hannah and Norman she was. She was Cinderella, and she was going to the ball!

"Let's see, Candy," Hannah called out, and Candy hurried out of the dressing room to show her.

"It's lovely on you," the owner of the shop said, but Candy was concerned about Hannah. Her new friend was buying her this dress and there wasn't any price tag. Candy had heard of sticker shock when people saw the prices of new cars. Was this dress so expensive that they had to hide the cost?

"You've got a great eye, Claire," Hannah complimented the owner. And then she turned to Candy. "It looks absolutely wonderful, and I think we should get it for the party tomorrow. What do you think?"

"It's beautiful," Candy said, sighing deeply. "But . . . is it too expensive?"

"No."

Both the owner and Hannah spoke at once, and then they burst out laughing. Even Candy had to smile.

"Claire gives me a discount because I'm her next-door neighbor," Hannah explained.

"It's only fair," the owner said. "Hannah brings me free cookies whenever she bakes my favorites."

Candy gave a delighted laugh, she was so happy. She was getting the dress of her dreams and it made her look like a princess. The only thing that could make this moment even more wonderful would be if Mom could see her now.

Chapter Ten

Candy had just refilled the carafe and was preparing to make the rounds of the tables when a pretty, very pregnant lady came in. "May I help you?" Candy asked, precisely the way Lisa and Hannah had coached her.

"Don't I wish! I need to see Hannah. Is she in the kitchen?"

"Yes, she is. But . . ."

"Hi, Sally," Lisa came up and took the carafe out of Candy's hand. "I'll do the coffee. You go see if you can round up any more Cherry Winks. We're running out. And take Sally back to the kitchen with you so she can talk to Hannah."

"I'm Sally, and I run the Lake Eden Inn," Sally said as Candy led her toward the kitchen.

"And I'm Candy. I'm helping Hannah and Lisa out over the holidays. Are you the one giving the big party tonight?"

"That's me. Or maybe I should say, 'That *was* me.'" Sally gave a little sigh as Candy pushed through the kitchen door and held it for her.

Hannah looked up from the tray of Lovely Lemon Cookie Bars she was cutting and nodded to Sally. "What are you doing here? I thought you'd be decorating for the party."

"I would be if I had some help. But I don't."

"I don't understand. You said you were going to hire three high school girls."

"I did, and all three of them called to cancel this morning. One's sick, one's grounded because she got home late from her date, and the third one slipped on the ice and broke her thumb. I managed to find one girl who said she'd help out, but she can't do it alone."

Hannah glanced at Candy. "Do you want to help Mrs. Laughlin and this other girl decorate for the party?"

"Sure, if you can spare me. But I don't know if I'd be any good at decorating."

"If you can throw tinsel at a tree and make it stick, you're good enough for me," Sally told her.

"Okay, then." Hannah grabbed Candy's parka and tossed it at her. "I'll pick you up in the lobby at five-thirty so we can drive back to the condo and get dressed. Sound good?"

Candy nodded. "Fine with me."

"Thanks, Hannah," Sally said, and then she turned to Candy. "And thank *you*, Candy. My car's parked in front and the clock's ticking. Let's go do it."

"Candy? Meet Sonny." Sally turned to the girl who was waiting in the lobby for them when they arrived at the inn. "Sonny? Meet Candy."

"Hi, Sonny," Candy said, giving the other girl a tentative smile. She was a little overweight and she wore a knit slacks-and-sweater outfit that was much too good for putting up decorations, but she looked friendly enough.

"Glad to meet you," Sonny said, returning the smile.

"Sonny has the pictures," Sally told her. "My husband hired a photographer to take photos of the decorations last year. We want it just the same, except we decided to use multi-colored lights on the trees instead of white. And we want gold balls instead of silver."

"Got it," Sonny said, and Candy was glad. Since she hadn't seen the pictures, she didn't really know what Sally was talking about.

"Come with me and I'll get you started," Sally said, and the two girls followed her to the dining room. She flicked on the lights and gestured toward the boxes that were stacked against the back wall. "Everything you need should be in those boxes. The busboys set up the tables this morning, and all you have to do is put on the tablecloths and the center-pieces. And that reminds me . . . on the centerpieces, take off the silver bows and replace them with gold."

"Where will you be if we have a question?" Sonny asked.

"In the kitchen. Just go out the door we came in and turn right. It's at the end of the hallway behind the swinging doors."

"Thanks, Mrs. Laughlin," Candy said, hoping that she would be up to the job.

"It's Sally. There's a cooler of soft drinks in the corner and I'll have one of my staff bring out a snack in an hour or so to keep up your energy."

Once Sally had left, Candy gazed around at the bare ta-bles that dotted the space and the dozen six-foot Christmas trees that sat in their stands, waiting for ornamentation. "It's a huge job," she said with a groan.

"Relax. It won't be that bad," Sonny told her. "We've got five hours."

"And we're going to need every second of it. Do you have those pictures so we know what it's supposed to look like when we're through?"

"Right here," Sonny plunked a folder on the table. Then she sat down in one of the chairs and motioned for Candy to take the other. "Let's spread out the pictures and leave them right here for reference. That way we won't make any mis-takes."

"Good idea." Candy was impressed.

"Thank you. I'm not just another pretty face."

Candy burst out laughing and then she wished she hadn't. What if she'd hurt Sonny's feelings? But she hadn't because Sonny was laughing, too. "Do you think we should work together? Or start in opposite corners and meet in the middle?"

"We should work together. That way all the decorations will look the same. Besides, it'll be more fun. What should we do first? The tables or the trees?"

Candy thought about that for a moment. "We should do the trees. That way we can use the tables to hold the boxes with the balls and the lights. They're probably dusty, especially if they were in storage all year."

"Good idea! You're not just another pretty face, either. Except you are."

"Are what?"

"Pretty. I'd kill for hair like yours. Mine's straight as a board."

"And I'd kill for eyes like yours. Your lashes are so long." Candy stopped and gave a little laugh. "Is this the grass is greener on the other side of the fence?"

Sonny stood up with a grin. "I think so. It's either that or something about walking a mile in somebody else's shoes. Let's go take a look at those boxes and see if we can find the lights."

"So how are they getting along?" Hannah asked, stretching out the phone cord so she could take another tray of Oatmeal Raisin Crisps from the oven.

"Like two peas in a pod. Every time I stick my head in, they're laughing about something or other."

"That's great. But are they getting any work done?"

"Tons of it. They've only got one tree left to go and then they're going to start on the tables. If they finish early, that'll give them even more time to talk."

* * *

"You're getting your outfit all dirty," Candy said, noticing the smudges on Sonny's slacks when she placed another box on the table. "You should have worn jeans."

"I'm not allowed."

"What?"

"Well I guess I am now, but I don't have any. I wasn't allowed to wear them at boarding school."

"What did you wear?" Candy asked, thoroughly shocked. She suspected she'd die if she couldn't wear jeans.

"We wore uniforms during school hours, and dress slacks or skirts after school and on the weekends. And pajamas to bed, of course."

Candy just shook her head. "Did they think jeans would corrupt you?"

"Maybe. We were supposed to act like ladies all the time. It was one of the rules. There were an awful lot of rules."

Candy just shook her head as she climbed the ladder and placed the last angel on top of the last tree. "I'm glad I never went to boarding school," she said, once she was back on the floor again. "I think it would have killed me."

"When I first got there I thought it was going to kill me, too. But it didn't and I learned a lot."

"Like what?"

"Like you really ought to carry that box of ornaments right side up, because I already opened it."

Chapter Eleven

The party was on, and their decorations looked great. Candy stood at the dessert table, feeling beautiful in her new dress, and watching her Three-Way Fudge disappear. Sally had put it on a round silver platter with a pedestal, and it looked every bit as good as it tasted. The bottom layer was dark chocolate, the middle layer was white chocolate mixed with chopped nuts, and the top layer was milk chocolate. When Norman had seen it, he'd taken a picture and promised to give her a print. And when she'd told Sonny about it, right after they'd finished decorating, Sonny had asked her to save her a piece.

There was a tap on her shoulder, and Candy whirled around to see Sonny standing there. She was wearing a powder blue sweater and skirt, and she was smiling. "Did you save me some?" she asked.

"I never break a promise." Candy patted the little gold purse she was carrying. "I grabbed two pieces before they carried it out, and I put them in here."

"I don't think two pieces will do it. It's not a proper taste test. I should probably have one right now, just to be fair of course. Fantastic dress, by the way. You look like a princess."

"Thanks. You look great, too," Candy said and she meant it. Light blue was a good color for Sonny, and her hair looked nice with a little curl at the tips.

"Okay. Here we go."

Candy watched as Sonny took a piece of fudge and tasted it. If the expression on her face was any indication, she liked it a lot. "So it passes the taste test?" she asked.

"What taste test? I'm in love." Sonny reached for another piece. "I've never tasted fudge this good before."

"It's really easy to make. I could teach you how to do it."

"Not me. I'm terrible in the kitchen. The one time I tried to make dinner for my dad, the neighbors called the fire department."

"I didn't even know Lake Eden *had* a fire department!"

"Oh, it wasn't here. We're just visiting Lake Eden. How about you? Do you live here?"

"I'm the same as you, just visiting." Candy remembered the cover story that Andrea had made up for her. "My boyfriend dumped me for my best friend, and I needed a change of scene."

"You also need a new boyfriend!"

"You're right about that," Candy said with a giggle. This party was a lot more fun now that Sonny had gotten here. "Let's grab a Coke and go sit at the table over by the last Christmas tree we decorated."

"Sounds good. I'll get the drinks. You stake out the table."

Candy made a beeline for the table and nabbed it before anyone else could claim it. When Sonny arrived with two Cokes and they'd popped them open, she asked, "How about you? Do you have a boyfriend?"

"Not yet, but I believe in miracles."

Candy laughed so hard, tears came to her eyes. "Too bad we don't go to the same school. There's a guy in my science class who'd be perfect for you."

"That won't do me much good unless he goes to Hamilton in Des Moines."

"That's my school!" Candy gasped, forgetting all about her cover story. "But I've never seen *you* there."

"That's because I'm not there yet. I don't start until January."

"Your folks just moved to Des Moines?"

"Not exactly. My dad's been there all along, but after Mom died, he put me in that boarding school I told you about. He just didn't know how to take care of me, you know? I mean . . . I was pretty little when it happened."

"That's awful! But now that you're older and you can take care of yourself, you're coming back to live with him?"

"Sort of."

Candy leaned forward. She knew there was more to the story than that. "What does *sort of* mean?"

"Dad got married again so he sent for me."

Candy felt a lump form in her throat. Sonny's story was eerily close to hers. They'd both faced the loss of a parent and their remaining parent had remarried.

"What's the matter? You look a little strange."

"It's just that we've got almost the same situation, except it's reversed. My dad's the one who died and my mom just got remarried. My situation's a little different, though, because my mom married a man with a daughter."

"So suddenly you've got a stepsister?"

"Right."

"So what do you think of her? Is she awful?"

Candy swallowed hard again. She really wanted someone to confide in and Sonny was awfully nice. "Larry, he's my stepdad, says she's perfect. She's beautiful, and she sings like a professional, and she's on the honor rolls, and . . ."

"But what do you think of her?" Sonny interrupted.

"I . . ." Candy stopped speaking and blinked away tears. "I don't know. I ran away the day before she came."

"Without even meeting her?"

Candy had the urge to break down and sob, but she stared

at the angel on top of the tree instead. "Yes. We're too different. She would have hated me."

"Are you sure?"

"I'm sure. She's not like you and me."

Sonny leaned forward. "If I could wave a magic wand and turn into your new stepsister, would that be okay?"

"That would be great. But you don't have a magic wand and this isn't a fairytale."

"I know that, but I'm your new stepsister anyway."

Candy's mouth dropped open. "But you can't be! Her name is Allison!"

"That's right. And Allison's nickname is Sonny."

For a moment, Candy was too shocked to do anything but sit there like a stone. And then she dropped her head in her hands and cried. "I really goofed, didn't I?"

"You could say that. I wouldn't say that because I'm a very nice person, but you could."

Candy's tears turned to laughter and she wiped her face with a napkin. "Is Mom here? I've missed her so much!"

"She's here, and so is my dad. They're waiting in the lobby. Do you want to see them now?"

Candy nodded. "You're coming, aren't you?"

"Sure, if you want me to."

"I want you to." Candy took a deep breath and regained some of her equilibrium. And then she said, "We might as well present a united front right away. That way it'll be easier for us to get away with murder."

"Looks like everything turned out all right," Norman said, watching Allison and Candy link arms and walk across the room.

"Sure did," Hannah said, giving a big sigh of relief.

"Where are they going?"

"To the lobby where Candy's mother and Allison's father are waiting for them."

Norman reached out to take her hand. "It's a good thing you took her under your wing, Hannah."

"It was my pleasure. She's a sweet girl, and her candy is incredible. Did you taste that fudge?"

Norman nodded. "It gives new meaning to the word *rich*. I have the feeling you're going to miss her a lot."

"I am, but not as much as Moishe. He's been sleeping in the guest room with her, and the comforter in there is down-filled silk. Now he's going to have to move back in with me and sleep on his lumpy foam pillow again."

THREE-WAY FUDGE

Hannah's 1st Note: You don't need a candy thermometer to make this fudge. If you've got a microwave, you don't even need a *stove* to make this fudge.

1 cup *(6-ounce pkg.)* semisweet chocolate chips *(I used Ghirardelli's.)*

1 cup *(6-ounce pkg.)* white chocolate chips *(I used Ghirardelli's.)*

1 cup *(6-ounce pkg.)* milk chocolate chips *(I used Ghirardelli's.)*

14-ounce can of sweetened condensed milk

6 Tablespoons butter

Line an 8-inch square pan with waxed paper, OR line it with foil and spray the foil with a nonstick cooking spray.

You can make this fudge on the stovetop or in the microwave. Either way will work just fine.

If you choose the stovetop method, use a heavy saucepan and stir constantly while you're melting the chocolate and other ingredients.

For the microwave, I combined my ingredients in a 2-cup Pyrex measuring cup and processed them for 70 seconds on HIGH. Remember that chocolate chips maintain their shape even after they're melted so don't go by appearance. You'll have to stir them to be sure.

Hannah's 2nd Note: A 14-ounce can of sweetened condensed milk contains approximately one and a third cups. You're going to be dividing the can in thirds, so make each third a bit less than a half-cup and you'll come out all right.

Melt the following together:
1 cup semisweet chocolate chips
scant half-cup sweetened condensed milk
2 Tablespoons butter

Stir to make sure everything's melted and then spread it out in the bottom of the 8-inch square pan you've prepared. Let it sit on the counter until it's cool and slightly hard to the touch and then . . .

Melt the following together:
1 cup white chocolate chips
scant half-cup sweetened condensed milk
2 Tablespoons butter

Stir to make sure everything's melted and then spread the second layer on top of the first. Let it sit on the counter until it's cool to the touch and slightly hardened and then . . .

Melt the following together:
1 cup milk chocolate chips
the remainder of the sweetened condensed milk
2 Tablespoons butter

Spread this third layer on top of the other two, smooth it out with a rubber spatula, and let it harden in the refrigerator for at least two hours. *(Overnight is even better.)* Then turn it out on a cutting board and cut it into bite size squares.

Hannah's 3rd Note: Mike really likes this fudge when I add chopped macadamia nuts to the middle layer. Norman thinks it's best with chopped pecans in the bottom layer. I suppose that should tell me something about their personalities, but I have no idea what it is!

Index of Recipes

Summertime has finally arrived in Lake Eden, Minnesota, and Hannah Swensen, owner of The Cookie Jar bakery, is looking forward to warm, lazy days, eating ice cream, and sharing picnics with friends. But when a family reunion takes a deadly turn, it's up to Hannah to find a killer . . .

Between baking up a storm for The Cookie Jar and unraveling the mystery of her cat Moishe's recent strange behavior, Hannah Swensen has a lot on her plate. But she'll always make time for her business partner, Lisa, who's in the midst of preparing for a big family reunion. Everyone is delighted when Lisa's long-lost uncle makes a surprise appearance. No one has heard from Gus in twenty-five years—and his arrival has everyone buzzing with excitement.

Uncle Gus is immediately the hit of the reunion, telling tales of his great success and flashing money for all to see. He's almost as popular as Hannah's scrumptious carrot cake, which is also Gus's favorite dessert. But the next morning, as the whole family gathers for the group photo, one person is missing. Hannah offers to track down Uncle Gus, but her search leads to a shocking find. Over by the bar at the pavilion, she spots two slices of her infamous carrot cake, frosting-side down on the floor—and Gus's corpse with an ice pick jutting out of his chest!

A little snooping reveals that not everyone was celebrating Gus's return. And when Hannah unearths more secrets from Gus's past, she discovers even more people with an axe to grind. Now Hannah's got to sift through a long list of suspects to find a killer—even if it could mean a recipe for her own demise . . .

**Please turn the page for an exciting sneak peek at
CARROT CAKE MURDER
now available!**

Hannah lowered the driver's window of her cookie truck to enjoy the gentle breeze wafting off the far shore of Eden Lake. Even thought the gravel road around the lake was showing wear from the tourists who'd towed heavy boat trailers and campers, she took the ruts at a fast clip to outrun the mosquitoes. She'd been through enough Minnesota summers to know that if she slowed to a crawl, they would descend on her arm in hungry hordes to gorge on a luncheon of A Negative with an Anti-B Antibody.

It was a perfectly lovely day. The air was scented with a wisp of smoke from a fisherman's shore lunch and a dampness that reminded her of wet swimming suits tossed over a porch rail to dry. The sun was almost straight overhead. When it reached its apex, the shadows of the tall pines that lined the lakeshore would be at their smallest: merely a darker circle on the ground around the tree truck, no larger than the branches that served as its pattern. It was the final Monday in August, and Hannah was playing hooky with her mother's blessing, an occurrence that had never happened during her school days at Jordan High. But today Delores and Carrie were also playing hooky. They'd closed their antique shop to attend the Beeseman-Herman Family Reunion, and sent their assistant, Luanne Hanks, next door to Hannah's cookie-and-coffee shop. She'd arrived to take charge just as Hannah was about to turn the CLOSED sign on the front door to OPEN, and now Hannah was free to enjoy this lazy, end-of-summer day.

Since she was in no hurry, Hannah took the long way around the lake. Attending Lisa and Herb's family reunion would be fun as long as she didn't get buttonholed by Uncle Gus again. She'd spent quite enough time with him at the dance last night, wedged into a round wooden booth at the Lake Pavilion with Marge Beeseman on one side and Uncle Gus on the other. Hannah had seriously been considering sliding under the table and crawling out when they weren't looking; but finally Gus had asked Marge to dance, and she was free to make her escape.

Gus Kaun, Marge's brother, was back in town after a twenty-five-year absence. To hear him tell about it, he'd gone off to make his fortune and was now a rich, successful businessman. Perhaps everything he'd told Hannah and Marge last night was true, but Hannah didn't like the way he bragged about everything he'd done and belittled everyone who'd stayed behind in Lake Eden. She especially didn't like the way he behaved toward Jack Herman, Lisa's father. There appeared to be bad blood between them, but neither man would talk about it, and no one knew what had caused the rift between the friends who had been inseparable in high school.

Hannah let out a groan as she came around a curve and saw that the public parking lot was full. In addition to the relatives who were staying at nearby lake cottages, it appeared that everyone in town had driven out for the day's festivities. It wasn't surprising, considering the size of both families. Lisa was the youngest daughter in the large Herman family. Most of the children had stayed in the area and married into other big families. The same was true for the Beesemans. At last count, over one hundred people had responded to the reunion invitation.

Since there weren't any vacant parking spots, Hannah created one of her own. That was the beauty of owning a four-wheel-drive cookie truck. When the proper gear was engaged, her Suburban climbed up the three-foot berm of dirt surrounding the parking lot and found a semilevel spot on top.

Hannah took the time to spray on mosquito repellent, a precaution she'd learned early in life. Then she retrieved the large box of cookies she'd packed to add to the lunch table. Kids loved cookies, and there were plenty of kids at the family reunion. She held the box with both hands, dug in her heels to walk down the berm, and then hurried toward the picnic tables, where a crowd was gathering by the shore.

Loud, merry voices floated up to greet her, and Hannah spied Lisa standing on top of a picnic table, holding a cheerleading megaphone to her lips. She was wearing a red T-shirt with the legend FAMILY IS EVERYTHING.

"It's time for the family portrait," Lisa called out. "We're going to have the lake in the background, so line up at the edge of the water behind the two chairs for your host and hostess. That's my dad, Jack Herman, and Herb's mom, Marge Beeseman. Norman and Herb will tell you what row you're in if you can't figure it out for yourself. We want the tallest in the back and the shortest in the front."

Hannah set the cookies down on the food table and headed for the shore to watch. She knew that Norman had offered to take the group pictures, and perhaps she could help.

"Hannah!"

Hannah knew that voice and thankfully it wasn't Uncle Gus. "Hi, Mother," she said, turning to greet the fashionable, dark-haired woman who would die rather than exceed the petite dress size she'd worn in high school.

"Hello, dear." Delores steadied herself against her eldest daughter's arm and shook the sand from one white high-heeled sandal. "I wish I hadn't worn these today, but I didn't think the beach would be quite this sandy."

Hannah laughed. "It's a beach, Mother. By definition it's sandy."

"You're right, of course. But I didn't think it would be *this* sandy." Delores paused for a moment and then she gave Hannah a smile. "Did you like the surprise we sent you this morning?"

For a brief moment Hannah was puzzled, but then she got it. "You mean Luanne. That was really thoughtful of you, Mother. I didn't think I'd be able to drive out here until we closed."

"Anything for my dearest daughter."

Uh-oh! Warning bells sounded in Hannah's head. Her mother wanted something . . . but what?

"I hope you can relax and have a good time today. You deserve a little break, Hannah."

The warning bells turned into klaxons, and yellow caution lights behind to blink on and off. "Thanks, Mother," Hannah responded. And then, just because she couldn't resist, she asked, "What do you want?"

Her mother reared back in surprise that could have been real or not, Hannah couldn't tell. "*Want?* What makes you think I *want* anything? Just because I called you my dearest daughter and I said you deserved to relax and have a good time doesn't mean I *want* anything."

"I'm sorry," Hannah said, backpedaling as fast as she could. "I thought there was something you wanted me to do for you."

"Well . . . now that you mention it . . ." Delores gave an elaborate shrug. "You could find Marge's brother for me. No one's seen him since the dance last night. When he didn't show up for the family picture, they sent me to find him. But my shoes . . ." She glanced down at the stylish sandals. "They're just not suitable for trying to locate someone. You know what I mean, don't you, dear?"

Caught like a rat in a trap, like a fly on a sticky spiral of flypaper, like a deer in the headlights, like a moth fluttering helpless against . . .

"Hannah?"

Delores interrupted her mental chain of similes and Hannah focused on the here and now. Delores *had* wanted something and now she knew what it was. "Okay, Mother," she said, bowing to the inevitable. "I'll go find Uncle Gus for you."

Nothing was ever easy. Hannah gazed around the small lake cabin. The only living creature inside was a small green frog who hopped determinedly toward the kitchen alcove. Unless Uncle Gus had met a witch who'd turned him into the Frog Prince, he wasn't here. And since his Jaguar was still parked in the driveway, he'd gone somewhere on foot. But where? Eden Lake was far from being the largest body of water in Minnesota, but it would still take several hours to walk around the perimeter searching for him.

The frog gave a croak and Hannah watched as he hopped up on the counter and into the sink. That was when she noticed that there were no dirty breakfast dishes. A quick peek in the refrigerator told her way. The only contents were a bottle of vodka and two cans of beer. If Uncle Gus had wanted something other than a boilermaker for breakfast, he'd probably walked over to the Eden Lake store to buy food.

Hannah ran a little in the sink for the frog and headed across the road to the store. It had been one of her favorite places as a child. The old-fashioned bell on the door tinkled as she pushed it open and stepped in. Some things never changed; and Hannah found that comforting. The interior of the store still smelled the way it always had, a curious mixture of ring bologna, dill pickles in a large jar on the counter, and bananas that had gotten too ripe for anything except banana bread.

"Hello, Hannah." Ava Schultz came out from the back, pushing aside the curtain that concealed her living quarters from her customers' view. She had been only a year or two behind Delores at Jordan High, and that meant Ava had passed middle age and was fast approaching what advertisers called "the golden years." A small woman prone to quick movements and rapid speech, she reminded Hannah of a small brown wren, flitting from one part of the store to another and seldom lighting in one place for long. Ava had fashionably cut, perfectly coifed dark brown hair without a touch of gray. Delores and her friends were certain that she wore a wig since Bertie Straub, the owner of the Cut 'n' Curl, insisted that Ava had never come in, not even once, to have her hair cut, styled, or colored.

"Hi, Ava." Hannah walked over to the main attraction, a shiny metal case filled with every available Popsicle flavor. "Anything new since I grew up?"

Ava gave a little laugh and joined her at the case. "See the three boxes in the middle?" she asked, pointing to them. "Those are Rainbows, Scribblers, and Great White."

"Never heard of them."

"Of course not. We didn't have them when you were a child. All we carried then were the double pops in variety of flavors."

"Rhubarb," Hannah said with a grin. "That was my favorite."

Ava's mouth dropped open. "They never made rhubarb!" she exclaimed. "You're pulling my leg, Hannah."

"You're right. I should have known I couldn't put one over on Winnetka County's leading Popsicle authority."

"I *do* like to keep up with it," Ava admitted. "The kids enjoy hearing about the new products and they've got so many." She pointed to another box. "Look at those Lifesaver Super Pops. From the bottom up, they're pineapple, orange, cherry, and raspberry. And over here are the Incredible Hulks. They're part of the Firecracker Super Heroes series. The Hulk is strawberry-kiwi, grape, and green apple. They've even got Big Foot." Ava reacted to Hannah's raised eyebrows and explained, "It's cherry and cotton candy swirled together and shaped like a foot with a gumball. Get it?"

Hannah nodded. "Big Foot. Cute. Popsicles have come along way since 1905 when Frank Epperson left his lemonade and stir stick out on the porch and it froze solid overnight."

"You remembered!" Ava gave her the same smile a teacher might bestow on a favorite student.

"Of course I did." Hannah smiled back. Ava had told her the story enough times. But she wasn't here to discuss Popsicles history. She had to find out if Ava had seen Uncle Gus. "Did Gus Kaun come in this morning?" she asked. "They're lining up for the family-reunion picture and they sent me to find him."

"I haven't seen him since he walked back here last night after the dance. And before you can ask, it's not what you think. He just wanted me to open up the store so he could get some milk to go with that carrot cake you gave him."

Hannah nodded, even though she hadn't been thinking what Ava thought she'd been thinking. "So you opened the store for him?"

"Of course I did. A customer's a customer, even after midnight. He bought eggs and bacon for breakfast, too. Then we had a drink and waited for the cars to clear out of the parking lot. He said he hid your cake behind the bar and he was going back to eat it as soon as no one else was around. I think that was so he wouldn't have to share. We went to school together, you know. Gus was never any good at sharing, not even in kindergarten."

Hannah thought about that for a moment. One the one hand, she was pleased that Gus liked her Special Carrot Cake so much that he hadn't wanted to give any away. On the other hand, she'd baked him a half-dozen pieces, one of which he could have given to Ava.

"Anyway," Ava went on, "the last time I saw Gus, he was heading back to the pavilion with his sack of groceries. He was supposed to come back to pay me for them this morning, but he never showed."

Ominous music began to play in the recesses of Hannah's mind. It sounded like a cross between Bach's "Toccatta and Fugue" and the soundtrack of a bad horror movie, but she didn't have time to think about that now. "What time was it when Gus left here last night?"

"A little after one-thirty. I got ready for bed, that takes about ten minutes, and I looked at the clock before I turned off the lights. It was a quarter to two."

Hannah reached reflexively for her steno pad, the kind she used for murder cases, but she quickly thought better of it. This was nothing more than a missing person, someone who hadn't shown up for the family-reunion picture. Uncle Gus hadn't left for good, for his car was still here; but he could have found a warmer, more hospitable place to sleep than the single bunk in his unheated lake cabin. There had been at least five dozen women at the dance last night. One of them might have thought a middle-aged braggart like Uncle Gus was irresistible. He could have waited until no one was around and walked to her cabin bearing gifts of carrot cake and breakfast. *Perhaps he'd decided to skip the group photo and was sitting at her kitchen table right now, eating bacon and eggs with her carrot cake for dessert . . .*

. . . or not, Hannah muttered under her breath, and then she turned to Ava. "I'd better get going. They'll be ready to take that photo soon."

"I hope you find Gus. If you do, will you do me a favor?"

"What?" Hannah asked, knowing better than to promise blindly.

"Right after they snap that picture, grab Gus by the ear

and march him back here to pay his bill. You can tell him I said that groceries don't grow on trees."

There was only one logical place to look, and Hannah headed straight for it. The Lake Pavilion was clearly deserted. The sandy parking lot was empty of cars and contained only a crumpled cigarette pack, the remnants of what had once been a blue-and-white bandanna, and a neatly clipped coupon for a two-fer dinner at Perkins' Pancake House.

As she approached the entrance to the white clapboard structure, Hannah felt an odd prickling at the back of her neck. She'd experienced that sensation before and it had preceded something unpleasant, something bad, something like discovering a dead body. She told herself that Uncle Gus was fine and she'd find nothing but the debris of a party inside, but her feet dragged a bit as she approached the front entrance.

Last night the pavilion had looked majestic, a gleaming white edifice in the moonlight, its open shutters spilling out warm yellow light into the humid blanket of summer darkness. Music had set up joyful vibrations in the walls, the wooden chairs, the old chrome barstools, and the revelers themselves, causing laughter and loud voices to peal out in a cacophony of raucous gaiety. Today it was . . . Hannah paused, both in mind and step, attempting to think of the word. *Sad.* The word was *sad.* The white paint was peeling, the shutters were warped from exposure to the elements, and there was a gaggle of brown beer bottles leaning up against the front of the building. The party was over. Everyone had left. All that remained was the abandoned pavilion with its curling shards of paint.

Hannah tried the front door, but it was locked just as she'd thought it would be. She knocked, calling out for Uncle Gus, but there was no answer. A nonlocal person might have gone back to ask Ava how to get the key, but Hannah had been born and raised in Lake Eden and she knew all about the Lake Pavilion. In a town where the lover's lane was regularly patrolled, and the parking lot at the rear of Jordan High was peppered with arc lights, the Lake Pavilion was the sole haven for teenage couples seeking privacy.

The loose shutter was at the back of the pavilion, the third from the corner. Hannah found the proper one, tugged on the padlock that had been rigged to open, and removed it. Gaining access to the pavilion was every bit as easy as her date for the high-school prom had told her it would be. She hadn't believed him at the time, and she wouldn't have gone out to the pavilion with him in any case—especially since she knew that her father had bribed him with the promise of a summer job if he'd invite Hannah to be his date for the dance.

Hannah lifted the shutter and propped it open with the stick that was attached to the side of the window frame. The opening was at waist height, and she swung her leg up and over the sill. A moment later she was sitting on the sill with both legs hanging down inside the building, preparing to push off with her hands and jump down.

She landed hard, which wasn't surprising. She'd never been the athletic type. Since the shutter was at the back of the pavilion, not visible from the road, she left it open for illumination.

All was quiet within. The interior had an air of abandonment, and the only sign of life Hannah heard was the buzzing of several flies that had been trapped inside. As a child she'd believed that if she recorded the high-pitched buzzing of houseflies and played it back ever so slowly, she'd hear tiny little voices saying things like, "Dig in. Hannah spilled strawberry jam on the kitchen table!" and "Watch out! Her mother's got a flyswatter!"

A phalanx of giant trash barrels sat against the wall. Several were close to overflowing with plastic plates and coffee-laden Styrofoam cups from the dessert buffet. Another barrel was marked with a familiar symbol, and it contained bottles and cans for recycling.

Hannah wrinkled up her nose. There was an odd combination of scents in the air: a spicy sweetness from the dessert buffet, the acrid scent of coffee that had perked too long in the pot, the lingering fragrance of perfumes and colognes, and the stale odor of spilled beer and liquor. Those smells were ordinary, what you might expect in a place where a large party had been held. But there was another scent under it all, cloying and sharp, and slightly metallic. It reminded Hannah of something unpleasant, something bad, something . . . but she didn't want to think about that now.

She fought the urge to dig in, to start picking up paper napkins, cups, glasses, and bottles and stuffing them into the appropriate trash barrels. She reminded herself that Lisa and Herb had organized a crew of relatives to clean the pavilion this afternoon, and nobody expected her to do it. Her number-one priority was to find Uncle Gus so that they could take the family picture.

A shaft of sunlight streamed through the open window, setting dust mites twirling. As Hannah watched, several more flies buzzed by the beam of sunlight on their way to the mahogany bar against the far wall. The top of the bar was empty except for a brown grocery sack, the type that Ava used at the Eden Lake Store. Uncle Gus had been here, and he must have forgotten to take his groceries when he left.

Another group of flies with the same destination flew in. If this kept up, Lisa and Herb would never get the insects out in time for the program they'd planned tonight. Hannah hurried to the kitchen, soaked a rag with water, and grabbed a bottle of degreaser. Last night they'd set out the dessert buffet on the bar, and it was apparent that whomever had wiped it down hadn't done a good job. She'd clean it thoroughly right now so that no more flies would come in.

Hannah had almost reached her goal when she noticed

something. She stopped abruptly and peered down at the floor. The flies weren't the only insect group attracted to this particular locale. There was a line of black carpenter ants streaming toward the bar and disappearing behind it. They must be looping around because there was a returning line of ants and they were carrying morsels of something. Carpenter ants seldom foraged for food during the daylight hours, but their scouts must have discovered something tasty enough to call out the troops.

Hannah moved closer and gave a groan when she saw what had attracted the ants. They were retrieving sweet crumbs from a piece of her carrot cake that had been dropped, cream cheese icing side down, and mashed to a pulp.

For a brief moment, Hannah was livid. Uncle Gus had dropped a piece of her Special Carrot Cake and stepped on it! What a waste! But then she spotted something sticking out from behind the bar, something that looked like . . . a foot. And the ominous organ music that had been playing in her mind increased in volume until the crashing chords were almost deafening.

"Oh, murder!" Hannah breathed, hoping that her words weren't prophetic. But she recognized the shoe, the rich buttery leather that shouted designer footwear with an exorbitant price tag. And the trousers. They were made of imported Italian silk and they matched a well-tailored jacket that had been paired with a cream silk shirt and a tie that had probably cost more than she made all week at The Cookie Jar. She'd seen the ensemble last night at the dance and she knew who had been wearing it.

Hannah took a bracing breath and made her feet move forward so that she could see behind the bar. Uncle Gus had come back to the pavilion to eat his carrot cake, but he'd only enjoyed a bit or two. And now, as she stood there staring, he was lying face down on the floor with the other pieces of cake scattered around him.

She shut her eyes and then opened them. Nothing had

changed. There was no doubt that Uncle Gus was dead. Blunt-force trauma had taken an extremely visible toll, and it wasn't a pretty sight. She wanted to find something to cover him, so the flies couldn't gather, but she knew she shouldn't touch anything. Uncle Gus hadn't cracked his own skull with the blood-splattered Louisville Slugger leaning up against a bar stool. This was a murder scene, and she had to call . . .

"Hannah?"

The voice startled her and she turned to look. Herb was standing at the open window.

"You can stop looking. We took the picture without Uncle Gus. If he shows up later, we'll take another one."

"He won't show up," Her voice sounded strained to her own ears, and Hannah cleared her throat.

"What do you mean, *He won't show up?*"

Hannah cleared her throat again. "He's . . . he . . . call Mike and Bill on your cell phone, will you? It's important."

"Okay, but why?"

"They need to come out here. Uncle Gus is . . . gone." She forced out the words, knowing full well that the woman who hated euphemisms had just used one.

"You mean he left the family reunion without even saying goodbye?"

"Not exactly." Hannah winced as she avoided a direct answer once again. "Just tell them to hurry. And don't let anyone in until they get here."